STONE MAN, by Fred —— ——
20,000 years into the pa——
Berserker Machines that ——
future time!

SCYLLA's DAUGHTER, by Fritz Leiber—Could even
the pitiless blade of Fafhrd's sword save the tribute
ship from unspeakable horror?

NOT LONG BEFORE THE END, by Larry
Niven—After the world's magic had worn thin,
could the sorcerer still guard his terrible secret—a
secret that could spell the end of civilization?

BEYOND THE BLACK RIVER, by Robert E.
Howard—Can Conan escape from a land ruled by a
magic more primitive and mysterious than anything he
has ever battled?

Out of legend come heroes and villains from less
civilized lands, from an unforgettable, golden age of
glory. . . .

BARBARIANS

Signet brings the stars to you . . .

BARBARIANS

EDITED BY
Robert Adams,
Martin H. Greenberg,
and Charles G. Waugh

A SIGNET BOOK
NEW AMERICAN LIBRARY

Acknowledgments

"Scylla's Daughter" by Fritz Leiber. Copyright © 1970 by Ultimate Publishing Company. Reprinted by permission of Richard Curtis Associates, Inc.

"Stone Man" by Fred Saberhagen. Copyright © 1967 by the Galaxy Publishing Corpora-
tion. Reprinted by permission of the author.

"Sand Sister" by Andre Norton. Copyright © 1979 by Gerald Page and Hank Reinhardt.
Reprinted by permission of the author and Larry Sternig Literary Agency.

"Swordsman of Lost Terra" by Poul Anderson. Copyright © 1951 by Love Romances
Publishing Company. Reprinted by permission of the Scott Meredith Literary Agency,
Inc., 845 Third Avenue, New York, NY 10022.

"Swords Against the Marluk" by Katherine Kurtz. Copyright © 1977 by Lin Carter.
First published in FLASHING SWORDS #4. Reprinted by permission of the authors.

"Not Long Before the End" by Larry Niven. Copyright © 1969 by Mercury Press, Inc.
Reprinted by permission of Kirby McCauley, Ltd.

"Maureen Birnbaum, Barbarian Swordsperson" by George Alec Effinger. Copyright ©
1982 by Mercury Press, Inc. From The Magazine of Fantasy and Science Fiction.
Reprinted by permission of Richard Curtis Associates, Inc.

"Thurigon Agonistes" by Ardath Mayhar. Copyright © 1983 by Ardath Mayhar.
Reprinted by permission of the author.

"Vault of Silence" by Lin Carter. Copyright © 1977 by Lin Carter. Reprinted by
permission of the author.

"The Other One" by Karl Edward Wagner. Copyright © 1977 by Charles W. Melvin
for ESCAPE! #1. Reprinted by permission of the author.

"The Age of the Warrior" by Hank Reinhardt. Copyright © 1979 by Gerald W. Page
and Hank Reinhardt. Reprinted by permission of the author.

"Beyond the Black River" by Robert E. Howard. Copyright 1935 by Robert E.
Howard. Reprinted by permission of Conan Properties, Inc.

CONTENTS

INTRODUCTION

Our concept of a barbarian is most often that of a skins-and-furs-clad, shaggy-haired and -bearded, unwashed, thick-thewed and often thick-headed human who hits anything strange to him with either a bark-on club, a stone axe or, at best, a huge and clumsy sword. But this concept, alas, dates at earliest from only about the first quarter of the seventeenth century, at least in English usage.

The original word was the Greek *barbaros*, and, as it only denoted a person who was not Greek and did not speak the Hellenic language, it was right often applied to persons and groups possessed of more culture for a good bit longer time than the haughty Greeks, themselves.

As time marched onward, Greek arrogance, disdain and hauteur proved to be no match for the strength, the well-honed steel and the vaunting ambition of the "barbaric" Romans. The Greeks were enslaved in droves, the land of Greece and all the Greek colonial settlements passed to Rome, as too did the Greek language. The Greek arrogance passed to the Romans, as well, for presently the word *barbaros* was metamorphosed into Latin *barbarus*; the word now meant anyone who was so unfortunate as to not be a Roman or to speak Latin. As the Roman Republic and Empire lasted much longer and covered much broader territories than did the Classical Period of Greece, they got a lot more opportunities to call considerably more peoples barbarians (or, more properly, *barbarii* [those old Romans were all greedy; they seldom were willing to settle for a single "i" to end a word when they could have two]).

The Romans threw this word at damned nearly anybody and everybody of the then-known world—Carthagenians, Garamantians, Egyptians, Mauretanians, Celt-Iberians, Lusitanians, Cyrenians, all manner of Gallic Celts, Belgae, Britons, Caledonian Picts, Germans, Franks, Goths, Alemannii, Alans, Huns, Scythians, Parthians, Galatians, Marcomannii, Quadii, Dacians,

Thracians, Armenians, Cilicians, Arabs, Numidians, Cappadocians, Lycians, Sarmatians and on and on.

Eventually, they even got around to calling the Greeks, who had started it all, barbarians. Certain of those Greeks were so upset by it that they pouted publicly and vowed to hold their breaths until they received a full apology; at last count, they had held their breaths for something over two thousand years. Isn't it truly amazing how much you can accomplish if you just put your mind to it?

The inheritors of the Roman Empire, after they finally got their respective acts together, adopted the word and applied it mostly to people who were not practicing Christians or not of the same brand of Christianity as was the person calling them barbarian. This is a practice even yet in usage, here and there, in barbarous backwaters of the world.

Principally, however, the modern-day use of the word has become one of war (diplomacy by other means) and/or geopolitics. It still goes to show that "barbarian" is definitely in the eye of the beholder.

This anthology, fortunately, has little to do with barbarism in the real world. These stories are heroic fantasies, pure and simple, intended to transport the reader from the deadly complexities of this twentieth-century world in which we live into a relatively simpler milieu of strong men, beautiful maidens, evil sorcerers, dark gods, savage beasts . . . but no nuclear-tipped missiles.

Barbarians brings you stories by the greatest names and about the most famous—or infamous—characters in the field—including Robert E. Howard, the doctor's son from Cross Plains, Texas, who left us Conan, the prototype "barbarian" who has captured the imagination of several generations of readers and made Arnold Schwarzenegger at least a minor film star; Fritz Leiber's wonderful barbarian Fafhrd and his fighting companion the Gray Mouser, who have starred in a series of entertaining stories that began in the pages of the late and lamented *Unknown Worlds* in 1939; Kane, a direct descendant of Conan and the creation of Karl Edward Wagner, the only psychiatrist we know who loves barbarian fiction; Poul Anderson, a man of many literary talents who can also handle a broadsword with the best of them; and Andre Norton (Alice Mary Norton), whose books of wizards, witches, and sorcery have thrilled millions of readers for decades.

Contained in the following pages are tales that are the adult equivalent of children's fairy-tales, pure, unadulterated escapism. I have for long been of the opinion that, in this day and age, adults need fairy-tale escapism far more than do children.

So, now, enter with me into the ultimate escape, the barbaric, barbarous worlds of BARBARIANS!

—Robert Adams

SCYLLA'S DAUGHTER

By Fritz Leiber

With the motherly-generous west wind filling their brown triangular sails, the slim war galley and the five broad-beamed grain ships, two nights out of Lankhmar, coursed north in line ahead across the Inner Sea of the ancient world of Nehwon.

It was late afternoon of one of those mild blue days when sea and sky are the same hue, providing irrefutable evidence for the hypothesis currently favored by Lankhmar philosophers: that Nehwon is a giant bubble rising through the waters of eternity with continents, islands, and the great jewels that at night are the stars all orderly afloat on the bubble's inner surface.

On the afterdeck of the last grain ship, which was also the largest, the Gray Mouser spat a plum skin to leeward and boasted luxuriously, "Fat times in Lankhmar! Not one day returned to the City of the Black Toga after months away adventuring and I procure us this cushy job from the Overlord himself."

"I have an old distrust of cushy jobs," Fafhrd replied, yawning and pulling his fur-trimmed jerkin open wider so that the mild wind might trickle more fully through the tangled hair-field of his chest. "And you got us out of Lankhmar so quickly that we had not even time to pay our respects to the ladies. Nevertheless I must confess that you might have done worse. A full purse is the best ballast for any man-ship, especially one bearing letters of marque against ladies."

Ship's Master Slinoor looked back with hooded appraising eyes at the small lithe gray-clad man and his tall, more gaudily accoutered barbarian comrade. The master of the *Squid* was a sleek black-robed man of middle years. He stood beside the two stocky black-tunicked bare-legged sailors who held steady the great high-arching tiller that guided the *Squid*.

"How much do you two rogues really know of your cushy job?" Slinoor asked softly. "Or rather, how much did the arch-noble Glipkerio choose to tell you of the purpose and dark antecedents of this voyaging?" Two days of fortunate sailing seemed at last to have put the closed-mouthed ship's master in a mood to exchange confidences, or at least trade queries and lies.

From a bag of netted cord that hung by the taffrail, the Mouser speared a night-purple plum with the hook-bladed dirk he called Cat's Claw. Then he answered lightly, "This fleet bears a gift of grain from Overlord Glipkerio to Movarl of the Eight Cities in gratitude for Movarl's sweeping the Mingol pirates from the Inner Sea and mayhap diverting the steppe-dwelling Mingols from assaulting Lankhmar across the Sinking Land. Movarl needs grain for his hunter-farmers turned cityman-soldiers and especially to supply his army relieving his border city of Klelg Nar, which the Mingols besiege. Fafhrd and I are, you might say, a small but mighty rear-guard for the grain and for certain more delicate items of Glipkerio's gift."

"You mean those?" Slinoor bent a thumb toward the larboard rail.

Those were twelve large white rats distributed among four silver-barred cages. With their silky coats, pale-rimmed blue eyes and especially their short, arched upper lips and two huge upper incisors, they looked like a clique of haughty, bored inbred aristocrats, and it was in a bored aristocratic fashion that they were staring at a scrawny black kitten which was perched with dug-in claws on the starboard rail, as if to get as far away from the rats as possible, and staring back at them most worriedly.

Fafhrd reached out and ran a finger down the black kitten's back. The kitten arched its spine, losing itself for a moment in sensuous delight, but then edged away and resumed its worried rat-peering—an activity shared by the two black-tunicked helmsmen, who seemed both resentful and fearful of the silver-caged afterdeck passengers.

The Mouser sucked plum juice from his fingers and flicked out his tongue-tip to neatly capture a drop that threatened to run down his chin. Then, "No, I mean not chiefly those high-bred gift rats," he replied, to Slinoor and kneeling lightly and unexpectedly and touching two fingers significantly to the scrubbed oak deck, he said, "I mean chiefly *she* who is below, who ousts you from your master's cabin, and who now insists that the gift-rats require sunlight and fresh air—which strikes me as a strange way of cosseting burrow- and shadow-dwelling vermin."

Slinoor's cropped eyebrows rose. He came close and whispered, "You think the Demoiselle Hisvet may not be merely the conductress of the rat-gift, but also herself part of Glipkerio's gift to Movarl? Why, she's the daughter of the greatest grain merchant in Lankhmar, who's grown rich selling tawny corn to Glipkerio.''

The Mouser smiled cryptically but said nothing.

Slinoor frowned, then whispered even lower, ''True, I've heard the story that Hisvet has already been her father Hisven's gift to Glipkerio to buy his patronage.''

Fafhrd, who'd been trying to stroke the kitten again with no more success than to chase it up the aftermast, turned around at that. ''Why, Hisvet's but a child,'' he said almost reprovingly. ''A most prim and proper miss. I know not of Glipkerio, he seems decadent''—the word was not an insult in Lankhmar—''but surely Movarl, a northerner albeit a forest man, likes only strong-beamed, ripe, complete women.''

''Your own tastes, no doubt?'' the Mouser remarked, gazing at Fafhrd with half-closed eyes. ''No traffic with childlike women?''

Fafhrd blinked as if the Mouser had dug fingers in his side. Then he shrugged and said loudly, ''What's so special about these rats? Do they do tricks?''

''Aye,'' Slinoor said distastefully. ''They play at being men. They've been trained by Hisvet to dance to music, to drink from cups, hold tiny spears and swords, even fence. I've not seen it—nor would care to.''

The picture struck the Mouser's fancy. He visioned himself small as a rat, dueling with rats who wore lace at their throats and wrists, slipping through the mazy tunnels of their underground cities, becoming a great connoisseur of cheese and smoked meats, perchance wooing a slim rat queen and being surprised by her rat-king husband and having to dagger-fight him in the dark. Then he noted one of the white rats looking at him intently through the silver bars with a cold inhuman blue eye and suddenly his idea didn't seem amusing at all. He shivered in the sunlight.

Slinoor was saying, ''It is not good for animals to try to be men.'' The *Squid*'s skipper gazed somberly at the silent white aristos. ''Have you ever heard tell of the legend of—'' he began, hesitated, then broke off, shaking his head as if deciding he had been about to say too much.

''A sail!'' The call winged down thinly from the crow's nest. ''A black sail to windward!''

''What manner of ship?'' Slinoor shouted up.

''I know not, master. I see only sail top.''

''Keep her under view, boy,'' Slinoor commanded.

''Under view it is, master.''

Slinoor paced to the starboard rail and back.

"Movarl's sails are green," Fafhrd said thoughtfully.

Slinoor nodded. "Ilthmar's are white. The pirates' were red, mostly. Lankhmar's sails once were black, but now that color's only for funeral barges and they never venture out of sight of land. At least I've never known . . ."

The Mouser broke in with, "You spoke of dark antecedents of this voyaging. Why dark?"

Slinoor drew them back against the taffrail, away from the stocky helmsmen. Fafhrd ducked a little, passing under the arching tiller. They looked all three into the twisting wake, their heads bent together.

Slinoor said, "You've been out of Lankhmar. Did you know this is not the first gift-fleet of grain to Movarl?"

The Mouser nodded. "We'd been told there was another. Somehow lost. In a storm, I think. Glipkerio glossed over it."

"There were two," Slinoor said tersely. "Both lost. Without a living trace. There was no storm."

"What then?" Fafhrd asked, looking around as the rats chittered a little. "Pirates?"

"Movarl had already whipped the pirates east. Each of the two fleets was galley-guarded like ours. And each sailed off into fair weather with a good west wind." Slinoor smiled thinly. "Doubtless Glipkerio did not tell you of these matters for fear you might beg off. We sailors and the Lankhmarines obey for duty and the honor of the City, but of late Glipkerio's had trouble hiring the sort of special agents he likes to use for second bow-strings. He has brains of a sort, our overlord has, though he employs them mostly to dream of visiting other world bubbles in a great diving-bell or sealed brass diving-ship, while he sits with trained girls watching trained rats and buys off Lankhmar's enemies with gold and repays Lankhmar's ever-more-impatient friends with grain not soldiers." Slinoor grunted. "Movarl grows most impatient, you know. He threatens, if the grain comes not, to recall his pirate patrol, league with the land-Mingols and set them at Lankhmar."

"Northerners, even though not snow-dwelling, league with Mingols?" Fafhrd objected. "Impossible!"

Slinoor looked at him. "I'll say just this, ice-eating northerner. If I did not believe such a leaguer both possible and likely—and Lankhmar thereby in dire danger—I would never have sailed with this fleet, honor and duty or no. Same's true of Lukeen who commands the galley. Nor do I think Glipkerio would otherwise be sending to Movarl at Kvarch Nar his noblest performing rats and dainty Hisvet.''

Fafhrd growled a little. ''You say both fleets were lost without a trace?'' he asked incredulously.

Slinoor shook his head. ''The first was. Of the second, some wreckage was sighted by an Ilthmar trader Lankhmar-bound. The deck of only one grain ship. It had been ripped off its hull, splinteringly—how or by what, the Ilthmart dared not guess. Tied to a fractured stretch of railing was the ship's-master, only hours dead. His face had been nibbled, his body gnawed.''

''Fish?'' the Mouser asked.

''Seabirds?'' Fafhrd inquired.

''Dragons?'' a third voice suggested, high, breathless, and as merry as a school girl's. The three men turned around, Slinoor with guilty swiftness.

The Demoiselle Hisvet stood as tall as the Mouser, but judging by her face, wrists, and ankles was considerably slenderer. Her face was delicate and taper-chinned with small mouth and pouty upper lip that lifted just enough to show a double dash of pearly tooth. Her complexion was creamy pale except for two spots of color high on her cheeks. Her straight fine hair, which grew low on her forehead, was pure white touched with silver and all drawn back through a silver ring behind her neck, whence it hung unbraided like a unicorn's tail. Her eyes had china whites but darkly pink irises around the large black pupils. Her body was enveloped and hidden by a loose robe of violet silk except when the wind briefly molded a flat curve of her girlish anatomy. There was a violet hood, half thrown back. The sleeves were puffed but snug at the wrists. She was barefoot, her skin showing as creamy there as on her face, except for a tinge of pink about the toes.

She looked them all three one after another quickly in the eye. ''You were whispering of the fleets that failed,'' she said accusingly. ''Fie, Master Slinoor. We must all have courage.''

''Aye,'' Fafhrd agreed, finding that a cue to his liking. ''Even dragons need not daunt a brave man. I've often watched the sea monsters, crested, horned, and some two-headed, playing in the waves of outer ocean as they broke around the rocks sailors call the Claws. They were not to be feared, if a man remembered always to fix them with a commanding eye. They sported lustily together, the man dragons pursuing the woman dragons and going—'' Here Fafhrd took a tremendous breath and then roared

out so loudly and wailingly that the two helmsmen jumped—
"Hoongk! Hoongk!"

"Fie, Swordsman Fafhrd," Hisvet said primly, a blush mantling her cheeks and forehead. "You are most indelicate. The sex of dragons—"

But Slinoor had whirled on Fafhrd, gripping his wrist and now crying, "Quiet, you monster-fool! Know you not we sail tonight by moonlight past the Dragon Rocks? You'll call them down on us!"

"There are no dragons in the Inner Sea," Fafhrd laughingly assured him.

"There's something that tears ships," Slinoor asserted stubbornly.

The Mouser took advantage of this brief interchange to move in on Hisvet, rapidly bowing thrice as he approached.

"We have missed the great pleasure of your company on deck, Demoiselle," he said suavely.

"Alas, sir, the sun mislikes me," she answered prettily. "Now his rays are mellowed as he prepares to submerge. Then too," she added with an equally pretty shudder, "these rough sailors—" She broke off as she saw that Fafhrd and the master of the *Squid* had stopped their argument and returned to her. "Oh, I meant not you, dear Master Slinoor," she assured him, reaching out and almost touching his black robe.

"Would the Demoiselle fancy a sun-warmed, wind-cooled black plum of Sarheenmar?" the Mouser suggested, delicately sketching in the air with Cat's Claw.

"I know not." Hisvet said, eyeing the dirk's needlelike point. "I must be thinking of getting the White Shadows below before the evening's chill is upon us."

"True," Fafhrd agreed with a flattering laugh, realizing she must mean the white rats. "But 'twas most wise of you, little mistress, to let them spend the day on deck, where they surely cannot hanker so much to sport with the Black Shadows—I mean, of course, their black free commoner brothers, and slim delightful sisters, to be sure, hiding here and there in the hold."

"There are no rats on my ship, sportive or otherwise," Slinoor asserted instantly, his voice loud and angry. "Think you I run a rat-brothel? Your pardon, Demoiselle," he added quickly to Hisvet. "I mean, there are no common rats aboard *Squid*."

"Then yours is surely the first grain ship so blessed," Fafhrd told him with indulgent reasonableness.

The sun's vermilion disk touched the sea to the west and flattened like a tangerine. Hisvet leaned back against the taffrail under the arching tiller. Fafhrd was to her right, the Mouser to

her left with the plums hanging just beyond him, near the silver
cages. Slinoor had moved haughtily forward to speak to the
helmsmen, or pretend to.

"I'll take that plum now, Dirksman Mouser," Hisvet said
softly.

As the Mouser turned away in happy obedience and with
many a graceful gesture, delicately palpating the net bag to find
the most tender fruit, Hisvet stretched her right arm out sideways
and without looking once at Fafhrd slowly ran her spread-fingered
hand through the hair on his chest, paused when she reached the
other side to grasp a fistful and tweak it sharply, then trailed her
fingers lightly back across the hair she had ruffled.

Her hand came back to her just as the Mouser turned around.
She kissed the palm lingeringly, then reached it across her body
to take the black fruit from the point of the Mouser's dirk. She
sucked delicately at the prick Cat's Claw had made and shivered.

"Fie, sir," she pouted. "You told me 'twould be sun-warmed
and 'tis not. Already all things grow chilly with evening." She
looked around her thoughtfully. "Why, Swordsman Fafhrd is all
goose-flesh," she announced, then blushed and tapped her lips
reprovingly. "Close your jerkin, sir. 'Twill save you from ca-
tarrh and perchance from further embarrassment a girl who is
unused to any sight of man-flesh save in slaves."

"Here is a toastier plum," the Mouser called from beside the
bag. Hisvet smiled at him and lightly tossed him backhanded the
plum she'd sampled. He dropped that overboard and tossed her
the second plum. She caught it deftly, lightly squeezed it, touched
it to her lips, shook her head sadly though still smiling, and
tossed back the plum. The Mouser, smiling gently too, caught it,
dropped it overboard and tossed her a third. They played that
way for some time. A shark following in the wake of the *Squid*
got a stomachache.

The black kitten came single-footing back along the starboard
rail with a sharp eye to larboard. Fafhrd seized it instantly as any
good general does opportunity in the heat of battle.

"Have you seen the ship's catling, little mistress?" he called,
crossing to Hisvet, the kitten almost hidden in his big hands.
"Or perhaps we should call the *Squid* the catling's ship, for she
adopted it, skipping by herself aboard just as we sailed. Here,
little mistress. It feels sun-tested now, warmer than any plum,"
and he reached the kitten out sitting on the palm of his right
hand.

But Fafhrd had been forgetting the kitten's point of view. Its
fur stood on end as it saw itself being carried toward the rats and

now, as Hisvet stretched out her hand toward it, showing her upper teeth in a tiny smile and saying, "Poor little waif," the kitten hissed fiercely and raked out stiff-armed with spread claws.

Hisvet drew back her hand with a gasp. Before Fafhrd could drop the kitten or bat it aside, it sprang to the top of his head and from there onto the highest point of the tiller.

The Mouser darted to Hisvet, crying meanwhile at Fafhrd, "Dolt! Lout! You knew the beast was half wild!" Then, to Hisvet, "Demoiselle! Are you hurt?"

Fafhrd struck angrily at the kitten and one of the helmsmen came back to bat at it too, perhaps because he thought it improper for kittens to walk on the tiller. The kitten made a long leap to the starboard rail, slipped over it, and dangled by two claws above the curving water.

Hisvet was holding her hand away from the Mouser and he was saying, "Better let me examine it, Demoiselle. Even the slightest scratch from a filthy ship's cat can be dangerous," and she was saying, almost playfully, "No, Dirksman, I tell you it's nothing."

Fafhrd strode to the starboard rail, fully intending to flick the kitten overboard, but somehow when he came to do it he found he had instead cupped the kitten's rear in his hand and lifted it back on the rail. The kitten instantly sank its teeth deeply in the root of his thumb and fled up the aftermast. Fafhrd with difficulty suppressed a great yowl. Slinoor laughed.

"Nevertheless, I will examine it," the Mouser said, masterfully and took Hisvet's hand by force. She let him hold it for a moment, then snatched it back and drawing herself up said frostily, "Dirksman, you forget yourself. Not even her own physician touches a demoiselle of Lankhmar, he touches only the body of her maid, on which the demoiselle points out her pains and symptoms. Leave me, Dirksman."

The Mouser stood huffily back against the taffrail. Fafhrd sucked the root of his thumb. Hisvet went and stood beside the Mouser. Without looking at him, she said softly, "You should have asked me to call my maid. She's quite pretty."

Only a fingernail clipping of red sun was left on the horizon. Slinoor addressed the crow's nest: "What of the black sail, boy?"

"She holds her distance, master," the cry came back. "She courses on abreast of us."

The sun went under with a faint green flash. Hisvet bent her head sideways and kissed the Mouser on the neck, just under the ear. Her tongue tickled.

"Now I lose her, master," the crow's nest called. "There's mist to the northwest. And to the northeast . . . a small black cloud . . . like a black ship specked with light . . . that moves through the air. And now that fades too. All gone, master."

Hisvet straightened her head. Slinoor came toward them muttering, "The crow's nest sees too much." Hisvet shivered and said, "The White Shadows will take a chill. They're delicate, Dirksman." The Mouser breathed, "You are Ecstasy's White Shadow, Demoiselle," then strolled toward the silver cages, saying loudly for Slinoor's benefit, "Might we not be privileged to have a show of them, Demoiselle, tomorrow here on the afterdeck? 'Twould be wondrous instructive to watch you control them." He caressed the air over the cages and said, lying mightily, "My, they're fine handsome fellows." Actually he was peering apprehensively for any of the little spears and swords Slinoor had mentioned. The twelve rats looked up at him incuriously. One even seemed to yawn.

Slinoor said curtly, "I would advise against it, Demoiselle. The sailors have a mad fear and hatred of all rats. 'Twere best not to arouse it."

"But these are aristos," the Mouser objected, while Hisvet only repeated, "They'll take a chill."

Fafhrd, hearing this, took his hand out of his mouth and came hurrying to Hisvet, saying, "Little Mistress, may I carry them below? I'll be gentle as a Kleshite nurse." He lifted between thumb and third finger a cage with two rats in it. Hisvet rewarded him with a smile, saying, "I wish you would, gallant Swordsman. The common sailors handle them too roughly. But two cages are all you may safely carry. You'll need proper help." She gazed at the Mouser and Slinoor.

So Slinoor and the Mouser, the latter much to his distaste and apprehension, must each gingerly take up a silver cage, and Fafhrd two, and follow Hisvet to her cabin below the afterdeck. The Mouser could not forbear whispering privily to Fafhrd, "Oaf! To make rat-grooms of us! May you get rat-bites to match your cat-bite!" At the cabin door Hisvet's dark maid Frix received the cages, Hisvet thanked her three gallants most briefly and distantly and Frix closed the door against them. There was the muffled thud of a bar dropping across it and the jangle of a chain locking down the bar.

Darkness grew on the waters. A yellow lantern was lit and hoisted to the crow's nest. The black war galley *Shark*, its brown sail temporarily furled, came rowing back to fuss at *Clam*, next ahead of *Squid* in line, for being slow in getting up its masthead light, then dropped back by *Squid* while Lukeen and Slinoor exchanged shouts about a black sail and mist and ship-shaped small black clouds and the Dragon Rocks. Finally the galley went bustling ahead again with its Lankhmarines in browned-iron chain mail to take up its sailing station at the head of the column. The first stars twinkled, proof that the sun had not deserted through the waters of eternity to some other world bubble, but was swimming as he should back to the east under the ocean of the sky, errant rays from him lighting the floating star-jewels in his passage.

After moonrise that night Fafhrd and the Mouser each found private occasion to go rapping at Hisvet's door, but neither profited greatly thereby. At Fafhrd's knock Hisvet herself opened the small grille set in the larger door, said swiftly, "Fie, for shame, Swordsman! Can't you see I'm undressing?" and closed it instantly. While when the Mouser asked softly for a moment with "Ecstasy's White Shadow," the merry face of the dark maid Frix appeared at the grille, saying, "My mistress bid me kiss my hand good night to you." Which she did and closed the grille.

Fafhrd, who had been spying, greeted the crestfallen Mouser with a sardonic, "Ecstasy's White Shadow!"

"Little Mistress!" the Mouser retorted scathingly.

"Black Plum of Sarheenmar!"

"Kleshite Nurse!"

Neither hero slept restfully that night and two-thirds through it the *Squid*'s gong began to sound at intervals, with the other ships' gongs replying or calling faintly. When at dawn's first blink the two came on deck, *Squid* was creeping through fog that hid the sail top. The two helmsmen were peering about jumpily, as if they expected to see ghosts. The sails hung slackly. Slinoor, his eyes dark-circled by fatigue and big with anxiety, explained tersely that the fog had not only slowed but disordered the grain fleet.

"That's *Tunny* next ahead of us, I can tell by her gong note. And beyond *Tunny*, *Carp*. Where's *Clam*? What's *Shark* about? And still not certainly past the Dragon Rocks! Not that I want to see 'em!"

"Do not some captains call them the Rat Rocks?" Fafhrd interposed. "From a rat colony started there from a wreck?"

"Aye," Slinoor allowed and then grinning sourly at the Mouser, observed, "Not the best day for a rat show on the afterdeck, is it? Which is some good from this fog. I can't abide the lolling white brutes. Though but a dozen in number they remind me too much of the Thirteen. Have you ever heard tell of the legend of the Thirteen?''

''I have,'' Fafhrd said somberly. ''A wise woman of the Cold Waste once told me that for each animal kind—wolves, bats, whales, it holds for all and each—there are always thirteen individuals having almost manlike (or demonlike!) wisdom and skill. Can you but find and master this inner circle, the Wise Woman said, then through them you can control all animals of that kind.''

Slinoor looked narrowly at Fafhrd and said, ''She was not an altogether stupid woman.''

The Mouser wondered if for men also there was an inner circle of Thirteen.

The black kitten came ghosting along the deck out of the fog forward. It made toward Fafhrd with an eager mew, then hesitated, studying him dubiously.

''Take for example, cats,'' Fafhrd said with a grin. ''Somewhere in Nehwon today, mayhap scattered but more likely banded together, are thirteen cats of superfeline sagacity, somehow sensing and controlling the destiny of all catkind.''

''What's this one sensing now?'' Slinoor demanded softly.

The black kitten was staring to larboard, sniffing. Suddenly its scrawny body stiffened, the hair rising along its back and its skimpy tail a-bush.

''HOONGK!''

Slinoor turned to Fafhrd with a curse, only to see the Northerner staring about shut-mouthed and startled.

Out of the fog to larboard came a green serpent's head big as a horse's, with white dagger teeth fencing red mouth horrendously a-gape. With dreadful swiftness it lunged low past Fafhrd on its endless yellow neck, its lower jaw loudly scraping the deck, and the white daggers clashed on the black kitten.

Or rather, on where the kitten had just been. For the latter seemed not so much to leap as to lift itself, by its tail perhaps, onto the starboard rail and thence vanished into the fog at the top of the aftermast in at most three more bounds.

The helmsmen raced each other forward. Slinoor and the Mouser threw themselves against the starboard taffrail, the unmanned tiller swinging slowly above them affording some sense of protection against the monster, which now lifted its nightmare head and swayed it this way and that, each time avoiding Fafhrd by inches. Apparently it was searching for the black kitten or more like it.

Fafhrd stood frozen, at first by sheer shock, then by the thought that whatever part of him moved first would get snapped off.

Nevertheless he was about to jump for it—besides all else the monster's mere stench was horrible—when a second green dragon's head, four times as big as the first with teeth like scimitars, came looming out of the fog. Sitting commandingly atop this second head was a man dressed in orange and purple, like a herald of the Eastern Lands, with red boots, cape and helmet, the last with a blue window in it, seemingly of opaque glass.

There is a point of grotesquerie beyond which horror cannot go, but slips into delirium. Fafhrd had reached that point. He began to feel as if he were in an opium dream. Everything was unquestionably real, yet it had lost its power to horrify him acutely.

He noticed as the merest of quaint details that the two greenish-yellow necks forked from a common trunk.

Besides, the gaudily garbed man or demon riding the larger head seemed very sure of himself, which might or might not be a good thing. Just now he was belaboring the smaller head, seemingly in rebuke, with a blunt-pointed blunt-hooked pike he carried, and roaring out, either under or through his blue red helmet, a gibberish that might be rendered as:

"*Gottverdammter Ungeheuer!*"*

The smaller head cringed away, whimpering like seventeen puppies. The man-demon whipped out a small book of pages and after consulting it twice (apparently he could see *out* through his blue window) called down in broken, outlandishly accented Lankhmarese, "What world is this, friend?"

Fafhrd had never been in his life heard that question asked, even by an awakening brandy guzzler. Nevertheless in his opium-dream mood he answered easily enough, "The world of Nehwon, oh sorcerer!"

"*Gott sei dank!*"† the man-demon gibbered.

Fafhrd asked, "What world do *you* hail from?"

This question seemed to confound the man-demon. Hurriedly consulting his book, he replied, "Do you know about other worlds? Don't you believe the stars are only huge jewels?"

Fafhrd responded, "Any fool can see that the lights in the sky are jewels, but we are not simpletons, we know of other worlds.

---

* "Goddam monster!" German is a language completely unknown in Nehwon.
† "Thank God!"

The Lankhmarts think they're bubbles in infinite waters. *I* believe we live in the jewel-ceilinged skull of a dead god. But doubtless there are other such skulls, the universe of universes being a great frosty battlefield.''

The tiller, swinging as *Squid* wallowed with sail a-flap, bumped the lesser head, which twisted around and snapped at it, then shook splinters from its teeth.

"Tell the sorcerer to keep it off!" Slinoor shouted, cringing.

After more hurried page-flipping the man-demon called down, "Don't worry, the monster seems to eat only rats. I captured it by a small rocky island where many rats live. It mistook your small black ship's cat for a rat.''

Still in his mood of opium-lucidity, Fafhrd called up, "Oh sorcerer, do you plan to conjure the monster to your own skull-world, or world-bubble?''

This question seemed doubly to confound and excite the man-demon. He appeared to think Fafhrd must be a mind-reader. With much frantic book-consulting, he explained that he came from a world called simply Tomorrow and that he was visiting many worlds to collect monsters for some sort of museum or zoo, which he called in his gibberish *Hagenbeck's Zeitgarten**. On this particular expedition he had been seeking a monster that would be a reasonable facsimile of a wholly mythical six-headed sea-monster that devoured men off the decks of ships and was called Scylla by an ancient fantasy writer named Homer.

"There never was a Lankhmar poet named Homer," muttered Slinoor, who seemed to have none too clear an idea of what was going on.

"Doubtless he was scribe of Quarmall or the Eastern Lands," the Mouser told Slinoor reassuringly. Then, grown less fearful of the two heads and somewhat jealous of Fafhrd holding the center of the stage, the Mouser leapt atop the taffrail and cried, "Oh sorcerer, with what spells will you conjure your Little Scylla back to, or perhaps I should say ahead to your Tomorrow bubble? I myself know somewhat of witchcraft. Desist, vermin!'' (This last remark was directed with a gesture of lordly contempt toward the lesser head, which came questing curiously toward the Mouser. Slinoor gripped the Mouser's ankle.)

The man-demon reacted to the Mouser's question by slapping himself on the side of his red helmet, as though he'd forgotten something most important. He hurriedly began to explain that he traveled between worlds in a ship (or space-time engine, what-

---

*Literally, in German, "Hagenbeck's Time-garden," apparently derived from *Tiergarten*, which means animal-garden, or zoo.

ever that might mean) that tended to float just above the water—"a black ship with little lights and masts"—and that the ship had floated away from him in another fog a day ago while he'd been absorbed in taming the newly captured sea-monster. Since then the man-demon, mounted on his now-docile monster, had been fruitlessly searching for his lost vehicle.

The description awakened a memory in Slinoor, who managed to nerve himself to explain audibly that last sunset *Squid*'s crow's nest had sighted just such a ship floating or flying to the northeast.

The man-demon was voluble in his thanks and after questioning Slinoor closely announced (rather to everyone's relief) that he was now ready to turn his search eastward with new hope.

"Probably I will never have the opportunity to repay your courtesies," he said in parting. "But as you drift through the waters of eternity at least carry with you my name: Karl Treuherz of Hagenbeck's."

Hisvet, who had been listening from the middeck, chose that moment to climb the short ladder that led up to the afterdeck. She was wearing an ermine smock and hood against the chilly fog.

As her silvery hair and pale lovely features rose above the level of the afterdeck, the smaller dragon's head, which had been withdrawing decorously, darted at her with the speed of a serpent striking. Hisvet dropped. Woodwork rended loudly.

Backing off into the fog atop the larger and rather benign-eyed head, Karl Treuherz gibbered as never before and belabored the lesser head mercilessly as it withdrew.

Then the two-headed monster with its orange-and-purple mahout could be dimly seen moving around *Squid*'s stern eastward into thicker fog, the man-demon gibbering gentlier what might have been an excuse and farewell: *"Es tut mir sehr leid! Aber dankeschoen, dankeschoen!"** With a last gentle "Hoongk!" the man-demon dragon-dragon assemblage faded into the fog.

Fafhrd and the Mouser raced a tie to Hisvet's side, vaulting down over the splintered rail, only to have her scornfully reject their solicitude as she lifted herself from the oaken middeck, delicately rubbing her hip and limping for a step or two.

"Come not near me, Spoonmen," she said bitterly. "Shame it is when a demoiselle must save herself from toothy perdition only by falling helter-skelter on that part of her which I would almost shame to show you on Frix. You are no gentle knights, else dragons' heads had littered the afterdeck. Fie, fie!"

---

*It was! "I am so very sorry! But thank you, thank you so nicely!"

Meanwhile patches of clear sky and water began to show to the west and the wind to freshen from the same quarter. Slinoor dashed forward, bawling for his bosun to chase the monster-scared sailors up from the forecastle before *Squid* did herself an injury.

Although that was yet little real danger of that, the Mouser stood by the tiller, Fafhrd looked to the mainsheet. Then Slinoor, hurrying back aft followed by a few pale sailors, sprang to the taffrail with a cry.

The fogbank was slowly rolling eastward. Clear water stretched to the western horizon. Two bowshots north of *Squid,* four other ships were emerging in a disordered cluster from the white wall: the war galley *Shark* and the grain ships *Tunny, Carp* and *Grouper.* The galley, moving rapidly under oars, was headed toward *Squid.*

But Slinoor was staring south. There, a scant bowshot away, were two ships, the one standing clear of the fogbank, the other half hid in it.

The one in the clear was *Clam,* about to sink by the head, its gunwales awash. Its mainsail, somehow carried away, trailed brownly in the water. The empty deck was weirdly arched upward.

The fog-shrouded ship appeared to be a black cutter with a black sail.

Between the two ships, from *Clam* toward the cutter, moved a multitude of tiny, dark-headed ripples.

Fafhrd joined Slinoor. Without looking away, the latter said simply, "Rats!" Fafhrd's eye-brows rose.

The Mouser joined them, saying, "*Clam*'s holed. The water swells the grain, which mightily forces up the deck."

Slinoor nodded and pointed toward the cutter. It was possible dimly to see tiny dark forms—rats surely!—climbing over its side from out of the water. "There's what gnawed holes in *Clam,*" Slinoor said.

Then Slinoor pointed between the ships, near the cutter. Among the last of the ripple-army was a white-headed one. A little later a small white form could be seen swiftly mounting the cutter's side. Slinoor said, "There's what commanded the hole-gnawers."

With a dull splintering rumble the arched deck of *Clam* burst upward, spewing brown.

"The grain!" Slinoor cried hollowly.

"Now you know what tears ships," the Mouser said.

The black cutter grew ghostlier, moving west now into the retreating fog.

The galley *Shark* went boiling past *Squid*'s stern, its oars moving like the legs of a leaping centipede. Lukeen shouted up, "Here's foul trickery! *Clam* was lured off in the night!"

The black cutter, winning its race with the eastward-rolling fog, vanished in whiteness.

The split-decked *Clam* nosed under with hardly a ripple and angled down into the black and salty depths, dragged by its leaden keel.

With war trumpet skirling, *Shark* drove into the white wall after the cutter.

Clam's masthead, cutting a little furrow in the swell, went under. All that was to be seen now on the waters south of *Squid* was a great spreading stain of tawny grain.

Slinoor turned brim-faced to his mate. "Enter the Demoiselle Hisvet's cabin, by force if need be," he commanded. "Count her white rats!"

Fafhrd and the Mouser looked at each other.

Three hours later the same four persons were assembled in Hisvet's cabin with the Demoiselle, Frix, and Lukeen.

The cabin, low-ceilinged enough so that Fafhrd, Lukeen and the mate must move bent and tended to sit hunch-shouldered, was spacious for a grain ship, yet crowded by this company together with the caged rats and Hisvet's perfumed, silver-bound baggage piled on Slinoor's dark furniture and locked sea chests.

Three horn windows to the stern and louver slits to starboard and larboard let in a muted light.

Slinoor and Lukeen sat against the horn windows, behind a narrow table. Fafhrd occupied a cleared sea chest, the Mouser an upended cask. Between them were racked the four rat cages, whose white-furred occupants seemed as quietly intent on the proceedings as any of the men. The Mouser amused himself by imagining what it would be like if the white rats were trying the men instead of the other way round. A row of blue-eyed white rats would make most formidable judges, already robed in ermine. He pictured them staring down mercilessly from very high seats at a tiny cringing Lukeen and Slinoor, round whom scuttled mouse pages and mouse clerks and behind whom stood rat pikemen in half armor holding fantastically barbed and curvy-bladed weapons.

The mate stood stooping by the open grille of the closed door, in part to see that no other sailors eavesdropped.

The Demoiselle Hisvet sat cross-legged on the swung-down sea-bed, her ermine smock decorously tucked under her knees, managing to look most distant and courtly even in this attitude. Now and again her right hand played with the dark wavy hair of Frix, who crouched on the deck at her knees.

Timbers creaked as *Squid* bowled north. Now and then the bare feet of the helmsmen could be heard faintly slithering on the afterdeck overhead. Around the small trapdoor-like hatches leading below and through the very crevices of the planking came the astringent, toastlike, all-pervasive odor of the grain.

Lukeen spoke. He was a lean, slant-shouldered, cordily muscled man almost as big as Fafhrd. His short coat of browned-iron mail over his simple black tunic was of the finest links. A golden band confined his dark hair and bound to his forehead the browned-iron five-pointed curvy-edged starfish emblem of Lankhmar.

"How do I know *Clam* was lured away? Two hours before dawn I twice thought I heard *Shark*'s own gong-note in the distance, although I stood then beside *Shark*'s muffled gong. Three of my crew heard it too. 'Twas most eerie. Gentlemen, I know the gong-notes of Lankhmar war galleys and merchantmen better than I know my children's voices. This that we heard was so like *Shark*'s I never dreamed it might be that of another ship—I deemed it some ominous ghost-echo or trick of our minds and I thought no more about it as a matter for action. If I had only had the faintest suspicion . . ."

Lukeen scowled bitterly, shaking his head, and continued, "Now I know the black cutter must carry a gong shaped to duplicate *Shark*'s note precisely. They used it, likely with someone mimicking my voice, to draw *Clam* out of line in the fog and get her far enough off so that the rat horde, officered by the white one, could work its will on her without the crew's screams being heard. They must have gnawed twenty holes in her bottom for *Clam* to take on water so fast and the grain to swell so. Oh, they're far shrewder and more persevering than men, the little spade toothed fiends!"

"Midsea madness!" Fafhrd snorted in interruption. "Rats make men scream? And do away with them? Rats seize a ship and sink it? Rats officered and accepting discipline? Why this is the rankest superstition!"

"You're a fine one to talk of superstition and the impossible, Fafhrd," Slinoor shot at him, "when only this morning you talked with a masked and gibbering demon who rode a two-headed dragon."

Lukeen lifted his eyebrows at Slinoor. This was the first he'd heard of the Hagenbeck episode.

Fafhrd said, "That was travel between worlds. Another matter altogether. No superstition in it."

Slinoor responded skeptically. "I suppose there was no superstition in it either when you told me what you'd heard from the Wise Woman about the Thirteen?"

Fafhrd laughed. "Why, I never believed one word the Wise Woman ever told me. She was a witchery old fool. I recounted her nonsense merely as a curiosity."

Slinoor eyed Fafhrd with slit-eyed incredulity, then said to Lukeen, "Continue."

"There's little more to tell," the latter said. "I saw the rat-battalions swimming from *Clam* to the black cutter. I saw, as you did, their white officer." This with a glare at Fafhrd. "Thereafter I fruitlessly hunted the black cutter two hours in the fog until cramp took my rowers. If I'd found her, I'd not boarded her but thrown fire into her! Aye, and stood off the rats with burning oil on the waters if they tried again to change ships! Aye, and laughed as the furred murderers fried!"

"Just so," Slinoor said with finality. "And what, in your judgment, Commander Lukeen, should we do now?"

"Sink the white arch-fiends in their cages," Lukeen answered instantly, "before they officer the rape of more ships, or our sailors go mad with fear."

This brought an instant icy retort from Hisvet. "You'll have to sink me first, silver-weighted, oh Commander!"

Lukeen's gaze moved past her to a scatter of big-eared silver unguent jars and several looped heavy silver chains on a shelf by the bed. "That too is not impossible, Demoiselle," he said, smiling hardly.

"There's not one shred of proof against her!" Fafhrd exploded. "Little mistress, the man is mad."

"No proof?" Lukeen roared. "There were twelve white rats yesterday. Now there are eleven." He waved a hand at the stacked cages and their blue-eyed haughty occupants. "You've all counted them. Who else but this devilish demoiselle sent the white officer to direct the sharp-toothed gnawers and killers that destroyed *Clam*? What more proof do you want?"

"Yes, indeed!" the Mouser interjected in a high vibrant voice that commanded attention. "There is proof aplenty . . . *if* there were twelve rats in the four cages yesterday." Then he added casually but very clearly, "It is my recollection that there were eleven."

Slinoor stared at the Mouser as though he couldn't believe his ears. "You lie!" he said. "What's more, you lie senselessly.

Why, you and Fafhrd and I all spoke of there being twelve white rats!''

The Mouser shook his head. ''Fafhrd and I said no word about the exact number of rats. *You* said there were a dozen,'' he informed Slinoor. ''Not twelve, but . . . a dozen. I assumed you were using the expression as a round number, an approximation.'' The Mouser snapped his fingers. ''Now I remember that when you said a dozen I became idly curious and counted the rats. And got eleven. But it seemed to me too trifling a matter to dispute.''

''No, there were twelve rats yesterday,'' Slinoor asserted solemnly and with great conviction. ''You're mistaken, Gray Mouser.''

''I'll believe my friend Slinoor before a dozen of you,'' Lukeen put in.

''True, friends should stick together,'' the Mouser said with an approving smile. ''Yesterday I counted Glipkerio's gift-rats and got eleven. Ship's Master Slinoor, any man may be mistaken in his recollections from time to time. Let's analyze this. Twelve white rats divided by four silver cages equals three to a cage. Now let me see . . . I have it! There was a time yesterday when between us, we surely counted the rats—when we carried them down to this cabin. How many were in the cage you carried, Slinoor?''

''Three,'' the latter said instantly.

''And three in mine,'' the Mouser said.

''And three in each of other two,'' Lukeen put in impatiently. ''We waste time!''

''We certainly do,'' Slinoor agreed strongly, nodding.

''Wait!'' said the Mouser, lifting a point-fingered hand. ''There was a moment when all of us must have noticed how many rats there were in one of the cages Fafhrd carried—when he first lifted it up, speaking while to Hisvet. Visualize it. He lifted it like this.'' The Mouser touched his thumb to his third finger. ''How many rats were in that cage, Slinoor?''

Slinoor frowned deeply. ''Two,'' he said, adding instantly, ''and four in the other.''

''You said three in each just now,'' the Mouser reminded him.

''I did not!'' Slinoor denied. ''Lukeen said that, not I.''

''Yes, but you nodded, agreeing with him,'' the Mouser said, his raised eyebrows the very emblem of innocent truth-seeking.

''I agreed with him only that we wasted time,'' Slinoor said. ''And we do.'' Just the same a little of the frown lingered between his eyes and his voice had lost its edge of utter certainty.

"I see," the Mouser said doubtfully. By stages he had begun to play the part of an attorney elucidating a case in court, striding about and frowning most professionally. Now he shot a sudden question: "Fafhrd, how many rats did you carry?"

"Five," boldly answered the Northerner, whose mathematics were not of the sharpest, but who'd had plenty time to count surreptitiously on his fingers and to think about what the Mouser was up to. "Two in one cage, three in the other."

"A feeble falsehood!" Lukeen scoffed. "The base barbarian would swear to anything to win a smile from the Demoiselle, who has him fawning."

"That's a foul lie!" Fafhrd roared, springing up and fetching his head such a great hollow thump on a deck beam that he clapped both hands to it and crouched in dizzy agony.

"Sit down, Fafhrd, before I ask you to apologize to the roof!" the Mouser commanded with heartless harshness. "This is solemn civilized court, no barbarous brawling session! Let's see—three and three and five make . . . eleven. Demoiselle Hisvet!" He pointed an accusing finger straight between her red-irised eyes and demanded most sternly, "How many white rats did you bring aboard *Squid*? The truth now and nothing but the truth!"

"Eleven," she answered demurely. "La, but I'm joyed someone at last had the wit to ask me."

"That I know's not true!" Slinoor said abruptly, his brow once more clear. "Why didn't I think of it before?—'twould have saved us all this bother of questions and counting. I have in this very cabin Glipkerio's letter of commission to me. In it he speaks verbatim of entrusting to me the Demoiselle Hisvet, daughter of Hisvin, and twelve witty white rats. Wait, I'll get it out and prove it to your faces!"

"No need, Ship's-Master," Hisvet interposed. "I saw the letter writ and can testify to the perfect truth of your quotation. But most sadly, between the sending of the letter and my boarding of *Squid*, poor Tchy was gobbled up by Glippy's giant boarhound Bimbat." She touched a slim finger to the corner of her eye and sniffed. "Poor Tchy, he was the most winsome of the twelve. 'Twas why I kept to my cabin the first two days." Each time she spoke the name Tchy, the eleven caged rats chittered mournfully.

"Is it Glippy you call our overlord?" Slinoor ejaculated, genuinely snocked. "Oh shameless one!"

"Aye, watch your language, Demoiselle," the Mouser warned severely, maintaining to the hilt his new role of austere inquisitor. "The familiar relationship between you and our overlord the arch-noble Glipkerio Kistomerces does not come within the province of this court.''

"She lies like a shrewd subtle witch!" Lukeen asserted angrily. "Thumbscrew or rack, or perchance just a pale arm twisted high behind her back would get the truth from her fast enough!"

Hisvet turned and looked at him proudly. "I accept your challenge, Commander," she said evenly, laying her right hand on her maid's dark head. "Frix, reach out your naked hand, or whatever other part of you the brave gentleman wishes to torture." The dark maid straightened her back. Her face was impassive, lips firmly pressed together, though her eyes searched around wildly. Hisvet continued to Slinoor and Lukeen, "If you know any Lankhmar law at all, you know that a virgin of the rank of demoiselle is tortured only in the person of her maid, who proves by her steadfastness under extreme pain the innocence of her mistress."

"What did I tell you about her?" Lukeen demanded of them all. "Subtle is too gross a term for her spiderwebby sleights!" He glared at Hisvet and said scornfully, his mouth a-twist, "Virgin!"

Hisvet smiled with cold long-suffering. Fafhrd flushed and although still holding his battered head, barely refrained from leaping up again. Lukeen looked at him with amusement, secure in his knowledge that he could bait Fafhrd at will and that the barbarian lacked the civilized wit to insult him deeply in return.

Fafhrd stared thoughtfully at Lukeen from under his capping hands. Then he said, "Yes, you're brave enough in armor, with your threats against girls and your hot imaginings of torture, but if you were without armor and had to prove your manhood with just one brave girl alone, you'd fail like a worm!"

Lukeen shot up enraged and got himself such a clout from a deck beam that he squeaked shudderingly and swayed. Nevertheless he gripped blindly for his sword at his side. Slinoor grasped that wrist and pulled him down into his seat.

"Govern yourself, Commander," Slinoor implored sternly, seeming to grow in resolution as the rest quarreled and quibbled. "Fafhrd, no more dagger words. Gray Mouser, this is not your court but mine and we are not met to split the hairs of high law but to meet a present peril. Here and now this grain fleet is in grave danger. Our very lives are risked. Much more than that, Lankhmar's in danger if Movarl gets not his gift-grain at this third sending. Last night *Clam* was foully murdered. Tonight it may be *Grouper* or *Squid, Shark* even, or no less than all our ships. The first two fleets went warned and well guarded, yet suffered only total perdition.''

He paused to let that sink in. Then, ''Mouser, you've roused some small doubts in my mind by your eleven-twelving. But small doubts are nothing where home lives and home cities are in peril. For the safety of the fleet and of Lankhmar we'll sink the white rats forthwith and keep close watch on the Demoiselle Hisvet to the very docks of Kvarch Nar.''

''Right!'' the Mouser cried approvingly, getting in ahead of Hisvet. But then he instantly added, with the air of sudden brilliant inspiration, ''*Or* . . . better yet . . . appoint Fafhrd and myself to keep unending watch not only on Hisvet but also on the eleven white rats. That way we don't spoil Glipkerio's gift and risk offending Movarl.''

''I'd trust no one's mere watching of the rats. They're too tricksy,'' Slinoor informed him. ''The Demoiselle I intend to put on *Shark*, where she'll be more closely guarded. The grain is what Movarl wants, not the rats. He doesn't know about them, so can't be angered at not getting them.''

''But he does know about them,'' Hisvet interjected. ''Glipkerio and Movarl exchange weekly letters by albatross-post. La, but Nehwon grows smaller each year, Ship's Master—ships are snails compared to the great winging mail-birds. Glipkerio wrote of the rats to Movarl, who expressed great delight at the prospective gift and intense anticipation of watching the White Shadows perform. Along with myself,'' she added, demurely bending her head.

''Also,'' the Mouser put in rapidly, ''I must firmly oppose— most regretfully, Slinoor—the transfer of Hisvet to another ship. Fafhrd's and my commission from Glipkerio, which I can produce at any time, states in clearest words that we are to attend the Demoiselle at all times outside her private quarters. He makes us wholly responsible for her safety—and also for that of the White Shadows, which creatures our overlord states, again in clearest writing, that he prizes beyond their weight in jewels.''

''You can attend her in *Shark*,'' Slinoor told the Mouser curtly.

''I'll not have the barbarian on my ship!'' Lukeen rasped, still squinting from the pain of his clout.

''I'd scorn to board such a tricked-out rowboat or oar-worm,'' Fafhrd shot back at him, voicing the common barbarian contempt for galleys.

''*Also*,'' the Mouser cut in again, loudly, with an admonitory gesture at Fafhrd, ''It is my duty as a friend to warn you,

Slinoor, that in your reckless threats against the White Shadows and the Demoiselle herself, you risk incurring the heaviest displeasure not only of our overlord but also of the most powerful grain merchant in Lankhmar.''

Slinoor answered most simply, "I think only of the city and the grain fleet. You know that," but Lukeen, fuming, spat out a "Hah!" and said scornfully, "the Gray Fool has not grasped that it is Hisvet's very father Hisvin who is behind the rat-sinkings, since he thereby grows rich with the extra nation's-ransoms of grain he sells Glipkerio!"

"Quiet, Lukeen!" Slinoor commanded apprehensively. "This dubious guess-work of yours has no place here."

"Guesswork? Mine?" Lukeen exploded. "It was *your* suggestion, Slinoor—Yes, and that Hisvin plots Glipkerio's overthrow—Aye, and even that he's in league with the Mingols! Let's speak truth for once!''

"Then speak it for yourself alone, Commander," Slinoor said most sober-sharply. "I fear the blow's disordered your brain. Gray Mouser, you're a man of sense," he appealed. "Can you not understand my one overriding concern? We're alone with mass murder on the high seas. We must take measures against it. Oh, will none of you show some simple wit?"

"La, and I will, Ship's-Master, since you ask it," Hisvet said brightly, rising to her knees on the sea-bed as she turned toward Slinoor. Sunlight striking through a louver shimmered on her silver hair and gleamed from the silver ring confining it. "I'm but a girl, unused to problems of war and rapine, yet I have an all-explaining simple thought that I have waited in vain to hear voiced by one of you gentlemen, wise in the ways of violence.

"Last night a ship was slain. You hang the crime on rats—small beasties which would leave a sinking ship in any case, which often have a few whites among them, and which only by the wildest stretch of imagination are picturable as killing an entire crew and vanishing their bodies. To fill the great gaps in this weird theory you make me a sinister rat-queen, who can work black miracles, and now even it seems, create my poor doting daddy an all-powerful rat-emperor.

"Yet this morning you met a ship's murderer if there ever was one and let him go honking off unchallenged. La, but the man-demon even confessed he'd been seeking a multi-headed monster that would snatch living men from a ship's deck and devour them. Surely he lied when he said his this-world foundling ate small fry only, for it struck at me to devour me—and might earlier have snapped up any of you, except it was sated!

"For what is more likely than that the two-headed long-neck dragon ate all *Clam*'s sailors off her deck, snaking them out of the forecastle and hold, if they fled there, like sweetmeats from a compartmented comfit-box, and then scratched holes in *Clam*'s planking? Or perhaps more likely still, that *Clam* tore out her bottom on the Dragon Rocks in the fog and at the same time met the sea-dragon? These are sober possibilities, gentlemen, apparent even to a soft girl and asking no mind-stretch at all."

This startling speech brought forth an excited medly of reactions. Simultaneously the Mouser applauded, "A gem of princess wit, Demoiselle, oh you'd make a rare strategist"; Fafhrd said stoutly, "Most lucid, Little Mistress, yet Karl Treuherz seemed to me an honest demon"; Frix told them proudly, "My mistress outthinks you all"; the mate at the door goggled at Hisvet and made the sign of the starfish; Lukeen snarled, "She conveniently forgets the black cutter"; while Slinoor cried them all down with, "Rat-queen you say jestingly? Rat-queen you are!"

As the others grew silent at that dire accusation, Slinoor, gazing grimly fearful at Hisvet, continued rapidly, "The Demoiselle has recalled to me by her speech the worst point against her. Karl Treuherz said his dragon, living by the Rat Rocks, ate only rats. It made no move to gobble us several men, though it had every chance, yet when Hisvet appeared it struck at her at once. It knew her true race."

Slinoor's voice went shudderingly low. "Thirteen rats with the minds of men rule the whole rat race. That's ancient wisdom from Lankhmar's wisest seers. Eleven are these silver-furred silent sharpies, hearing our every word. The twelfth celebrates in the black cutter his conquest of *Clam*. The thirteenth"—and he pointed finger—"is the silver-haired, red eyed Demoiselle herself!"

Lukeen slithered to his feet at that, crying, "Oh most shrewdly reasoned, Slinoor! And why does she wear such modest shrouding garb except to hide further evidence of the dread kinship? Let me but strip off that cloaking ermine smock and I'll show you a white furred body and ten small black dugs instead of proper maiden breasts!"

As he came snaking around the table toward Hisvet, Fafhrd sprang up, also cautiously, and pinned Lukeen's arms to his sides in a bear-hug, calling, "Nay, and you touch her, you die!"

Meantime Frix cried, "The dragon was sated with *Clam*'s crew, as my mistress told you. It wanted no more coarse-fibered men, but eagerly seized at my dainty-fleshed darling for a dessert mouthful!''

Lukeen wrenched around until his black eyes glared into Fafhrd's green ones inches away. "Oh most foul barbarian!" he grated. "I forego rank and dignity and challenge you this instant to a bout of quarterstaves on middeck. I'll prove Hisvet's taint on you by trial of battle. That is, if you dare face civilized combat, you great stinking ape!" And he spat full in Fafhrd's taunting face.

Fafhrd's only reaction was to smile a great smile through the spittle running gummily down his cheek, while maintaining his grip of Lukeen and wary lookout for a bite at his own nose.

Thereafter, challenge having been given and accepted, there was naught for even the head-shaking, heaven-glancing Slinoor to do but hurry preparation for the combat or duel, so that it might be fought before sunset and leave some daylight for taking sober measures for the fleet's safety in the approaching dark of night.

As Slinoor, the Mouser and mate came around them, Fafhrd released Lukeen, who scornfully averting his gaze instantly went on deck to summon a squad of his marines from *Shark* to second him and see fair play. Slinoor conferred with his mate and other officers. The Mouser, after a word with Fafhrd, slipped forward and could be seen gossiping industriously with *Squid*'s bosun and the common members of her crew down to cook and cabin boy. Occasionally something might have passed rapidly from the Mouser's hand to that of the sailor with whom he spoke.

Despite Slinoor's urging, the sun was dropping down the western sky before *Squid*'s gongsman beat the rapid brassy tattoo that signalized the imminence of combat. The sky was clear to the west and overhead, but the sinister fogbank still rested a Lankhmar league (twenty bowshots) to the east, paralleling the northward course of the fleet and looking almost as solid and dazzling as a glacier wall in the sun's crosswise rays. Most mysteriously neither hot sun nor west wind dissipated it.

Black-suited, brown-mailed and brown-helmeted marines facing aft made a wall across *Squid* to either side of the mainmast. They held their spears horizontal and crosswise at arm's-length down, making an additional low fence. Black-tunicked sailors peered between their shoulders and boots, or sat with their own brown legs adangle on the larboard side of the foredeck, where the great sail did not cut off their view. A few perched in the rigging.

The damaged rail had been stripped away from the break in the afterdeck and there around the bare aftermast sat the three judges: Slinoor, the Mouser, and Lukeen's sergeant. Around them, mostly to larboard of the two helmsmen, were grouped *Squid*'s officers and certain officers of the other ship on whose presence the Mouser had stubbornly insisted, though it had meant time-consuming ferrying by ship's boat.

Hisvet and Frix were in the cabin with the door shut. The Demoiselle had wanted to watch the duel through the open door or even from the afterdeck, but Lukeen had protested that this would make it easier for her to work an evil spell on him, and the judges had ruled for Lukeen. However the grille was open and now and again the sun's rays twinkled on a peering eye or silvered fingernail.

Between the dark spear-wall of marines and the afterdeck stretched a great square of white oaken deck, empty save for the crane-fittings and like fixed gear and level except for the main hatch, which made a central square of deck a hand's span above the rest. Each corner of the larger square was marked off by a black-chalked quarter circle. Either contestant stepping inside a quarter circle after the duel began (or springing on the rail or grasping the rigging or falling over the side) would at once forfeit the match.

In the forward larboard quarter circle stood Lukeen in black shirt and hose, still wearing his gold-banded starfish emblem. By him was his second, his own hawkfaced lieutenant. With his right hand Lukeen gripped his quarterstaff, a heavy wand of close-grained oak as tall as himself and thick as Hisvet's wrist. Raising it above his head he twirled it till it hummed, smiling fiendishly.

In the after starboard quarter circle, next the cabin door, were Fafhrd and his second, the mate of *Carp*, a grossly fat man with a touch of the Mingol in his sallow features. The Mouser could not be judge and second both, and he and Fafhrd had diced more than once with *Carp*'s mate in the old days at Lankmar—losing money to him, too, which at least indicated that he might be resourceful.

Fafhrd took from him now his own quarterstaff, gripping it cross-handed near one end. He made a few slow practice passes with it through the air, then handed it back to *Carp*'s mate and stripped off his jerkin.

Lukeen's marines sniggered to each other at the Northerner handling a quarterstaff as if it were a two-handed broadsword, but when Fafhrd bared his hairy chest *Squid*'s sailors set up a rousing cheer and when Lukeen commented loudly to his second, "What did I tell you? A great hairy-pelted ape, beyond question," and spun his staff again, the sailors booed him lustily.

"Strange," Slinoor commented in a low voice. "I had thought Lukeen to be popular among the sailors."

Lukeen's sergeant looked around incredulously at that remark. The Mouser only shrugged. Slinoor continued to him, "If the sailors knew your comrade fought on the side of rats, they'd not cheer him." The Mouser only smiled.

The gong sounded again.

Slinoor rose and spoke loudly: "A bout at quarterstaves with no breathing spells! Commander Lukeen seeks to prove on the Overlord's mercenary Fafhrd certain allegations against a demoiselle of Lankhmar. First man struck senseless or at mercy of his foe loses. Prepare!"

Two ship's boys went skipping across the middeck, scattering handfuls of white sand.

Sitting, Slinoor remarked to the Mouser, "A pox of this footling duel! It delays our action against Hisvet and the rats. Lukeen was a fool to bridle at the barbarian. Still, when he's drubbed him, there'll be time enough."

The Mouser lifted an eyebrow. Slinoor said lightly, "Oh didn't you know? Lukeen will win, that's certain," while the sergeant, nodding soberly, confirmed. "The Commander's a master of staves. 'Tis no game for barbarians."

The gong sounded a third time.

Lukeen sprang nimbly across the chalk and onto the hatch, crying, "Ho, hairy ape! Art ready to double-kiss the oak? —first my staff, then the deck?"

Fafhrd came shambling out, gripping his wand most awkwardly and responding, "Your spit has poisoned my left eye, Lukeen, but I see some civilized target with my right."

Lukeen dashed at him joyously then, feinting at elbow and head, then rapidly striking with the other end of his staff at Fafhrd's knee to tumble or lame him.

Fafhrd, abruptly switching to conventional stance and grip, parried the blow and swung a lightning riposte at Lukeen's jaw.

Lukeen got his staff up in time so that the blow hit only his cheek glancingly, but he was unsettled by it and thereafter Fafhrd was upon him, driving him back in a hail of barely parried blows while the sailors cheered.

Slinoor and the sergeant gaped wide-eyed, but the Mouser only knotted his fingers, muttering, "Not so fast, Fafhrd."

Then, as Fafhrd prepared to end it all, he stumbled stepping off the hatch, which changed his swift blow to the head into a slow blow at the ankles. Lukeen leaped up so that Fafhrd's staff passed under his feet, and while he was still in the air rapped Fafhrd on the head.

The sailors groaned. The marines cheered once, growlingly.

The unfooted blow was not of the heaviest, nonetheless it three-quarters stunned Fafhrd and now it was his turn to be driven back under a pelting shower of swipes. For several moments there was no sound but the rutch of soft-soled boots on sanded oak and the rapid dry musical *bong* of staff meeting staff.

When Fafhrd came suddenly to his full senses he was falling away from a wicked swing. A glimpse of black by his heel told him that his next inevitable backward step would carry him inside his own quarter circle.

Swift as thought he thrust far *behind* him with his staff. Its end struck deck, then stopped against the cabin wall, and Fafhrd heaved himself forward with it, away from the chalk line, ducking and lunging to the side to escape Lukeen's blows while his staff could not protect him.

The sailors screamed with excitement. The judges and officers on the afterdeck kneeled like dice-players, peering over the edge.

Fafhrd had to lift his left arm to guard his head. He took a blow on the elbow and his left arm dropped limp to his side. Thereafter he had to handle his staff like a broadsword indeed, swinging it one-handed in whistling parries and strokes.

Lukeen hung back, playing more cautiously now, knowing Fafhrd's one wrist must tire sooner than his two. He'd aim a few rapid blows at Fafhrd, then prance back.

Barely parrying the third of these attacks, Fafhrd riposted recklessly, not with a proper swinging blow, but simply gripping the end of his staff and lunging. The combined length of Fafhrd and his staff overtook Lukeen's retreat and the tip of Fafhrd's staff poked him low in the chest, just on the nerve spot.

Lukeen's jaw dropped, his mouth stayed open wide, and he wavered. Fafhrd smartly rapped his staff out of his fingers and as it clattered down, toppled Lukeen to the deck with a second almost casual prod.

The sailors cheered themselves hoarse. The marines growled surlily and one cried, "Foul!" Lukeen's second knelt by him, glaring at Fafhrd. *Carp*'s mate danced a ponderous jig up to Fafhrd and wafted the wand out of his hands. On the afterdeck *Squid*'s officers were glum, though those of the other grain ships seemed strangely jubilant. The Mouser gripped Slinoor's elbow, urging, "Cry Fafhrd victor," while the sergeant frowned prodigiously, hand to temple, saying, "Well, there's nothing I know of in the *rules* . . ."

At that moment the cabin door opened and Hisvet stepped out, wearing a long scarlet, scarlet-hooded silk robe.

The Mouser, sensing climax, sprang to starboard, where *Squid*'s gong hung, snatched the striker from the gongsman and clanged it wildly.

Squid grew silent. Then there were pointings and questioning cries as Hisvet was seen. She put a silver recorder to her lips and began to dance dreamily toward Fafhrd, softly whistling with her recorder a high haunting tune of seven notes in a minor key. From somewhere tiny tuned bells accompanied it tinklingly. Then Hisvet swung to one side, facing Fafhrd as she moved around him, and the questioning cries changed to ones of wonder and astonishment and the sailors came crowding as far as they could and swinging through the rigging, as the procession became visible that Hisvet headed.

It consisted of eleven white rats walking in single file on their hind legs and wearing little scarlet robes and caps. The first four carried in each forepaw clusters of tiny silver bells which they shook rhythmically. The next five bore on their shoulders, hanging down between them a little, a double length of looped gleaming silver chain—they were very like five sailors lugging an anchor chain. The last two each bore slantwise a slim silver wand as tall as himself as he walked erect, tail curving high.

The first four halted side by side in rank facing Fafhrd and tinkling their bells to Hisvet's piping.

The next five marched on steadily to Fafhrd's right foot. There their leader paused, looked up at Fafhrd's face with upraised paw, and squeaked three times. Then, gripping his end of the chain in one paw, he used his other three to climb Fafhrd's boot. Imitated by his four fellows, he then carefully climbed Fafhrd's trousers and hairy chest.

Fafhrd stared down at the mounting chain and scarlet-robe rats without moving a muscle, except to frown faintly as tiny paws unavoidably tweaked clumps of his chest-hair.

The first rat mounted to Fafhrd's right shoulder and moved behind his back to his left shoulder, the four other rats following in order and never letting slip the chain.

When all five rats were standing on Fafhrd's shoulders, they lifted one strand of the silver chain and brought it forward over his head, most dexterously. Meanwhile he was looking straight ahead at Hisvet, who had completely circled him and now stood piping behind the bell-tinklers.

The five rats dropped the strand, so that the chain hung in a gleaming oval down Fafhrd's chest. At the same instant each rat lifted his scarlet cap as high above his head as his foreleg would reach.

Someone cried, "Victor!"

The five rats swung down their caps and again lifted them high, and as if from one throat all the sailors and most of the marines and officers cried in a great shout: "VICTOR!"

The five rats led two more cheers for Fafhrd, the men aboard *Squid* obeying as if hypnotized—though whether by some magic power or simply by the wonder and appropriateness of the rats' behavior, it was hard to tell.

Hisvet finished her piping with a merry flourish and the two rats with silver wands scurried up onto the afterdeck and standing at the foot of the aftermast where all might see, began to drub away at each other in most authentic quarterstaff style, their wands flashing in the sunlight and chiming sweetly when they clashed. The silence broke in rounds of exclamation and laughter. The five rats scampered down Fafhrd and returned with the bell-tinklers to cluster around the hem of Hisvet's skirt. Mouser and several officers were leaping down from the afterdeck to wring Fafhrd's good hand or clap his back. The marines had much ado to hold back the sailors, who were offering each other bets on which rat would be the winner in this new bout.

Fafhrd, fingering his chain, remarked to the Mouser, "Strange that the sailors were with me from the start," and under cover of the hubbub the Mouser smiling explained, "I gave them money to bet on you against the marines. Likewise I dripped some hints and made some loans for the same purpose to the officer of the other ships—a fighter can't have too big a claque. Also I started the story going round that the whiteys are anti-rat rats, trained exterminators of their own kind, sample of Glipkerio's latest device for the safety of the grain fleets—sailors eat up such tosh."

"Did you first cry victor?" Fafhrd asked.

The Mouser grinned. "A judge take sides? In *civilized* combat? Oh, I was prepared to, but 'twasn't needful."

At that moment Fafhrd felt a small tug at his trousers and looking down saw that the black kitten had bravely approached through the forest of legs and was now climbing him purposefully. Touched at this further display of animal homage, Fafhrd rumbled gently as the kitten reached his belt, "Decided to heal our quarrel, eh, small black one?" At that the kitten sprang up his chest, sunk his little claws in Fafhrd's bare shoulder and, glaring like a black hangman, raked Fafhrd bloodily across the jaw, then sprang by way of a couple of startled heads to the mainsail and rapidly climbed its concave taut brown curve. Someone threw a belaying pin at the small black blot, but it was negligently aimed and the kitten safely reached the mast-top.

"I forswear all cats!" Fafhrd cried angrily, dabbling at his chin. "Henceforth rats are my favored beasties."

"Most properly spoken, Swordsman!" Hisvet called gayly from her own circle of admirers, continuing, "I will be pleased by your company and the Dirksman's at dinner in my cabin an hour past sunset. We'll conform to the very letter of Slinoor's stricture that I be closely watched and the White Shadows too." She whistled a little call on her silver recorder and swept back into her cabin with the nine rats close at her heels. The quarterstaving scarlet-robed pair on the afterdeck broke off their drubbing with neither victorious and scampered after her, the crowd parting to make way for them admiringly.

Slinoor, hurrying forward, paused to watch. The *Squid*'s skipper was a man deeply bemused. Somewhere in the last half hour the white rats had been transformed from eerie poison-toothed monsters threatening the fleet into popular, clever, harmless animal-mountebanks, whom *Squid*'s sailors appeared to regard as a band of white mascots. Slinoor seemed to be seeking unsuccessfully but unceasingly to decipher how and why.

Lukeen, still looking very pale, followed the last of his disgruntled marines (their purses lighter by many a silver smerduk, for they had been coaxed into offering odds) over the side into *Shark*'s long dinghy, brushing off Slinoor when *Squid*'s skipper would have conferred with him.

Slinoor vented his chagrin by harshly commanding his sailors to leave off their disorderly milling and frisking, but they obeyed him right cheerily, skipping to their proper stations with the happiest of sailor smirks. Those passing the Mouser winked at him and surreptitiously touched their forelocks. The *Squid* bowled smartly northward a half bowshot astern of *Tunny*, as she'd been doing throughout the duel, only now she began to cleave the blue water a little more swiftly yet as the west wind freshened and her after sail was broken out. In fact, the fleet began to sail so swiftly now that *Shark*'s dinghy couldn't make the head of the line, although Lukeen could be noted bullying his marine-oarsmen into back-cracking efforts, and the dinghy had finally to signal

Shark herself to come back and pick her up—which the war galley achieved only with difficulty, rolling dangerously in the mounting seas and taking until sunset, oars helping sails, to return to the head of the line.

"*He*'ll not be eager to come to *Squid*'s help tonight, or much able to either," Fafhrd commented to the Mouser where they stood by the larboard middeck rail. There had been no open break between them and Slinoor, but they were inclined to leave him the afterdeck, where he stood beyond the helmsmen in bent-head converse with his three officers, who had all lost money on Lukeen and had been sticking close to their skipper ever since.

"Not still expecting *that* sort of peril tonight, are you, Fafhrd?" the Mouser asked with a soft laugh. "We're far past the Rat Rocks."

Fafhrd shrugged and said frowningly, "Perhaps we've gone just a shade too far in endorsing the rats."

"Perhaps," the Mouser agreed. "But then their charming mistress is worth a fib and false stamp or two, aye and more than that, eh, Fafhrd?"

"She's a brave sweet lass," Fafhrd said carefully.

"Aye, and her maid too," the Mouser said brightly. "I noted Frix peering at you adoringly from the cabin entryway after your victory. A most voluptuous wench. Some men might well prefer the maid to the mistress in this instance. Fafhrd?"

Without looking around at the Mouser, the Northerner shook his head.

The Mouser studied Fafhrd, wondering if it were politic to make a certain proposal he had in mind. He was not quite certain of the full nature of Fafhrd's feelings toward Hisvet. He knew the Northerner was a goatish man enough and had yesterday seemed quite obsessed with the lovemaking they'd missed in Lankhmar, yet he also knew that his comrade had a variable romantic streak that was sometimes thin as a thread yet sometimes grew into a silken ribbon leagues wide in which armies might stumble and be lost.

On the afterdeck Slinoor was now conferring most earnestly with the cook, presumably (the Mouser decided) about Hisvet's (and his own and Fafhrd's) dinner. The thought of Slinoor having to go to so much trouble about the pleasures of three persons who today had thoroughly thwarted him made the Mouser grin and somehow also nerved him to take the uncertain step he'd been contemplating.

"Fafhrd," he whispered, "I'll dice you for Hisvet's favors."

"Why, Hisvet's but a gir—" Fafhrd began in accents of
rebuke, then cut off abruptly and closed his eyes in thought.
When he opened them, they were regarding the Mouser with a
large smile.

"No," Fafhrd said softly, "for truly I think this Hisvet is so
balky and fantastic a miss it will take both our most heartfelt and
cunning efforts to persuade her to aught. And, after that, who
knows? Dicing for such a girl's favors were like betting when a
Lankhman night-lilly will open and whether to north or south."

The Mouser chuckled and lovingly dug Fafhrd in the ribs,
saying, "There's my shrewd true comrade!"

Fafhrd looked at the Mouser with sudden dark suspicions.
"Now don't go trying to get me drunk tonight," he warned, "or
sifting opium in my drink."

"Hah, you know me better than that, Fafhrd," the Mouser
said with laughing reproach.

"I certainly do," Fafhrd agreed sardonically.

Again the sun went under with a green flash, indicating crystal
clear air to the west, though the strange fogbank, now an ominous dark wall, still paralleled their course a league or so to the
east.

The cook, crying, "My mutton!" went racing forward past
them toward the galley, whence a deliciously spicy aroma was
wafting.

"We've an hour to kill," the Mouser said. "Come on, Fafhrd.
On our way to board *Squid* I bought a little jar of wine of
Quarmall at the Silver Eel. It's still sealed."

From just overhead in the ratlines, the black kitten hissed
down at them in angry menace or perhaps warning.

Two hours later the Demoiselle Hisvet offered to the Mouser,
"A golden rilk for your thoughts, Dirksman."

She was on the swung-down sea-bed once more, half reclin-
ing. The long table, now laden with tempting viands and tall
silver wine cups, had been placed against the bed. Fafhrd sat
across from Hisvet, the empty silver cages behind him, while the
Mouser was at the stern end of the table. Frix served them all
from the door forward, where she took the trays from the cook's
boys without giving them so much as a peep inside. She had a
small brazier there for keeping hot such items as required it and
she tasted each dish and set it aside for a while before serving it.
Thick dark pink candles in silver sconces shed a pale light.

The white rats crouched in rather disorderly fashion around a
little table of their own set on the floor near the wall between the

sea-bed and the door, just aft of one of the trapdoors opening down into the grain-redolent hold. They wore little black jackets open at the front and little black belts around their middles. They seemed more to play with than eat the bits of food Frix set before them on their three or four little silver plates and they did not lift their small bowls to drink their wine-tinted water but rather lapped at them and that not very industriously. One or two would always be scampering up onto the bed to be with Hisvet, which made them most difficult to count, even for Fafhrd, who had the best view. Sometimes he got eleven, sometimes ten. At intervals one of them would stand up on the pink coverlet by Hisvet's knees and chitter at her in cadences so like those of human speech that Fafhrd and the Mouser would have to chuckle.

"Dreamy Dirksman, two rilks for your thoughts!" Hisvet repeated, upping her offer. "And most immodestly I'll wager a third rilk they are of me."

The Mouser smiled and lifted his eyebrows. He was feeling very light-headed and a bit uneasy, chiefly because contrary to his intentions he had been drinking much more than Fafhrd. Frix had just served them the main dish, a masterly yellow curry heavy with dark-tasting spices and originally appearing with "Victor" pricked on it with black capers. Fafhrd was devouring it manfully though not voraciously, the Mouser was going at it more slowly, while Hisvet all evening had merely toyed with her food.

"I'll take your two rilks, White Princess," the Mouser replied airily, "for I'll need one to pay the wager you've just won and the other to fee you for telling me *what* I was thinking of you."

"You'll not keep my second rilk long, Dirksman," Hisvet said merrily, "for as you thought of me you were looking not at my face, but most impudently somewhat lower. You were thinking of those somewhat nasty suspicions Lukeen voiced this day about my secretest person. Confess it now, you were!"

The Mouser could only hang his head a little and shrug helplessly, for she had most truly divined his thoughts. Hisvet laughed and frowned at him in mock anger, saying, "Oh, you are most indelicate-minded, Dirksman. Yet at least you can see that Frix, though indubitably mammalian, is not fronted like a she-rat."

This statement was undeniably true, for Hisvet's maid was all dark smooth skin except where black silk scarves narrowly circled her slim body at breasts and hips. Silver net tightly confined her black hair and there were many plain silver bracelets on each wrist. Yet although garbed like a slave, Frix did not seem one

tonight, but rather a lady-companion who expertly played at
being slave, serving them all with perfect yet laughing, wholly
unservile obedience.

Hisvet, by contrast, was wearing another of her long smocks,
this of black silk edged with black lace, with a lace-edged hood
half thrown back. Her silvery white hair was dressed high on her
head in great smooth swelling sweeps. Regarding her across the
table, Fafhrd said, "I am certain that the Demoiselle would be
no less than completely beautiful to us in whatever shape she
chose to present herself to the world—wholly human or somewhat otherwise."

"Now that was most gallantly spoken, Swordsman," Hisvet
said with a somewhat breathless laugh. "I must reward you for
it. Come to me, Frix." As the slim maid bent close to her,
Hisvet twined her white hands round the dark waist and im-
printed a sweet slow kiss on Frix's lips. Then she looked up and
gave a little tap on the shoulder to Frix, who moved smiling
around the table and, half kneeling by Fafhrd, kissed him as she
had been kissed. He received the token graciously, without
unmannerly excitement, yet when Frix would have drawn back,
prolonged the kiss, explaining a bit thickly when he released her:
"Somewhat extra to return to the sender, perchance." She grinned
at him saucily and went to her serving table by the door, saying,
"I must first chop the rats their meat, naughty barbarian." While
Hisvet discoursed, "Don't seek too much, Bold Swordsman.
That was in any case but a small proxy reward for a small gallant
speech. A reward with the mouth for words spoken with the
mouth. To reward you for drubbing Lukeen and vindicating my
honor were a more serious matter altogether, not to be entered on
lightly if at all. I'll think of it."

At this point the Mouser, who just had to be saying something
but whose fuddled brain was momentarily empty of suitably
venturesome yet courteous wit, called out to Frix, "Why chop
you the rats their mutton, dusky minx? 'Twould be rare sport to
see them slice it for themselves." Frix only wrinkled her nose at
him, but Hisvet expounded gravely, "Only Skwee carves with
any great skill. The others might hurt themselves, particularly
with the meat shifting about in the slippery curry. Frix, reserve a
single chunk for Skwee to display us his ability. Chop the rest
fine. Skwee!" she called, setting her voice high. "Skwee-
skwee-skwee!"

A tall rat sprang onto the bed and stood dutifully before her
with forelegs folded across his chest. Hisvet instructed him, then
took from a silver box behind her a most tiny carving set of

knife, steel and fork in joined treble scabbard and tied it carefully to his belt. Then Skwee bowed low to her and sprang
nimbly down to the rats' table.

The Mouser watched the little scene with clouded and heavy-
lidded wonder, feeling that he was falling under some sort of
spell. At times thick shadows crossed the cabin, at times Skwee
grew tall as Hisvet or perhaps it was Hisvet tiny as Skwee. And
then the Mouser grew small as Skwee too and ran under the bed
and fell into a chute that darkly swiftly slid him, not into a dark
hold of sacked or loose delicious grain, but into the dark spacious low-ceilinged pleasance of a subterranean rat metropolis,
lit by phosphorus, where robed and long-skirted rats whose
hoods hid their long faces moved about mysteriously, where rat
swords clashed behind the next pillar and rat money chinked,
where lewd female rats danced in their fur for a fee, where rat
spies and rat informers lurked, where everyone—every-*furry*-one—
was cringingly conscious of the omniscient overlordship of a
supernally powerful Council of Thirteen, and where a rat Mouser
sought everywhere a slim rat princess named Hisvet-sur-Hisvin.

The Mouser woke from his dinnerdream with a jerk. Somehow he'd surely drunk even more cups than he'd counted, he
told himself haltingly. Skwee, he saw, had returned to the rats'
table and was standing before the yellow chunk Frix had set on
the silver platter at Skwee's end. With the other rats watching
him, Skwee drew forth knife and steel with a flourish. The
Mouser roused himself more fully with another jerk and shake
and was inspired to say, "Ah, were I but a rat, White Princess,
so that I might come as close to you, serving you!"

The Demoiselle Hisvet cried, "A tribute indeed!" and laughed
with delight, showing—it appeared to the Mouser—a tongue half
splotched with bluish black and an inner mouth similarly pied.
Then she said rather soberly, "Have a care what you wish, for
some wishes have been granted," but at once continued gayly,
"Nevertheless, 'twas most gallantly said, Dirksman. I must
reward you. Frix, sit at my right side here."

The Mouser could not see what passed between them, for
Hisvet's loosely smocked form hid Frix from him, but the merry
eyes of the maid peered steadily at him over Hisvet's shoulder,
twinkling like the black silk. Hisvet seemed to be whispering
into Frix's ear while nuzzling it playfully.

Meanwhile there commenced the faintest of high *skirrings* as
Skwee rapidly clashed steel and knife together, sharpening the
latter. The Mouser could barely see the rat's head and shoulders
and the tiny glimmer of flashing metal over the larger table

intervening. He felt the urge to stand and move closer to observe the prodigy—and perchance glimpse something of the interesting activities of Hisvet and Frix—but he was held fast by a great lethargy, whether of wine or sensuous anticipation or pure magic he could not tell.

He had one great worry—that Fafhrd would out with a cleverer compliment than his own, one so much cleverer that it might even divert Frix's mission to him. But then he noted that Fafhrd's chin had fallen to his chest, and there came to his ears along with the silvery *klirring* the barbarian's gently rumbling snores.

The Mouser's first reaction was pure wicked relief. He remembered gloatingly past times he'd gamboled while his comrade snored sodden. Fafhrd must after all have been sneaking many extra swigs or whole drinks!

Frix jerked and giggled immoderately. Hisvet continued to whisper in her ear while Frix giggled and cooed again from time to time, continuing to watch the Mouser impishly.

Skwee scabbarded the steel with a tiny *clash*, drew the fork with a flourish, plunged it into the yellow-coated meat-chunk, big as a roast for him, and began to carve most dexterously.

Frix rose at last, received her tap from Hisvet, and headed around the table, smiling the while at the Mouser.

Skwee up with a paper-thin tiny slice of mutton on his fork and flapped it this way and that for all to see, then brought it close to his muzzle for a sniff and a taste.

The Mouser in his dreamy slump felt a sudden twinge of apprehension. It had occurred to him that Fafhrd simply couldn't have sneaked *that* much extra wine. Why, the Northerner hadn't been out of his sight the past two hours. Of course blows on the head sometimes had a delayed effect.

All the same his first reaction was pure angry jealousy when Frix paused beside Fafhrd and leaned over his shoulder and looked in his forward-tipped face.

Just then there came a great squeak of outrage and alarm from Skwee and the white rat sprang up onto the bed, still holding carving knife and fork with the mutton slice dangling from it.

From under eyelids that persisted in drooping lower and lower, the Mouser watched Skwee gesticulate with his tiny implements, as he chittered dramatically to Hisvet in most manlike cadences, and finally lift the petal of mutton to her lips with an accusing squeak.

Then, coming faintly through the chittering, the Mouser heard a host of stealthy footsteps crossing the middeck, converging on the cabin. He tried to call Hisvet's attention to it, but found his lips and tongue numb and unobedient to his will.

Frix suddenly grasped the hair of Fafhrd's forehead and jerked his head up and back. The Northerner's jaw hung slackly, his eyes fell open, showing only whites.

There was a gentle rapping at the door, exactly the same as the cook's boys had made delivering the earlier courses.

A look passed between Hisvet and Frix. The latter dropped Fafhrd's head, darted to the door, slammed the bar across it and locked the bar with the chain (the grille already being shut) just as something (a man's shoulder, it sounded) thudded heavily against the thick panels.

That thudding continued and a few heartbeats later became much more sharply ponderous, as if a spare mast-section were being swung like a battering ram against the door, which yielded visibly at each blow.

The Mouser realized at last, much against his will, that something was happening that he ought to do something about. He made a great effort to shake off his lethargy and spring up.

He found he could not even twitch a finger. In fact it was all he could do to keep his eyes from closing altogether and watch through lash-blurred slits as Hisvet, Frix and the rats spun into a whirlwind of silent activity.

Frix jammed her serving table against the jolting door and began to pile other furniture against it.

Hisvet dragged out from behind the sea-bed various dark long boxes and began to unlock them. As fast as she threw them open the white rats helped themselves to the small blued-iron weapons they contained: swords, spears, even most wicked-looking blued-iron crossbows with belted canisters of darts. They took more weapons than they could effectively use themselves. Skwee hurriedly put on a black-plumed helmet that fitted down over his furry cheeks. The number of rats busy around the boxes was ten—that much the Mouser noted clearly.

A split appeared in the middle of the piled door. Nevertheless Frix sprang away from there to the starboard trapdoor leading to the hold and heaved it up. Hisvet threw herself on the floor toward it and thrust her head down into the dark square hole.

There was something terribly animal-like about the movements of the two women. It may have been only the cramped quarters and the low ceiling, but it seemed to the Mouser that they moved by preference on all fours.

All the while Fafhrd's chest-sunk head kept lifting very slowly and then falling with a jerk as he went on snoring.

Hisvet sprang up and waved on the ten white rats. Led by Skwee, they trooped down through the hatch, their blued-iron weapons flashing and once or twice clashing, and were gone in a twinkling. Frix grabbed dark garments out of a curtained niche. Hisvet caught her by the wrist and thrust the maid ahead of her down the trap and then descended herself. Before pulling the hatch down above her, she took a last look around the cabin. As her red eyes gazed briefly at the Mouser, it seemed to him that her forehead and cheeks were grown over with silky white hair, but that may well have been a combination of eyelash-blue and her own disordered hair streaming and streaking down across her face.

The cabin door split and a man's length of thick mast boomed through, overturning the bolstering table and scattering the furniture set on and against it. After the mast end came piling in three apprehensive sailors followed by Slinoor holding a cutlass low and Slinoor's starsman (navigation officer) with a crossbow at the cock.

Slinoor pressed ahead a little and surveyed the scene swiftly yet intently, then said, "Our poppy-dust curry has taken Glipkerio's two lust-besotted rogues, but Hisvet's hid with her nymphy slavegirl. The rats are out of their cages. Search, sailors! Starsman, cover us!"

Gingerly at first, but soon in a rush, the sailors searched the cabin, tumbling the empty boxes and jerking the quilts and mattress off the sea-bed and swinging it up to see beneath, heaving chests away from walls and flinging open the unlocked ones, sweeping Hisvet's wardrobe in great silken armfuls out of the curtained niches in which it had been hanging.

The Mouser again made a mighty effort to speak or move, with no more success than to widen his blurred eye-slits a little. A sailor louted into him and he helplessly collapsed sideways against an arm of his chair without quite falling out of it. Fafhrd got a shove behind and slumped face-down on the table in a dish of stewed plums, his great arms outsweeping unconsciously upsetting cups and scattering plates.

The starsman kept crossbow trained on each new space uncovered. Slinoor watched with eagle eye, flipping aside silken fripperies with his cutlass point and using it to overset the rats' table, peering the while narrowly.

"There's where the vermin feasted like men," he observed

disgustedly. "The curry was set before them. Would they had gorged themselves senseless on it."

"Likely they were the ones to note the drug even through the masking spices of the curry, and warn the women," the starsman put in. "Rats are prodigiously wise to poisons."

As it became apparent neither girls nor rats were in the cabin, Slinoor cried with angry anxiety, "They can't have escaped to the deck—here's the sky-trap locked below besides our guard above. The mate's party bars the after hold. Perchance the stern-lights—"

But just then the Mouser heard one of the horn windows behind him being opened and the *Squid*'s arms-master call from there, "Naught came this way. Where are they, captain?"

"Ask someone wittier than I," Slinoor tossed him sourly. "Certain they're not here."

"Would that these two could speak," the starsman wished, indicating the Mouser and Fafhrd.

"No," Slinoor said dourly. "They'd just lie. Cover the larboard trap to the hold. I'll have it up and speak to the mate."

Just then footsteps came hurrying across the middeck and the *Squid*'s mate with blood-streaked face entered by the broken door, half dragging and half supporting a sailor who seemed to be holding a thin stick to his own bloody cheek.

"Why have you left the hold?" Slinoor demanded of the first. "You should be with your party below."

"Rats ambushed us on our way to the after hold," the mate gasped. "There were dozens of blacks led by a white, some armed like men. The sword of a beam-hanger almost cut my eye across. Two foamy-mouthed springers dashed out our lamp. 'Twere pure folly to have gone on in the dark. There's scarce a man of my party not bitten, slashed or jabbed. I left them guarding the foreway to the hold. They say their wounds are poisoned and talk of nailing down the hatch."

"Oh monstrous cowardice!" Slinoor cried. "You've spoiled my trap that would have scotched them at the start. Now all's to do and difficult. Oh scarelings! Daunted by rats!"

"I tell you they were armed!" the mate protested and then, swinging the sailor forward, "Here's my proof with a spearlet in his cheek."

"Don't drag her out, captain, sir," the sailor begged as Slinoor moved to examine his face. " 'Tis barbed for certain and poisoned too, I wot."

"Hold still, boy," Slinoor commanded. "And take your hands away—I've got it firm. The point's near the skin. I'll drive it out forward so the barbs don't catch. Pinion his arms, mate. Don't move your face, boy, or you'll be hurt worse. If it's poisoned, it must come out the faster. There!''

The sailor squeaked. Fresh blood rilled down his cheek.

'' 'Tis a nasty needle indeed,'' Slinoor commended, inspecting the bloody point. "Doesn't look poisoned. Mate, gently cut off the shaft aft of the wound, draw out the rest forward.''

"Here's further proof, most wicked,'' said the starsman, who'd been picking about in the litter. He handed Slinoor a tiny crossbow.

Slinoor held it up before him. In the pale candlelight it gleamed bluely, while the skipper's dark-circled eyes were like agates.

"Here's evil's soul,'' he cried. "Perchance 'twas well you were ambushed in the hold. 'Twill teach each mariner to hate and fear all rats again, like a good grain-sailor should. And now by a swift certain killing of all rats on *Squid* wipe out today's traitorous foolery, when you clapped for rats and let rats lead your cheers, seduced by a scarlet girl and bribed by that most misnamed Mouser.''

The Mouser, still paralyzed and perforce watching Slinoor a-slant as Slinoor pointed at him, had to admit it was a well-turned reference to himself.

"First off,'' Slinoor said, "drag those two rogues on deck. Truss them to mast or rail. I'll not have them waking to botch my victory.''

"Shall I up with a trap and loose a dart in the after hold?'' the starsman asked eagerly.

"You should know better,'' was all Slinoor answered.

"Shall I gong for the galley and run up a red lamp?'' the mate suggested.

Slinoor was silent two heartbeats, then said, "No. This is *Squid*'s fight to wipe out today's shame. Besides, Lukeen's a hotheaded botcher. Forget I said that, gentlemen, but it is so.''

"Yet we'd be safer with the galley standing by,'' the mate ventured to continue. "Even now the rats may be gnawing holes in us.''

"That's unlikely with the Rat Queen below,'' Slinoor retorted. "Speed's what will save us and not stand-by ships. Now hearken close. Guard well all ways to the hold. Keep traps and hatches shut. Rouse the off watch. Arm every man. Gather on middeck all we can spare from sailing. Move!''

The Mouser wished Slinoor hadn't said "Move!'' quite so vehemently, for the two sailors instantly grabbed his ankles and dragged him most enthusiastically out of the littered cabin and across the middeck, his head bumping a bit. True, he couldn't feel the bumps, only hear them.

To the west the sky was a quarter globe of stars, to the east a mass of fog below and thinner mist above, with the gibbous moon shining through the latter like a pale misshapen silver ghost-lamp. The wind had slackened. *Squid* sailed smoothly.

One sailor held the Mouser against the mainmast, facing aft, while the other looped rope around him. As the sailors bound him with his arms flat to his sides, the Mouser felt a tickle in his throat and life returning to his tongue, but he decided not to try to speak just yet. Slinoor in his present mood might order him gagged.

The Mouser's next divertissement was watching Fafhrd dragged out by four sailors and bound lengthwise, facing inboard with head aft and higher than feet, to the larboard rail It was quite a comic performance, but the Northerner snored through it.

Sailors began to gather then on middeck, some palely silent but most quipping in low voices. Pikes and cutlasses gave them courage. Some carried nets and long sharp-tined forks. Even the cook came with a great cleaver, which he hefted playfully at the Mouser.

"Struck dumb with admiration of my sleepy curry eh?"

Meanwhile the Mouser found he could move his fingers. No one had bothered to disarm him, but Cat's Claw was unfortunately fixed far too high on his left side for either hand to touch, let alone get out of its scabbard. He felt the hem of his tunic until he touched, through the cloth, a rather small flat round object thinner along one edge than the other. Gripping it by the thick edge through the cloth, he began to scrape with the thin edge at the fabric confining it.

The sailors crowded aft as Slinoor emerged from the cabin with his officers and began to issue low-voiced orders. The Mouser caught "Slay Hisvet or her maid on sight. They're not women but were-rats or worse," and then the last of Slinoor's orders: "Poise your parties below the hatch or trap by which you enter. When you hear the bosun's whistle, move!"

The effect of this "Move!" was rather spoiled by a tiny *twing* and the arms-master clapping his hand to his eye and screaming. There was a flurry of movement among the sailors. Cutlasses struck at a pale form that scurried along the deck. For an instant a rat with a crossbow in his hands was silhouetted on the starboard rail against the moonpale mist. Then the starsman's crossbow twanged and the dart winging with exceptional accuracy or luck knocked the rat off the rail into the sea.

"That was a whitey, lads!" Slinoor cried. "A good omen!"

Thereafter there was some confusion, but it was quickly settled, especially when it was discovered that the starsman had not been struck in the eye but only near it, and the beweaponed parties moved off, one into the cabin, two forward past the mainmast, leaving on deck a skeleton crew of four.

The fabric the Mouser had been scraping parted and he most carefully eased out of the shredded hem an iron tik (the Lankhmar coin of least value) with half its edge honed to razor sharpness and began to slice with it in tiny strokes at the nearest loop of the line binding him. He looked hopefully toward Fafhrd, but the latter's head still hung at a senseless angle.

A whistle sounded faintly, followed some ten breaths later by a louder one from another part of the hold, it seemed. Then muffled shouts began to come in flurries, there were two screams, something thumped the deck from below, and a sailor swinging a rat squeaking in a net dashed past the Mouser.

The Mouser's fingers told him he was almost through the first loop. Leaving it joined by a few threads, he began to slice at the next loop, bending his wrist acutely to do it.

An explosion shook the deck, stinging the Mouser's feet. He could not conjecture its nature and sawed furiously with his sharpened coin. The skeleton crew cried out and one of the helmsmen fled forward but the other stuck by the tiller. Somehow the gong clanged once, though no one was by it.

Then *Squid*'s sailors began to pour up out of the hold, half of them without weapons and frantic with fear. They milled about. The Mouser could hear sailors dragging *Squid*'s boats, which were forward of the mainmast, to the ship's side. The Mouser gathered that the sailors had fared most evilly below, assaulted by battalions of black rats, confused by false whistles, slashed and jabbed from dark corners, stung by darts, two struck in the eye and blinded. What had completed their rout was that, coming to a hold of unsacked grain, they'd found the air above it choked with grain dust from the recent churnings and scatterings of a horde of rats, and Frix had thrown in fire from beyond, exploding the stuff and knocked them off their feet though not setting fire to the ship.

At the same time as the panic-stricken sailors, there also came on deck another group, noted only by the Mouser—a most quiet and orderly file of black rats that went climbing around him up the mainmast. The Mouser weighed crying an alarm, although he wouldn't have wagered a tik on his chances of survival with hysterical be-cutlassed sailors rat-slashing all around him.

In any case his decision was made for him in the negative by Skwee, who climbed on his left shoulder just then. Holding on by a lock of the Mouser's hair, Skwee leaned out in front of him, staring into the Mouser's left eye with his own two wally blue ones under his black-plumed silver helmet. Skwee touched pale paw to his buck-toothed lips, enjoying silence, then patted the little sword at his side and jerked his rat-thumb across his rat-throat to indicate the penalty for silence broken. Thereafter he retired into the shadows by the Mouser's ear, presumably to watch the routed sailors and wave on and command his own company—and keep close to the Mouser's jugular vein. The Mouser kept sawing with his coin.

The starsman came aft followed by three sailors with two white lanterns apiece. Skwee crowded back closer between the Mouser and the mast, but touched the cold flat of his sword to the Mouser's neck, just under the ear, as a reminder. The Mouser remembered Hisvet's kiss. With a frown at the Mouser the starsman avoided the mainmast and had the sailors hang their lanterns to the aftermast and the crane fittings and the forward range of the afterdeck, fussing about the exact positions. He asserted in a high babble that light was the perfect military defense and counterweapon, and talked wildly of light-entrenchments and light palisades, and was just about to set the sailors hunting more lamps, when Slinoor limped out of the cabin bloody-foreheaded and looked around.

"Courage, lads," Slinoor shouted hoarsely. "On deck we're still masters. Let down the boats orderly, lads, we'll need 'em to fetch the marines. Run up the red lamp! You there, gong the alarm!"

Someone responded, "The gong's gone overboard. The ropes that hung it—gnawed!"

At the same time thickening waves of fog came out of the east, shrouding *Squid* in deadly moonlit silver. A sailor moaned. It was a strange fog that seemed to increase rather than diminish the amount of light cast by the moon and the starsmen's lantern. Colors stood out, yet soon there was only white wall beyond the *Squid*'s rails.

Slinoor ordered, "Get up the spare gong! Cook, let's have your biggest kettles, lids and pots—anything to beat an alarm!"

There were two splashing thumps as *Squid*'s boats hit the water.

Someone screamed agonizingly in the cabin.

Then two things happened together. The mainsail parted from the mast, falling to starboard like a cathedral ceiling in a gale, its lines and ties to the mast gnawed loose or sawed by tiny swords. It floated darkly on the water, dragging the boom wide. *Squid* lurched to starboard.

At the same time a horde of black rats spewed out of the cabin door and came pouring over the taffrail, the latter presumably by way of the stern lights. They rushed at the humans in waves, springing with equal force and resolution whether they landed on pike points or tooth-clinging to noses and throats.

The sailors broke and made for the boats, rats landing on their backs and nipping at their heels. The officers fled too. Slinoor was carried along, crying for a last stand. Skwee out with his sword on the Mouser's shoulder and bravely waved on his suicidal soldiery, chittering high, then leaped down to follow in their rear. Four white rats armed with crossbows knelt on the crane fittings and began to crank, load and fire with great efficiency.

Splashings began, first two and three, then what sounded like a half dozen together, mixed with screams. The Mouser twisted his head around and from the corner of his eye saw the last two of *Squid*'s sailors leap over the side. Straining a little further around yet, he saw Slinoor clutch to his chest two rats that worried him and follow the sailors. The four white-furred arbalasters leaped down from the crane fittings and raced toward a new firing position on the prow. Hoarse human cries came up from the water and faded off. Silence fell on *Squid* like the fog, broken only by the inevitable chitterings and those few now.

When the Mouser turned his head aft again, Hisvet was standing before him. She was dressed in close-fitting black leather from neck to elbows and knees, looking most like a slim boy, and she wore a black leather helmet fitting down over her temples and cheeks like Skwee's silver one, her white hair streaming down in a tail behind making her plume. A slim dagger was scabbarded on her left hip.

"Dear, dear Dirksman," she said softly, smiling with her little mouth, "you at least do not desert me," and she reached out and almost brushed his cheek with her fingers. Then, "Bound!" she said, seeming to see the rope for the first time and drawing back her hand. "We must remedy that, Dirksman."

"I would be most grateful, White Princess," the Mouser said humbly. Nevertheless, he did not let go his sharpened coin, which although somewhat dulled had now sliced almost halfway through a third loop.

"We must remedy that," Hisvet repeated a little absently, her gaze straying beyond the Mouser. "But my fingers are too soft and unskilled to deal with such mighty knots as I see. Frix will release you. Now I must hear Skwee's report on the afterdeck. Skwee-skwee-skwee!"

As she turned and walked aft the Mouser saw that her hair all went through a silver-ringed hole in the back top of her black helmet. Skwee came running past the Mouser and when he had almost caught up with Hisvet he took position to her right and three rat-paces behind her, strutting with forepaw on sword-hilt and head held high, like a captain-general behind his empress.

As the Mouser resumed his weary sawing of the third loop, he looked at Fafhrd bound to the rail and saw that the black kitten was crouched fur-on-end on Fafhrd's neck and slowly raking his cheek with the spread claws of a forepaw while the Northerner still snored garglingly. Then the kitten dipped its head and bit Fafhrd's ear. Fafhrd groaned piteously, but then came another of the gargling snores. The kitten resumed its cheek-raking. Two rats, one white, one black, walked by and the kitten wauled at them softly yet direly. The rats stopped and stared, then scurried straight toward the afterdeck, presumably to report the unwholesome condition to Skwee or Hisvet.

The Mouser decided to burst loose without more ado, but just then the four white arbalasters came back dragging a brass cage of frightenedly cheeping wrens the Mouser remembered seeing hanging by a sailor's bunk in the forecastle. They stopped by the crane fittings again and started a wren-shoot. They'd release one of the tiny terrified flutterers, then as it winged off bring it down with a well-aimed dart—at distances up to five and six yards, never missing. Once or twice one of them would glance at the Mouser narrowly and touch the dart's point.

Frix stepped down the ladder from the afterdeck. She was now dressed like her mistress, except she had no helmet, only the tight silver hairnet, though the silver rings were gone from her wrists.

"Lady Frix!" the Mouser called in a light voice, almost gaily. It was hard to say how one should speak on a ship manned by rats, but a high voice seemed indicated.

She came towards him smiling, but "Frix will do better," she said. "Lady is such a corset title."

"Frix then," the Mouser called, "on your way would you

scare that black witch cat from our poppy-sodden friend? He'll rake out my comrade's eye."

Frix looked sideways to see what the Mouser meant, but still kept stepping toward him.

"I never interfere with another person's pleasures or pains, since it's hard to be certain which are which," she informed him, coming close. "I only carry out my mistresses's directives. Now she bids me tell you be patient and of good cheer. Your trials will soon be over. And this withal she sends you as a remembrancer." Lifting her mouth, she kissed the Mouser softly on each upper eyelid.

The Mouser said, "That's the kiss with which the green priestess of Djil seals the eyes of those departing this world."

"Is it?" Frix asked softly.

"Aye, 'tis," the Mouser said with a little shudder, continuing briskly. "So now undo me these knots, Frix, which is something your mistress has directed. And then perchance give me a livelier smack—after I've looked to Fafhrd."

"I only carry out the directives of my mistress' own mouth," Frix said, shaking her head a little sadly. "She said nothing to me about untying knots. But doubtless she will direct me to loose you shortly."

"Doubtless," the Mouser agreed, a little glumly, forbearing to saw with his coin at the third loop while Frix watched him. If he could but sever at once three loops, he told himself, he might be able to shake off the remaining ones in a not impossibly large number of heartbeats.

As if on cue, Hisvet stepped lightly down from the afterdeck and hastened to them.

"Dear mistress, do you bid me undo the Dirksman his knots?" Frix asked at once, almost as if she wanted to be told to.

"I will attend to matters here," Hisvet replied hurriedly. "Go you to the afterdeck, Frix, and harken and watch for my father. He delays overlong this night." She also ordered the white crossbow-rats, who'd winged their last wren, to retire to the afterdeck.

After Frix and the rats had gone, Hisvet gazed at the Mouser for the space of a score of heartbeats, frowning just a little, studying him deeply with her red-irised eyes.

Finally she said with a sigh, "I wish I could be certain."

"Certain of what, White Princesship?" the Mouser asked.

"Certain that you love me truly," she answered softly yet downrightly, as if he surely knew. "Many men—aye and women too and demons and beasts—have told me they loved me truly, but truly I think none of them loved me for myself (save Frix, whose happiness is in being a shadow) but only because I was young or beautiful or a demoiselle of Lankhmar or dreadfully clever or had a rich father or was dowered with power, being blood-related to the rats, which is a certain sign of power in more worlds than Nehwon. Do you truly love me for myself, Gray Mouser?"

"I love you most truly indeed, Shadow Princess," the Mouser said with hardly an instant's hesitation. "Truly I love you for yourself alone, Hisvet. I love you more dearly than aught else in Nehwon—aye, and in all other worlds too and heaven and hell besides."

Just then Fafhrd, cruelly clawed or bit by the kitten, let off a most piteous groan indeed with a dreadful high note in it, and the Mouser said impulsively, "Dear Princess, first chase me that were-cat from my large friend, for I fear it will be his blinding and death's bane, and then we shall discourse of our great loves to the end of eternity."

"*That* is what I mean," Hisvet said softly and reproachfully. "If you loved me truly for myself, Gray Mouser, you would not care a feather if your closest friend or your wife or mother or child were tortured and done to death before your eyes, so long as my eyes were upon you and I touched you with my fingertips. With my kisses on your lips and my slim hands playing about you, my whole person accepting and welcoming you, you could watch your large friend there scratched to blindness and death by a cat—or mayhap eaten alive by rats—and be utterly content. I have touched few things in this world, Gray Mouser. I have touched no man, or male demon or larger male beast, save by the proxy of Frix. Remember that, Gray Mouser."

"To be sure, Dear Light of my Life!" the Mouser replied most spiritedly, certain now of the sort of self-adoring madness with which he had to deal, since he had a touch of the same mania and so was well-acquainted with it. "Let the barbarian bleed to death by pinpricks! Let the cat have his eyes! Let the rats banquet on him to his bones! What skills it while we trade sweet words and caresses, discoursing to each other with our entire bodies and our whole souls!"

Meanwhile, however, he had started to saw again most fiercely with his now-dulled coin, unmindful of Hisvet's eyes upon him. It joyed him to feel Cat's Claw lying against his ribs.

"That's spoken like my own true Mouser," Hisvet said with most melting tenderness, brushing her fingers so close to his cheek that he could feel the tiny chill zephyr of their passage.

Then, turning, she called, "Holla, Frix! Send to me Skwee and the White Company. Each may bring with him two black comrades of his own choice. I have somewhat of a reward for them, somewhat of a special treat. Skwee! Skwee-skwee-skwee!"

What would have happened then, both instantly and ultimately, is impossible to say, for at that moment Frix hailed, "Ahoy!" into the fog and called happily down, "A black sail! Oh Blessed Demoiselle, it is your father!"

Out of the pearly fog to starboard came the shark's-fin triangle of the upper portion of a black sail, running alongside *Squid* aft of the dragging brown mainsail. Two boathooks a small ship's length apart came up and clamped down on the starboard middeck rail while the black sail flapped. Frix came running lightly forward and secured to the rail midway between the boathooks the top of a rope ladder next heaved up from the black cutter (for surely this must be that dire craft, the Mouser thought).

Then up the ladder and over the rail came nimbly an old man of Lankhmar dressed all in black leather and on his left shoulder a white rat clinging with right forepaw to a cheek-flap of his black leather cap. He was followed swiftly by two lean bald Mingols with faces yellow-brown as old lemons, each shoulder-bearing a large black rat that steadied itself by a yellow ear.

At that moment, most coincidentally, Fafhrd groaned again, more loudly, and opened his eyes and cried out in the faraway moan of an opium-dreamer. "Millions of black monkeys! Take him off, I say! 'Tis a black fiend of hell torments me! Take him off!"

At that the black kitten raised up, stretched out its small evil face, and bit Fafhrd on the nose. Disregarding this interruption, Hisvet threw up her hand at the newcomers and cried clearly, "Greetings, oh Cocommander my Father! Greetings, peerless rat captain Grig! *Clam* is conquered by you, now *Squid* by me, and this very night, after small business of my own attended to, shall see the perdition of all this final fleet. Then it's Movarl estranged, the Mingols across the Sinking Land, Glipkerio hurled down, and the rats ruling Lankhmar under my overlordship and yours!"

The Mouser, sawing ceaselessly at the third loop, chanced to note Skwee's muzzle at that moment. The small white captain had come down from the afterdeck at Hisvet's summoning along with eight white comrades, two bandaged, and now he shot Hisvet a silent look that seemed to say there might be doubts about the last item of her boast, once the rats ruled Lankhmar.

Hisvet's father Hisvin had a long-nosed, much wrinkled face patched by a week of white, old-man's beard, and he seemed permanently stooped far over, yet he moved most briskly for all that, taking very rapid little shuffling steps.

Now he answered his daughter's bragging speech with a petulant sideways flirt of his black glove close to his chest and a little impatient "Tsk-tsk!" of disapproval, then went circling the deck at his odd scuttling gait while the Mingols waited by the ladder-top. Hisvin circled by Fafhrd and his black tormenter ("Tsk-tsk!") and by the Mouser (another "Tsk!") and stopping in front of Hisvet said rapid and fumingly, still crouched over, jogging a bit from foot to foot, "Here's confusion indeed tonight! You catsing and romancing with bound men!—I know, I know! The moon coming through too much! (I'll have my astrologer's liver!) *Shark* oaring like a mad cuttlefish through the foggy white! A black balloon with little lights scudding above the waves! And but now ere we found you, a vast sea monster swimming about in circles with a gibbering demon on his head—it came sniffing at us as if we were dinner, but we evaded it!

"Daughter, you and your maid and your little people must into the cutter at once with us, pausing only to slay these two and leave a suicide squad of gnawers to sink *Squid*!"

"Sink *Squid*?" Hisvet questioned. "The plan was to slip her to Ilthmar with a Mingol skeleton crew and there sell her cargo."

"Plans change!" Hisvin snapped. "Daughter, if we're not off this ship in forty breaths, *Shark* will ram us by pure excess of blundering energy or the monster with the clown-clad mad mahout will eat us up as we drift here helpless. Give orders to Skwee! Then out with your knife and cut me these two fools' throats! Quick, quick!"

"But Daddy," Hisvet objected, "I had something quite different in mind for them. Not death, at least not altogether. Something far more artistic, even loving—"

"I give you thirty breaths each to torture ere you slay them!" Hisvin conceded. "Thirty breaths and not one more, mind you! I know your somethings!"

"Dad, don't be crude! Among new friends! *Why* must you always give people a wrong impression of me? I won't endure it longer!"

"Chat-chat-chat! You pother and pose more than your rat-mother."

"But I tell you I won't endure it. This time we're going to do things *my* way for a change!"

"Hist-hist!" her father commanded, stooping still lower and

cupping hand to left ear, while his white rat Grig imitated his gesture on the other side.

Faintly through the fog came a gibbering. *"Gottverdammter Nebel! Freunde, wo sind Sie?"**

" 'Tiz the gibberer!" Hisvin cried under his breath. "The monster will be upon us! Quick, daughter, out with your knife and slay, or I'll have my Mingols dispatch them!"

Hisvet lifted her hand against that villainous possibility. Her proudly plumed head literally bent to the inevitable.

"I'll do it," she said. "Skwee, give me your crossbow. Load with silver."

The white rat captain folded his forelegs across his chest and chittered at her with a note of demand.

"No, you can't have him," she said sharply. "You can't have either of them. They're mine now."

Another curt chitter from Skwee.

"Very well, your people may have the small black one. Now quick with your crossbow or I'll curse you! Remember, only a smooth silver dart."

Hisvin had scuttled to his Mingols and now he went around in a little circle, almost spitting. Frix glided smiling to him and touched his arm but he shook away from her with an angry flirt.

Skwee was fumbling into his canister rat-frantically. His eight comrades were fanning out across the deck toward Fafhrd and the black kitten, which leaped down now in front of Fafhrd, snarling defiance.

Fafhrd himself was looking about bloody-faced but at last lucid-eyed, drinking in the desperate situation, poppy-languor banished by nose-bite.

Just then there came another gibber through the fog. *"Gottverdammter Nirgendswelt!"*†

Fafhrd's blood-shot eyes widened and brightened with a great inspiration. Bracing himself against his bonds, he inflated his mighty chest.

"HOONGK!" he bellowed. "HOONGK!"

Out of the fog came eager answer, growing each time louder: "Hoongk! *Hoongk!* HOONGK!"

Seven of the eight white rats that had crossed the deck now returned carrying stretched between them the still-snarling black

---

*"Goddamn fog! Friends, where are you?" Evidently Karl Treuherz' Lankhmarese dictionary was unavailable to him at the moment.
†"Goddamn Nowhere-World!"

kitten spread-eagled on its back, one to each paw and ear while the seventh tried to master but was shaken from side to side by the whipping tail. The eighth came hobbling behind on three legs, shoulder paralyzed by a deep-stabbing cat-bite.

From cabin and forecastle and all corners of the deck, the black rats scurried in to watch gloatingly their traditional enemy mastered and delivered to torment, until the middeck was thick with their bloaty dark forms.

Hisvin cracked a command at his Mingols. Each drew a wavy-edged knife. One headed for Fafhrd, the other for the Mouser. Black rats hid their feet.

Skwee dumped his tiny darts on the deck. His paw closed on a palely gleaming one and he slapped it in his crossbow, which he hurriedly handed up toward his mistress. She lifted it in her right hand toward Fafhrd, but just then the Mingol moving toward the Mouser crossed in front of her, his kreese point-first before him. She shifted crossbow to left hand, whipped out her dagger and darted ahead of the Mingol.

Meanwhile the Mouser had snapped the three cut loops with one surge. The others still confined him loosely at ankles and throat, but he reached across his body, drew Cat's Claw and slashed out at the Mingol as Hisvet shouldered the yellow man aside.

The dirk sliced her pale cheek from jaw to nose.

The other Mingol, advancing his kreese toward Fafhrd's throat, abruptly dropped to the deck and began to roll back across it, the black rats squeaking and snapping at him in surprise.

"HOONGK!"

A great green dragon's head had loomed from the moon-mist over the larboard rail just at the spot where Fafhrd was tied. Strings of slaver trailed on the Northerner from the dagger-toothed jaws.

Like a ponderous jack-in-the-box, the red-mawed head dipped and drove forward, lower jaw rasping the oaken deck and sweeping up from it a swathe of black rats three rats wide. The jaws crunched together on their great squealing mouthful inches from the rolling Mingol's head. Then the green head swayed aloft and a horrid swelling traveled down the greenish yellow neck.

But even as it poised there for a second strike, it shrank in size by comparison with what now appeared out of the mist after it—a second green dragon's head fourfold larger and fantastically crested in red, orange and purple (for at first sight the rider seemed to be part of the monster). This head now drove forward as if it were that of the father of all dragons, sweeping up a

black-rat swathe twice as wide as had the first and topping off its
monster gobble with the two white rats behind the rat-carried
black kitten.

It ended its first strike so suddenly (perhaps to avoid eating the
kitten) that its particolored rider, who'd been waving his pike
futilely, was hurled forward off its green head. The rider sailed
low past the mainmast, knocking aside the Mingol striking at the
Mouser, and skidded across the deck into the starboard rail.

The white rats let go of the kitten, which raced for the
mainmast.

Then the two green heads, famished by their two days of small
fishy pickings since their last real meal at the Rat Rocks, began
methodically to sweep *Squid*'s deck clean of rats, avoiding humans for the most part, though not very carefully. And the rats,
huddled in their mobs, did little to evade this dreadful mowing.
Perhaps in their straining toward world-dominion they had grown
just human and civilized enough to experience imaginative,
unhelpful, freezing panic and to have acquired something of
humanity's talent for inviting and enduring destruction. Perhaps
they looked on the dragons' heads as the twin red maws of war
and hell, into which they must throw themselves willy-nilly. At
all events they were swept up by dozens and scores. All but three
of the white rats were among those engulfed.

Meanwhile the larger people aboard *Squid* faced up variously
to the drastically altered situation.

Old Hisvin shook his first and spat in the larger dragon's face
when after its first gargantuan swallow it came questing toward
him, as if trying to decide whether this bent black thing were
(ugh!) a very queer man or (yum!) a very large rat. But when the
stinking apparition kept coming on, Hisvin rolled deftly over the
rail as if into bed and swiftly climbed down the rope ladder,
fairly chittering in consternation, while Grig clung for dear life
to the back of the black leather collar.

Hisvin's two Mingols picked themselves up and followed him,
vowing to get back to their cozy cold steppes as soon as Mingolly
possible.

Fafhrd and Karl Treuherz watched the melee from opposite
sides of the middeck, the one bound by ropes, the other by
outwearied astonishment.

Skwee and a white rat named Siss ran over the heads of their
packed apathetic black fellows and hopped on the starboard rail.
There they looked back. Siss blinked in horror. But Skwee, his

black-plumed helmet pushed down over his left eye, menaced with his little sword and chittered defiance.

Frix ran to Hisvet and urged her to the starboard rail. As they neared the head of the rope ladder, Skwee went down it to make way for his empress, dragging Siss with him. Just then Hisvet turned like someone in a dream. The smaller dragon's head drove toward her viciously. Frix sprang in the way, arms wide, smiling, a little like a ballet dancer taking a curtain call. Perhaps it was the suddenness or seeming aggressiveness of her move that made the dragon sheer off, fangs clashing. The two girls climbed the rail.

Hisvet turned again, Cat's Claw's cut a bold red line across her face, and sighted her crossbow at the Mouser. There was the faintest silvery flash. Hisvet tossed the crossbow in the black sea and followed Frix down the ladder. The boathooks let go, the flapping black sail filled, and the black cutter faded into the mist.

The Mouser felt a little sting in his left temple, but he forgot it while whirling the last loops from his shoulders and ankles. Then he ran across the deck, disregarding the green heads lazily searching for last rat morsels, and cut Fafhrd's bonds.

All the rest of that night the two adventurers conversed with Karl Treuherz, telling each other fabulous things about each other's worlds, while Scylla's sated daughter slowly circled *Squid*, first one head sleeping and then the other. Talking was slow and uncertain work, even with the aid of the little Lankhmarese-German Dictionary for Space-Time Travelers, and neither party really believed a great deal of the other's tales, yet pretended to for friendship's sake.

"Do all men dress as grandly as you do in Tomorrow?" Fafhrd once asked, admiring the German's purple-and-orange garb.

"No, Hagenbeck just has his employees do it, to spread his monster zoo's fame," Karl Treuherz explained.

The last of the mist vanished just before dawn and they saw, silhouetted against the sea silvered by the sinking gibbous moon, the black ship of Karl Treuherz hovering not a bowshot west of *Squid*, its little lights twinkling softly.

The German shouted for joy, summoned his sleepy monster by thwacking his pike against the rail, swung astride the larger head, and swam off calling after him, "*Auf Wiedersehen!*"

Fafhrd had learned just enough Gibberish—German, during the night to know this meant, "Until we meet again."

*   *   *

When the monster and the German had swum below it, the space-time engine descended, somehow engulfing them. Then a little later the black ship vanished.

"It dove into the infinite waters toward Karl's Tomorrow bubble," the Gray Mouser affirmed confidently. "By Ning and by Sheel, the German's a master magician!"

Fafhrd blinked, frowned, and then simply shrugged. . . .

The black kitten rubbed his ankle. Fafhrd lifted it gently to eye level, saying, "I wonder, kitten, if you're one of the Cats' Thirteen or else their small agent, sent to wake me when waking was needful?" The kitten smiled solemnly into Fafhrd's cruelly scratched and bitten face and purred.

Clear gray dawn spread across the waters of the Inner Sea, showing them first *Squid*'s two boats crowded with men and Slinoor sitting dejected in the stern of the nearer but standing up with uplifted hand as he recognized the figures of the Mouser and Fafhrd; next Lukeen's war galley *Shark* and the three other grain ships *Tunny*, *Carp* and *Grouper*; lastly, small on the northern horizon, the green sails of two dragon-ships of Movarl.

The Mouser, running his left hand back through his hair, felt a short, straight, rounded ridge in his temple under the skin. He knew it was Hisvet's smooth silver dart, there to stay.

STONE MAN

By Fred Saberhagen

Derron Odegard took a moment to wipe his sweaty palms on the legs of his easy-fitting duty uniform, and to minutely shift the position of his headset on his skull. Then he leaned forward in his contour chair, hunting the enemy again.

After just half an hour on watch he was bone-tired. The weight of his planet and its forty million surviving inhabitants rested crushingly on the back of his neck. He didn't want to bear the weight of forty million lives, but at the moment there was nowhere to set them down.

The responsibility was very real. One gross error by Derron, or anyone else in Time Operations, could be enough to tumble the people who still survived on the planet Sirgol into nothingness, to knock them out of real-time and end them for good, end them so completely that they would never have existed at all.

Derron's hunter's hands settled easily to rest on the molded controls of his console. Like those of a trained musician, his fingers followed his thought. The pattern on the curved viewscreen before him, a complex weaving of green cathode-traces, dissolved at his touch on the controls, then steadied, then shifted again—grass put carefully aside by the touch of a cautious stalker. In the screen pattern, Derron's educated eye saw represented the lifelines of animals and plants, a tangle which made up his assigned small segment of his planet's prehistorical ecology.

Surrounding Derron Odegard's chair and console were those of other sentries, all aligned in long, subtly curving rows. This arrangement pleased and rested the momentarily lifted eye—and then led the eye back to the job, where it belonged. The same effect resulted from the gentle modulations that sometimes passed cloudlike across the artificial light flowing from the strongly vaulted ceiling; and from the insistent psych-music, a murmur of melody that now and then shifted into a primitive heavy beat.

A thousand men stood guard with Derron in his buried chamber while the music murmured and the fake cloud-shadows passed, and through the huge room there wafted fresh-smelling air; breezes scented convincingly with green fields, sometimes with the tang of the sea, with all the varieties of living soil and water that no longer existed up above the miles of rock, on the surface of the planet.

Again the cathode traces symbolizing interconnected life rippled past Derron on his screen.

Like a good soldier he avoided predictability in his own moves while patrolling his post. He sent his recon-device a decade further into the past, then five miles north, then two years presentward, and a dozen miles southwest. At every pause he watched and listened, so far in vain. No predator's passage had yet disturbed this green symbolic grass.

"Nothing yet," he said aloud, feeling his supervisor's presence at his elbow. When the presence stayed put, Derron glanced back for a moment at Captain—?

It irritated him that he could not think of the captain's name, though perhaps it was understandable. Time Operations had only been in business for about a month and during all that period had been in a state of organizational flux.

Whoever he was, the captain had his eyes fixed fiercely on Derron's screen. "Your section right here," the captain said, showing his nervousness, "this is the hot spot." The captain's only reassuring aspect was that his dark jowly face seemed set like a bulldog's, to bite and hold on. Derron turned back to work.

His assigned segment of spacetime was set about twenty thousand years in the past, near the time of the First Men's coming to Sirgol. Its duration was about a century, and in space it comprised a square of land roughly a hundred miles on a side, including the lower atmosphere above the square. On the screen every part of it appeared as an enormously complex thicket of events.

Derron had not yet found a human lifeline woven into this thicket of the past, but he was not looking for humans especially. What mattered was that he had not yet discovered the splash of disruptive change that would have signaled the presence of an invading berserker machine.

The infraelectronic recon-device which served as Derron's sense-extension into the past did not stir the branches of forests, or startle animals. Rather it hovered just outside reality, seeing real-time through the fringe of things that almost were, dipping into real-time for an ano-second and then dropping back again to peer at it from just around the local curves of probability.

*   *   *

The first intimation that battle had been joined came to Derron not through his screen or even his earphones, but through the sound of his captain moving away in soft-footed haste, to whisper excitedly with the supervisor of the next rank.

If the fight was really on in Time Operations at last, a man might well feel frightened. Derron did, in a remote and withdrawn sort of way. He was not badly frightened as yet, and did not expect to be. He thought he would stay on his job and do it well.

There were advantages in not caring very much.

A few seconds later the start of an action was confirmed by a calm girl's voice that came into his earphones. She also told him in which dimensions and by how much to shift his pattern of search. All the sentries would be shifting now, as those nearest the enemy penetration closed in and the rest spread their zones to maintain coverage. The first attack might be only a diversion.

Present-time passed slowly. Derron's orders were changed and changed again, by the unshakable girl-voice that might be only a recording. For a while he could only guess at how things were going. Men had never tried to fight in the past before, but all the men of Sirgol who were still alive were used to war in one form or another. And this game of Time Operations would also be new to the enemy—though of course he had no emotions to get in his way.

"Attention, all sentries," said a new, drawling male voice in Derron's headset. "This is Time Ops Command, to let you all know what's going on. First, the enemy's sunk a beachhead down about twenty-one thousand years in probability-time. Looks like they're going to take things down there and then launch 'em up into history."

A few seconds later, the voice added: "We got our first penetration already spotted, somewhere around twenty-and-a-half down. Keep your eyes sharp and find us the keyhole."

At some time more than twenty thousand years in the past, at some spot not yet determined high in Sirgol's atmosphere, six berserker devices the size of aircraft had come bursting into reality. If men's eyes had been able to watch the event directly, they would have seen the six missile-shaped killing machines materialize out of nothing and then explode from their compact formation like precision flyers. Like an aerobatic team they scattered at multisonic speed away from their "keyhole"—the point of spacetime through which they had entered reality, and where one perfect counterblow could still destroy them all.

As the six enemy machines flew at great speed away from one

another, they seeded the helpless world below them with poison. Radioactives, antibiotic chemicals—it was hard from a distance of twenty thousand years to say just what they were using. Derron Odegard, patrolling like the other sentries, saw the attack only in its effects. He perceived it as a diminishing in probability of the existence of life in his own sector, a morbid change following certain well-defined directions that would in time reduce the probability of any life at all in the sector to zero.

If the planet was dead and poisoned when the First Men arrived, groping and wandering as helpless as babies, why then there could be no human civilization on Sirgol, no one in Modern times to resist the berserkers. The planet would still be dead today. Derron knew that the dark tide of nonexistence was rising in each cell of his own body, in each cell of every living creature.

Derron's findings with those of every other sentry were fed to Time Ope Command. Men and computers worked together, tracing back the vectors along which the deadly changes in probability advanced.

The system worked to Command's satisfaction, this time. The computers announced that the keyholes of the six flying machines had been pinpointed.

In the catacomb of Operations' Stage Two, the missiles waited, blunt simple shapes surrounded by complexities of control and launching mechanism. As Command's drawling voice announced: "Firing one for the keyhole," massive steel arms extended the missile sideways from its rack, while on the dark stone floor beneath it there appeared a silvery circle, shimmering like troubled liquid.

The arms dropped the missile, and in the first instant of its fall it disappeared. Even as it fell into the past it was propelled as a wave of probability through the miles of rock to the surface. The guidance computers made constant corrections, steering their burden of fusible hydrogen through the mazes of the half-real, toward the right point on the edge of normal existence. . . .

Derron saw the malignant changes that had been creeping ominously across his screen begin suddenly to reverse themselves. It looked like a trick, like running the projector backward, like some stunt with no relevance to the real world.

"Right in the keyhole!" yelped Command's voice in his ear, drawling no longer. The six berserker flyers now shared their point of entry into real-time with an atomic explosion, neatly tailored to fit.

As the waves of death were seen to recede on every screen, jubilation spread in murmurous waves of its own up and down the curved rows of sentry-positions. But experience, not to mention discipline, kept the rejoicing muted.

The rest of the six-hour watch passed like a routine training exercise in the techniques of mopping-up. All the i's were dotted and the t's crossed, the tactical success tied down and made certain by observations and tests. Men were relieved on schedule for their customary breaks, and passed one another smiling and winking. Derron went along and smiled when someone met his eye; it was the easiest thing to do.

When the shift ended and there was still no sign of any further enemy action, there was no doubt left that the berserkers' first attempt to get at the Moderns through their past had been beaten back into nonexistence.

But the damned machine would be back, as always. Stiff and sweaty and tired, and not conscious of any particular elation, Derron rose from his chair to make room for the sentry on the next shift.

"I guess you guys did all right today," the replacement said, a touch of envy in his voice.

Derron made himself smile again. "You can have the next chance for glory." He pressed his thumbprint on the console's scanner as the other man did the same. Then, his responsibility officially over, he walked at a dragging pace out of the sentry room. Other members of his shift were moving in the same direction; once outside the area of enforced quiet they formed excited groups and started to whoop it up a little.

Nodding cheerfully to the others, and replying appropriately to their jokes, Derron stood in line to hand in the recording cartridge with its record of his shift activity. Then he waited in another short line, to make a final oral report to a debriefing officer. After that he was free; as free as any citizen of Sirgol could be, these days.

II

When the huge passenger elevator lifted Derron and a crowd of others out of the deeper caves of Time Operations to the housing level, there were still ten miles of rock overhead.

The pampered conditions of the sentry room were not to be found here, or anywhere where a maximum-efficiency environment was not absolutely necessary. Here the air smelled stale and the lighting was just tolerable. The corridor in which Derron

had his bachelor-cubicle was one of the main streets of the
buried world-city, the fortress in which the surviving population
of Sirgol was armed and maintained and housed and fed. Given
the practically limitless power of hydrogen fushion to labor for
them, and the mineral wealth of the surrounding rock, the be-
sieged planet-garrison at least had no fear of starvation.

The corridor was two stories high and as wide as a main street
in one of the cities of the old surface-world. People who traveled
this corridor for any considerable distance rode upon the moving
belts laid down in its center. On the moving belt now rushing
past Derron a pair of black-uniformed police were checking the
identity cards of travelers. Planetary Command must be cracking
down again on work-evaders.

As usual, the belts and the broad statwalk strips on either side
were moderately crowded. Men and women were going to their
jobs or leaving them, at a pace neither hurried nor slow, wearing
work uniforms that were mostly monotonously alike. A few
other people, wearing lighter and gayer off-duty clothes, were
strolling or standing in line before stores or places of amusement.

One of the shorter lines was that in front of the local branch of
the Homestead Office. Derron paused on the statwalk there,
looking at the curling posters and the shabby models on display.
All depicted various plans for the rehabilitation of the surface of
the planet after the war. Apply *now* for the land you want . . .
they said there would be new land, then, nourished and protected
by new oceans of air and water, which were to be somehow
squeezed out of the planet's deep rocks.

The people standing in line looked at the models with wistful,
half-hopeful eyes, and most of those passing glanced in with
something more than indifference. They were all of them able to
forget, if they had ever really understood it, the fact that the
world was dead. The real world was dead and cremated, along
with nine out of ten of the people who had made it live. . . .

To control his thoughts Derron had to turn away from the
dusty models and the people waiting in line to believe. He
started toward his cubicle but then on impulse turned aside, down
a narrow branching passage.

He knew where he was going. Likely there would be only a
few people there at this time of day. A hundred paces ahead of
him, the end of the passage framed in its arch the living green of
real treetops—

The tremor of a heavy explosion raced through the living rock
from which this passage had been carved.

*   *   *

Ahead, Derron saw two small red birds streak in alarm across the greenery of the trees. Now the sound came, dull and muffled, but heavy. It had been a small missile penetration, then, one hitting fairly close by. The enemy threw down through the shielding rock probability-waves that turned into missiles, even as men fired them upward at the enemy fleet in space.

Without hesitating or breaking stride Derron paced on to the end of the passage. There he halted, leaning his hands heavily on a protective railing of natural logs, while he looked out over the park from two levels above the grass. From six levels higher yet, an artificial sun shone down almost convincingly on three or four acres of real trees and real grass, on varicolored birds that were held inside the park by curtain-jets of air. Across the scene there passed a gurgling brook of real water. Today its level had fallen so that the concrete sides of its bed were revealed halfway down.

A year ago—a lifetime ago, that is, in the real world—Derron Odegard had been no nature-lover. Then he had been thinking of finishing his schooling and settling down to the labors of a professional historian. Even on holidays he had gone to historic places . . . he thrust out of his memory now certain thoughts, and a certain face, as he habitually did. Yes, a year ago he had spent most of his days with history texts and films and tapes, and in the usual academic schemes for academic advancement. In those days the first hints of the possibility that historians might be allowed to take a first-hand look at the past had been promises of pure joy. The warnings of Earthmen were decades old, and the defenses of Sirgol had been decades in the building, all part of the background of life. The Berserker War itself was other planets' business.

In the past year, Derron thought, he had learned more about history than in all the years of study that had gone before. Now when the last moment of history came on Sirgol, if he could know it was the last, he would get away if he could come to one of these parks with a little bottle of wine he had been keeping stowed under his cot. He would finish history by drinking whatever number of toasts circumstances allowed, to whatever dead and dying things seemed to him then the most worthy.

The tension was just beginning to drain from his fingers into the hand-worn bark of the railing, and he had actually forgotten the recent explosion, when the first of the wounded came into the park below him.

The first was a man with his uniform jacket gone and the remains of his clothing all torn and blackened. One of his arms was burnt and raw and swelling. He tottered forward half-blindly among the trees, and then like an actor in some wilderness drama he fell full length at the edge of the brook and began to drink from it ravenously.

Next came another man, older, this one probably some kind of clerk or administrator, though he was too far away for Derron to make out his insignia. This man stood in the park as if lost, seemingly unwounded but more dazed than the burned man. Now and then the second man raised his hands to his ears; there was something wrong with his hearing.

A pudgy woman entered, moaning in bewilderment as she held the flap of her torn scalp in place. Two more women came in; a trickle of injured people began to spill steadily from a small park entrance at grass level. They flowed in and defiled the false peace of the park. Their voices, growing in number, built a steadily rising murmur of complaint against the injustice of the universe. Everyone knew it was a rare event for a berserker missile to get past all the defenses and penetrate to the depth of an inhabited level.

Why did it have to happen today, and to them?

There were a couple of dozen people in the park now, walking wounded from what must have been a relatively harmless explosion. Down the nearby passages there echoed authoritarian yells, and the whine and rumble of heavy machines. Damage Control was on the job; the walking wounded were being sent here to get them out from under foot while more urgent matters were being taken care of.

A slender girl of eighteen or twenty, clad in the remnants of a simple paper dress, came into the park and leaned against a tree as if she could walk no further. The way her dress was torn . . .

Derron turned away, squeezing his eyes shut and shaking his head in a spasm of self-disgust. He stood up here like some ancient tyrant, remotely entertained and critically lustful.

He would have to decide, one of these days, whether he was really still on the side of the human race or not. He hurried down some nearby stairs and came out on the ground level of the park. The badly burned man was bathing his raw arm in the cool running water. No one seemed to have stopped breathing, or to be bleeding to death. The girl looked as if she might fall away from her supporting tree at any moment.

Derron went to her, pulling off his jacket. He wrapped her in the garment and eased her away from the tree.

"Where are you hurt?"

She shook her head and refused to sit down, so they did a little off-balance dance while he held her up. She was tall and slim and ordinarily she would be lovely . . . no, not really lovely, or at least not standard-pretty. But good to look at. Her dark hair was cut in the short simple style most favored by Planetary Command, as most women's was these days. No jewelry or makeup. Plainly she was in some kind of shock.

She came out of it somewhat to look in bewilderment at the jacket that had been wrapped around her; her eyes focused on the collar insignia. She said: "You're an officer." Her voice was low and blurry.

"In a small way. Hadn't you better lie down somewhere?"

"No. First tell me what's going on. . . . I've been trying to get home . . . or somewhere. Can't you tell me where I am? What's going on?" Her voice was rising.

"Easy, take it easy. There was a missile strike. Here, now, this insignia of mine is supposed to be a help with the girls. So behave! Won't you sit down?"

"No! First I must find out . . . I don't know who I am, or where, or why."

"I don't know those things about myself." That was the most honest communication he had made to anyone in a long time.

He was afraid that when the girl came out of her dazed condition it would be into panic. More people, passersby and medics, were running into the park now, aiding the wounded and creating a scene of confusion. The girl looked wildly around her and clung to Derron's arm. He supposed the best thing was to walk her to a hospital. Where? Of course—there was the one adjoining Time Operations, just a short way from here.

"Come along," he said. The girl walked willingly beside him, clinging to his encircling arm. "What's your name?" he asked, as they boarded the elevator. The other people stared at her in his jacket.

"I . . . don't know." Now she looked more frightened than ever. Her hand went to her throat, but there was no dog-tag chain around her neck. Many people didn't like to wear them. "Where are you taking me?"

"To a hospital. You need some looking-after." He would have liked to give some wilder answer for the onlookers' benefit, but he didn't want to terrify the girl.

She had little to say after that. He led her off the elevator and another short walk brought them to the hospital's emergency door. Other casualties from the explosion, stretcher cases, were arriving now.

Inside the emergency room an old nurse started to peel Derron's jacket off the girl and what was left of her dress came with it. "You just come back for your jacket tomorrow, young man," the woman ordered sharply, rewrapping.

"Gladly." Then he could only wave good-by to the girl as a horde of stretcher-bearers and other busy people swept him with them back out into the corridor. He found himself laughing to himself about the nurse and the jacket. It was a while since he had laughed about anything.

He had a spare jacket in his locker in the sentry officers' ready room in Time Ops, and he went there to pick it up. There was nothing new on the bulletin board. He would like to get off sentry duty and into something where you didn't just sit still under strain for six hours a day.

He went to the nearest officers' gym and talked to acquaintances and played two rounds of handball, winning an ersatz soft drink that he preferred not to collect. The others were talking about the missile strike; Derron mentioned that he had seen some of the wounded, but he said nothing about the girl.

From the gym he went with a couple of the others to a bar, where he had one drink, his usual limit, and listened without real interest to their talk of some new girls at a local uplevel dive called the Red Garter. Private enterprise still flourished in certain areas.

He ate a meal in the local officers' mess, with a better appetite than usual. Then he took the elevator back up to housing level and at last reached his bachelor's cubicle. He stretched out on his cot and for once went sound asleep before he could even consider taking a pill.

III

He was awake earlier than usual, feeling well rested. The little clock on his cubicle wall had just jumped to oh-six-thirty hours, Planetary Emergency Time.

This morning none of Time's aspects worried him particularly. He had enough time to stop by the hospital and see what had happened to her, before he went on duty.

He was carrying yesterday's jacket over his arm when, following a nurse's directions, he found the girl seated in a patients' lounge. The TV was on, tuned to Channel Gung-Ho, the one devoted to the war effort and associated government propaganda, and she was frowning at it with a look of naiveté. Today she was wearing a plain dress that did not exactly fit. Her sandaled feet were curled beside her on her chair. At this time of the morning she had the lounge pretty much to herself.

At the sound of Derron's step she turned her head quickly, then got to her feet, smiling. "Oh, it's you! It's a good feeling to recognize someone."

"It's a good feeling for me, to have someone recognize me."

She thanked him for yesterday's help. He introduced himself.

She wished she could tell him her name, but the amnesia was persisting. "Outside of that, I feel fine."

"That's good, anyway," he said as they sat down in adjacent chairs.

"Actually I do have a name, of sorts. For the sake of their computer records the people here at the hospital have tagged me Lisa Gray, next off some list they keep handy. Evidently a fair number of people go blank in the upper story these days."

"I don't doubt it."

"They tell me that when the missile hit yesterday I was with a number of people from an upper-level refuge camp that's being closed down. A lot of the records were destroyed in the blast. They can't find me, or they haven't yet." She laughed nervously.

Derron tried a remark or two meant to be reassuring, but they didn't sound very helpful in his own ears. He got off the subject. "Have you had your breakfast?"

"Yes. There's a little automat right here if you want something. Maybe I could use some more fruit juice."

In a couple of minutes Derron was back with two glasses of the orange-colored liquid called fruit juice and a couple of standard sweetrolls. Lisa was again studying the war on the TV screen; the commentator's stentorian voice was turned mercifully low.

Derron set the repast on a low table, pulled his own chair closer, and asked: "Do you remember what we're fighting against?"

On screen at the moment was a deep-space scene in which it was hard to make anything out. Lisa hesitated, then shook her head. "Not really."

"Does the word 'berserker' mean anything to you?"

"No."

"Well, they're machines. Some of them are bigger than any spaceships we Earth-descended men have ever built. Others come in many shapes and sizes, but all of them are deadly. The first berserkers were built ages ago, to fight in some war we've never heard of, between races we've never met.

"Sometimes men have beaten the berserkers in battle, but

some of them always survived, to hide out somewhere and build more of their kind, with improvements. They're programmed to destroy life anywhere they can find it, and they've come halfway across the galaxy doing a pretty good job. They go on and on like death itself.''

"No," said Lisa, not liking the plot.

"I'm sorry, I didn't mean to start raving. We on Sirgol were alive, and so the berserkers had to get rid of us. They boiled away our oceans, and burned our air and our land and nine tenths of our people. But since they're only machines, it's all an accident, a sort of cosmic joke. An act of the Holy One, as people used to say. We have no one to take revenge on.'' His voice choked slightly in his tight throat; he sipped at his orange-colored water and then pushed it away.

"Won't men come from other planets to help us?"

"Some of them are fighting berserkers near their own systems, too. And a really big relief fleet will have to be put together to do us any good. And polities must be played between the stars as usual. I suppose some help will come eventually, maybe in another year.''

The TV announcer began to drone aggressively about victories on the moon, while an appropriate videotape was shown. The chief satellite of Sirgol was said to much resemble the moon of Earth. Its round face had been pocked by impact craters into an awed expression long before men or berserkers existed. During the last year a rash of new craters had wiped away the face of Sirgol's moon, together with all human bases there.

"I think that help will come to us in time," said Lisa.

In time for what? Derron wondered. "I suppose so," he said and felt it was a lie.

Lisa was looking anxiously at the TV. "It seems to me I can remember . . . Yes! I can remember seeing the old moon, the funny face in it! It did look like a face, didn't it?''

"Oh, yes.''

"I remember it!" she cried in a burst of joy. Like a child she jumped up from her chair and kissed Derron on the cheek.

While she sat down again, looking at him happily, a line of ancient poetry sang through his mind. He swallowed.

Now on the TV they were showing the dayside surface of Sirgol. Cracked dry mudflats stretched away to a horizon near which there danced whirlwinds of yellow dust—there was a little atmosphere left—under a sky of savage blue. Rising gleaming from the dried mud in the middle distance were the bright steel bones of some invading berserker device, smashed and twisted last ten-day or last month by some awesome energy of defense. Another victory for the droning voice to try to magnify.

Derron cleared his throat. "Do you remember about our planet here being unique?"

"No . . . I doubt that I ever understood science." But she looked interested. "Go on, tell me about it."

"Well." Derron put on his little-used teacher's voice. "If you catch a glimpse of our sun on the screen there, you'll see it looks much like any other star that has an Earth-type planet. But looks are deceiving. Oh, our daily lives are the same as they would be elsewhere. And interstellar ships can enter and leave our system—if they take precautions. But our local spacetime is tricky.

"We were colonized through a weird accident. About a hundred years ago an exploring ship from Earth fell into our peculiar spacetime unawares. It dropped back through about twenty thousand years of time, which must have wiped clean the memories of everyone aboard." He smiled at Lisa. "Our planet is unique in that time travel into the past is possible here, under certain conditions. First, anyone who travels back more than about five hundred years suffers enough mental devolution to have their memories wiped out. They go blank in the upper story, as you put it. Our First Men must have crawled around like babies after their ship landed itself."

"The First Men . . . that's familiar."

"There were First Women, too, of course. Somehow the survivors kept on surviving, and multiplied, and over the generations started building up civilizations. When the second exploring ship arrived, about ten years Earth-time after the first, we'd built up a thriving planet-wide civilization and were getting started on space travel ourselves. In fact it was signals from our early interplanetary probes that drew the second Earthship here. It approached more carefully than the first one had and landed successfully.

"Pretty soon the men from Earth figured out what had happened to our first ship. They also brought us warning of the berserkers. Took some of our people to other systems and showed them what galactic war was like. The people of other worlds were tickled to have four hundred million new allies, and they deluged us with advice on weapons and fortifications, and we spent the next eighty years getting ready to defend ourselves. Then about a year ago the berserker fleet came. . . ." Derron's voice trailed off.

Lisa drank some of her "juice" as if she liked it. She prompted: "What do you do now, Derron?"

"Oh, various odd jobs in Time Operations. See, if the berserkers can delay our historical progress at some vital point—the invention of the wheel, say—everything following would be slowed down. When galactic civilization contacted us, we might be still in the Middle Ages, or further back, without any technological base on which to build defenses for ourselves. And in the new real-time, the present would see us entirely wiped out."

Derron looked at the version of Time he wore on his wrist. "Looks like I'd better go right now and start my day's heroic fighting."

The officer in charge of that morning's briefing was Colonel Borss. He took his job very seriously in all its details, with the somber expectancy of a prophet.

"As we all know, yesterday's defensive action was tactically successful."

In the semidarkness of the briefing room the colonel's pointer skipped luminously across the glowing symbols on his big display screen. "*But,* strategically speaking, we must admit that the situation has deteriorated somewhat."

The colonel went on to explain that this gloomy view was due to the existence of the enemy's beachhead, his staging area some twenty-plus-thousand years down, from whence more berserker devices would undoubtedly be propelled up into historical real-time. For technical reasons, these devices moving presentward would be almost impossible to stop until they had finally emerged.

All was not entirely lost, however. "After the enemy has broken three more times into our history, we should be able to get a fix on his beachhead and smash it with a few missiles.

"That'll pretty well put an end to his whole Time Operations program.

"Of course we have first to face the little detail of repelling the next three attacks."

As his dutiful audience of junior officers made faint laughing sounds, the colonel produced on his screen a type of graph of human history on Sirgol, a glowing treelike shape. He tapped with his pointer far down on the slender trunk. "We rather suspect that the first attack will fall somewhere near here, near the First Men, where our history is still a tender shoot."

IV

Matt, sometimes also called Lion-Hunter, felt the afternoon sun hot on his bare shoulders as he turned away from the last familiar landmarks of his country, the territory in which he had lived all his twenty-five years.

Matt had climbed up on a rock to get a better view of the unknown land ahead, into which he and the rest of The People were fleeing. Ahead he could see swamps, and barren hills, and nothing very inviting. Everywhere the land wavered with the spirits of heat.

The little band of The People, as many in number as a man's fingers and toes, were shuffling along in a thin file beside the rock which Matt had mounted. No one was hanging back, or even trying to argue the others out of making the journey. For though there might be strange dangers in the new land ahead, everyone agreed that nothing there was likely to be as terrible as what they were fleeing—the new beasts, the lions with flesh of stone who could not be hurt by stones or arrows, who could kill with only a glance from their fiery eyes.

In the past two days, ten of The People had been caught and killed. The others had been able to do nothing but hide, hardly daring to look for a puddle to drink from or to pull up a root to eat.

Matt gripped with one hand the bow slung over his shoulder, the only bow now left to the survivors of The People; the others had been burned, with the men who had tried to use them against a stone-lion. Tomorrow, Matt thought, he would try hunting for meat in the new country. No one was carrying any food now. Some of the young were wailing in hunger until the women pinched their mouths and noses shut to quiet them.

The file of the surviving People had passed Matt now. He ran his eye along it, then hopped down from his rock, frowning.

A few strides brought him up to those in the rear of the march. "Where is Dart?" he asked, frowning.

Dart was an orphan, and no one was overly concerned. "He kept telling us how hungry he was," a woman said. "And then he ran on toward those swampy woods ahead. I suppose he went to look for something to eat."

Matt grunted. He had no idea of trying to keep any firm control over the action of any of The People. Someone who wanted to run ahead just did so.

Derron was just buying Lisa some lunch—from the hospital automat, since she was still being kept under observation—when the public address speakers began to broadcast a list of names of

Time Operation people who were to report for duty at once. Derron's name was included.

He scooped up a sandwich and ate it as he went. This was something more than another practice alert. When Derron reached the briefing room, Colonel Borss was already on the dais and speaking, pausing to glare at each new arrival.

"Gentlemen, the first assault has fallen just about as predicted, within a few hundred years of the First Men." To Derron's slight surprise, the colonel paused momentarily to bow his head at the mention of those beings sacred to Orthodoxy. These days there were few religionists traditional enough to make such gestures.

"Certainly," the colonel went on, "the berserkers would like to catch the First Men and eliminate them. But this, as we know, must prove impossible."

On this one point at least, science and Orthodox religion were still in firm agreement. The first men entering the ecology on any planet constituted the beginning of an evolutionary peduncle, said science, and as such were considered practically impossible of discovery, time travel or not.

Colonel Borss smoothed his mustache and went on: "As in the first attack, we are faced by six enemy machines breaking into real-time. But in this case the machines are not flyers, or at least they seem not to be operating in an airborne mode. Probably they are slightly smaller than the flyers were. We think they are antipersonnel devices that move on legs and rollers and are of course invulnerable to any means of self-defense possessed by the Neolithic population.

"Evidently the berserker's game here is *not* to simply kill as many people as possible. We could trace the disturbance of a mass slaughter back to their new keyhole and blast them again. This time we think they'll concentrate on destroying some historically important individual, or small group. Just who in the invaded area is so important we don't know yet, but if the berserkers can read their importance in them we certainly can, and we soon will.

"Now here is Commander Nolos, to brief you on your part in our planned countermeasures."

Nolos, an earnest young man with a rasping voice, came right to the point. "You twenty-four men all have high scores in training on the master-slave androids. No one has any real combat experience with them yet, but you soon will. You're all relieved of other duties as of now."

Expressing various reactions, the two dozen men were hurried to a near-by ready room, and there left to wait for some minutes. At length they were taken down by elevator to Operations Stage Three, on one of the lowest and most heavily defended levels yet dug.

Stage Three was a great echoing cave, the size of an aircraft hangar. A catwalk spanned the cave close up under its reinforced ceiling, and from this walk were suspended the two dozen master units. They looked like spacesuits on puppet-strings.

Like a squad of armored infantry the slave-units stood on the floor below, each slave directly beneath its master. The slaves were the bigger, standing taller and broader than men, dwarfing the technicians who were now busy giving them final precombat checks.

Derron and his fellow operators were given individual briefings, with maps of the terrain where they were to be dropped, and such information as was available on the Neolithic nomads they were to try to protect. Generally speaking this information did not amount to much. After this the operators were run through a brief medical check, dressed in leotards and marched up onto the high catwalk.

At this point the word was passed to delay things momentarily. A huge screen on one wall of the stage lit up with an image of the bald, massive head of the Planetary Commander himself

"Men . . ." boomed the familiar amplified voice. Then the image paused, frowning off-camera. "You've got them *waiting* for me? Get on with it, man, get on with the operation! I can make speeches anytime!"

The Planetary Commander's voice was still rising as it was turned off. Derron got the impression that it had a good deal more to say, and he was glad that it was not being said to him. A pair of technicians came and helped him into his master, as into a heavy diving suit. But once inside he could wave the master's arms and legs and twist its thick body with perfect freedom and servo-powered ease.

"Power coming on," said a voice in Derron's helmet. And it seemed to him that he was no longer suspended in the free-moving puppet. All his senses were transferred in an instant into the body of his slave-unit on the floor below. He felt the slave starting to tilt as its servos moved it into conformity with the master's posture, and he moved the slave's foot as naturally as his own to maintain balance. Tilting back his head, he could look up through the slave-unit's eyes to see the master-unit, himself inside it, holding the same attitude on its complex suspension.

"Form ranks for launching!" came the command in his helmet. Around Derron the cavernous chamber came alive with the echoes of the Technicians who trotted and jumped to get out of the way. The squad of metal man-shapes formed a single serpentine file, and at the head of the file the floor of the stage suddenly blossomed into a bright mercurial disk.

". . . three, two, one, launch."

All of Derron's senses told him that he inhabited one of a line of tall bodies, all running with immense and easy power in their winding file toward the circle on the dark floor. The figure ahead of Derron reached the circle and disappeared. Then he himself leaped out over the silvery disk.

His metal feet came down on grass. He staggered briefly on uneven ground, through shadowy daylight in the midst of a leafy forest.

He moved at once to the nearest clearing from which he could get a good look at the sun. It was low in the western sky—he checked a compass in the slave's wrist—which indicated that he had missed his planned moment of arrival by some hours, if not by days or months or years.

He reported this at once, subvocalizing inside his helmet to keep the slave's speaker silent. If the slave had after all landed in the right place and time, the enemy was somewhere near it.

"All right then, Odegard, start coursing, and we'll try to get a fix."

"Understand."

He began to walk a spiral path through the woods. He of course kept alert for sign of the enemy, but the primary purpose of this maneuver was to splash up some waves in reality—to create minor disturbances in the local life-history, which a skilled sentry some twenty thousand years in the future should be able to see and pinpoint.

After he had spiraled for some ten minutes, alarming perhaps a hundred small animals and perhaps crushing a thousand insects underfoot without knowing it, the impersonal voice spoke again.

"All right, Odegard, we've got you spotted. You're in the right place but between four and five hours late. The sun should be getting low."

"It is."

"All right. Bear about two hundred forty degrees from magnetic north. It's hard to tell at this range just where your people are, but if you hold that course for about half an hour you should come somewhere near them."

"Understand."

Derron got his bearings and set off in a straight line. The wooded land ahead sloped gradually downward into a swampy area, beyond which there rose low rocky hills, a mile or two distant.

"Odegard, we're getting indication of another minor disturbance right there in your area. Probably caused by a berserker. We can't pin it down any more closely than that, sorry."

"Understand." He was not really there in the past, about to risk his own skin in combat; but the weight of forty million lives was on his neck again.

Some minutes passed. Derron was moving slowly ahead, trying to keep a lookout in all directions while planning a good path for the heavy slave-unit through the marshy ground, when he heard trouble in plain and simple form: a child screaming.

"Operations? I'm onto something." The scream was repeated; the slave-unit's ears were keen and directionally accurate; Derron changed course and began to move the unit at a run, leaping it across the softest-looking spots of ground, striving for both speed and silence.

In a few more seconds, he slid as silently as possible to a halt. In a treetop a stone's throw ahead was the source of the screams—a boy of about twelve, who was clinging tightly to the tree's thin upper trunk with bare arms and legs, clinging tightly to keep from being shaken down. Whenever his yelling ceased for lack of breath, another sharp tremor would run up through the tree and start him off again. The tree's lower trunk was thick, but the bush around its base concealed something that could shake it like a sapling. An animal would have to have the strength of an elephant, and there were no such living creatures here. It would be the berserker, using the boy in the tree as bait, hoping that his cries would bring the adults of his group to try a rescue.

Derron's mission was to protect a particular group of people, and at least one of them was in immediate danger. He moved forward without delay. But the berserker spotted the slave-unit before he saw the berserker.

Only an accidental slip of the slave's foot on the soft soil saved it from taking the first hit right there. As Derron slipped, a pinkish laser beam crackled like straightened lightning past his left ear.

In the next instant the brush around the tree heaved. Derron caught just one glimpse of something charging him, something four legged and low and wide as a groundcar. He snapped open his jaw, which pressed down inside his helmet on the trigger of his own laser weapon. From the center of the slave's forehead a pale lance cracked out, aimed automatically at the spot where the slave's eyes were focused. The beam smote the charging berserker amid the knobs of metal that served it for a face and glanced off to explode a small tree into a cloud of flame and steam.

The shot might have done damage, for the enemy broke off its rush in midstride and dove for cover behind a hillock, a grass-tufted hump of ground not five feet high.

Derron was somewhat surprised by his own aggressiveness. He found himself moving quickly to the attack, running the slave-unit in a crouch around the tiny hill. Two voices from Operations were trying at the same time to give him advice, but even if they had gone about it sensibly it was too late now for him to do anything but go his own way.

He charged right round onto the berserker, yelling inside his helmet as he fired his laser. The thing before him looked like a metal lion, but squat and very broad; given a second to hesitate, Derron might have flinched away, for in spite of all his training the illusion was very strong that he was actually hurling his own precious flesh upon this monster.

As it was, circumstances gave him no time to flinch. The slave ran at full speed into the berserker, and the trees in the swamp shook as the machines collided.

It was soon plain that wrestling was not likely to succeed against this enemy, which was not limited in its reactions by the slowness of protoplasmic nerves. For all the slave-unit's fushion-powered strength, Derron could only hang on desperately, gripping the berserker in a sort of half nelson while it bucked and twisted like a wild loadbeast to throw him off.

Since the fight had started everybody wanted to watch. The voices of at least two senior Operations officers screamed orders and abuse into Derron's ears, while the green forest spun around him faster than his eyes and brain could sort it out. In a detached fraction of a second of thought he noticed how his feet were flying uselessly on the end of his steel legs, breaking down small trees as the monster spun him. He tried to turn his head to bring the cyclops' eye of his laser to bear, but somehow could not manage to do so. He tried desperately to get a more solid grip for his steel arms on the berserker's thick neck, but then his grip was broken and he flew.

Before the slave-unit could even bounce the berserker was on top of it, moving faster than any maddened bull. Derron fired wildly with his laser. That the berserker should trample and batter the slave-unit and he should feel no pain gave him a giddy urge to laugh. In a moment now the fight would be lost and he would be able to give up.

But then the berserker was running away from Derron's wildly slashing laser. It leaped among the trees as lightly as a deer and vanished.

Dizzily—for the master-unit had of course spun on its mountings even as the slave was spun—Derron tried to sit up, on the peculiar little hillside where he had been flung. Now he discovered why the berserker had retired so willingly. Some important part had been broken in the slave, so its legs trailed as limp and useless as those of a man with a broken spine.

But the slave-unit's laser still worked. The berserker computer-brain had decided it could gain nothing by staying around to trade zaps with a crippled but still dangerous antagonist, not when it could be busy at its programmed task of killing people.

The voices had their final say: "Odegard, why in the—?" "Oh, do what you can!" Then with a click they were gone from his helmet, leaving their disgust behind.

Derron's own disgust with his failure was even sharper. Gone were the thoughts of getting things settled quickly one way or the other. Now all he wanted was another crack at 'em.

With the slave's arms alone, he got it into a sitting position, halfway down the conical side of a soggy sandpit.

He looked about him. The nearby trees were nearly all in bad shape; those not broken during the wrestling-match were black and smoking furiously from his wildly aimed laser.

What about the boy?

Working hard with his arms, Derron churned his way up to a spot near the rim of the funnel-shaped pit, where the sides were steepest. He could recognize, a little distance away, the tall tree in which the youngster had been clinging for his life. He was not in sight now, living or dead.

In a sudden little avalanche the crippled slave slid down once more toward the bottom of the sandy funnel.

A funnel?

Derron at last recognized the place where the slave-unit had been thrown.

It was the trap of a poison-digger, a species of carnivore that had been—or would be—exterminated in early historical times. Even now, there reared up a frightful grayish head from the watery mess that filled the bottom of the pit.

V

Matt stood just behind the boy Dart, while both of them peered very cautiously through the bushes toward the poison-digger's trap. The rest of The People were waiting, resting from their march while they ate some grubs and roots, a few hundred paces away.

Matt caught just a glimpse of a head above the lip of the funnel. Not a poison-digger's head, certainly. This one was curved almost as smoothly as a drop of water, but was still hard-looking.

"I think it is a stone-lion," Matt whispered very softly.

"Ah no," whispered Dart. "It's a man, a big man, the stone-man I told you about. Ah, what a fight he made against the stone-lion! But I didn't wait to see the end, I jumped from the tree and ran."

Matt beckoned Dart with a motion of his head. The two of them bent down and crept forward, them peered from behind another bush. Now they could see down into the pit.

Matt gasped, and almost called aloud in wonder. Poison-Digger down in the pit had reared up from his slime and lunged. And Stone-Man simply slapped Digger's nose with casual force, like someone swatting a child; and with a howl like that of a punished child, the Bad One splashed down under his water again.

In a strange tongue, Stone-Man muttered disconsolate words, like a man invoking spirits, at the same time slapping at his legs which seemed to be dead. Then with his arms he started trying to dig his way up and out of the pit. Stone-Man made the sand fly, and Matt thought maybe he would eventually make it, though it looked like a very hard struggle.

"Now do you believe me?" Dart was whispering fiercely. "He did fight the stone-lion, I saw him."

Matt hushed the young one and led him away. As they retreated it occurred to Matt that the stone-lion might have been mortally hurt in the fight, and he circled through the trees looking hopefully for a huge shiny corpse. He wanted very much before his own death to see a stone-lion somehow defeated and slain. But all he saw were burnt and broken trees.

When they got back to where the others were waiting, Matt talked things over with the more intelligent adults.

"You think we should approach this Stone-Man?" one asked.

"I would like to help him," said Matt. He was eager to join forces if he could with any power that was able to oppose a stone-lion.

The oldest woman of The People opened her lizard-skin pouch, in which she also kept the seed of fire, and took out the finger-bones of her predecessor. Three times she shook the bones and threw them on the ground, and studied the pattern in which they fell.

At last she pointed to Matt. "You will die," she announced, "fighting a strange beast, the likes of which none of us has ever seen."

Like most prophecies Matt had heard, this one was more interesting than helpful. "If you are right," he answered, "this stone-man can't kill me, since we have now seen him."

The others muttered doubtfully.

The more he thought about it, the more determined Matt became. "If he does turn out to be hostile, he can't chase us on his dead legs. I want to help him."

This time the slave's keen ears detected the approach of The People, though they were obviously trying to be quiet. Derron's helmet had been free of Modern voices for some minutes now; the too-many chiefs of Time Operations were evidently busy harassing some other operator.

Derron hated to draw their attention back to himself, but the approach of The People was something that he had to report.

"I'm getting some company," he subvocalized. No immediate reply was granted. Now the heads of the bolder ones among The People came into sight, peering nervously around treetrunks at the slave-unit. Derron made a gentle gesture to them with one open metal hand; he had to use the other to maintain the slave in a sitting position. If he could only get his visitors to remain until more help arrived, he could give them some degree of protection. The berserker had evidently gone away after some false scent, but it might be back at any time.

The People were reassured by the slave's quiescence, its crippled condition and its peaceful gestures. Soon all two dozen of them were out in the open, whispering among themselves as they looked down into the pit.

"Anybody listening?" Derron subvocalized, calling for help. "I've got a crowd of people here. Get me a linguist!"

Lately the Moderns had made a desperate effort to learn all the languages of Sirgol's past, through the dropping of disguised microphones into the divers parts of real-time where there were people to be studied. This had been a crash program, only undertaken in recent months when it had become apparent to both sides that the war could be moved from present-time into the past. There were one or two Moderns who had managed to learn something about the speech of The People and the other bands of the area—and those Moderns were very busy people today.

"Odegard!" The blast in his helmet made him wince. It sounded like Colonel Borss. "Don't let those people get away, try to protect them!"

Derron sighed, sub-subvocally. "Understood. How about getting me a linguist?"

"We're trying to get you one. You're in a vital area there. Try to protect those people until we can get you some help."

"Understood." ·

"Anyone that size is bound to eat a lot of food," one of the older men was complaining to Matt.

"With dead legs I don't suppose he'll live long enough to eat very much," Matt answered. He was trying to talk someone into giving him a hand in pulling the stone-man up out of the pit. Stone-Man sat watching calmly, as if he felt confident of getting some help.

The man debating against Matt cheerfully switched arguments. "If he won't live long, there's no use trying to help him. Anyway he's not one of The People."

"No, he's not. But still . . ." Matt searched for words, for ways of thought, to clarify his own feelings. This stone-man who had tried to help Dart was part of some larger order, to which The People also belonged. Part of something opposing all the wild beasts and demons that killed men by day or night.

"There may be others of his band around here," put in another man. "They would be strong friends to have."

"This one wants to be our friend," the boy Dart piped up.

The oldest woman scoffed: "So would anyone who was crippled and needed help."

VI

A girl linguist's voice joined the muted hive buzzing in Derron's helmet and gave him a rather halting translation of part of the debate. But after only a couple of minutes she was ordered away to work with another operator, who had managed to terrify the band he was supposed to be protecting.

"Tell him to pretend he's crippled," Derron advised. "All right, I'll do without a linguist. But how about dropping some of those self-defense weapons for these people of mine? If we wait until that berserker comes back it'll be too late. And make it grenades, not arrows. There's only one man in the bunch who has a bow."

"The weapons are being prepared. It's dangerous to hand them out until they're absolutely needed. Suppose they use 'em on each other, or on the slave?"

"You can at least drop them into the slave now." Inside the slave-unit's big torso was a hollow receptacle into which small items could be dropped from the future as required.

"They're being prepared."

Derron didn't know if he could believe that or not, the way things were going today.

The people seemed to be still discussing the slave-unit, while he kept it sitting in what he hoped was a patient and trustworthy attitude. According to the brief translation Derron had heard, the tall young man with the bow slung over his shoulder was arguing in favor of helping the "stone-man."

At last this man with the bow, who seemed to be the nearest thing to a chief that these people had, talked one of the other men into helping him. Together they approached one of the saplings splintered in the fight, and twisted it loose from its stump, hacking through the tough bark strings with a hand-axe. Then the two bold men came right up to the edge of the poison-digger's trap, holding the sapling by its branches so its splintered end was extended, rather shakily, down to where the slave could grasp it.

The two men pulled, then grunted with surprise at the weight they felt. Two more men were now willing to come and lend a hand.

"Odegard, this is Colonel Borss," said a helmet-voice, in urgent tones. "We can see now what the berserkers' target is. The first written language developed on the planet originates very near your present location. Possibly with the people you're with right now. We can't be sure of that and neither can the enemy, but certainly your band is in the target group."

Derron was hanging on with both hands as the slave-unit was dragged up the side of the pit. "Thanks for the word, Colonel. Now how about those grenades I asked for?"

"We're rushing two more slaves toward you, but we're having technical problems. Grenades?" There was a brief pause. "They tell me some grenades are coming up." The colonel's voice clicked off.

When the slave came sliding up over the rim of the pit, The People all retreated a few steps, falling silent and watching the machine carefully. Derron repeated his peaceful gestures.

As soon as his audience was slightly reassured about the slave,

they went back to worrying about something else. The setting
sun made them nervous, and they kept looking over their shoulders at it as they talked to one another.

In another minute they had gathered up their few belongings
and were on the march, with the air of folk resuming a practiced
activity. Stone-Man, it seemed, was to be allowed to choose his
own course of action.

Derron trailed along at the end of the file. He soon found that
on level ground he could keep the slave-unit moving pretty well,
walking on the knuckles of its hands like a broken-backed ape.
The People cast frequent backward glances at this pathetic monstrosity, showing mixed emotions. But even more frequently
they looked farther back, fearful about something that might be
on their trail.

Quite possibly, Derron thought, these people had already seen
the berserker, or found the bodies of their friends who had met
it. Sooner or later it would pick up their trail, in any case. The
slave-unit's leg-dragging track would make the berserker use a
bit more caution, but certainly, it would still come on.

Colonel Borss came back to talk. "You're right, Odegard,
your berserker's still in your area. It's the only one we haven't
bagged yet, but it's in the most vital spot. What I think we'll do
is this—the two slaves being sent as reinforcements will be in
place in a few minutes now. They'll follow your line of march
one on each side and a short distance ahead. Then when your
people stop somewhere for the night we'll set up the two new
slaves for an ambush."

Falling dusk washed the scene in a kind of dark beauty. The
People hiked with the swampy, half-wooded valley on their right
and low rocky hills close by on their left. The man with the bow,
whose name seemed to be something like Matt, kept scanning
these hills as he walked.

"What about those grenades? Operations? Anybody there?"

"We're setting up this ambush now, Odegard. We don't want
your people pitching grenades at *our* devices."

There was some sense to that, Derron supposed. But he had
no faith.

The leader, Matt, turned and went trotting up a hillside, the
other people following briskly. Derron saw that they were headed
for a narrow cave entrance, which was set into a steep low cliff
like a door in the wall of a house. A little way from the cave
everyone halted. Matt unslung his bow and nocked an arrow
before pitching a rock into the darkness of the cave. Just inside

the entrance was an L-bend that made it practically impossible to see any further.

Derron was reporting these latest developments to Operations, when out of the cave there reverberated a growl that made The People scatter like the survival experts they were.

When the cave-bear came to answer the door, it found Derron's proxy waiting alone on the porch.

The slave in its present condition had no balance to speak of, so the bear's first slap bowled it over. From a supine position Derron slapped back, clobbering the bear's nose and provoking a blood-freezing roar.

Made of tougher stuff than poison-diggers, the bear strained its fangs on the slave-unit's face. Still flat on his back, Derron lifted the bear with his steel arms and pitched it downhill. Go away!

The first roar had been only a tune-up for this second one. Derron didn't want to break even an animal's lifeline here if he could help it, but time was passing. He threw the bear a little further this time; it bounced once, landed on its feet, and without slowing down kept right on going into the swamp. Its howls trailed in the air for half a minute.

The People slowly gathered round again, for once forgetting to look over their shoulders. Derron had the feeling they were all about to fall down and worship him; before anything like this could happen, he dragged his proxy into the cave and made sure that it was now unoccupied. Matt had made a good discovery here; there was plenty of room inside the high narrow cavern to shelter the whole band.

When he came out he found The People gathering dead branches from under the trees at the edge of the swamp, getting ready to build a good-sized fire at the mouth of the cave. Far across the swampy valley a small spark of orange marked the encampment of some other band, in the thickening purplish haze of falling night.

"Operations, how's that ambush coming?"

"The other two units are taking up ambush positions now. They have you in sight at the cave-mouth."

"Good."

Let The People build their fire, then, and draw the berserker. They would be safe in a guarded cave while it walked into a trap.

From a pouch made of what looked like tough lizard-skin one of the old women produced a bundle of bark, which she unwrapped to reveal a smoldering center. With incantations and a judicious use of wood chips, she soon had the watchfire blazing. Its first tongues gave more light than did the fast-dimming sky.

The slave-unit moved last into the cave, right after Matt. Derron sat it leaning against the wall just inside the L-bend and sighed. He could use a rest—

Without warning the night outside erupted with the crackle of lasers and the clang of armored battle. Inside the cave the people jumped to their feet.

In the lasers' reflected glare Derron saw Matt with his bow ready, the other men grabbing up stones—and Dart, high up on a rock in the rear of the cave. There was a small window in the wall of rock back there, and the boy was looking out, the laser-glare bright on his awed face.

The flashing and crashing outside came to a sudden halt. The world sank into a deathlike silence. Long seconds passed.

"Operations? Operations? What's going on? What happened outside?"

"Oh, Holy One . . ." The voice was shaken. "Scratch two slave-units. Looks like the damn' thing's reflexes are just too good. Odegard, do the best you can . . ."

The watchfire came exploding suddenly into the cave, kicked probably by a clawed steel foot, so that a hail of sparks and brands bounced from the curving wall of stone just opposite the narrow entrance. The berserker would walk right in. Its cold brain had learned contempt for all the Moderns were able to do against it.

But there came a heavy grating sound; evidently the cave mouth was just a bit too narrow for it.

"Odegard, a dozen of the arrows are ready to drop through to you now. Shaped charges in the points, set to fire on sharp contact."

"*Arrows*? I wanted grenades, I told you we've only one bow, and there's no room . . ." But the window in the rear of the cave might serve as an archery port. "Send arrows, then. Send something!"

"Dropping arrows now. Odegard, we have a relief operator standing by in another master-unit, so we can switch . . ."

"Never mind that. I'm used to operating this broken-backed thing now, and he isn't."

The berserker was scraping and hammering at the bulge of rock that kept it from its prey, raising a hellish racket. With the slave-unit's hands Derron undid the catches and opened the door in its metal torso. While a bank of faces surrounded him, staring solemnly through the gloom, he took out the arrows and offered them to Matt.

VII

With reverence the hunter accepted the weapons. Since the firelight had vanished the slave's eyes had shifted into the infrared; Derron could see well enough to tell that the arrows looked to be well constructed, their straight wooden shafts fletched with plastic feathers, their heads a good imitation of hand-chipped flint. Now if they only worked . . .

Matt needed no instructions on what to do with the arrows, not after their magical manner of appearance. Dart getting under his feet, he dashed to the rear of the cave; there he put the youngster behind him and scrambled up the rocks to the natural window. It would have given him a fine safe spot to shoot from, if there had been no such thing as laser beams.

Since lasers did exist, it would be the slave-unit's task to take the first beam itself and keep the berserker's attention on it as much as possible. Derron inched his crippled metal body toward the bend of the L. When he saw Matt nock an arrow to his bow, he lunged out, with his ridiculous hand-walking movement, around the corner.

The berserker had just backed away to take a fresh run at the entrance. It of course was quicker than Derron with its beam. But the slave's armor held for the moment, and Derron scrambled forward, firing back at point-blank range. If the berserker saw Matt, it ignored him, thinking arrows meant nothing.

But now the first one struck. Derron saw the shaft spin softly away, while the head vanished in a momentary fireball that left a fist-sized hole in the berserker's armor at the shoulder of one foreleg.

The machine lurched off balance even as its laser flicked toward Matt. Derron kept scrambling after it on steel hands, keeping his own beam on it like a spotlight. The bushes atop the little cliff had been set afire, but Matt popped up bravely and shot his second arrow, as accurately as the first. The shaped charge hit the berserker in the side, and staggered it on its three legs. And then it could fire its laser no more, for Derron was close enough to swing a heavy metal fist and crack the thick glass of the projector-eye.

And then the wrestling-match was on again. The strength of the slave's two arms matched that of the berserker's one functional foreleg. But the enemy reflexes were still more than human. Derron hung on as best he could, but the world was soon spinning round him again, and again he was thrown.

Derron gripped one of the trampling legs and hung on some-how, trying to immobilize the berserker as a target. Where were the arrows now? Derron's laser was smashed. The berserker was still too big, too heavy, too quick. While Derron gripped one of its functional legs the other two still stomped and tore—there went one of the slave-unit's useless feet, ripped clean off. The metal man was going to be pulled to pieces. For some reason no more arrows were being shot—

Derron caught just a glimpse of a hurtling body as Matt leaped directly into the fight, raising in each hand a cluster of magic-arrows. Yelling, seeming to fly like a god, he stabbed his thunderbolts down against the enemy's back.

The blasts were absorbed in full by the berserker's interior. And then something inside the monster let go in an explosion that bounced both machines. And with that, the fight was over.

Derron crawled from the overheated wreck of the slave-unit, out from under the mass of glowing, twisting, spitting metal that had been the enemy. Then he had to pause for a few seconds in exhaustion. He saw Dart come running from the cave, tears streaking his face, in his hand Matt's bow, with its broken string dangling.

Most of the rest of The People were gathering around some-thing on the ground nearby. Matt lay where the enemy's last convulsion had thrown him. He was dead, his belly torn open, hands charred, face smashed out of shape—then the eyes opened in that ruined face. Matt drew a shaky breath and shuddered and went on breathing.

Derron no longer felt his own exhaustion. The People made way as he crawled his battered metal proxy to Matt's side and gently lifted him. Two of the younger women were wailing. Matt was too far gone to wince at the touch of hot metal.

"Good work, Odegard!" Colonel Borss's voice had regained strength. "That wraps up the operation. We can lift your unit back to present-time now; better put that fellow down."

Derron held onto Matt. "His lifeline is breaking off here no matter what we do. Bring him up with the machine."

"It's not authorized to bring anyone. . . ." The voice faded in hesitation.

"He won the fight for us, and now his guts are hanging out. He's finished in this part of history. Sir."

"All right, we'll bring him up. Stand by while we readjust."

The People meanwhile had formed a ring of awe around the slave-unit and its dying burden. Somehow the scene would probably be assimilated into one of the extant myths; myths were tough bottles, Derron thought, stretching to hold many kinds of wine.

Up at the mouth of the cave, the old woman was having trouble with her tinder as she tried to get the watch-fire started again. A young girl with her hesitated, then ran down to the glowing berserker-shell and on its heat kindled a dry branch into flame. Waving the branch to keep it bright, she went back up the hill in a sort of dance.

And then Derron was sitting in a fading circle of light on the dark floor of Operations Stage Three. The circle vanished, and two men with a stretcher ran toward him. He opened his metal arms to let the medics take Matt, then inside his helmet his teeth found the power switch and he turned off the master-unit.

He let the end-of-mission checklist go hang. In a few seconds he had extricated himself from the master, and in his sweat-soaked leotard was skipping down the stairs from the catwalk. The other slaves were being brought back too, and the Stage was busy. He pushed his way through a confusion of technicians and miscellaneous folk and reached Matt's side just as the medics were picking up the stretcher with him on it. Wet cloths had already been draped over the wounded man's bulging intestines, and some kind of an intravenous had been started.

Matt's eyes were open, though of course they were stupid with shock. To him Derron could be no more than another strange shape among many; but Derron's shape walked along beside him, gripping his forearms above his burned hand, until consciousness faded away.

The word was spreading, as if by public announcement, that a man had been brought up alive from the deep past. When they carried Matt into the nearest hospital it was only natural that Lisa, like everyone else who had the chance, should come hurrying to see him.

"He's lost," she murmured, looking down at the swollen face, in which the eyelids now and then flicked open. "Oh, so lost. Alone." She turned anxiously to a doctor. "He'll live, now, won't he?"

The doctor smiled faintly. "If he's lasted this far I think we'll save him."

Lisa sighed in deep relief. Of course her concern was natural and kind. The only difficulty was that she hardly noticed Derron at all.

SAND SISTER

By Andre Norton

The moment of birth came in the early dawning when the mists of Tormarsh night still curled thick and rank about the walls of Kelva's hall. This in itself was an ill thing, for, as all well knew, a child who is to have the foresight and the forereach must come into the world at that time: the last moment of one day and the first of the next; while under a full moon of the Shining One is indeed the best time to welcome a new Voice among the People.

Also this was no lusty child who entered the world crying a demand for life and the fullness thereof. Rather the wrinkled skin on its undersized body was dusky, and it lay across the two hands of the healer limply. Nor did it seek to draw a breath. But because all children were necessary for the Torfolk and each new life was a barrier against the twilight of their kind, they labored to save this one.

The healer set lips upon the cold flaccid ones of the baby and strove to breathe air into its lungs. They warmed it and nursed it, until at last it cried feebly—not to welcome life but to protest that it must receive it. At the sound of that cry Mafra's head inclined to one side as she listened to that plaint which was more like the cry of a luckless bird trapped in a net than that of any true child of Tor.

Though her eyes were long since blind to what the Folk could see, being covered with a film which no light could hope now to pierce, Mafra had the other sight. When they brought the child to her for the blessing of the Clan and House Mother, she did not hold out her hands to receive the small body. Rather she shook her head and spoke:

"Not of the kindred is this one. The spirit who was chosen to fill this body came not. What you have drawn to life in it is—"

She fell silent then. While the women who had brought the child drew away from the Healer, now staring at the baby she held as if the wrap cloth of the clan birthing enfolded some slimy thing out of the encroaching bog land.

Mafra turned her head slowly so that her blind eyes faced each for the space of a breath.

"Let no one think of the Dark Death for this one." She spoke sharply. "The body is blood of our blood, bone of our bone. This much I also say to you: what now dwells within that body we must bind to us, for there is a strength indwelling in it which the child must learn to use for herself. Then when she uses it for those she favors it will be both a mighty tool and a weapon."

"But you have not named her, Clan Mother. How can she dwell in the clan house if she bears not our name freely given?" ventured then the boldest of those who had faced Mafra.

"It is not in my gift to name her," Mafra said slowly. "Ask that of the Shining One."

It was now morning and the mist was curtain-heavy, blanking out the sky. However as if her very words had summoned the creature out of the air, there swooped across the women there gathered one of the large silver-gray moths that were dancers in the night air. This settled for an instant on the wrapping of the child, fanning gently its palm-wide wings. Thus the healer spoke:

"Tursla—" Which was a name of the Moth-maid in the very ancient song-tale of Tursla and the Toad Devil. Thus it was that the child who-was-not-of-the-clan spirit was given a name which was in itself uncanny and even a little tinged with ill-fortune.

Tursla lived among the Torpeople. After the fashion of their ways she who had borne the child was never known to her as "mother" for that was not the custom. Rather all the children of one clan were held in love by the elders of their House and all were equal. Since Mafra had spoken for her, and the Tormarsh itself had sent her a name, there was no difference made between Tursla and the other children—who were very few now.

For the Torfolk were very old indeed. They spoke in their Remember Chants of a day when they had been near unthinking beasts (even less than some of the beasts of this old land) and how Volt, The Old One (he who was not human at all but the last of a much older and greater race than man dared to aspire to equal) had come to be their guide and leader. For he was lonely and found in them some spark of near thought which intrigued him so he would see what he might make of them.

Volt's half-avian face still was one they carved on the guard totems set about the fields of loquths and in their dwelling places. To his memory they offered the first fruits of their fields, the claws and teeth of the dire wak-lizard, if they were lucky enough to slay such. By Volt's name they swore such oaths as they must say for weighty reasons.

Thus Tursla grew in body, and in knowledge of Tormarsh. What lay across its borders was of no consequence to the Torfolk, though there was land and sea and many strange peoples beyond. Not as old naturally as Torfolk, nor with the same powers, for they had not been blessed by Volt and his learning in the days their clans were first shaped.

But Tursla was different in that she dreamed. Even before she knew the words with which she might tell those dreams they caught her up and gave her another life. So that many times the worlds which encased her periods of sleep were far more vivid and real than Tormarsh itself.

She discovered as she grew older that the telling of her dreams to those of her own age made them uncomfortable and they left her much to herself. She was hurt, and then angered. Later, perhaps out of the dreams, there came to her a newer thought that these were for her alone and could not be shared. This brought a measure of loneliness until she discovered that Tormarsh itself (though it might not be the worlds through which her dreams led her) was a place of mystery and delight.

Such opinion, however, could only be that of one who wore a Tor body and was reared in a Tor Clan; for Tormarsh was a murky land in which there were great stretches of noisome bog from which reared the twisted skeletons of long-dead trees—and those were oftentimes leprous seeming with growths of slimy substances.

There were the remnants of very ancient roads, which tied together in a network the islands raised from these marshy lands, and age-old stone walls enclosed the fields of the Torfolk, rearing also to form the clan halls. Always the mists gathered at night and early morning and wreathed around the crumbling stones.

But to Tursla the mists were silver veiling, and in the many sounds of the hidden boglands she could single out and name the cries of birds, the toads, frogs, and lizards, though even those were not like their distant kin to be found other places.

Best of all she loved the moths which had given her her own name. She discovered they were drawn to the scent of certain pale flowers which bloomed only at night. This scent she came to love also and would place the blossoms in the silvery fluff to her shoulder-length hair, weave garlands of them to wear about her neck. Also she learned to dance, swaying as did the marsh reeds under the winds, and as she danced the moths gathered about her, brushing against her body, flying back and forth in their own measures about her upheld, outstretched arms.

But this was not the way of the other Tormaidens, and when Tursla danced she did so apart and for her own pleasure.

The years are all the same in Tormarsh and they pass with a slow and measured beat. Nor do the Torfolk reckon them in any listing. For when Volt left his people they no longer cared to reckon time. They knew that there was war and much trouble in the outer world. Tursla had heard that before she had been born a war leader of that other land had been brought into Tormarsh by treachery and had been taken away again by his enemies with whom the Torfolk had made an uneasy and quickly broken pact.

Also there was still an older story—but that was whispered and could only be learned if one plucked a hint there, added a word here. Even further back in time there had been a man from outside whose ship had floundered on the strip of shore where Tormarsh actually came down in a point to the sea. And there he had been found by one who was a clan mother.

She had taken pity on the man, who had been sore hurt, and had, against all custom, brought him to the healers. But the end to that had been sadness, for he had laid a spell of caring on the First Maiden of that clan and she had chosen, against all custom, to go forth with him when he was healed.

There had come a time when she returned—alone. Though to her clan she had said the name of a child. Later she had died. Yet the name of the child remained in the chant of the Rememberer. Now it was said that he, too, was a great warrior and a ruler in a land no Torfolk would ever see.

Tursla often wondered about that story. To her it had more meaning (though why she could not have said) than any of the other legends of her people. She wondered about the ruler who was half Tor. Did he ever feel the pull of his part blood? Did the moon at night and perhaps one of the lesser mists which might lie in his land awake in him some dream as real as the strange ones which haunted her? Sometimes she said his name as she danced.

"Koris! Koris!" She wondered if his mate among the stranger people held his heart in truth and if so, what was she like? Did he feel divided in his heart as Tursla did? She was by all the rights of blood fully of Tor and yet had this ache in her spirit which would never be stilled and which waxed stronger with every year of her life.

She grew out of childhood and she set herself obediently to the learning which she should have. Her fingers were clever at the loom and her weaving was smooth, with delicate pale patterns quite new among the Torfolk. Yet no one remarked upon any strangeness in those designs and she had long since ceased to mention her dreams. Lately she had indeed come to feel that there was a certain danger in allowing herself to become too deeply immersed in such. For sometimes they filled her with an odd feeling that if she were not careful she would lose herself in that other world, unable to return.

There was an urgency in those dreams, which plucked at her, wishing her to do this or that. The Torfolk themselves had strange powers. Among them such talent was not accounted in any way alien. Not all of them could use these—but that, too, was natural. Was it not true that all had each his or her own gift? That one could work in wood, another weave, a third prove a hunter or huntress skilled in tracking the quarry. Just so could Mafra, or Elkin, or Unnanna, transport a thing here or there by will alone. The range of such talents was limited, and the use of them drew upon the inner strength of the user to a high degree so that they were not for common employment.

In her dreams lately Tursla had not roamed afar in those strange landscapes. Rather she had come always to stand beside a pool of water, not murky or half overgrown with reed and plant as were the pools of Tormarsh, but rather a clear green blue.

More important, what she had felt in each of those recurring dreams was that the reddish sand which rimmed it around, as the old soft gold the Torfolk used would rim a gem, had great meaning. It was the sand which drew her—always the sand.

Twice with the coming of the Shining One in full sighting, she had awakened suddenly, not in Kelva's House but in the open, awakened and was afraid for she knew not how she had come there. So mused that she might have wandered into one of the sucking bogs and been trapped forever. She came to be afraid of the night and sleep, although she did not share with any the burden she bore. It was as if one of the geas set by Volt himself bound her thoughts, laid a silencing finger across her lips. She grew unhappy and restless. The isle of the clan houses began to feel like a prison.

It was on the night of the highest and brightest coming of the Shining One that the women of the Torfolk must gather and bathe in the radiance of the One's lamp (for so was the body quickened and made ready that children might come forth) and there were too few children. But Tursla had never come to the Shining One's place of blessing, nor had this been urged upon her. This night when the others arose to go she stirred, meaning to follow. But out of the darkness there came a quiet voice: "Tursla—"

She turned and saw now that some of the light insects had crawled from their crevices to form a circle on the wall, giving the light of their bodies to illuminate the woman sitting on the bed place there. Tursla bowed her head even though that woman could not see her.

"Clan Mother—I am here."

"It is not for you—"

Tursla did not need Mafra to tell her what was not for her. But in her was the heat of shame, and also a little anger. For she had not chosen to be what she was; that fate had instead been thrust upon her from the hour of her birthing.

"What then is for me, Clan Mother? Am I to go unfulfilled and give no new life to this House?"

"You must seek your own fulfillment, moth-child. It lies not among us. Yet there is a purpose in what you are and a greater purpose in what awaits you—out there." Mafra's hand pointed to the open door of the House.

"Where do I find it, Clan Mother?"

"Seek and it will find you, moth-child. Part of it already lies within you. When that awakes you will learn and learning—know."

"That is all you will tell me then, Clan Mother?"

"It is all I can tell you. I can foresee for the rest. But between your spirit and mine rolls a mist thicker and darker than any Tormarsh gives birth to in the night. There is this—" She hesitated a long time before she spoke again.

"Darkness lies before us all, moth-child. We who forsee can see, in truth, only one of many paths. From every action there issue at least two ways, one in which one decision is followed, one in opposition to that. I can see that such a decision now lies before the folk. Ill, great ill may come from it. There is one among us who chooses even now to ask for the Greater Power."

Tursla gasped. "Clan Mother, how can this thing be? The Greater Power comes not by a single asking. It is called only when there is danger to all whom Volt taught."

"True enough in the past, moth-child. But time changes all things and even a geas may fade to a dried reed easily snapped between the fingers. Such a calling needs blood to feed it. This I say to you now, moth-child. Go you out this night—not to seek the place of the Shining One—there are those there who tend strange thoughts within. Rather go where your dreams point you and do what you have learned within those dreams."

"My dreams!" Tursla wondered. "Are they of use, Clan Mother?"

"Dreams are born of thought—ours—or another's. All thought is of some use. That which entered into you at your birthing cannot be denied, moth-daughter. You are now ripe to seek it out and deal with it. Go. Now!"

Her last word had the force of an order. Tursla still hesitated however. "Clan Mother, have I your blessing, the goodwill of this House?"

When Mafra did not reply at once Tursla shivered. This was like being before the House and seeing the door barred, shutting one out of all touch with kin and heart-ties.

But Mafra was raising her hand.

"Moth-daughter, for what it may be worth to you as you go to fulfill the future laid before you, you have the good-willing of this House. In return you must open your mind to patience and to understanding. No, I will not tell this foreseeing, for you must be guided not by any words of mine but by what comes from your own heart and mind when you are put to the test. Now, go. Trust to what the dreams have laid in your mind and go!"

Tursla went into the moonlight, into a world which was the black of bog-buried wood, the silver of mist and the pallid moonlight. But where was she to go? She flung out her arms. This night no moths came to dance with her.

Trust to what the dreams had laid in her mind. Would such point her in the direction she must take? Following the discipline of those who used the talent, she strove to clear her mind of all conscious thought.

Tursla began to walk, steadily, as one who has a purpose and a definite goal. She did not turn to the east, but faced westward, her feet on the blocks of one of the lesser roads. Though her eyes were open, she was not aware of what she saw, or even of her moving body. Somewhere before her lay the pool of her dreams and about it the all important sand.

The mist clung about her like a veiling, now concealing what lay ahead, what she had left behind. She crossed one of the islands and another. The road failed at last but unerringly her feet found tussocks and hillocks of solid land to support her. At last the mist itself was tattered by a wind, strong, carrying in it a scent which was not that of the Tormarsh.

That wind awoke Tursla from her trance. She slowed to a halt at the highest point of a hillock covered with grass, shaped like the finger of a giant, pointing due west. The girl used both hands to keep the silk soft strands of her hair out of her eyes. Now the moon was bright enough to show her that this ridge of land ran on to farther rises beyond.

Then, she began to run—lightly. In her some barrier had broken and she was swallowed up by this great need to find what lay ahead; that which had waited for her so long—so very long!

Nor was she surprised to come at last into that very place of her dreams. Here was the clear pool, and the sand. Though in the moonlight the colors of her dream had been leached away, the sand was dark and so was the pool.

She tore off her robe, letting the length of cloth, spattered with the mud and slime of her marsh journey, fall from her. But she did not allow it to drop onto the sand. It was as if nothing must sully or mark that sand.

Nor did Tursla step upon its smooth surface. Rather she climbed a small rock just beyond its edge and from that sprang out, to dive into the waiting water. That closed about her body, neither cold nor hot, but rather silken smooth, caressing. It held her as might a giant hand cupped about her, soothing, gentle. She surrendered to the water, floating on the surface of the pool.

Did she sleep then, or was she entranced by some magic beyond the knowledge of those who had bred her? Tursla was never quite sure. But she was aware that there came a change within her. Doors opened and would never close again. What lay behind those doors she was not yet sure, but she was free to explore, to use. Only the first thing—

As she lay floating on the soft cushion of the water Tursla began to hum, and then to sing. There were no words in her song, rather she trilled as might a bird, first gently, quietly, then with a rising—call? Yes, a call!

Though she lay with her face turned up to the sky, the moon, the stars, those far-off night jewels, she was aware that about her was a stirring; not in the water which cradled her, but in the sand. It was arising, partly to her will, or rather her call, partly to the need of—of—someone.

Still Tursla sang. Now she dared to turn her head a little. There was a pillar of sand from which came a tinkling, a faint chiming, caused as one grain of its substance rubbed against the other in a whirl so fast it would seem that there was no sand but only a solid column of the dark grit. Louder grew Tursla's song, more and more the pillar thickened. It no longer reached skyward, rather kept to a height no greater than her own.

The contours of the pillar began to alter, to thin here, thicken there. It took on the appearance of a statue—crude at first, a head which was a ball, a body with no grace or shape to it. But still the sand changed, the figure it formed became more and more human-like.

At last the sense of movement was gone. A figure stood there on rock from which her birth had drawn all the sleeping sand. Tursla trod water, drew into the shore and climbed out to front this being for whom her song had opened the door and wrought a shaping.

Into her mind there came the name she must now speak—the name which would anchor this other, make sure and safe the bridge between her world and another one that she could not even imagine, so alien was its existence.

"Xactol!"

The sand woman's eyelids quivered, raised. Eyes which were like small red-gold coals of fire regarded Tursla. The girl saw the rise and fall of the stranger's breasts, the moonlight was reflected from a dark skin as smooth seeming as her own.

"Sister—"

The word from the other was hardly more than a whisper. It held in it still some of the sound of sand slipping over sand. But neither woman nor voice wrought any fear in Tursla. Her open hands went out, offering kinship to the sand woman. Hands as firm to the touch as her own caught and held, in a clasp which welcomed her in return.

"I have hungered—" Tursla said, realizing in this moment that she spoke the truth. Until those hands closed about hers there had been this deep lack, this hunger in her which she had not even truly known she carried until it was so assuaged.

"You have hungered," Xactol repeated. "Hunger no more, sister. You have come—you will have what you seek. You shall do thereafter what must be done."

"So be it."

Tursla took another step forward. Their hands fell apart, but their arms were wide. They embraced as indeed close kin welcomed one another after some long time apart. Tursla found tears on her cheeks.

2

"What is asked of me?" The girl drew back from that embrace, studied the face so close to her own. It was calm and still as the sand had been before her power had troubled it.

"Only what you yourself choose," came the murmured reply. "Open your mind, and your heart, sister-one, and it shall be shown to you in the appointed time. Now—" The right hand of the sand woman arose, and the slightly rough fingertips touched Tursla's forehead, held so for the space of several heartbeats.

Then they slid down, over the eyelids the girl instinctively closed and again held so, before going on to her lips. The touch withdrew, came again to her breast over the faster beating of her heart.

From each of those touches there issued an inflowing of strength so that Tursla's breathing quickened; she felt a kind of impatience, of a need to be busy, though with what task she could not have said. This inflow of energy made her flesh tinkle, alive in a way she had never experienced.

"Yes—" her voice was swift, her words a little slurred. "Yes, yes! But how—and when? Oh, how and when, sand sister?"

"The how you shall know. The when is shortly."

"Then—then I shall find the door? I shall be free in the place of my dreaming?"

"Not so. For each her own place, sister-one. Seek not any gate until the time. There is that for you to do here and now. The future is the threaded loom upon which there is not yet any weaving. Sit before it, sister-kin, and fix the pattern you desire in your mind, then take up the shuttle and begin your task. In one sense we, in turn, are shuttles in the service of a greater purpose and we are moved to form a pattern we cannot see, for to its weaving we are too close. We can know the knotting and the breakage and perhaps even mend and reweave a little—but we are not that Great One who views it all. The time has come for you to set your portion of the pattern into the unseen design."

"But with you—"

"Younger sister, my bridging of the space between us cannot be held for long. We must hasten to the task set upon us both. Your mind is open, your eyes can now see, your lips are ready for the words, and your heart is prepared for what must come. Listen!"

So there by the dream pool Tursla listened. It was as if her mind was porous and empty as one of those leaves of the draw-well, a sponge ready to be filled when one dipped it into water. She drew in strange words, and heard stranger sounds which she must shape her lips to form. Though that was a difficult thing, for it would seem that some of those sounds were never meant for her to utter. Her hands moved to pattern designs in the air. While following the movements of her fingers there remained for an instant thereafter a faint tracing of color—that which was red-brown like the sand which had formed the body of her teacher, or else green-blue as the pool beside which they sat.

Again she got to her feet and moved her body in the measures of a dance—to no music save that which seemed to be locked into her own mind. All this had a meaning, though she was not sure what that might be, save that what she learned now was her true birthright and also both a weapon and a tool.

At last her companion was silent and Tursla, now slumped upon the sand, felt as if that energy which had filled her had slipped away little by little, driven out of her again by the burning which she had so eagerly grasped.

"Sand-sister, you have given me much. To what purpose? I cannot set aside Volt's ways and be ruler here."

"That was never intended. In what manner you can serve these people—that you will see from time to time. Give them what is best for their needs, but not openly, not claiming for yourself any powers. Give it only when such giving shall not be marked. There will be a time when your giving will set another part of the design to work—then, oh, younger sister, give with all your heart!"

She who answered to the name Xactol and whose true form and kind Tursla only dimly could perceive (and then only in her mind) arose. She began to turn, and that turning became faster and faster, a blur of movement. Just as she had put on the substance of the sand so now she lost it. Tursla covered her face with her hands, protecting her eyes against the trails of grit which spun out and away from what was becoming once more only a pillar.

The girl sank forward, feeling the drift of the sand over her. She was so tired, so very tired. Let her sleep now dreamlessly, she asked something beyond, the nature of which she recognized no more than she did the real form of Xactol. As the sand arose about her body, covered her lightly as might a soft cloth of spider silk, she indeed slept without dreams, even as she had petitioned to do.

It was the warmth of the midday sun beaming down upon her which roused her at last. She sat up, sand cascading from her. The colors of her dream were here, bright—green of pool, red of sand. But last night had not been a dream. It could not be. Tursla gathered up a palmful of the sand and allowed it to sift between her fingers. It was very fine, more like powder ash than the grit she expected.

She brushed it from her body and then she knelt by the pool, troubling its mirror-smooth surface to wash the sand from her hand, her arms, her face, splashing the water over her body. The wind blew steadily and, after she had retrieved the robe she had discarded, she went on, past the rocks which rimmed the pool site.

So she came to the sea and for the first time looked out onto that part of the outside world which she had heard spoken of but had never seen. The play of the waves as they crashed in shore and broke, leaving that which had formed them to drain away, enchanted her. She ventured out upon the water-smoothed sand. The wind, so much stronger here, whipped her robe and tugged at her hair. She flung her arms wide to welcome the wind which had none of the marsh scent.

It was good to be in the open. Tursla settled down on the sand to watch the breaking waves, singing softly to herself in wordless sounds which were not meant to evoke any answer but which were an attempt to match the music of wind and wave.

She saw shells in the sand and picked them up in wonder and delight. Like and yet unlike they were for, seeing them closely, she could perceive that each had some small difference to set it apart from its kind. Not unlike those of her own species—each with some part of him or her which was only his or hers.

At last she reluctantly turned her face from the sea to the Tormarsh. The sun was already westering. For the first time Tursla wondered if any had sought her and what she must say when she returned which might cloak this thing which had happened to her.

Slowly she dropped her harvest of shells. There was no need to advertise her visit to a place which custom forbade any to see. But that was no reason why she might not come this way again. No rule of Volt said definitely that the sea was forbidden to those who followed his ancient rules of living.

Tursla found the marsh oddly confining as she passed swiftly along the trail toward the House island. So as she went she plucked certain leaves which were for dyeing, glad that fortune favored her in that several plants were of the Corfil—a rarity much prized as it produced a scarlet dye which was mainly used for the curtains of Volt's own shrine, thus was always eagerly sought.

As Tursla came along the westward road she had her skirt upheld into a bag, a goodly harvest in that. But one moved out to intercept her before she gained Kelva's House.

"So, moth-sister—you have thought to return to us? Did the winged ones tire of you so soon, night walker?"

Tursla tensed. Of all those she wished the least to meet Affric was the one. He leaned now on his spear, his eyes regarding her mockingly. There was a belt with a fringe of wak-lizard teeth about his middle, attesting to both his courage and skill. For only a man with both nearly supernormal reflex and cunning dared hunt those great lizards.

"Fair day to you, Affric." She did not warm her words. He flouted custom in his familiar greeting. The very fact he did so was disturbing.

"Fair day—" he repeated. "And what of the night, moth-sister? Others danced with the moon."

She was more than startled. For any Torman to speak of the Calling, and to such as her who had not named any man before Volt for a choosing!

He laughed. "Send me no spears from your eyes, moth-sister. Only daughters of Volt—true daughters—need make a man watch his tongue by custom." He took a step nearer. "No, you did not seek the moon last night, so then whom *did* you seek, moth-sister?" There was an ugly set to his mouth.

She did not make any answer. To do so would be indeed lessening herself in the eyes of all. For there were those who listened, if from a distance. What Affric said and did was a raw affront.

Tursla looked away and walked forward. He would not dare, she was sure, attempt to stop her. And he did not. But the fact that he could publicly address her in that manner was frightening. Also, not one of those listening had spoken up in rebuke. It was almost as if this had been deliberately arranged to insult her. Her hands tightened on her improvised bag of leaves. Why—?

None stood before the door of Kelva's House and she walked head high, back straight, from the day into the dusk.

"Back at last, are you, then?" Parua, who tended the store cupboards and served as eyes for Mafra, regarded her sourly. "What have you there which needed to be cropped by night? A night when your duty lay elsewhere?"

Tursla shook out the leaves to fall upon a mat.

"Parua—do you really think that such as I should dance for the Shining One's favor?" she asked in a voice from which she was able to keep all emotion.

"What do you mean? You are woman grown. It is your duty to bring forth children—if you can!"

"If I can—you yourself say that, Mother-one. Have I not heard otherwise all my life? That I am one who is not true Tor born, and therefore I must not give life to a child because of the strangeness which is a part of me?"

"We grow too few—" Parua began.

"So thus the clan will welcome even the flawed? But that is

not custom, Parua. And when custom is broke it must be done openly before Volt's shrine, with all his People assenting.''

"If we grow few enough,'' Parua countered, ''Volt will have none here to raise his name. There are to be changes, even in custom. There will be a Calling, a Great Calling. So it has been decided.''

Tursla was astounded. Great Callings she had heard talked of; the last had been years ago when the Torfolk had allowed their stronghold to be invaded for a short time by strangers. It was then that the war leader of the outside lands had been prisoner here—together with her who, it was whispered, had been Koris' chosen lady. There had come no great ill from that, save that it had reached them later that, even as they had closed the marsh, so was now the outer world closed to them in turn. But even then there had been two minds about the right and the wrong of what they did.

It was true that births grew fewer each year. She had heard that Mafra and one or two of the other Clan Mothers speculated as to the reason for that. Perhaps even that their race was too old, had taken mates only among themselves too long so that their blood thinned, their creative powers were dimming. Thus it might be a fact that they would try to force her to their purposes. For it would only be by force that she would come to a Choosing— there was no Torman she had ever looked upon with favor. And now, she was not conscious she was pressing her hands against her breast; even less was she a daughter of Volt!

"So, moth-one,'' Parua continued, looking at her, Tursla thought, slyly and near maliciously, ''your body being Torborn, that might well serve Volt's purposes. Consider that.''

Tursla turned quickly toward that wall alcove which was Mafra's. The Clan Mother seldom left her private niche nowadays. She had hands whose skill had outrun her vanished sight, and, by touch alone, she made those useful to her people, shaping small pots to be fired, or spinning fibers more smoothly than any of her house descendants could.

Now Tursla saw that those hands lay strangely still, loosely clasped in the old woman's lap. Her head was held up, just slightly a-tip as if she listened. As the girl stood hesitantly before her, uncertain if she dared break into that trancelike state, Mafra spoke: "Fair day, moth-child. Fair be your going, fair be your coming, firm your steps upon the crossing places, full your hands with good labor, your heart with warmth, your mind with thoughts which will serve you.''

Tursla sank to her knees. That was no common greeting! It

was—it was that given to any clan daughter who knew she was at last with child! But—why—

Mafra raised one hand, stretched it forth. Tursla quickly bent her head to kiss those long, age-thinned fingers.

"Clan Mother—I am not—not as you have welcomed me," she said hurriedly.

"You are filled," Mafra said. "Not all filling is with a life which will separate itself in time from yours and become all in all to itself. There is life within you now and, in due time, it will come forth. If it does so in a different fashion, then that is the will of Volt, or of what power stood behind him when he came to lead our people up out of savagery. It shall be with you as with the Filled. So shall it be said in this House and Clan. And if it is said so among those who are your own, then it will be the same elsewhere among the Folk."

"But, Clan Mother, if my body does not contain a life they will understand, and the time passes when I should bear the fruit which House and Clan need, then will there not be a reckoning? What can be said then for one who had misled House and Clan?"

"There will be no misleading. There is set before you a task that you shall do by virtue of the life you hold. What will follow from that will lead to the two roads of which I told you—one this way—" Her hand swept to the right. "One that way." She indicated the left. "I cannot foresee past that choice which shall be yours. But I think what you will choose shall be of wisdom. Parua—" she raised her voice and the other woman came near, going to her knees as did Tursla.

"Parua, this Tursla, moth-daughter, is Filled and so let House and Clan be guarded according to custom."

"But she—there was no Choosing, no moon dance," Parua protested.

"She was sent out by my wisdom, Parua. Do you question that?" Mafra's tone was chill. "Into the night she went with my blessing. What she sought—and found—was by the will of Volt as revealed to me in foresight. She has returned, filled. I recognize it so, and, by my Volt-given gift, I proclaim that now."

Parua's mouth opened again as if she would protest and then it closed. Clan Mother had spoken, she had said that Tursla was Filled. And, if she who had the farsight for her own said this, then no one dared question the truth of it. Parua bowed her head submissively and kissed the hand held out to her. She backed away, her gaze still on Tursla, and the girl sensed that she might have to admit openly Mafra's judgment was right, but her own reservations were still stubbornly alive.

"Clan Mother," the girl said quickly, as soon as she was sure Parua must be beyond hearing the murmur of a voice she held to the edge of a whisper, "I do not know what is expected of me."

"This much I can tell you, moth-child. There will soon come one whom Unnanna will summon—not with voice or message— but by the Calling itself. He has such blood ties that this calling can catch and hold him as one snared in a net. But the purpose for which they would bring him—" There was a new note in Mafra's voice. "That is, in the end, death. If his blood is spilt upon the ground before Volt's shrine, that blood shall call aloud. And *its* calling will bring the forces of the outer world upon us with fire and steel. Volt's people will die and Tormarsh shall be a barren and cursed place.

"We count our children as the fruit of all of us together. No one claims any child as his or hers alone. But this is not the way of the Outside. There they hold not to House Clans, but are split into smaller gatherings. There a child has but two on which to call in trouble—she who gave him birth and he who filled her at some time of choosing. This seems strange and wrong to us, a breaking up of the bonds which are our strength. But it is their way of life.

"However, this different way also gives other bonds which we do not understand. Strange indeed are these bonds. Let anyone there raise hand against a child—and the mother-one and he who filled her will take up the hunt with the fury of a wak-lizard who sights man. The one whom Unnanna would summon for her purposes is son to a man who is perhaps the greatest threat the Outside can raise against us. I fear for our people, moth-child.

"It is true that we grow fewer, that only a hand-finger count of children may be born after any choosing. But that is our sorrow and perhaps the will of life itself. To bring in blood-giving—no."

"And my part in this, Clan Mother?" Tursla asked. "Do you wish me to stand against Unnanna then? But even though you have named me Filled, who would listen to my words? She is a Clan Mother, and, since you go no more to the moon dance, it is she who leads."

"That is so. No, I lay no task on you, moth-daughter. When the time comes for you to do as you must, you yourself will know it, for that knowledge will be inside you. Give me now your hands."

Mafra held out both of her own palms up, and Tursla placed

hers thereupon, palms down. Again, just as it had been when she and Xactol had communed with one another, there was a feeling of quickening within her, a stirring of energy she longed to use but did not yet know how to put to any testing.

"So—" Mafra's voice was but a whisper, as if this were a very secret thing. "I knew that you were from elsewhere at your birthing, but this is indeed a strange thing."

"Why did this happen to me, Clan Mother?" Tursla voiced her old protest.

"Why do many things happen—those for which we can see no meaning or root? Somewhere there is a master pattern of which we must all be a part."

"So did *she* say also—"

"She? Ah, think of her, picture her in your mind, moth-child!" There was an eagerness in Mafra now. "See her for me!" she ordered.

Obediently Tursla pictured the spinning pillar of sand, and she who had been formed by that.

"Indeed you have been Filled, moth-child," sighed Mafra after a long moment. "Filled with such knowledge that perhaps you alone in this world can begin to comprehend. I wish we might talk of this and of your learning, but that cannot be. For it was not meant for me to gain any other than I have. Do not share it, moth-daughter, even if you are so moved. A basket woven to hold loquth seeds, no matter how skillfully made, cannot carry water which is intended to fill a fired clay jar. Go you now and rest. And live after the manner of the Filled until the time comes and you know it."

So dismissed, Tursla went to her own portion of the clan house—that small section given to her when she was judged more girl than child. She pulled close the woven reed mats which made it into a private place and sat upon her double cushion to think.

Mafra's pronouncement would not only excuse her from any Moon dancing, but would speedily put to punishment any speeches such as Affric had made to her, any gesture even from any man of any House. She would be excused also from certain kinds of work. The only difficulty she might face at first would be that she could not leave the settlement island alone from now on. The Filled were ever under guard for their own protection.

She ran her hands down her own slender body. How long before the fact that her belly did not swell would be noted? The women were sharp-eyed about such matters, since birth was their great mystery and they were jealous of the keeping of it. Perhaps she could devise some sort of padding within her robe. Also the Filled often had unusual desires for different food, altered their habits of living. Maybe she could turn such fancies to her account.

But eventually the time would come when she would be found out. Then what? To her knowledge no one among the Folk had ever made a false statement concerning such a thing. It would strike at the very root of all of their long-held beliefs. What punishment could be harsh enough for that? Why had Mafra done this?

No one of the Torfolk, Tursla was sure, would accept the idea of a Filling with knowledge. And Mafra—she, Tursla, had not made the claim—it had been the Clan Mother. Such a deliberate flouting of custom, just so that she would be left to hold herself ready for this other action of which Mafra had only given her hints.

A Calling for the purpose of blood. Tursla drew a deep breath. If Mafra meant by that what Tursla could guess, then that was a great breaking of custom also. Sacrifice—of a—*man*? But there were no such sacrifices ever made to Volt; a man whose killing might bring down a doom of ending on Tormarsh and Torfolk. What part would she have?

She could—no, something within Tursla forbade that for now. This was no time to open that door in her mind which guarded what she had learned from Xactol.

Patience must be hers and this role must be played well. The girl drew aside her private curtain and arose. What she wanted most was food and drink. Suddenly she was very hungry and thirst made her mouth dry. She started for the supply jars, intent only on tending her body, sternly closing down the whirl of thoughts in her mind.

3

Three days went by; Tursla spent the time quietly at work with her spindle in her hands, but, more to her own desires, also with her thoughts. Mafra's word had been accepted by the House clan—how could it not be? She was given the deference accorded the Filled, served first with the choicest of foods, left to her own thoughts since she seemed to wish it so.

But on the third day the girl aroused from the half trance in which she had allowed herself to drift as she attempted to sort out and store what she had learned. Most of what she discovered lay only in hints. Yet she was sure that such hints were only way markers to deeper knowledge that she must have and that she still could not now remember. The struggle to do so only made her tense and restless, her head ache, and sleep hard to come by.

Nor could she summon up any of her dreams. When she slept now it was fitfully, more like a light doze from which she could be awakened by such a small thing as a sleeper in the next mat place turning over.

Knowledge was of no help if one could not tap it, Tursla believed with an ever growing distress. What lay before her?

Wishing to be alone with that spark of fear which was fast growing into a flame, she arose from her stool before the loom and went from the Kelva's House. She neared the group of women before she noted them, so entangled was she in her thoughts.

Unnanna stood there, the others facing her as if she were laying upon them some duty. Now her gaze rested on Tursla, and a small smile—a smile which held no kindness in it—lifted the corners of her thin-lipped mouth.

"Fair be the day—" She raised her voice a little, plainly to address the girl. "Fair be your going. Fair be the end of the waiting for you."

"I give thanks for your good wishing, Clan Mother," Tursla replied.

"You have not spoken before Volt the name of your Choosing—" Unnanna's smile grew wider. "Are you not proud enough for that, Filled One?"

"If I choose to spread Volt's cloak about me and am challenged for doing so," Tursla returned, hoping to hold her pretense of serenity, "then there must be a changing of custom."

Unnanna nodded. Her outer pose was one of good will. It was not unheard of that some maid at her first Filling chose not to announce the name of her partner in the moon ritual. Though generally it was a matter of common knowledge as soon as her Clan Mother proclaimed the fact to the satisfaction of the clan.

"Wear Volt's cloak then, moth-daughter. In days to come you will have sisters in aplenty." There was an assenting murmur from the women about her, an eager assenting.

But Unnanna was not yet through with Tursla.

"Do not go a-roaming, moth-daughter. You are precious to us all now."

"I go only to the fields, Clan Mother. To Volt's shrine that I may give thanks."

That was a worthy enough reason for leaving the place of Houses and no one could deny her such a small journey. She passed Unnanna and started down the moss-greened pavement of the ancient road. Nor did any follow her there, for again custom decreed that one who so sought Volt's shrine should be granted privacy for any petition or thanks the worshipper desired to raise.

Volt's shrine—time had not dealt well with it. Walls had sunk into the ever hungry softer ground of the marsh, or else tumbled the stone of their making across pavement, because no man could put hand to any rebuilding here.

For these were the very stones which Volt himself had laid hands upon in the very long ago, set up to make his shelter. It had been a large hall, Tursla guessed, as she traced the lines of those crumbling walls. But by all legend Volt himself was larger in body than any of the Torfolk.

Now she wove a way between those crumbling walls. Under her feet the earth and stone were beaten hard into a path during the countless years Torfolk had sought comfort here. Thus she came into the inner room. Though the roof was gone, and the light of sun shone down upon what was the very heart of Volt's domain—a massive chair seemingly carved of wood (but such a wood—strange to Tormarsh—which no damp could rot). On either side of the chair stood tall vases wrought of stone and set in them, ready for any call to Volt, the quick firing pith of those trees waterlogged in the marsh whose spongy outer bark could be flaked away, leaving an inner hardness which burned so brightly. Here were no light insects, but fire which destroyed and yet was so brilliant in its death.

For a long moment Tursla hesitated. What she would do now was allowed by custom, yes, but only if one were greatly moved by some happening which could not be understood and from which there seemed to be no answer in any human mind. Was that her case now? She believed she could claim it was.

Tursla put out her hand, setting her palm flat on the petrified wood of the chair's wide arm. Then she drew herself up the one shallow step which raised the seat about the flooring of that near destroyed hall, and seated herself upon the chair of Volt.

It was as if she were a small child settling herself into the chair of some large-boned adult. Tall as she was among the Torfolk, here her feet did not meet the pavement as she wriggled back until her shoulders touched the wood behind her. To lay her hands out upon the arms was a strain but this she did before she closed her eyes.

Did Volt indeed listen from wherever he had gone when he withdrew from Tormarsh? Did that essence of Volt which might just still exist somewhere in the world care now what happened to those he had once protected and cherished? She had no answer to those questions, nor could any within the bounds of Tor give her more than such guesses as she herself might make.

"Volt"—her thought shaped words as she did not speak aloud—"we give you honor and call upon your good will in times of need. If you still look upon us— No, I do not cry now for help as a helpless child calls upon those of the clan house. I wish only to know who or what I am, and how I must or may use what has Filled me as Mafra swears I have been Filled. It is no child that I carry in truth; perhaps it is more—or less. But I would know!"

She had closed her eyes, and her head rested now upon the back of the chair. There was the faint scent of the tree candles from either hand, less than they would give off at their igniting. She had seen the Clan Mothers hold such before them and the smoke had wreathed them around while they chanted.

She—

Where was she? Green grass grew out before her, a fan which stretched to the feet of rises of gray rock. Scattered in the grass, as if someone had carelessly flung wide a handful of bright and shining stones, were flowers, their petals wide, their shapes and colors differing as the shells on the shore had differed. Above the flowers fluttered moths—or winged things which resembled moths. Those were also brightly colored, sometimes bearing more than one shade or hue on their wings.

There was nothing of Tormarsh in this place. Nor was it, she was sure, another sighting of her dream land. She willed to move forward and her will gave birth to action for she passed, not on her feet step by step, but rather drifted in the air, as might those flying things.

So Tursla was wafted by her will to those rocks which rose above the grass. Again her desire lifted her higher, to the topmost pinnacle of the rocks. Now she gazed down into a greater valley wherein there ran a river. Across that wide ribbon of water spanned a bridge of stone, and the bridge served a road which ran across the green of the land.

While on the road, approaching the bridge, there was—

Horse—that was a horse. Though Tursla had never seen such an animal, she knew it. And on the horse—a man.

Her will to see drew him to her sight in a strange way, though in truth she had not moved from her place on the hill, nor had he yet come upon the bridge. Still she saw him as clearly as if he and his mount were within such distance that she could put forth a hand and lay it on the horse's shoulder.

He wore metal like a silken shirt, for it had been fashioned of small rings linked one upon the other. Above that a cloak dropped down his shoulders, fastened at his throat with a large brooch set with dull green and gray stones. There was a belt with like stones about his waist and from that hung a sheathed sword.

His head was covered with a cap also of metal, but this was a solid piece, not chained rings. It had a ridge beginning above the wearer's forehead and running back to a little below the crown of his head. This ridge possessed sockets into which were fastened upstanding feathers of a green color.

But Tursla's attention only marked that in passing, for it was the man himself she would see. So she studied the face beneath the shadow of the cap.

He was young, his skin was fair, hardly darker than a Torman's. There was strength in his face, as well as comeliness. He would make a good friend or clan brother, she decided, and a worse enemy.

As he rode he had been looking ahead, not truly as if he saw the road, but rather as if he were busied with his thoughts, and those not pleasant ones. Now, suddenly, his head jerked up a fraction and his eyes were aware—and they looked upon her! While a quick frown marked a sharp line between his brows.

Tursla saw his lips move, but she heard nothing, if he had spoken. Then one hand lifted, was held out toward her. At that same moment all was gone. She whirled away in a dizzy, giddy retreat. When she opened her eyes she sat once more in Volt's chair, and she saw nothing save the time-breached walls of his shrine. But now—now she knew! Volt had indeed answered her wish! She was linked with the horseman and in no easy way. Their meeting lay before her and from it would come danger and such a trial of strength as she could not now measure.

Slowly the girl arose, drawing a deep breath, as one preparing for a struggle, though she knew that the time for that was not yet. He had been aware of her, that horseman, nor did he in the mind's eye grow blurred with the passing of moments. No, somewhere he rode and was real!

In the later afternoon she sought out Mafra again. Perhaps the Clan Mother could or would give her no answers, yet she must share Volt's vision with someone. And in all this place only Mafra did she trust without reservation.

"Moth-child—" Though Mafra turned sightless eyes in her direction never was she mistaken concerning the identity of those who came to her. "You are a seeker—"

"True, Clan Mother. I have sought in other places and other

ways, and I do not understand. But this I have seen; from Volt's own chair did I venture out in a strange way beyond explaining.'' Swiftly she told Mafra of the rider.

For a long moment the Clan Mother sat silent. Then she gave a quick nod as if she affirmed some thought of her own.

"So it begins. How will it then end? The foreseeing reaches not to that. He whom you saw, moth-child, is one tied to us by part blood—"

"Koris!"

Mafra's hand, where it rested upon her knee, tightened, her head jerked a fraction as if she strove to avoid a blow.

"So that old tale still holds meaning," she said. "But Koris was not your rider. This is he whom I told you about—the child of those who would move mountains with spells, slay men with steel, that naught comes to harm him. He is Koris's son, and his name is Simond, which in part was given by that Outlander who fought so valiantly beside his father to free Estcarp of the Kolder.''

Mafra paused and then continued. "If you wonder how these things are known: when I was younger, strong in my powers, I sometimes visited in thought beyond the edge of Tormarsh, even as this day you have done. It was Koris's friend Simon Tregarth who was brought hither through stranger's magic and delivered to his enemies. Also with him was she who was Koris's choice of mate after the manner of the Outlanders. Then we chose ill, so that in turn the Outlands set their own barriers against us. We cannot go, even if we wish, outside the Marsh, nor can anyone come to us.''

"Is the seashore also barred, Clan Mother?"

"Most of the shore, yes. One may look at it, but the mist which rises between is a wall as firm as the stone ones about us now.''

"But, Clan Mother. I have trod the sand beside the sea, found shells within it—"

"Be silent!" Mafra's voice was a whisper. "If this much was given you let no other know it. The time may come when it will be of worth to you.''

Tursla allowed her voice to drop also. "Is that a foreseeing, Clan Mother?"

"Not a clear one, I only know that you will have need for all your strength and wit. This I can tell you, Unnanna calls tonight and, if she is answered, then—'' Mafra lifted her hands and let them fall again to her lap. "Then I leave it to your wit, moth-daughter. To your wit and that which is in you from that other place.''

She gave the sign of dismissal and Tursla went to her own place and took up her spindle, but if any watched her for long they would know that she had little profit from her labors.

Night came and around her the women of the clan stirred and spoke to one another in whispers. None addressed her; being Filled she was carefully set apart that nothing might threaten that which she was supposed now to carry. Nor did they approach Mafra either, rather ranged themselves with Parua and slipped quietly away.

There were no guards set about the House isle, save on the two approaches by which a wak-lizard might come. No one would watch those bound for the Shrine in any case, so that Tursla, pulling a drab cloak about her, even over the soft silver of her hair, thought she could follow behind without note.

Once more she crept along the same path she had taken earlier that day. Those ahead carried no lighted torches; there was no gleam save the moonlight, but she saw that every house must be represented. This could not be a complete Calling after all for there were no men. Or so she had thought until she caught sight of moon gleam on a spear head and noted those cloaked men, ten of them, standing in a line facing the Chair. While in that seat huddled a figure who raised her face to the light even as Tursla found a hiding place back behind a pile of fallen rock.

Unnanna sat in the place of Seeking. Her eyes were closed, her head turned slowly from side to side. Those standing below began to croon, first so softly that it was hardly to be heard over the lap of water, the wing rustle of some flying thing. Then that hum grew stronger—no words, but rather a sound which made Tursla's skin tingle, her hair move against her neck. She found that her head was swinging also in the same way as Unnanna's and, at that moment, realized the danger which lay in being trapped into becoming a part of what they would do here.

She raised her hands and covered her eyes so that she might not see that swaying, while she thought, as one catches a line of safety thrown wide, of the sand sister, or the racing sea waves. Though a pulse now beat within her, Tursla also fought her own body; and, without being fully conscious of what she did, she rose to her full height and began to move her feet, not in the pattern Unnanna's head had set, but in another fashion, to break for herself the spell the Clan Mother was rising.

There was power building here; her body answered to it. Force pressed in upon her like a burden, trying to crush her. Still

Tursla countered that, her lips moving in words which sprang from behind those doors in her mind which she had earlier tried to open and could not. Only such danger as this would free them for her.

She opened her eyes. All was as before—save that Unnanna had moved forward on the chair of Volt. One after another those waiting men came to her. She touched them on the forehead, on the eyes. Then each made way for his fellow. From the tips of those fingers which she used to touch them came small cones of light, and those who stepped back from her anointing carried now a mark on the forehead of the same eerie radiance.

When all had been so marked they turned and made their way from the hall, the women giving back to open their path. As they passed by Tursla she saw that their eyes were set and they stared as men entranced. Their leader was Affric; and those who followed him were all young, the most skilled of the hunters.

When they had gone from her sight, Tursla looked back to the hall. Once more Unnanna sat with closed eyes. Power surged; it came from each of them there. Unnanna, in some manner, drew that unseen energy from them, consolidated it, shaped from it a weapon, aimed that weapon, and sent out on course.

Tursla was not one of them. Now she stood tense, seeking within herself something she sensed must be ready to answer her call. She used her thought to mold it, thinking of what she would hurl—not as the spear Unnanna's wish had fostered—no, what then? A shield? She did not hold strength enough in herself to interpose any lasting barrier. But perhaps there was something else she could mind-fashion. She thought of the likenesses of all the weapons known to the Torfolk, and fastened in the space of a breath upon—a net!

Clenching her hands until her nails cut into her own flesh, the girl centered all of her unknown energies, untested to their full extent since that night by the pool, and thought of a net—a net to entangle feet, to impede those who marched by night, those who would set a trap. They themselves would be now entrapped.

As blood draining from a grievous mortal wound, the energy Tursla summoned seeped from her. If she could only call upon that greater well of strength which Unnanna could tap for herself! But a net—surely a net! Let it catch about the feet of Affric; let it ensnare him where he would go. Let it *be*!

The girl stumbled back against the wall, weakness in her legs, her arms hanging heavily by her sides, as she had neither the will not strength now to raise them. With her back against the rough stone she slipped downward, the ruins rising around her like a protective shield. Her head fell forward on her breast as she made her last attempt to send what remained in her to reinforce the net her vivid mind picture had set about Affric's stumbling feet.

It was cold and she was shivering. Dark lay about her, and she no longer heard that sound which had built up the energy for Unnanna's mind dart. Rather what came was the whisper of wings. Lifting her head, Tursla looked upward to the night sky above the pocket in the ruins where she rested.

There were two moths a-dance, their beautiful shadowy wings outlined with the faint night shine which was theirs when they flew in the deep dark. Back and forth they wove their meetings and partings. Then the large spiraled down, and for just a moment it clung to the dew-wet robe on her breast, fanning its wings, tiny eyes which were alight looking into hers . . . or so it seemed to the bemused girl.

"Sister," Tursla whispered. "I give you greeting. Fair flying for your night. May the blessing of Volt himself be with you!"

The moth clung for another instant and then flew away. Stiffly Tursla pulled herself up. Her body ached as if she had done a full day's stooping at the loom, or at harvest in the fields. She felt stupid, also, when she tried to think clearly.

She tottered along, one hand against the wall to support her. There was no one here—Volt's chair was empty. For a moment she wavered as she gazed upon that seat. Should she try again? There was a longing in her, a strange longing. She wanted to see how the rider fared. What had Mafra named him? Simond, an odd name. Tursla repeated it in a whisper as if a name could be tasted, said to be either sweet or sour.

"Simond!"

But there was no answer. And she knew that, even if she mounted Volt's chair again, this time there would be no answer. What she had done or tried to do here this night had exhausted for a time her power. She had nothing to aid her to reach out.

Walking slowly, catching now and then on some half-broken wall or pile of stones, she won out of Volt's hall. But she needed to sit and rest several times before she got back to the clan house.

Then it took all the skill she had to be able to make her way through Mafra's house to her own corner. Should she tell the Clan Mother what had been done this night? Perhaps—but not in this hour. To rouse any of the nearby sleepers would be the last thing she wished.

She lowered herself onto the sleeping mat. In her mind then

there was only one picture, already becoming fuzzed with sleep—the image of Affric fighting a web about his feet, his sneering mouth open as if he shouted aloud in fear. Though she was not conscious of it, Tursla smiled as she fell asleep.

4

Mist was heavy about the island where the ancient clan houses stood, hanging curtains between house and house, turning those who went outside into barely seen shadows moving in and around through the fog. The moisture in it pearled on every surface in large drops which gathered substance and then trickled downward. That same damp clung to skin, matted hair, made clammy all garments.

Such fen mists had been known to Tursla all her life. Still this one was far thicker than any she could remember; and it would seem her uneasiness was matched within the clan house for no hunters went forth, while those within stirred higher the fires, drawing in closer for the light and heat. Perhaps they did this not for any warmth to send their garments steaming but because the very brightness of the flames themselves had a kind of cheer.

Tursla had sought out Marfra again. But the Clan Mother appeared unwilling to talk. Rather she sat very still, her blind eyes staring unwinking at the fire and those about it, though she made no move to add herself to the circle of company there. At length Tursla's foreboding of a shadow to come made her greatly daring and she touched timidly one of Mafra's hands where it lay palm up on the woman's lap.

"Clan Mother—?"

Mafra's head did not turn, yet Tursla was sure she knew that the girl was beside her. Then she spoke, in so low a voice Tursla was sure it could not carry beyond her own ears.

"Moth-child, it comes close now—"

What—the fog? Or that other thing which Tursla felt, though she had no part of Mafra's powers.

"What may be done, Clan Mother?" The girl shifted her body restlessly.

"Nothing to stop these witless ones. Not now." There was a bitter note in that. "You cannot trust in anything or anyone save yourself, moth-child. The ill act has been begun."

At that moment there sounded, through the doorway of the clan house (like the bellow of some great beast), a call which brought Tursla and all the rest sheltering within to their feet. Never before had the girl heard such a sound.

Then the cries of those by the fire, who were now all turning to the mist-hidden doorway, running toward that, made her understand. That had been the Great Alarm, which had never been sounded in her lifetime, perhaps even in the lifetimes of all now here. Only some action of overpowering peril could have brought the sentries on the outer road to give that alert.

"Girl!" Mafra was also standing. Her hand tightened about Tursla's arm. "Give me your strength, daughter. Ill, thrice ill, has been this thing! Dark the ending thereof!"

Then she, who so seldom left her own alcove nowadays, tottered beside Tursla. At first her slight body bore heavily upon the girl's support. Then she straightened, and it appeared that strength returned to her limbs as she took one step and then another.

They came into the open but there the mist was very thick. Figures could only be half seen and that just when close by. Mafra's pressure on her arm drew Tursla in a way which it would seem the blind woman knew well.

"Where—?"

"To Volt's Hall," Mafra answered her. "They would carry this through to the end—profane the very place which is the heart of all we are, have ever been. They will slay, in the name of Volt. And, if such a slaying comes, why, then their own deaths must follow! They have decided upon their road—and evil is the end of it!"

"To stop—" Tursla got out no more than those two words when her companion interrupted her.

"Stop—yes. Girl, open now your inner thoughts, give yourself freely to what may lie within you. That is the only way! But it must be quick."

She had never believed that Mafra's strength might still be such as to send the Clan Mother at so fast a pace. There were others around them, all were heading in the same direction. The stones of the ancient road under their feet were slimed with water, yet Mafra, for all her lack of sight, made no missteps.

About them loomed the broken walls of Volt's Hall. Still on they pressed, until they were in the place of the chair. Here through some trick perhaps of emanations from the ancient stones themselves, the mist thinned, raised, to lie above their heads like a ceiling, yet allow them full sight of all which was below.

Those torches set upright in the vases to either side of the chair were ablaze. Other brands were in the hands of those standing along the walls. In Volt's chair sat Unnanna once again.

Braced with a hand on either arm of the giant seat she leaned forward, an eager, avid expression on her face.

Those she so eyed were gathered immediately below. Affric stood there; but he had not the arrogant pride which he had worn so confidently when he had strode forth from this place at the Clan Mother's bidding. He was pale of countenance, and his clothing was smeared with swamp slime, while one arm was bound to his side with vine fiber, as if bones had been broken that must be straightened and protected for healing.

Seeing him so brought a picture into Tursla's mind: that of Affric unsure of foot as if he had been caught in some snare, stumbling and falling, falling against one of the upright pillars which bore Volt's own face deep carven. Her wish—dream! Had that indeed left Affric like this?

If so, she had not done all that she had wished. For between two of Affric's followers was the stranger she had seen mounted on the road, the one Mafra had named Simond.

His helm was gone, so his fair hair, near as bleached as her own, shown in the torch light. But his head rolled limply forward on his breast. It was plain his legs would not support him and he had to be kept on his feet by the help of his guards. There was a matting of blood in his hair.

"Done!" Unnanna's voice rang out, silencing the murmurs of those gathered there, producing a quiet through which the sounds of the marsh life without could be heard. "Done, well done! Here is that which shall give us new life! Did I not say it? Into our hands has Volt brought this one that we may drink of his strength and—"

Tursla did not know if she had made some signal but the guards suddenly released their hold upon Simond and he fell forward. There must have remained some spark of awareness in him, for he put out his hands, though he was on his knees, to catch at the edge of the step on which the chair stood. Now he raised his head by visible effort and lurched forward and up, for he grasped at the chair itself, and dragged himself to his feet.

The girl could not see his face. Without knowing she had done so, she broke from Mafra's side and edged along, pushing by others, seeing none of them, coming closer to where the captive stood.

"What do you want of me?" he asked as he edged around, so that he half faced the Torfolk.

Affric took a step forward and spat. His mouth was a vicious slit.

"Half-blood! We want from you what you have no right to—that part which is of Tormarsh!"

There was a sound like the far-off squall of a wak-lizard. Unnanna laughed.

"They are right, half-blood. You are part of Tor. Let that part now give us what we need." Her tongue curled over her lower lip, swept from side to side as if she licked moss-honey and savored the sweetness of that delicacy.

"We need life," she leaned closer to the arm of the chair where Simond still had his hand, using that hold to support him. "Blood is life, half-breed. By Volt's word we dare not take it from our own kind, and we cannot take from one who is full Outlander, for between the twain of us there is no common heritage. You are neither one nor the other; therefore you are ripe for our purpose."

"You know of what House I am." Simond held his head high and now his eyes caught the Clan Mother's in a compelling stare. "I am the son of him who took Volt's axe—by Volt's own wishing. Do you think then that Volt will look with approval on the fate you would give me?"

"Where is the axe now?" Unnanna demanded. "Yes, Koris of Gorm took it; but is it not now gone from him? Volt's favor follows the axe. With it destroyed, he has lost interest in you."

The murmur which had begun at Simond's words died away. Tursla pushed closer. She had done as Mafra had urged, laid her mind open to whatever power lay in her. But she felt no swelling of force, no new warmth within. How then could she stop this thing which was of dark evil and which would indeed bring an end to the Torfolk?

"Take him—" Unnanna was on her feet, her arms spread wide. In her pale face there was exultation.

Tursla moved. Those about her were so intent upon the scene before them that they were not aware of her until she was through their line and had shoved past one of Affric's followers to reach Simond. Once there she stationed herself before him, facing the man moving in to obey Unnanna's order.

"Touch me if you dare," she said. "I am one Filled. And this one I take under my protection."

The nearest man had raised his hands to sweep her aside. Now he stood as rooted as one of the dead trees, while those behind him retreated a step or two. Unnanna leaned closer from her perch upon the chair.

"Take him!" She lifted her hand as if to strike Tursla in the face, so drive her away. The girl did not flinch.

"I am one Filled," she repeated.

The Clan Mother's face twisted with stark rage. "Stand aside," she hissed as might one of the pallid vipers of the deep muck. "In Volt's name, I order, stand aside! And if you are truly Filled—"

"Ask it of Mafra!" challenged the girl. "She has said it—"

"Shall it be needful then"—Mafra's voice rang out from the gathering of the Torfolk—"for a Clan Mother to state this again? Do you aver that on such a thing there can be a false swearing, Unnanna?"

The crowd stirred, fell away to form a lane. Along that Mafra advanced. She did not totter now, but walked as firmly as if she could indeed see what lay before her, bumping into no one, but keeping straight course down that open way until she, too, came to stand before the chair of Volt.

"You take much upon you, Unnanna, very much."

"You take more!" Unnanna shrilled. "Yes, once you sat here and spoke for Volt, but that day is past. Rule your own clan house as you may until the messenger of Volt comes to call you. But do not try to speak for all in this time."

"I say no more than is my right, Unnanna. If I say this house daughter is Filled, then do you deny it?"

Unnanna's mouth worked. "It is your word before Volt, then? You take on you much in that, Mafra. This one came not to the moon dancing—who then filled her?"

"Unnanna—" Mafra raised her right hand. Her fingers moved in the air as if gathering threads of mist and rolling them into a ball. In the silence which now fell between them, she made a tossing motion, as if what she had pulled out of invisibility had indeed substance. Unnanna shrank back until her shoulders touched the high back of the chair.

Suddenly she flung both hands up before her face. From behind that slight defense she sputtered words which had no meaning as far as Tursla was concerned. But that Unnanna was, for a moment, at bay, the girl understood. Turning a little she caught at Simond's arm which was closest to her.

"Come!" she ordered.

Whether they could win from Volt's Hall, and if so what she might do then, Tursla had no idea. For the moment all she could think of was to get away from this place where only the slender thread spun by custom had so far protected her.

She did not even look to Simond. But he apparently yielded to her urging, for when she stepped away from Volt's chair he did in truth come with her. Hoping that he would continue to be able to stay on his feet, Tursla led him forward.

Affric moved into their path. His good arm raised, he balanced a short stabbing spear. Tursla met his gaze squarely and moved closer to Simond. She said no word but her intention was plain. Any attack upon the stranger would be met by her. To raise a weapon against a Filled One—Affric snarled, but he gave way when she did not, just as those others made a path for her, even as they had for Mafra.

Somehow they reached the outer wards of the Hall. Tursla was breathing as fast as if she had run all the way. Where now—? They could not return to the clan houses. Not even Mafra could hold back the weight of outraged custom long enough for Simond to escape. And the trails out from here would be speedily covered.

The trail to the pool, the sea! That flashed into her mind even as if some voice out of the mist had reminded her. For the first time she spoke to her companion:

"We dare not stay here. I do not think even Mafra can long hold Unnanna. We must go on. Can you do it?"

She had noted that he staggered though he kept his feet. Now she could only hope.

"Lady—by the Death of the Kolder—I shall try!"

So they went into the boiling of that strange, heavy mist. She could not even see beyond the length of an out-held hand before her. This was the strongest folly. If they missed the road, the step-tussocks farther on, the marsh itself might claim them and no one would ever know how they passed.

Still she walked, and brought him with her. After a space they went side by side, as she drew his arm about her shoulders, took a measure of his weight. He muttered now and then—broken words without any meaning.

They were well away from the clan-house isle when once again the deep-throated alarm trumpet of the Torfolk aroused echoes across the marsh. Now they could expect pursuit. Would this mist which enclosed them work as well to delay the hunters? She feared because such as Affric knew the outer ways of the Tormarsh far better than she.

On and on, Tursla fought a desire to hurry. For he whom she now half supported could never step up the pace. The surface of the road was still under them. She was, she realized, trusting in an inner guide which was an instinct and something she had never called upon before. Unless it was that same feeling of rightness which had led her this way when she had met Xactol

under the moon. Always she listened, after the echoes of the
alarm died away, for any sounds which might mean they were
closely followed.

There were ploppings from swamp sloughs where small creatures, disturbed by their passing, leapt into hiding; and the
hoarse cries and calls of other life. They did not move out of the
mist, nor did that grow any thinner.

Time lost any measurement. From one moment to the next
Tursla could only hope that they were still well ahead of any
pursuers. That she had been proclaimed Filled would save her,
for a space, until her false claims would be proven. But she
could not hope to protect Simond.

Why did she risk all for this stranger? Tursla could not have
answered that. But when she had seen him in that vision which
had visited her in Volt's Hall she had known that, in some way,
they were linked. It was as if some geas of power had been laid
upon her; there was no avoiding what must be done.

They were nearly to the end of the pavement now. Though she
could see nothing, the girl could sense that in an odd way as if
the knowledge came to her by a talent which had nothing to do
with sight, hearing or touch. She halted and spoke sharply to her
companion, striving to bring him, by the very force of her will,
out of the daze of mind in which he walked.

"Simond!" Names had power; the use of his might well
awaken him to reality. "Simond!"

His head raised, turned a little so he could eye her. Like the
Tormarsh men he was of a height such that they could see each
other on a level. His mouth hung a little open; there was a runnel
of blood from one temple clotting on his cheek. But in his eyes
there was also the look of intelligence.

"We must take to the swamp itself here." She spoke slowly,
pausing between words as one might do with a small child or a
person gravely ill. "I cannot hold you—"

He closed his mouth and his jaw line firmed. Then he tried to
nod, winced and his eyes blinked in pain.

"What I can do—that I shall," he promised.

She looked on into the mist. Folly to venture so blindly. But
this mist might lie for hours. With the Torfolk aroused they had
no hours; they might not even have more than the space of a
dozen breaths. She had as yet heard no sounds of pursuit, for
Torfolk were wily and had learned long since to move with
practiced silence through their territory.

"You must come directly behind me." Tursla bit her lip. That

they could do this at all she was dubious. But there was no other
choice.

He drew himself straight. "Go—I'll follow," he told her
quietly.

With a last glance at him the girl stepped out into the mist.
That inner guide had led her aright; her foot came down on the
firmness of the hassocks he could not see. She went slowly,
lingering before she took each step to make sure that he saw her,
though for him this blind journey must be much worse, for he
did not have the same certainty which was hers.

Step by step she wove a way, trying hard to remember how
long this most perilous part of their flight must last. Still he did
not call to her, and each time she turned her head she could see
him well upright, safely balanced on a foothold.

Then she stumbled out on firm ground, the tenseness of her
body leading to pain in her back and shoulders, a warning
tremble in her legs. This was, at last, that island like a finger
which marked the last part of the way to the pool. With her feet
firmly planted she waited once more for him to draw close to
her. When he gained that solid stretch of land he fell to his knees
and his body swayed from side to side. Swiftly she knelt beside
him, steadied him.

There was the sheen of sweat across his face and the clotting
blood melted under that. He breathed heavily through his mouth,
and his eyes, when he looked at her, were dull. He frowned as if
she were difficult to see and he must expend much effort to hold
her within his range of vision.

"I—am—near—done—Lady—" he gasped, word by painful
word.

"There is no more. From here the footing is good. It is only a
little way."

His mouth stretched in a stark shadow of a smile. "I can—
crawl—if—it—not—be—too far—"

"You can walk!" she said firmly. Rising, she stooped and
locked both her hands under his nearer armpit. Exerting the full
of her remaining strength, Tursla indeed brought him to his feet.
Then, pulling his arm once more about her shoulders, she led
him on, until they were on the rocks above the silent pool
encircled in sand.

Her hands fumbled first with the fastenings of her robe. She
moved now in answer to her knowledge of what must be done.
The answer slipped into her mind as the maker of dye might
measure and add a handful of this, a counter of that, while intent
on boiling some fire-cradled mixture. There was custom to be

faced here also. Only by a certain ritual might that which she
must summon be approached.

Tursla's robe fell about her feet. Now she stooped once more
above the recumbent man, her fingers seeking buckles, the fas-
tening of mail. His eyes opened and he looked up to her,
puzzled.

"What—do—?"

"These—" She tugged at the mail where it lay across his
shoulders, her other hand picking at the stuff of his breeches.
"Off—we must go where these cannot be worn."

He blinked. "One of the Old Powers?" he asked.

Tursla shrugged. "I know not of your Old Powers. But I
know a little of what we can summon here. If—" She put her
forefinger to her mouth and bit upon that as she considered a
point which had only that moment occurred to her. This place
would welcome her, had welcomed her, because she was what
she was (and what in truth was she? one small part of her now
asked. But the time for any such questioning was not now).
Would he also be accepted? There was no way of proving that
except to try.

"We must"—she made the decision firm—"do this thing.
For I have no other way of escape for you."

She helped his fumbling hands with the fastenings, the clasps,
and belting until his body with the wide powerful shoulders, the
long arms which marked him as of Torblood, was bare. Then she
pointed to the rock from which she had leaped that other time.

"Do not tread upon the sand," she cautioned. "Not while it
lies thus. We must leap from there—into the pool."

"If I can—" but he pulled himself along as she mounted the
rock.

Out she leapt and down. Once more that water closed about
her. But she moved swiftly away toward the farther side of the
pool, clearing the spot where he should land. Then she looked up
as she trod water.

"Come!"

His body looked as white as the mist curling behind him. He
had climbed onto the stone she had just quitted, and she saw his
muscles tense. Then he stretched out his arms and dove, cleaving
the water with a loud splash.

Tursla turned on her back and floated as she had before. He
was no longer her charge for she had brought him to what safety
her instinct told her was all they could hope for, and the pool had
not repelled him.

Tursla, her eyes up to the sky which she could see through

ragged patches of mist which was being tattered by the sea wind, began to sing—without words—the notes rising and falling like the call of some bird.

5

As before at her call that sand stirred. The girl could feel no wind, yet the grains of powdery stuff arose, began to twirl as she had seen them on that night. A pillar was born, now moving faster and faster, each turn making it more solid to the eyes. Now came the rounding of a head, the modeling of the body below that.

Still Tursla sang her hymn without words as the vessel was formed to hold that which she summoned. She had half forgotten Simond. If he watched in astonishment he made no sound to disturb the voice spell she wove with the same certainty as her hands could follow a design upon her loom.

At last Xactol stood there. Seeing her waiting, Tursla came from the pool, standing erect on stone from which the forming of that other had swept the last minute grain of sand.

"Sand-sister—" The girl raised her arms, but did not quite embrace the other.

"Sister—" echoed the other, in her hissing, sand-sliding voice. "What is your need?" Now her hands came forth also and Tursla's lay palm down upon them, flesh meeting sand.

"There is this one." Tursla did not turn her head to look upon Simond in the water still. "He is hunted. They must not find him."

"This is your choice, sister?" inquired that other. "Think well, for from such a choice may come many things you could have reason to look upon as ills in the future."

"Ills alone, Xactol?" asked the girl slowly.

"Nothing is altogether ill, sister. But you must think of this— you are now of Tor. If you go forth there will be no return. And those of Tor are not well looked upon by the Outlanders."

"Of Tor," Tursla repeated. "Only part of me, Sand sister. Only part of me. Even as it is with him. I have the body of Tor but the—"

"Do not say it!" commanded Xactol, interrupting her sharply. "But even if it be so, Tor body may betray you. There is a spell set upon the Marsh boundaries. Torfolk cannot go forth—and live."

"And this one?"

"He is divided. He was drawn in by the spelling of Tor, for

there was that in him which answered to such a call. But his Outland blood will help him to win forth again. Do you try to go with him—'' Now it was the woman of sand who left unfinished a warning.

"What will happen to me?"

"I do not know. This spelling is none of ours. The Outlanders have their own witcheries and their learning in such is very old and very deep. You would go at your own peril."

"I stay at even more, sand sister. You know what cloak of safety Mafra dared to throw over me; and, in the way they understand that claim, it is false."

"The decision is yours. What now would you have of me?"

"Can you buy us time, sand sister? There are those who will trail us to the death."

"That is so. Their rage and fear reaches out even to this place. It is like the mists which they love." The woman withdrew her right hand from where it rested under Tursla's. Now she raised that so that her finger touched the girl's forehead between and just above her eyes.

"This I give you. Use it as you will," she said in a soft voice. "I must go—''

"Will I see you again?" Tursla asked.

"Not if this choice is yours, sister, this choice I read in your thoughts. My door between the worlds is here alone."

"Then I can't—'' Tursla cried out.

"But you have already chosen, sister. In your spirit's innermost place that choice lies. Go with peace. Accept what may lie before you with the courage of your spirit. There is a meaning behind what has happened to you. If we don't see it now, all will be made clear in time. Do as you know how to do."

Her arms dropped to her sides and Tursla fell once more to her knees, and veiled her eyes with one hand. But the other she rested on one knee, palm up and slightly cupped.

Xactol began to turn, her spin grew ever faster. The fine sand which had formed her whirled out and away as the body became a pillar, and the pillar, in turn, sand falling to the rock. But in Tursla's hand there remained a small pile of the sand.

When the rest of that substance was once more spread out upon the rim of pool she arose, cupping her fingers tightly about what she held. Now she hailed Simond.

"You may come forth. We must go on."

Her head jerked around. There was a sound behind. The hunters may have been questing, at last they had the trail. Like Xactol, she could now sense the rage and fear which drove them.

Not even her claim of being Filled would be a protection against what moved them now. She shivered. Never before had emotions other than her own been fed to her in this way. The alienness of this was frightening. But there was no time to hesitate, to learn fear fostered by that hate.

Simnond came ashore. He walked more steadily, his head was up, but his attention was not for her, rather on their back trail as if he, too, had picked up some emanation from their pursuers.

Tursla climbed the rock to where she had left her robe. She held it up in one hand and spoke:

"Can you tear from this a portion of cloth? What I carry" —she showed him the fist which grasped the sand-dust—"must be safe until we have need for it."

He caught the cloth from her and tore a portion from the mud-stained him. Into this she emptied the sand, making a packet of it. Then she drew on her robe. But though he had breeches and boots on now, he fastened on only the leather undershirt, left his mail lying.

When he caught her attention he stirred the mail with his boot. "It will slow me. Where do we go?"

"To the sea." Already she was on her way.

The stay in the pool might have refreshed Simond's body, brought beginning healing to his wound, for he kept pace with her as she climbed and slipped among the rocks. She could hear the come and go of the waves, the wind sweeping mist and marsh air away from her.

They came to the shore. Simond looked north and then south, finally standing to face south. "That is the way for Estcarp. Let us go—"

If I can, she thought. *How strong is that spell laid upon the Torfolk? Does it rule body only, or body and spirit both? Can my spirit break a bond laid upon the body?* But she asked none of this aloud.

So they sped along the sand just beyond the reach of the waves. From behind came a shout, and a spear flashed over the wash of the water. A warning, Tursla guessed. The hunters wanted them not dead but captive. Perhaps Unnanna still would have her sacrifice.

Suddenly the girl gasped and cried out, stumbling back. It was as if she had run into a wall and rebounded, her body bruised from the force of that encounter. Simond was already several strides farther on. He whirled about at her cry and started back.

Tursla put out her hands. There was a surface there—invisible—

but as tight as the stone side of her place in the clan house. She could feel its substance.

The wall the Outlanders had set about the Tormarsh! It would seem that it was indeed a barrier she could not pierce.

"Come!" Simond was back at her side; apparently what was the wall for her did not exist for him. He caught at her, tried to drag her on.

The force of his attempt again brought her hard against that barrier.

"No—I cannot! The spells of your people—" she gasped. "Go—they cannot follow you through this!"

"Not without you!" His face was grim as he stood beside her. "Try by sea. Can you swim?"

"Not well enough." She had splashed now and then in some of the marsh pools, but to entrust herself to the sea was another matter. Yet what choice had she? That heat of hate behind was warning enough of what might happen!

"Come—"

"Stand!" That shout was from behind. Affric— She did not even have to look around to know who led the hunters.

"Go—" Tursla tried to push her companion on, through that wall which was no wall for him.

"The sea!" he repeated.

But it would seem they were too late. Another spear, expertly thrown, flashed between them, struck the unseen wall and rebounded. Tursla faced around, her hand going to the breast of her robe, closing upon what she had brought from the pool side.

Affric, yes, and Brunwol, and Gawan. Behind them a score of others, closing in, their eyes avid with a lust of hatred such as she had never met before. Consciously or unconsciously they were using that hatred as a weapon, beating at her; and the hurtful blows of it made her sway, sick and spirit wounded.

But Tursla still had strength enough to bring out the packet she had made. With one hand she tore that open as she balanced the fold of cloth upon the palm of the other. Now that the sand was uncovered, she raised it level with her lips and gathered a great breath to blow it outward. As it swirled she cried aloud. Not a word, for such spelling as this was not summoned by the words of the world. Rather she shaped a sound which seemed to roar, even as the alarm trumpet of the Torfolk had done.

There was no sighting the disappearance of the sand that her breath had dispersed. From the shore itself there uprose small curlings of the white grit. Those began to whirl, even as Xactol had formed her body. Higher they grew by the instant, drawing more and more of the shore's substance into them. But they remained pillars, not taking on any other form. Far taller they were now than any of those who stood there.

Affric and his men backed away a little, eyeing the pillars with the uncertainty of men who face a hitherto-unknown menace. Yet they did not retreat far, and Tursla knew well that they still held their deadly purpose.

The top of the tallest pillar began to nod—toward the Tormen. Tursla caught at Simond's shoulder. The strength that moved the pillars was draining from her. That she could order them much longer she doubted.

"The sea!"

Had she cried that aloud, or had he read it in her mind? She was not sure. But Simond's arm was about her and he was striding toward the wash of the waves, bearing her with him.

As the waves struck against her, the water rising from knee to waist, Tursla strove still to keep her mind upon the columns of sand. But she did not turn her head to watch how effectively her energy wrought.

There was shouting there, not now aimed at the fugitives. Some of the voices were muffled or ceased abruptly. The water was high about her now. Simond, sparing no glance for what might be happening on the shore, gave an order:

"Turn on your back. Float! Leave it to me!"

She tried to do as he wanted. So far there had been no barrier. Now as she splashed she could see the shoreline again. There was a mist. No, not a mist—that must be a whirl of sand thick enough to half hide the figures struggling in it as if they could not win forth from its enbrace, rather were caught fast held in the storm of grit.

Then she was on her back and Simond was swimming, towing her with him. No longer did he head out to sea, but rather altered course to parallel the shore. Tursla had held the sand, sent it raging as long as she could. She was drained now, not able to move to aid herself even if she had known how to swim.

That shouting grew louder. Then—

Force—force pushing her back, sending her under the water. She gasped, and the salt flood was in her mouth, drawn chokingly into her lungs. She fought for breath. The barrier! This was the barrier. She wanted to shout to Simond, tell him that all his efforts were useless. There was no escape for her.

No escape! Her body, her body was sealed into Tormarsh by the spells of the outlanders! No—hope—

Aroused to a frenzy by the danger of drowning, Tursla tried to get free of the hold upon her, to strike at Simond and make him let go before she was pushed completely under the water.

"—go! Let me go!" Her mind shrieked and water once more flooded into her mouth and nose.

Out of nowhere came a blow. She felt a flash of pain as it landed. Then, nothing at all.

Slowly she came back from that place of darkness. Water— she was drowning! Simond must let her go.

But there was no water. She lay on a surface which was steady, which did not swing as did the waves. And she could breathe. No water filled her nose, covered her head. For a long moment it was enough to know that she was indeed safe from being drawn under. But—

They must be back on the shore then. With her releasing of mind control the sand would have gone. Perhaps Affric was—

Tursla opened her eyes. Above her the sky arched—clear except for a drifting cloud or two. There was no hint of the Tormarsh mist about. She raised her head—though that small action seemed very hard—she was weak, drained.

Sand, white, marked with the ripples of waves which curled in, drained away again. And rocks. And the sea. But no Affric, no Torman standing over her. She was— Tursla sat up, bracing herself by her hands.

Her wet robe was plastered thick with sand. She could even taste the grit between her teeth. There was no one—no one at all. Yet a few moments of study showed her that this was not that tongue of beach to which the Tormarsh reached.

She inched around to face inland. To her left now, a goodly distance away, rising into the air as if a hundred—no, a thousand fires burned (for it stretched along there inland as far as she could see), the mists of the marsh arose like smoke, cloaking well what might lie on the other side.

They had passed the barrier! This was the Outland.

Tursla wavered to her knees, striving to see more of this unknown world. The sand of the beach stretched for a space. Then there was a sparse growth of tough grass; beyond that, bushes. But there was no smell of the swamp.

Where was Simond?

Her loneliness, which had been good when she feared Affric and the others, now was a source of uneasiness. Where had he gone—and why?

His desertion, for her, was frightening. Was it that she was of the Torfolk? Could it be that the Outlanders' hatred for the marsh dwellers was so great, that having saved her life, he felt he had paid any debts between them and had wished no more of her company?

Bleakly Tursla settled on that fact. Perhaps in the Outlands Koris himself hated his Tor blood and his son had been raised to find it a matter of shame. Just as a Torman might, in turn, look upon half Outland blood as something to lessen him among his fellows.

She was Tor—as much as Simond knew. And as Tor—

Tursla supported her head upon her hands and tried to think. It might well be that, having made one of those decisions she had been told to consider seriously, she had cut herself totally adrift from all people now. Xactol had warned her fairly. When she left the country of the pool she would no longer have communication with that one mind?—spirit?—entity?—who could understand what she was.

Mafra—for the first time Tursla wondered, with a little catch of breath, how had it gone with the Clan Mother who had faced Unnanna and worked some magic of her own to cover their escape; though what manner of Torfolk would dare to raise either hand or voice against Mafra? The girl wished passionately at that moment that she could reverse all that had happened to her, be once-more in the clan house—as it had been on the night before she had gone to keep her meeting with the sand-sister.

To look back, Tursla shook her head, that was only a waste of effort. No man or woman might ever turn again and decide upon some other path once their feet were firm set on one of their choice. She had made her decision, now by that she must live—or perhaps die.

Bleakly she looked landward. The sea was empty and she expected no help to arise out of that. Now she was hungry. Already the sun was well down in the western sky. She had not even a knife at her belt; and who knew what manner of danger might prowl the Outland at the coming of true darkness?

But if she tried to go hence it must be on hands and knees. When she attempted to rise to her feet she found herself so weak and giddy that she tottered and fell. Hunger and thirst—both were an emptiness crying to be filled.

Filled! At least now the clan would never discover her deception. If she had been filled with something else as Mafra had averred, what *was* it?

She brought her knees up against her breast, put her arms about them, huddling in upon herself, for the wind was growing colder and had a bite to it which the winds of Tormarsh never held. Now she tried to think. What was good fortune for her now? What was ill? The latter seemed a longer list. But the good—she had escaped Affric and the rest—the anger of the Torfolk which would have been dire when they discovered she would bring forth no child to swell their dwindling numbers. She had certain knowledge which she as yet did not know how to use, that which Xactol had granted her.

But if the sand-sister was forever barred from her, when and how could she ever learn?

And where might she go for shelter? Where was there food? Water? Would the hands of all dwellers in this land be raised against her when they knew her for Tor?

She—

"Holla!"

Tursla's head came up instantly.

There was a mounted man—riding through the inland brush! His head—bare head—Simond! Somehow she wobbled to her feet, called out in return though her voice sounded very thin and weak in answer to that shout of his:

"Simond!"

Now, it was as if something tight and hurting inside her had suddenly broken apart. She wavered to her feet, staggered, one foot before the other. She was not alone! He had not left her here!

The horse was coming at a trot. She could sight a second animal following; Simond had it on lead. He came in a shower of sand sent up by the pounding feet of his mount. Then he was out of the saddle and to her, his arms around her.

Tursla could only repeat his name in a witless fashion, letting him take the weight of her worn out and aching body.

"Simond! Simond!"

"It is well. All is well." He held her steady, letting the very fact that he was there, that she was not alone, seep into her mind and bring her peace.

"I had to go," he told her. "We needed horses. There is a watchtower only a little away. I came back as soon as I could."

Now she gained a measure of control.

"Simond." She made herself look directly into his eyes, sure that he would in no way try to soothe her with any false promise. "Simond, I am of Tormarsh. I do not know how you brought me past that spell your people used as a barrier to keep us from the Outland. But I remain Tor. Will your people give me any welcome?"

His hands now cupped her face, and his eyes did not shift.

"Tor chose to stand our enemy, but in return we have never

sought that enmity. Also, I am partly Tor. And ██
Torblood a blessing not a curse in Estcarp, as all men ██
held the Axe of Volt which would come only to him. A██
intended that Estcarp not be meat for those who were worse tha██
any winter wolf! Tor holds no stigma here.''

Then he laughed, and the lightness of his smile made his
whole face different.

"This is an odd thing. You know my name, but I do not know
yours. Will you trust me with that much to show your belief in
my goodwill?''

She found that her face, sticky with seawater and rough with
sand, stretched an answering smile.

"I am Tursla of— No, I am no longer of any clan house. Just
what I am now—or whom—that I must learn.''

"It will not be hard that learning. There will be those to
help," he promised her.

Tursla's smile grew wider. "That I do not doubt," she replied
with conviction.

Anderson

I

The third book of the Story of the Men of Killorn. How Red Bram fought the Ganasthi from the lands of darkness, and Kery son of Rhiach was angered, and the pipe of the gods spoke once more.

Now it must be told of those who fared forth south under Bram the Red. This was the smallest of the parties that left Killorn, being from three clans only—Broina, Dagh, and Heorran. That made some thousand warriors, mostly men with some women archers and slingers. But the pipe of the gods had always been with Clan Broina, and so it followed the Broina on this trek. He was Rhiach son of Glyndwyrr, and his son was Kery.

Bram was a Heorran, a man huge of height and thew, with eyes like blue ice and hair and beard like a torch. He was curt of speech and had no close friends, but men agreed that his brain and his spirit made him the best leader for a journey like this, though some thought that he paid too little respect to the gods and their priests.

For some five years these men of Killorn marched south. They went over strange hills and windy moors, through ice-blinking clefts in gaunt-cragged mountains and over brawling rivers chill with the cold of the Dark lands.

They hunted and robbed to live, or reaped the gain of foreigners, and cheerfully cut down any who sought to gainsay them. Now and again Bram dickered with the chiefs of some or other city and hired himself and his wild men out to fight against another town. Then there would be hard battle and rich booty and flames red against the twilight sky.

Men died and some grew weary of roving and fighting. There was a sick hunger within them for rest and a hearthfire and the eternal sunset over the Lake of Killorn. These took a house and a woman and stayed by the road. In such ways did Bram's army shrink. On the other hand most of his warriors finally took some or other woman along on the march and she would demand more for herself and the babies than a roof of clouds and wind. So there came to be tents and wagons, with children playing between the turning wheels. Bram grumbled about this, it made his army slower and clumsier, but there was little he could do to prevent it.

Those who were boys when the trek began became men with the years and the battles and the many miles. Among these was the Kery of whom we speak. He grew tall and lithe and slender, with the fair skin and slant blue eyes and long ash-blond hair of the Broina, broad of forehead and cheekbones, straight-nosed, beardless like most of his clan.

He was swift and deadly with sword, spear, or bow, merry with his comrades over ale and campfire, clever to play harp or pipe and make verses—not much different from the others, save that he came of the Broina and would one day carry the pipe of the gods. And while the legends of Killorn said that all men are the offspring of a goddess whom a warrior devil once bore off to his lair, it was held that the Broina had a little more demon blood in them than most.

Always Kery bore within his heart a dream. He was still a stripling when they wandered from home. He had reached young manhood among hoofs and wheels and dusty roads, battle and roaming and the glimmer of campfires, but he never forgot Killorn of the purple hills and the far thundering sea and the lake where it was forever sunset. For there had been a girl of the Dagh sept, and she had stayed behind.

But then the warriors came to Ryvan and their doom.

It was a broad fair country into which they had come. Trending south and east, away from the sun, they were on the darker edge of the Twilight Lands and the day was no longer visible at all. Only the deep silver-blue dusk lay around them and above, with black night and glittering stars to the east and a few high clouds lit by unseen sunbeams to the west. But it was still light enough for Twilight Landers' eyes to reach the horizon—to see fields and woods and rolling hills and the far metal gleam of a river. They were well into the territory of Ryvan city.

Rumor ran before them on frightened feet, and peasants often fled as they advanced. But never had they met such emptiness as now. They had passed deserted houses, gutted farmsteads, and the bones of the newly slain, and had shifted their course eastward to get into wilder country where there should at least be game. But such talk as they had heard of the invaders of Ryvan made them march warily. And when one of their scouts galloped back to tell of an army advancing out of the darkness against them, the great horns screamed and the wagons were drawn together.

For a while there was chaos, running and yelling men, crying children, bawling cattle, and tramping hests. Then the carts were drawn into a defensive ring atop a high steep ridge and the warriors waited outside. They made a brave sight, the men of Killorn, tall barbarians in the colorful kilts of their septs with plundered ornaments shining around corded throat or sinewy arm.

Most of them still bore the equipment of their homeland— horned helmets, gleaming ring-byrnies, round shields, ax and bow and spear and broadsword, worn and dusty with use but ready for more. The greater number went afoot, though some rode the small shaggy hests of the north. Their women and children crouched behind the wagons, with bows and slings ready and the old battle banners of Killorn floating overhead.

Kery came running to the place where the chiefs stood. He wore only a helmet and a light leather corselet, and carried sword and spear and a bow slung over his shoulders. "Father," he called. "Father, who are they?"

Rhiach of Broina stood near Bram with the great bagpipes of the gods under one arm—old beyond memory, those pipes, worn and battered, but terror and death and the avenging furies crouched in them, power so great that only one man could ever know the secret of their use. A light breeze stirred the warlock's long gray hair about his gaunt face, and his eyes brooded on the eastern darkness.

The scout who had brought word turned to greet Kery. He was painting with the weariness of his hard ride. An arrow had wounded him, and he shivered as the cold wind from the Dark Lands brushed his sweat-streaked body. "A horde," he said. "An army marching out of the east toward us, not Ryvan but such a folk as I never knew of. Their outriders saw me and barely did I get away. Most likely they will move against us, and swiftly."

"A host at least as great as ours," added Bram. "It must be a part of the invading Dark Landers who are laying Ryvan waste. It will be a hard fight, though I doubt not that with our good sword-arms and the pipe of the gods we will throw them back."

"I know not." Rhiach spoke slowly. His deep eyes were somber on Kery. "I have had ill dreams of late. If I fell in this battle, before we won . . . I did wrong, son. I should have told you how to use the pipe."

"The law says you can only do that when you are so old that

you are ready to give up your chiefship to your first born," said Bram. "It is a good law. A whole clan knowing how to wield such power would soon be at odds with all Killorn."

"But we are not in Killorn now," said Rhiach. "We have come far from home, among alien and enemy peoples, and the lake where it is forever sunset is a ghost to us." His hard face softened. "If I fall, Kery, my own spirit, I think, will wander back thither. I will wait for you at the border of the lake, I will be on the windy heaths and by the high tarns, they will hear me piping in the night and know I have come home . . . but seek your place, son, and all the gods be with you."

Kery gulped and wrung his father's hand. The warlock had ever been a stranger to him. His mother was dead these many years and Rhiach had grown grim and silent. And yet the old warlock was dearer to him than any save Morna who waited for his return.

He turned and sped to his own post, with the tyrs.

The cows of the great horned tyrs from Killorn were for meat and milk and leather, and trudged meekly enough behind the wagons. But the huge black bulls were wicked and had gored more than one man to death. Still Kery had gotten the idea of using them in battle. He had made iron plates for their chests and shoulders. He had polished their cruel horns and taught them to charge when he gave the word. No other man in the army dared go near them, but Kery could guide them with a whistle. For the men of Broina were warlocks.

They snorted in the twilight as he neared them, stamping restlessly and shaking their mighty heads. He laughed in a sudden reckless drunkenness of power and moved up to his big lovely Gorwain and scratched the bull behind the ears.

"Softly, softly," he whispered, standing in the dusk among the crowding black bulks. "Patient, my beauty, wait but a little and I'll slip you, O wait, my Gorwain."

Spears blinked in the shadowy light and voices rumbled quietly. The bulls and the hests snorted, stamping and shivering in the thin chill wind flowing from the lands of night. They waited.

Presently they heard, faint and far, the skirling of war pipes. But it was not the wild joyous music of Killorn, it was a thin shrill note which ran along the nerves, jagged as a saw, and the thump of drums and the clangor of gongs came with it. Kery sprang up on the broad shoulders of Gorwain and tyr and strained into the gloom to see.

Over the rolling land came marching the invaders. It was an army of a thousand or so, he guessed with a shiver of tension,

moving in closer ranks and with tighter discipline than the
barbarians. He had seen many armies, from the naked yelling
savages of the upper Norlan hills to the armored files of civilized
towns, yet never one like this.

Dark Landers, he thought bleakly. *Out of the cold and the
night that never ends, out of the mystery and the frightened
legends of a thousand years, here at last are the men of the Dark
Lands, spilling into the Twilight like their own icy winds, and
have we anything that can stand against them?*

They were tall, as tall as the northerners, but gaunt, with a
stringy toughness born of hardship and suffering and bitter chill.
Their skins were white, not with the ruddy whiteness of the
northern Twilight Landers but dead-white, blank and bare, and
the long hair and beards were the color of silver.

Their eyes were the least human thing about them, huge and
round and golden, the eyes of a bird of prey, deep sunken in the
narrow skulls. Their faces seemed strangely immobile, as if the
muscles for laughter and weeping were alike frozen. As they
moved up, the only sound was the tramp of their feet and the
demon whine of their pipes and the clash of drum and gong.

They were well equipped, Kery judged, they wore close-
fitting garments of fur-trimmed leather, trousers and boots and
hooded tunics. Underneath he glimpsed mail, helmets, shields,
and they carried all the weapons he knew—no cavalry, but they
marched with a sure tread. Overhead floated a strange banner, a
black standard with a jagged golden streak across it.

Kery's muscles and nerves tightened to thrumming alertness.
He crouched by his lead bull, one hand gripping the hump and
the other white-knuckled around his spearshaft. And there was a
great hush on the ranks of Killorn as they waited.

Closer came the strangers, until they were in bowshot. Kery
heard the snap of tautening strings. *Will Bram never give the
signal? Gods, is he waiting for them to walk up and kiss us?*

A trumpet brayed from the enemy ranks, and Kery saw the
cloud of arrows rise whistling against the sky. At the same time
Bram winded his horn and the air grew loud with war shouts and
the roar of arrow flocks.

Then the strangers locked shields and charged.

II

The men of Killorn stood their ground, shoulder to shoulder,
pikes braced and swords aloft. They had the advantage of high
ground and meant to use it. From behind their ranks came a
steady hail of arrows and stones, whistling through the air to

crack among the enemy ranks and tumble men to earth—yet still the Dark Landers came, leaping and bounding and running with strange precision. They did not yell, and their faces were blank as white stone, but behind them the rapid thud of their drums rose to a pulse-shaking roar.

"Hai-ah!" bellowed Red Bram. "Sunder them!"

The great long-shafted ax shrieked in his hands, belled on an enemy helmet and crashed through into skull and brain and shattering jawbone. Again he smote, sideways, and a head leaped from its shoulders.

A Dark Land warrior thrust for his belly. He kicked one booted foot out and sent the man lurching back into his own ranks. Whirling, he hewed down one who engaged the Killorner beside him. A foeman sprang against him as he turned, chopping at his leg. With a roar that lifted over the clashing racket of battle, Bram turned, the ax already flying in his hands, and cut the stranger down.

His red beard blazed like a torch over the struggle as it swayed back and forth. His streaming ax was a lighting bolt that rose and fell and rose again, and the thunder of metal on breaking metal rolled between the hills.

Kery stood by his tyrs, bow in hand, shooting and shooting into the masses that roiled about him. None came too close, and he could not leave his post lest the unchained bulls stampede. He shuddered with the black fury of battle. When would Bram call the charge. How long? Zip, zip, gray-feathered death winging into the tide that rolled up to the wagons and fell back and resurged over its corpses.

The men of Killorn were yelling and cursing as they fought, but the Dark Landers made never a sound save for the hoarse gasping of breath and the muted groans of the wounded. It was like fighting demons, yellow-eyed and silver-bearded and with no soul in their bony faces. The northerners shivered and trembled and hewed with a desperate fury of loathing.

Back and forth the battle swayed, roar of axes and whine of arrows and harsh iron laughter of swords. Kery stood firing and firing, the need to fight was a bitter catch in his throat. How long to wait, how long, how long?

Why didn't Rhiach blow the skirl of death on the pipes? Why not fling them back with the horror of disintegration in their bones, and then rush out to finish them?

Kery knew well that the war-song of the gods was only to be played in time of direst need, for it hurt friend almost as much as

foe—but even so, even so! A few shaking bars, to drive the
enemy back in death and panic, and then the sortie to end them!

Of a sudden he saw a dozen Dark Landers break from the
main battle by the wagons and approach the spot where he stood.
He shot two swift arrows, threw his spear, and pulled out his
sword with a savage laughter in his heart, the demoniac battle
joy of the Broina. Ha, let them come!

The first sprang with downward-whistling blade. Kery twisted
aside, letting speed and skill be his shield, his long glaive
flickered out and the enemy screamed as it took off his arm.
Whirling, Kery spitted the second through the throat. The third
was on him before he could withdraw his blade, and a fourth
from the other side, raking for his vitals. He sprang back.

"Gorwain!" he shouted. "*Gorwain!*"

The huge black bull heard. His fellows snorted and shivered,
but stayed at their place—Kery didn't know how long they
would wait, he prayed they would stay a moment more. The lead
tyr ran up beside his master, and the ground trembled under his
cloven hoofs.

The white foemen shrank back, still dead of face but with fear
plain in their bodies. Gorwain snorted, an explosion of thunder,
and charged them.

There was an instant of flying bodies, tattered flesh ripped by
the horns, and ribs snapping underfoot. The Dark Landers thrust
with their spears, the points glanced off the armor plating and
Gorwain turned and slew them.

"Here!" cried Kery sharply. "Back, Gorwain! Here!"

The tyr snorted and circled, rolling his eyes. The killing
madness was coming over him, if he were not stopped now he
might charge friend or foe.

"Gorwain!" screamed Kery.

Slowly, trembling under his shining black hide, the bull returned.

And now Rhiach the warlock stood up behind the ranks of
Killorn. Tall and steely gray, he went out between them, the
pipes in his arms and the mouthpieces at his lips. For an instant
the Dark Landers wavered, hesitating to shoot at him, and then
he blew.

It was like the snarling music of any bagpipe, and yet there
was more in it. There was a boiling tide of horror riding the
notes, men's hearts faltered and weakness turned their muscles
watery. Higher rose the music, and stronger and louder, screaming in the dales, and before men's eyes the world grew unreal,
shivering beneath them, the rocks faded to mist and the trees
groaned and the sky shook. They fell toward the ground, holding

their ears, half blind with unreasoning fear and with the pain of the giant hand that gripped their bones and shook them, shook them.

The Dark Landers reeled back, falling, staggering, and many of those who toppled were dead before they hit the earth. Others milled in panic, the army was becoming a mob. The world groaned and trembled and tried to dance to the demon music.

Riach stopped. Bram shook his bull head to clear the ringing and the fog in it. "At them!" he roared. *"Charge!"*

Sanity came back. The land was real and solid again, and men who were used to the terrible drone of the pipes could force strength back into shuddering bodies. With a great shout, the warriors of Killorn formed ranks and moved forward.

Kery leaped up on the back of Gorwain, straddling the armored chine and gripping his knees into the mighty flanks. His sword blazed in the air. "Now kill them, my beauties!" he howled.

In a great wedge, with Gorwain at their lead, the tyrs rushed out on the foe. Earth shook under the rolling thunder of their feet. Their bellowing filled the land and clamored at the gates of the sky. They poured like a black tide down on the Dark Land host and hit it.

"Hoo-ah!" cried Kery.

He felt the shock of running into that mass of men and he clung tighter, holding on with one hand while his sword whistled in the other. Bodies fountained before the rush of the bulls, horns tossed men into the heavens and hoofs pounded them into the earth. Kery swung at dimly glimpsed heads, the hits shivered along his arm but he could not see if he killed anyone, there wasn't time.

Through and through the Dark Land army the bulls plowed, goring a lane down its middle while the Killorners fell on it from the front. Blood and thunder and erupting violence, death reaping the foe, and Kery rode onward.

"Oh, my beauties, my black sweethearts, horn them, stamp them into the ground. Oh, lovely, lovely, push them on, my Gorwain, knock them down to hell, best of bulls!"

The tyrs came out on the other side of the broken host and thundered on down the ridge. Kery fought to stop them. He yelled and whistled, but he knew such a charge could not expend itself in a moment.

As they rushed on, he heard the high brazen call of a trumpet, and then another and another, and a new war-cry rising behind him. What was that? What had happened?

They were down in a rocky swale before he had halted the charge. The bulls stood shivering then, foam and blood streaked their heaving sides. Slowly, with many curses and blows, he got them turned, but they would only walk back up the long hill.

As he neared the battle again he saw that another force had attacked the Dark Landers from behind. It must have come through the long ravine to the west, which would have concealed its approach from those fighting Southern Twilight Landers, Kery saw, well trained and equipped though they seemed to fight wearily. But between men of north and south, the easterners were being cut down in swathes. Before he could get back the remnants of their host was in full fight. Bram was too busy with the newcomers to pursue and they soon were lost in the eastern darkness.

Kery dismounted and led his bulls to the wagons to tie them up. They went through a field of corpses, heaped and piled on the blood-soaked earth, but most of the dead were enemies. Here and there the wounded cried out in the twilight, and the women of Killorn were going about succoring their own hurt. Carrion birds hovered above on darkling wings.

"Who are those others?" asked Kery of Bram's wife Eiyla. She was a big raw-boned woman, somewhat of a scold but stouthearted and the mother of tall sons. She stood leaning on an unstrung bow and looking over the suddenly hushed landscape.

"Ryvanians, I think," she replied absently. Then, "Kery—Kery, I have ill news for you."

His heart stumbled and there was a sudden coldness within him. Mutely, he waited.

"Rhiach is dead, Kery," she said gently. "An arrow took him in the throat even as the Dark Landers fled."

His voice seemed thick and clumsy. "Where is he?"

She led him inside the laager of wagons. A fire had been lit to boil water, and its red glow danced over the white faces of women and children and wounded men where they lay. To one side the dead had been stretched, and white-headed Lochly of Dagh stood above them with his bagpipes couched in his arms.

Kery knelt over Rhiach. The warlock's bleak features had softened a little in death, he seemed gentle now. But quiet, so pale and quiet. And soon the earth will open to receive you, you will be laid to rest here in an alien land where the life slipped from your hands, and the high windy tarns of Killorn will not know you ever again, O Rhiach the Piper.

Farewell, farewell, my father. Sleep well, goodnight, goodnight!

Slowly, Kery brushed the gray hair back from Rhiach's forehead, and knelt and kissed him on the brow. They had laid the god-pipe beside him, and he took this up and stood numbly, wondering what he would do with this thing in his hands.

Old Lochly gave him a somber stare. His voice came so soft you could scarce hear it over the thin whispering wind.

"Now you are the Broina, Kery, and thus the Piper of Killorn."

"I know," he said dully.

"But you know not how to blow the pipes, do you? No, no man does that. Since Broina himself had them from Lugan Longsword in heaven, there has been one who knew their use, and he was the shield of all Killorn. But now that is ended, and we are alone among strangers and enemies."

"It is not good. But we must do what we can."

"Oh, aye. 'Tis scarcely your fault, Kery. But I fear none of us will ever drink the still waters of the lake where it is forever sunset again."

Lochly put his own pipes to his lips and the wild despair of the old coronach wailed forth over the hushed camp.

Kery slung the god-pipes over his back and wandered out of the laager toward Bram and the Ryvanians.

III

The southern folk were more civilized, with cities and books and strange arts, though the notherners thought it spiritless of them to knuckle under to their kings as abjectly as they did. Hereabouts the people were dark of hair and eyes, though still light of skin like all Twilight Landers, and shorter and stockier than in the north. These soldiers made a brave showing with polished cuirass and plumed helmet and oblong shields, and they had a strong cavalry mounted on tall hests, and trumpeters and standard bearers and engineers. They outnumbered the Killorners by a good three to one, and stood in close, suspicious ranks.

Approaching them, Kery thought that his people were, after all, invaders of Ryvan themselves. If this new army decided to fall on the tired and disorganized barbarians, whose strongest weapon had just been taken from them, it could be slaughter. He stiffened himself, thrusting thought of Rhiach far back into his mind, and strode boldly forward.

As he neared he saw that however well armed and trained the Ryvanians were they were also weary and dusty, and they had many hurt among them. Beneath their taut bearing was a hollowness. They had the look of beaten men.

Bram and the Dagh, tall gray Nessa, were parleying with the

Ryvanian general, who had ridden forward and sat looking coldy down on them. The Heorran carried his huge ax over one mailed shoulder, but had the other hand lifted in sign of peace. At Kery's approach, he turned briefly and nodded.

"Well you came," he said. "This is a matter for the heads of all three clans, and you are the Broina now. I grieve for Rhiach, and still more do I grieve for poor Killorn, but we must put a bold face on it lest they fall on us."

Kery nodded, gravely as fitted an elder. The incongruity of it was like a blow. Why, he was a boy—there were men of Broina in the train twice and thrice his age—and he held leadership over them!

But Rhiach was dead, and Kery was the last living of his sons. Hunger and war and the coughing sickness had taken all the others, and so now he spoke for his clan.

He turned a blue gaze up toward the Ryvanian general. This was a tall man, big as a northerner but quiet and graceful in his movements, and the inbred haughtiness of generations was stiff within him. A torn purple cloak and a gilt helmet were his only special signs of rank, otherwise he wore the plain armor of a mounted man, but he wore it like a king. His face was dark for a Twilight Lander, lean and strong and deeply lined, with a proud high-bridged nose and a long hard jaw and close-cropped black hair finely streaked with gray. He alone in that army seemed utterly undaunted by whatever it was that had broken their spirits.

"This is Kery son of Rhiach, chief of the third of our clans," Bram introduced him. He used the wisespread Aluardian language of the southlands, which was also the tongue of Ryvan and which most of the Killorners had picked up in the course of their wanderings. "And Kery, he says he is Jonan, commander under Queen Sathi of the army of Ryvan, and that his is a force sent out from the city which became aware of the battle we were having and took the opportunity of killing a few more Dark Landers."

Nessa of Dagh looked keenly at the southerners. "Methinks there's more to it than that," he said, half to his fellows and half to Jonan. "You've been in a stiff battle and come off second best, if looks tell aught. Were I to make a further venture, it would be that while you fought clear of the army that beat you and are well ahead of pursuit, it's still on your tail and you have to reach the city fast."

"That will do," snapped Jonan. "We have heard of you plundering bandits from the north, and have no intention of permitting you on Ryvanian soil. If you turn back at once, you may go in peace, but otherwise . . ."

Casting a glance behind him, Bram saw that his men were swiftly reforming their own lines. If the worst came to the worst, they'd give a fearsome account of themselves. And it was plain that Jonan knew it.

"We are wanderers, yes," said the chief steadily, "but we are not highwaymen save when necessity drives us to it. It would better fit you to let us, who have just broken a fair-sized host of your deadly enemies, proceed in peace. We do not wish to fight you, but if we must it will be all the worse for you."

"Ill-armed barbarians, a third of our number, threatening us?" asked Jonan scornfully.

"Well, now, suppose you can overcome us," said Nessa with a glacial cheerfulness. "I doubt it, but just suppose so. We will not account for less than one man apiece of yours, you know, and you can hardly spare so many with Dark Landers ravaging all your country. Furthermore, a battle with us could well last so long that those who follow you will catch up, and there is an end to all of us."

Kery took a breath and added flatly, "You must have felt the piping we can muster at need. Well for you that we only played it a short while. If we chose to play you a good long dirge . . ."

Bram cast him an approving glance, nodded, and said stiffly, "So you see, General Jonan, we mean to go on our way, and it would best suit you to bid us a friendly goodbye."

The Ryvanian scowled blackly and sat for a moment in thought. The wind stirred his hest's mane and tail and the scarlet plume on his helmet. Finally he asked them in a bitter voice, "What do you want here, anyway? Why did you come south?"

"It is a long story, and this is no place to talk," said Bram. "Suffice it that we seek land. Not much land, nor for too many years, but a place to live in peace till we can return to Killorn."

"Hm." Jonan frowned again. "It is a hard position for me. I cannot simply let a band famous for robbery go loose. Yet it is true enough that I would not welcome a long and difficult fight just now. What shall I do with you?"

"You will just have to let us go," grinned Nessa.

"No! I think you have lied to me on several counts, barbarians. Half of what you say is bluff, and I could wipe you out if I had to."

"Methinks somewhat more than half of your words are bluff," murmured Kery.

Jonan gave him an angry look, then suddenly whirled on Bram. "Look here. Neither of us can well afford a battle, yet neither trusts the other out of its sight. There is only one answer. We must proceed together to Ryvan city."

"Eh? Are you crazy, man? Why, as soon as we were in sight of your town, you could summon all its garrison out against us."

"You must simply trust me not to do that. If you have heard anything about Queen Sathi, you will know that she would never permit it. Nor can we spare too many forces. Frankly, the city is going to be under siege very soon."

"Is it that bad?" asked Bram.

"Worse," said Jonan gloomily.

Nessa nodded his shrewd gray head. "I've heard some tales of Sathi," he agreed. "They do say she's honorable."

"And I have heard that you people have served as mercenaries before now," said Jonan quickly, "and we need warriors so cruelly that I am sure some arrangement can be made here. It could even include the land you want, if we are victorious, for the Ganasthi have wasted whole territories. So this is my proposal—march with us to Ryvan, in peace, and there discuss terms with her majesty for taking service under her flag." His harsh dark features grew suddenly cold. "Or, if you refuse, bearing in mind that Ryvan has very little to lose after all, I will fall on you this instant."

Bram scratched his red beard, and looked over the southern ranks and especially the engines. Flame-throwing ballistae could make ruin of the laager. Jonan galled him, and yet—well—however they might bluff about it, the fact remained that they had very little choice.

And anyway, the suggestion about payment in land sounded good. And if these—Ganasthi—had really overrun the Ryvanian empire, then there was little chance in any case of the Killorners getting much further south.

"Well," said Bram mildly, "we can at least talk about it—at the city."

Now the wagons, which the barbarians would not abandon in spite of Jonan's threats, were swiftly hitched again and the long train started its creaking way over the hills. Erelong they came on one of the paved imperial roads, a broad empty way that ran straight as a spearshaft southwestward to Ryvan city. Then they made rapid progress.

In truth, thought Kery, they went through a wasted land. Broad fields were blackened with fire, corpses sprawled in the embers of farmsteads, villages were deserted and gutted—everywhere folk had fled before the hordes of Ganasth. Twice they saw red glows on the southern horizon and white-lipped soldiers told Kery that those were burning cities.

As they marched west the sky lightened before them until at

last a clear white glow betokened that the sun was just below the curve of the world. It was a fair land of rolling plains and low hills, fields and groves and villages, but empty—empty. Now and again a few homeless peasants stared with frightened eyes at their passage, or trailed along in their wake, but otherwise there was only the wind and the rain and the hollow thudding of their feet.

Slowly Kery got the tale of Ryvan. The city had spread itself far in earlier days, conquering many others, but its rule was just. The conquered became citizens themselves and the strong armies protected all. The young queen Sathi was nearly worshipped by her folk. But then the Ganasthi came.

"About a year ago it was," said one man. "They came out of the darkness in the east, a horde of them, twice as many as we could muster. We've always had some trouble with Dark Landers on our eastern border, you know, miserable barbarians making forays which we beat off without too much trouble. And most of them told of pressure from some power forcing them to fall on us. But we never thought too much of it. Not before it was too late.

"We don't know much about Ganasth. It seems to be a fairly civilized state, somewhere out there in the cold and the dark. How they ever became civilized with nothing but howling savages around them I'll never imagine. But they've built up a power like Ryvan's, only bigger. It seems to include conscripts from many Dark Land tribes who're only too glad to leave their miserable frozen wastes and move into our territory. Their armies are as well trained and equipped as our own, and they fight like demons. Those war-gongs, and those dead faces . . ."

He shuddered.

"The prisoners we've taken say they aim to take over all the Twilight Lands. They're starting with Ryvan—it's the strongest state, and once they've knocked us over the rest will be easy. We've appealed for help to other nations but they're all too afraid, too busy raising their own silly defenses, to do anything. So for the past year the war's been raging up and down our empire." He waved a hand, wearily, at the blasted landscape. "You see what that's meant. Famine and plague are starting to hit us now—"

"And you could never stand before them?" asked Kery.

"Oh, yes, we had our victories and they had theirs. But when we won a battle they'd just retreat and sack some other area. They've been living off the country—our country—the devils!" The soldier's face twisted. "My own little sister was in Aquilaea when they took that. When I think of those white-haired fiends—

"Well about a month ago, the great battle was fought. Jonan led the massed forces of Ryvan out and caught the main body of Ganasthi at Seven Rivers, in the Donam Hills. I was there. The fight lasted, oh, four sleeps maybe, and nobody gave quarter or asked it. We outnumbered them a little, but they finally won. They slaughtered us like driven cattle. Jonan was lucky to pull half his forces out of there. The rest left their bones at Seven Rivers. Since then we've been a broken nation.

"We're pulling all we have left back toward Ryvan in the hope of holding it till a miracle happens. Do you have any miracles for sale, Northman?" The soldier laughed bitterly.

"What about this army here?" asked Kery.

"We still make sorties, you know. This one went out from Ryvan city a few sleeps past to the relief of Tusca, which our scouts said the Ganasthi were besieging with only a small force. But an emeny army intercepted us on the way. We cut our way out and shook them, but they're on our tail in all likelihood. When we chanced to hear the noise of your fight with the invaders we took the opportunity . . . Almighty Dyuus, it was good to hack them down and see them run!"

The soldier shrugged. "But what good did it do, really? What chance have we got? That was a good magic you had at the fight. I thought my heart was going to stop when that demon music started. But can you pipe your way out of hell, barbarian? Can you?"

IV

Ryvan was a fair city, with terraced gardens and high shining towers to be seen over the white walls, and it lay among wide fields not yet ravaged by the enemy. But around it, under its walls, spilling out over the land, huddled the miserable shacks and tents of those who had fled hither and could find no room within the town till the foe came over the horizon—the broken folk, the ragged horror-ridden peasants who stared mutely at the defeated army as it streamed through the gates.

The men of Killorn made camp under one wall and soon their fires smudged the deep silver-blue sky and their warriors stood guard against the Ryvanians. They did not trust even these comrades in woe, for they came of the fat southlands and the wide highways and the iron legions, and not of Killorn and its harsh windy loneliness.

Before long word came that the barbarian leaders were expected at the palace. So Bram, Nessa, and Kery put on their polished byrnies, and over them tunics and cloaks of their best plunder. They slung their swords over their shoulders and mounted their hests and rode between two squads of Ryvanian guardsmen through the gates and into the city.

It was packed and roiling with those who had fled. Crowds surged aimlessly around the broad avenues and spilled into the colonnaded temples and the looming apartments and even the gardens and villas of the nobility.

There was the dusty, bearded peasant, clinging to his wife and his children and looking on the world with frightened eyes. Gaily decked noble, riding through the mob with patrician hauteur and fear underneath it. Fat merchant and shaven priest, glowering at the refugees who came in penniless to throng the city and must, by the queen's orders, be fed and housed. Patrolling soldiers, striving to keep order in the mindless whirlpool of man, their young faces drawn and their shoulders stooped beneath their mail. Jugglers, mountebanks, thieves, harlots, tavern-keepers, plying their trades in the feverish gaiety of doom; a human storm foaming off into strange half-glimpsed faces in darkened alleys and eddying crowds, the unaccountable aliens who flit through all great cities—the world seemed gathered at Ryvan, and huddling before the wrath that came.

Fear rode the city, Kery could feel it, he breathed and the air was dank with terror, he bristled animal-like and laid a hand to his sword. For an instant he remembered Killorn, the wide lake rose before him and he stood at its edge, watching the breeze ruffle it and hearing the whisper of reeds and the chuckle of water on a pebbled shore. Miles about lay the hills and the moors, the clean strong smell of ling was a drunkenness in his nostrils. It was silent save for the small cool wind that ruffled Morna's hair. And in the west it was sunset, the mighty sun-disc lay just below the horizon and a shifting, drifting riot of colors, flame of red and green and molten gold, burned in the twilit heavens.

He shook his head, feeling his longing as a sharp clear pain, and urged his hest through the crowds. Presently they reached the palace.

It was long and low and gracious, crowded now since all the nobles and their households had moved into it and, under protest, turned their own villas over to the homeless. Dismounting, the northerners walked between files of guardsmen, through fragrant gardens and up the broad marble steps of the building— through long corridors and richly furnished rooms, and finally into the audience chamber of Queen Sathi.

It was like a chalice of white stone, wrought in loveliness and brimming with twilight and stillness. That deep blue dusk lay cool and mysterious between the high slim pillars, and somewhere came the rippling of a harp and the singing of birds and fountains. Kery felt suddenly aware of his uncouth garments and manners and accent. His tongue thickened and he did not know what to do with his hands. Awkwardly he took off his helmet.

"Lord Bram of Killorn, your majesty," said the chamberlain.

"Greeting, and welcome," said Sathi.

Word had spread far about Ryvan's young queen but Kery thought dazedly that the gossips had spoken less of her than was truth. She was tall and lithe and sweetly formed, with strength slumbering deep under the wide soft mouth and the lovely curves of cheeks and forehead. Blood of the Sun Lands darkened her hair to a glowing blue-black and tinted her skin with gold, there was fire from the sun within her. Like other southern women, she dressed more boldly than the girls of Killorn, a sheer gown falling from waist to ankles, a thin veil over the shoulders, little jewelry. She needed no ornament.

She could not be very much older than he, if at all, thought Kery. He caught her great dark eyes on him and felt a slow hot flush go up his face. With an effort he checked himself and stood very straight, with his strange blue eyes like cold flames.

Beside Sathi sat the general, Jonan, and there were a couple of older men who seemed to be official advisors. But it soon was clear that only the queen and the soldier had much to say in this court.

Bram's voice boomed out, shattering the peace of the blue dusk. For all his great size and ruddy beard he seemed lost in the ancient grace of the chamber. He spoke too loudly. He stood too stiff. "Thank you, my lady. But I am no lord, I simply head this group of the men of Killorn." He waved clumsily at his fellows. "These are Nessa of Dagh and Kery of Broina."

"Be seated, then, and welcome again." Sathi's voice was low and musical. She signaled her servants to bring wine.

"We have heard of great wanderings in the north," she went on, when they had drunk. "But those lands are little known to us. What brought you so far from home?"

Nessa, who had the readiest tongue, answered. "There was famine in the land, your majesty. For three years drought and cold lay like iron over Killorn. We hungered and the coughing sickness came over many of us. Not all our magics and sacrifices availed to end our misery, they seemed only to raise great storms that destroyed what little we had kept.

"Then the weather smiled again, but as often happens the gray blight came in the wake of the hard years. It reaped our grain before we could, the stalks withered and crumbled before our eyes, and wild beasts came in hunger-driven swarms to raid our dwindling flocks. There was scarce food enough for a quarter of our starving folk. We knew, from what had happened in other lands, that the gray blight will waste a country for years, five or ten, leaving only perhaps a third part of the crop alive at each harvest. Then it passes away and does not come again. But meanwhile the land will not bear many folk.

"So in the end the clans decided that most must move away leaving only the few who could keep alive through the niggard years to hold the country for us. Hearts broke in twain, your majesty, for the hills and the moors and the lake where it is forever sunset were part of us. We are of that land and if we die away from it our ghosts will wander home. But go we must, lest all die."

"Yes, go on," said Jonan impatiently when he paused.

Bram gave him an angry look and took up the story. "Four hosts were to wander out of the land and see what would befall. If they found a place to stay they would abide there till the evil time was over. Otherwise they would live however they could. It lay with the gods, my lady, and we have traveled far from the realms of our gods.

"One host went eastward, into the great forest of Norla. One got ships and sailed west, out into the Day Lands where some of our adventurers had already explored a little way. One followed the coast southwestward, through country beyond our ken. And ours marched due south. And so we have wandered for five years."

"Homeless," whispered Sathi, and Kery thought her eyes grew bright with tears.

"Barbarian robbers!" snapped Jonan. "I know of the havoc they have wrought on their way."

"And what would you have done," growled Bram. Jonan gave him a stiff glare, but he rushed on. "Your majesty, we have taken only what we needed . . ."

And whatever else struck our fancy, thought Kery in a moment's wryness.

"—and much of our fighting has been done for honest pay. We want only a place to live a few years, land to farm as free yeomen, and we will defend the country which shelters us as long as we are in it. We are too few to take that land and hold it against a whole nation—that is why we have not settled down ere this—but on the march we will scatter any army in the world or leave our corpses for carrion birds. The men of Killorn keep faith with friends and foes alike, help to the one and harm to the other.

"Now we saw many fair fields in Ryvan where we could be at home. The Ganasthi have cleared off the owners for us and we may be able to make friends with the Dark Landers instead. For friends we must have."

"You see?" snarled Jonan. "He threatens banditry."

"No, no, you are too hasty," replied Sathi. "He is simply telling the honest truth. And the gods knew we need warriors."

"This general was anxious enough for our help out there in the eastern marches," said Kery suddenly.

"Enough, barbarian," said Jonan with ice in his tones.

Color flared in Sathi's cheeks. "Enough of you, Jonan. These are brave and honest men, and our guests, and our sorely needed allies. We will draw up the treaty at once."

The general shrugged, insolently. Kery was puzzled. There was anger here, crackling under a hard-held surface, but it seemed new and strange. *Why?*

They haggled for a while over terms, Nessa doing most of the talking for Killorn. He and Bram would not agree that clansmen would owe fealty or even respect to any noble of Ryvan save the queen herself. Also they should have the right to go home whenever they heard the famine was over. Sathi was willing enough to concede it but Jonan had to be almost beaten down. Finally he gave grudging assent and the queen had her scribes draw the treaty up on parchment.

"That is not how we do it in Killorn," said Bram. "A tyr must be sacrificed and vows made on the ring of Llugan and the pipes of the gods."

Sathi smiled. "Very well, Red One," she nodded. "We will make the pledge thusly too, if you wish." With a sudden flame of bitterness, "What difference does it make? What difference does anything make now?"

V

Now the armies of Ganasth moved against Ryvan city itself. From all the plundered empire they streamed in, to ring the town in a living wall and hem the defenders with a fence of spears. And when the whole host was gathered, which took about ten sleeps from the time the Killorners arrived, they stormed the city.

Up the long slope of the hills on which Ryvan stood they came, running, bounding, holding up shields against the steady hail of missiles from the walls. Forward, silent and blank-faced, no noise in them save the crashing of thousands of feet and the high demon-music of their warmaking—dying, strewing the ground with their corpses, but leaping over the fallen and raging against the walls.

Up ladders! Rams thundering at the gates! Men springing to the top of walls and toppling before the defenders and more of them snarling behind!

Back and forth the battle raged, now the Ryvanians driven back to the streets and rooftops, now the Dark Landers pressed to the edge of the walls and pitchforked over. Houses began to burn, here and there, and it was Sathi who made fire brigades out of those who could not fight. Kery had a glimpse of her from afar, as he battled on the outer parapets, a swift and golden loveliness against the leaping red.

After long and vicious fighting the northern gate went down. But Bram had forseen this. He had pulled most of his barbarians thither, with Kery's bulls in their lead. He planted them well back and had a small stout troop on either side of the great buckling doors. When the barrier sagged on its hinges, the Ganasthi roared in unopposed, streaming through the entrance and down the broad bloody avenue.

Then the Killorners thrust from the side, pinching off the several hundred who had entered. They threw great jars of oil on the broken gates and set them ablaze, a barrier of flame which none could cross. And then Kery rode his bulls against the enemy, and behind him came the might of Killorn.

It was raw slaughter. Erelong they were hunting the foe up and down the streets and spearing them like wild animals. Meanwhile Bram got some engineers from Jonan's force who put up a temporary barricade in the now open gateway and stood guard over it.

The storm faded, grumbled away in surges of blood and whistling arrows. Shaken by their heavy losses, the Dark Landers pulled back out of missile range, ranged the city with their watchfires, and prepared to lay siege.

There was jubilation in Ryvan. Men shouted and beat their dented shields with nicked and blunted swords. They tossed their javelins in the air, emptied wineskins, and kissed the first and best girl who came to hand. Weary, bleeding, reft of many good comrades, and given at best a reprieve, the folk still snatched at what laughter remained.

Bram came striding to meet the queen. He was a huge and terrible figure stiff with dried blood, the ax blinking on his shoulder and the other hairy paw clamped on the neck of a tall Dark Lander whom he helped along with an occasional kick. Yet

Sathi's dark eyes trailed to the slim form of Kery, following in the chief's wake and too exhausted to say much.

"I caught this fellow in the streets, my lady," said Bram merrily, "and since he seemed to be a leader I thought I'd better hang on to him for a while."

The invader stood motionless, regarding them with a chill yellow stare in which there lay an iron pride. He was tall and well-built, his black mail silver-trimmed, a silver star on the battered black helmet. The snowy hair and beard stirred faintly in the breeze.

"An aristocrat, I would say," nodded Sathi. She herself seemed almost too tired to stand. She was smudged with smoke and her dress was torn and her small hands bleeding from their recent burdens. But she pulled herself erect and fought to speak steadily. "Yes, he may well be of value to us. That was good work. Aye, you men of Killorn fought nobly, without you we might well have lost the city. It was a good month when you came."

"It was no way to fight," snapped Jonan. He was tired and wounded himself, but there was no comradeship in the look he gave the northerners. "The risk of it—why, if you hadn't been able to seal the gate behind them, Ryvan would have fallen then and there."

"I did not see you doing much of anything when the gate was splintering before them," answered Bram curtly. "As it is, my lady, we've inflicted such heavy losses on them that I doubt they'll consider another attempt at storming. Which gives us, at least, time to try something else." He yawned mightily. "Time to sleep!"

Jonan stepped up close to the prisoner and they exchanged a long look. There was no way to read the Dark Lander's thoughts but Kery thought he saw a tension under the general's hard-held features.

"I don't know what value a food-eating prisoner is to us when he can't even speak our language," said the Ryvan. "However, I can take him in charge if you wish."

"Do," she nodded dully,

"Odd if he couldn't talk any Aluardian at all," said Kery. "Wanderers through alien lands almost have to learn. The leaders of invading armies ought to know the tongue of their enemy, or at least have interpreters." He grinned with the cold savagery of the Broina. "Let the women of Killorn, the ones who've lost husbands today, have him for a while. I daresay he'll soon discover he knows your speech—whatever is left of him."

"No," said Jonan flatly. He signaled to a squad of his men. "Take this fellow down to the palace dungeons and give him something to eat. I'll be along later."

Kery started to protest but Sathi laid a hand on his arm. He felt how it was still bleeding a little and grew silent.

"Let Jonan take care of it," she said, her voice flat with weariness. "We all need rest now—O gods, to sleep!"

The Killorners had moved their wagons into the great forum and camped there, much to the disgust of the aristocrats and to the pleasure of whatever tavern keepers and unattached young women lived nearby. But Sathi had insisted that their three chiefs should be honored guests at the palace and it pleased them well enough to have private chambers and plenty of servants and the best of wine.

Kery woke in his bed and lay for a long while, drowsing and thinking the wanderous thoughts of half-asleep. When he got up he groaned for he was stiff with his wounds and the long fury of battle. A slave came in and rubbed him with oil and brought him a barbarian-sized meal, after which he felt better.

But now he was restless. He felt the letdown which is the aftermath of high striving. It was hard to fight back the misery and loneliness that rose in him. He prowled the room unhappily, pacing under the glowing cressets, flinging himself on a couch and then springing to his feet again. The walls were a cage.

The city was a cage, a trap, he was caught like a snared beast and never again would he walk the moors of Killorn. Sharply as a knife thrust, he remembered hunting once out in the heath. He had gone alone, with spear and bow and a shaggy half-wild cynor loping at his heels, out after antlered prey somewhere beyond the little village. Long had they roamed, he and his beast, until they were far from sight of man and only the great gray and purple and gold of the moors were around them.

The carpet under his bare feet seemed again to be the springy, pungent ling of Killorn. It was as if he smelled the sharp wild fragrance of it and felt the leaves brushing his ankles. It had been gray and windy, clouds rushed out of the west on a mounting gale. There was rain in the air and high overhead a single bird of prey had wheeled and looped on lonely wings. O almighty gods, how the wind had sung and cried to him, chilled his body with raw wet gusts and skirled in the dales and roared beneath the darkening heavens! And he had come down a long rocky slope into a wooded glen, a waterfall rushed and foamed along his path, white and green and angry black. He had sheltered in a mossy cave, lain and listened to the wind and the rain and the crystal, ringing waterfall, and when the weather cleared he had gotten up and gone home. There had been no quarry, but by Morna of Dagh, that failure meant more to him than all his victories since!

He picked up the pipe of the gods, where it lay with his armor, and turned it over and over in his hands. Old it was, dark with age, the pipes were of some nameless ironlike wood and the bag of a leather such as was never seen now. It was worn with the uncounted generations of Broinas who had had it, men made hard and stern by their frightful trust.

It had scattered the legions of the southerners who came conquering a hundred years ago and it had quelled the raiding savages from Norla and it had gone with one-eyed Alrigh and shouted down the walls of a city. And more than once, on this last dreadful march, it had saved the men of Killorn.

Now it was dead. The Piper of Killorn had fallen and the secret had perished with him and the folk it had warded were trapped like animals to die of hunger and pestilence in a strange land—*O Rhiach, Rhiach my father, come back from the dead, come back and put the pipe to your cold lips and play the war-song of Killorn!*

Kery blew in it for the hundredth time and only a hollow whistling sounded in the belly of the instrument. Not even a decent tune, he thought bitterly.

He couldn't stay indoors, he had to get out under the sky again or go mad. Slinging the pipe over his shoulder he went out the door and up a long stairway to the palace roof gardens.

They slept all around him, sleep and silence were heavy in the long corridors, it was as if he were the last man alive and walked alone through the ruins of the world. He came out on the roof and went over to the parapet and stood looking out.

The moon was near the zenith which meant, at this longitude, that it was somewhat less than half full and would dwindle as it sank westward. It rode serene in the dusky sky adding its pale glow to the diffused light which filled all the Twilight Lands and to the white pyre of the hidden sun. The city lay dark and silent under the sky, sleeping heavily, only the muted tramp of sentries and their ringing calls drifted up to Kery. Beyond the town burned the ominous red circle of the Ganasthi fires and he could see their tents and the black forms of their warriors.

They were settling down to a patient death watch. All the land had become silent waiting for Ryvan to die. It did not seem right that he should stand here among fragrant gardens and feel the warm western breeze on his face, not when steadfast Lluwynn and Boroda the Strong and gay young Kormak his comrade were ashen corpses with the women of Killorn keening over them. *O Killorn, Killorn, and the lake of sunset, have their ghosts gone home to you? Greet Morna for me, Kormak, whisper in the wind that I love her, tell her not to grieve.*

He grew aware that someone else was approaching, and turned with annoyance. But his mood lightened when he saw that it was Sathi. She was very fair as she walked toward him, young and lithe and beautiful, with the dark unbound hair floating about her.

"Are you up, Kery?" she asked, sitting down on the parapet beside him.

"Of course, my lady, or else you are dreaming," he smiled with a tired humor.

"Stupid question wasn't it?" She smiled back with a curving of closed lips that was lovely to behold. "But I am not feeling very bright just now."

"None of us are, my lady."

"Oh, forget that sort of address, Kery. I am too lonely as it is, sitting on a throne above all the world. Call me by my name, at least."

"You are very kind—Sathi."

"That is better." She smiled again, wistfully. "How you fought today! How you reaped them! What sort of a warrior are you, Kery, to ride wild bulls as if they were hests?"

"We of clan Broina have tricks. We feel things that other men do not seem to." Kery sat down beside her feeling the frozenness within him ease a little. "Aye, it can be lonely to wield power and you wonder if you are fit for it, not so? My father died in our first battle with the Ganasthi, and now I am the Broina, but who am I to lead my clan? I cannot even perform the first duty of my post."

"And what is that?" she asked.

He told her about the god-pipe. He showed it to her and gave her the tales of its singing. "You feel your flesh shiver and your bones begin to crumble, rocks dance and mountains groan and the gates of hell open before you, but now the pipes are forever silent, Sathi. No man knows how to play them."

"I heard of your music at that battle," she nodded gravely, "and wondered why it was not sounded again this time." Awe and fear were in her eyes, the hand that touched the scarred sack trembled a little. "And this is the pipe of Killorn! You cannot play it again? You cannot find out how? It would be the saving of Ryvan and of your own folk and perhaps of all the Twilight Lands, Kery.''

"I know. But what can I do? Who can understand the powers of heaven or unlock the doors of hell save Llugan Longsword himself?''

"I do not know. But Kery—I wonder. This pipe . . . Do you really think that gods and not men wrought it?''

"Who but a god could make such a thing, Sathi?''

"I do not know, I say. And yet—tell me, have you any idea of what the world is like in Killorn? Do you think it a flat plain with the sun hanging above, forever fixed in one spot?''

"Why I suppose so. Though we have met men in the southlands who claimed the world was a round ball and went about the sun in such a manner as always to turn the same face to it.''

"Yes, the wise men of Ryvan tell us that that must be the case. They have learned it by studying the fixed stars and those which wander. Those others are worlds like our own, they say, and the fixed stars are suns a very long ways off. And we have a very dim legend of a time once, long and long and long ago, when this world did not eternally face the sun either. It spun like a top so that each side of it had light and dark alternately.''

Kery knitted his brows trying to see that for himself. At last he nodded. "Well, it may have been. What of it?''

"The barbarians all think the world was born in flame and thunder many ages ago. But some of our thinkers believe that this creation was a catastrophe which destroyed the older world I speak of. There are dim legends and here and there we find very ancient ruins, cities greater than any we know today but buried and broken so long ago that even their building stones are almost weathered away. These thinkers believe that man grew mighty on this forgotten world which spun about itself, that his powers were like those we today call divine.

"Then something happened. We cannot imagine what, though a wise man once told me he believed all things attract each other—that is the reason why they fall to the ground, he said—and that another world swept so close to ours that its pull stopped the spinning and yanked the moon closer than it had been.''

Kery clenched his fist. "It could be,'' he murmured. "It could well be. For what happens to an unskillful rider when his hest stops all at once? He goes flying over its head, right? Even so, this braking of the world would have brought earthquakes greater than we can imagine, quakes that leveled everything!''

"You have a quick wit. That is what this man told me. At any rate, only a very few people and animals lived and nothing remained of their great works save legends. In the course of many ages, man and beasts alike changed, the beasts more than man who can make his own surroundings to suit. Life spread from the Day Lands through the Twilight Zone. Plants got so they could use what little light we have here. Finally even the Dark Lands were invaded by the pallid growths which can live there. Animals followed and man came after the animals until today things are as you see.''

She turned wide and serious eyes on him. ''Could not this pipe have been made in the early days by a man who knew some few of the ancient secrets? No god but a man even as you, Kery. And what one man can make another can understand!''

Hope rose in him and sagged again. ''How?'' he asked dully. And then, seeing the tears glimmer in her eyes: ''Oh, it may all be true. I will try my best. But I do not even know where to begin.''

''Try,'' she whispered. ''Try!''

''But do not tell anyone that the pipe is silent, Sathi. Perhaps I should not even have told you.''

''Why not? I am your friend and the friend of your folk. I would we had all the tribes of Killorn here.''

''Jonan is not,'' he said grimly.

''Jonan—he is a harsh man, yes. But . . .''

''He does not like us. I do not know why but he doesn't.''

''He is a strange one,'' she admitted. ''He is not even of Ryvanian birth, he is from Guria, a city which we conquered long ago, though of course its people have long been full citizens of the empire. He wants to marry me, did you know?'' She smiled. ''I could not help laughing for he is so stiff. One would soon wed an iron cuirass.''

''Aye—wed—'' Kery fell silent, and there was a dream in his gaze as he looked over the hills.

''What are you thinking of?'' she asked after a while.

''Oh—home,'' he said. ''I was wondering if I would ever see Killorn again.''

She leaned over closer to him. One long black lock brushed his hand and he caught the faint fragrance of her. ''Is it so fair a land?'' she asked softly.

''No,'' he said. ''It is harsh and gray and lonely. Storm winds sweep in and the sea roars on rocky beaches and men grow gnarled with wrestling life from the stubborn soil. But there is space and sky and freedom, there are the little huts and the great halls, the chase and the games and the old songs around leaping fires, and—well—'' His voice trailed off.

"You left a woman behind, didn't you?" she murmured gently.

He nodded. "Morna of Dagh, she of the sun-bright tresses and the fair young form and the laughter that was like rain showering on thirsty ground. We were very much in love."

"But she did not come too?"

"No. So many wanted to come that the unwed had to draw lots and she lost. Nor could I stay behind for I was heir to the Broina and the god-pipes would be mine someday." He laughed, a harsh sound like breaking iron. "You see how much good that has done me!"

"But even so—you could have married her before leaving?"

"No. Such hasty marriage is against clan law and Morna would not break it." Kery shrugged. "So we wandered out of the land, and I have not seen her since. But she will wait for me and I for her. We'll wait till—till—" He had half raised his hand but as he saw again the camp of the besiegers it fell helplessly to his lap.

"And you would not stay?" Sathi's tones were so low he had to bend his head close to hear. "Even if somehow Ryvan threw back its foes and valiant men were badly needed and could rise to the highest honors of the empire, you would not stay here?"

For a moment Kery sat motionless, wrapping himself about his innermost being. He had some knowledge of women. There had been enough of them along the dusty way, brief encounters and a fading memory.

His soul had room only for the bright image of one unforgotten girl. It was plain enough what this woman, who was young and beautiful and a queen, was saying and he would not ordinarily have hung back.

Especially when the folk of Killorn were still strangers in a camp of allies who did not trust them very far, when Killorn needed every friend it could find. And the Broina were an elvish clan who had never let overly many scruples hold them.

Only—only he liked Sathi as a human being. She was brave and generous and wise and she was, really, so pitiably young. She had had so little chance to learn the hard truths of living in the loneliness of the imperium and only a scoundrel would hurt her.

She sighed, ever so faintly, and moved back a little. Kery thought he saw her stiffening. One does not reject the offer of a queen.

"Sathi," he said, "for you, perhaps, even a man of Killorn might forget his home."

She half turned to him, hesitating, unsure of herself and him. He took her in his arms and kissed her.

"Kery, Kery, Kery—" she whispered, and her lips stole back toward his.

He felt rather than heard a footfall and turned with the animal alertness of the barbarian. Jonan stood watching them.

"Pardon me," said the general harshly. His countenance was strained. Then suddenly, "Your majesty! This savage mauling you . . ."

Sathi lifted a proud dark head. "This is the prince consort of Imperial Ryvan," she said haughtily. "Conduct yourself accordingly. You may go."

Jonan snarled and lifted an arm. Kery saw the armed men step from behind the tall flowering hedges and his sword came out with a rasp of steel.

"Guards!" screamed Sathi.

The men closed in. Kery's blade whistled against one shield. Another came from each side. Pikeshafts thudded against his bare head—

He fell, toppling into a roaring darkness while they clubbed him again. Down and down and down, whirling into a chasm of night. Dimly, just before blankness came, he saw the white beard and the mask-like face of the prince from Ganasth.

VI

It was a long and hard ride before they stopped and Kery almost fell from the hest to which they had bound him.

"I should have thought that you would soon awake," said the man from Ganasth. He had a soft voice and spoke Aluardian well enough. "I am sorry. It is no way to treat a man, carrying him like a sack of meal. Here . . ." He poured a glass of wine and handed it to the barbarian. "From now on you shall ride erect."

Kery gulped thirstily and felt a measure of strength flowing back. He looked around him.

They had gone steadily eastward and were now camped near a ruined farmhouse. A fire was crackling and one of the score or so of enemy warriors was roasting a haunch of meat over it. The rest stood leaning on their weapons and their cold amber eyes never left the two prisoners.

Sathi stood near bleak-faced Jonan and her great dark eyes never left Kery. He smiled at her shakily and with a little sob she took a step toward him. Jonan pulled her back roughly.

"Kery," she whispered. "Kery, are you well?"

"As well as could be expected," he said wryly. Then to the Ganasthian prince, "What is this, anyway? I woke up to find myself joggling eastward and that is all I know. What is your purpose?"

"We have several," answered the alien. He sat down near the fire pulling his cloak around him against the chill that blew out of the glooming east. His impassive face watched the dance of flames as if they told him something.

Kery sat down as well, stretching his long legs easily. He might as well relax he thought. They had taken his sword and his pipes and they were watching him like hungry beasts. There was never a chance to fight.

"Come, Sathi," he waved to the girl. "Come over here by me."

"No!" snapped Jonan.

"Yes, if she wants to," said the Ganasthian mildly.

"But that filthy barbarian . . ."

"None of us have washed recently." The gentle tones were suddenly like steel. "Do not forget, General, that I am Mongku of Ganasth and heir apparent to the Throne."

"And I rescued you from the city," snapped the man. "If it weren't for me you might well be dead at the hands of that red savage."

"That will do," said Mongku. "Come over here and sit by us, Sathi."

His guardsmen stirred, unacquainted with the Ryvanian tongue but sensing the clash of wills. Jonan shrugged sullenly and stalked over to sit opposite them. Sathi fled to Kery and huddled against him. He comforted her awkwardly. Over her shoulder he directed a questioning look at Mongku.

"I suppose you deserve some explanation," said the Dark Lander. "Certainly Sathi must know the facts." He leaned back on one elbow and began to speak in an almost dreamy tone.

"When Ryvan conquered Guria, many generations ago, some of its leaders were proscribed. They fled eastward and so eventually wandered into the Dark Lands and came to Ganasth. It was then merely a barbarian town but the Gurians became advisors to the king and began teaching the people all the arts of civilization. It was their hope one day to lead the hosts of Ganasth against Ryvan, partly for revenge and partly for the wealth and easier living to be found in the Twilight Lands. Life is hard and bitter in the eternal night, Sathi. It is ever a struggle merely to keep alive. Can you wonder so very much that we are spilling into your gentler climate and your richer soul?

"Descendants of the Gurians have remained aristocrats in Ganasth. But Jonan's father conceived the idea of moving back with a few of his friends to work from within against the day of conquest. At that time we were bringing our neighbors under our heel and looked already to the time when we should move against the Twilight Lands. At any rate he did this and nobody suspected that he was aught but a newcomer from another part of Ryvan's empire. His son, Jonan, entered the army and, being shrewd and strong and able, finally reached the high post which you yourself bestowed on him, Sathi."

"Oh, no—Jonan—" She shuddered against Kery.

"Naturally when we invaded at last he had to fight against us, and for fear of prisoners revealing his purpose very few Ganasthians know who he really is. A risk was involved, yes. But it is convenient to have a general of the enemy on your side! Jonan is one of the major reasons for our success.

"Now we come to myself, a story which is very simply told. I was captured and it was Jonan's duty as a citizen of Ganasth to rescue his prince—quite apart from the fact that I do know his identity and torture might have loosened my tongue. He might have effected my escape easily enough without attracting notice, but other factors intervened. For one thing, there was this barbarian alliance, and especially that very dangerous new weapon they had which he had observed in use. We clearly could not risk its being turned on us. Indeed we almost had to capture it. Then, too, Jonan is desirous of marrying you, Sathi, and I must say that it seems a good idea. With you as a hostage Ryvan will be more amenable. Later you can return as nominal ruler of your city, a vassal of Ganasth, and that will make our conquest easier to administer. Though not too easy, I fear. The Twilight Landers will not much like being transported into the Dark Lands to make room for us."

Sathi began to cry, softly and hopelessly. Kery stroked her hair and said nothing.

Mongku sat up and reached for the chunk of meat his soldier handed him. "So Jonan and his few trusty men let me out of prison and we went up to the palace roof after you, who had been seen going that way shortly before. Listening a little while to your conversation we saw that we had had the good luck to get that hell-pipe of the north, too. So we took you. Jonan was for killing you, Kery my friend, but I pointed out that you could be useful in many ways such as a means for making Sathi listen to reason. Threats against you will move her more than against herself, I think."

"You crawling louse," said Kery tonelessly.

Mongku shrugged. "I'm not such a bad sort but war is war and I have seen the folk of Ganasth hungering too long to have much sympathy for a bunch of fat Twilight Landers.

"At any rate, we slipped out of the city unobserved. Jonan could not remain for when the queen and I were both missing, and he responsible for both, it would be plain to many whom to accuse. Moreover, Sathi's future husband is too valuable to lose in a fight. And I myself would like to report to my father the king as to how well the war has gone.

"So we are bound for Ganasth."

There was a long silence while the fire leaped and crackled and the stars blinked far overhead. Finally Sathi shook herself and sat erect and said in a small hard voice, "Jonan, I swear you will die if you wed me. I promise you that."

The officer did not reply. He sat brooding into the dusk with a look of frozen contempt and weariness on his face.

Sathi huddled back against Kery's side and soon she slept.

On and on.

They were out of the Twilight Lands altogether now. Night had fallen on them and still they rode eastward. They were tough, these Ganasthi, they stopped only for sleep and quickly gulped food and a change of mounts and the miles reeled away behind them.

Little was said on the trail. They were too tired at the halts and seemingly in too much of a hurry while riding. With Sathi there could only be a brief exchange of looks, a squeeze of hands, and a few whispered words with the glowing-eyed men of Ganasth looking on. She was a gallant girl, thought Kery. The cruel trek told heavily on her but she rode without complaint—she was still queen of Ryvan!

Ryvan, Ryvan, how long could it hold out now in the despair of its loss? Kery thought that Red Bram might be able to seize the mastery and whip the city into fighting pitch but warfare by starvation was not to the barbarians' stomachs. They could not endure a long siege.

But what lay ahead for him and her and the captured weapon of the gods?

Never had he been in so grim a country. It was dark, eternally dark, night and cold and the brilliant frosty stars lay over the land, shadows and snow and a whining wind that ate and ate and gnawed its way through furs and flesh down to the bone. The moon got fuller here than it ever did over the Twilight Belt, its chill white radiance spilled on reaching snowfields and glittered like a million pinpoint stars fallen frozen to earth.

He saw icy plains and tumbled black chasms and fanged crags sheathed in glaciers. The ground rang with cold. Cramped and shuddering in his sleeping bag, he heard the thunder of frost-split rocks, the sullen boom and rumble of avalanches, now and again the faint far despairing howl of prowling wild beasts of prey.

"How can anyone live here?" he asked Mongku once. "The land is dead. It froze to death ten thousand years ago."

"It is a little warmer in the region of Ganasth," said the prince. "Volcanoes and hot springs. And there is a great sea which has never frozen over. It has fish, and animals that live off them, and men that live off the animals. But in truth only the broken and hunted of man can ever have come here. We are the disinherited and we are claiming no more than our rightful share of life in returning to the Twilight Lands."

He added thoughtfully: "I have been looking at that weapon of yours, Kery. I think I know the principle of its working. Sound does many strange things and there are even sounds too low or too high for the human ear to catch. A singer who holds the right note long enough can make a wine glass vibrate in sympathy until it shatters. We built a bridge once, over Thunder Gorge near Ganasth, but the wind blowing between the rock walls seemed to make it shake in a certain rhythm that finally broke it. Oh, yes, if the proper sympathetic notes can be found much may be done.

"I don't know what hell's music that pipe is supposed to sound. But I found that the reeds can be tautened or loosened and that the shape of the bag can be subtly altered by holding it in the right way. Find the proper combination and I can well believe that even the small noise made with one man's breath can kill and break and crumble."

He nodded his gaunt half-human face in the ruddy blaze of fire. "Aye, I'll find the notes, Kery, and then the pipe will play for Ganasth."

The barbarian shuddered with more than the cold, searching wind. Gods, gods, if he did—if the pipes should sound the final dirge of Killorn!

For a moment he had a wild desire to fling himself on Mongku, rip out the prince's throat and kill the score of enemy soldiers with his hands. But no—no—it wouldn't do. He would die before he had well started and Sathi would be alone in the Dark Lands.

He looked at her, sitting very quiet near the fire. The wavering light seemed to wash her fair young form in blood. She gave him a tired and hopeless smile.

Brave girl, brave girl, wife for a warrior in all truth. But there was the pipe and there was Killorn and there was Morna waiting for him to come home.

They were nearing Ganasth, he knew. They had ridden past springs that seethed and bubbled in the snow, seen the red glare of volcanos on the jagged horizon, passed fields of white fungus-growths which the Dark Landers cultivated. Soon the iron gates would clash shut on him and what hope would there be then?

He lay back in his sleeping bag trying to think. He had to escape. Somehow he must escape with the pipe of the gods. But if he tried and went down with a dozen spears in him there was an end of all hope.

The wind blew, drifting snow across the sleepers. Two men stood guard and their strangely glowing eyes never left the captives. They could see in this realm of shadows where he was half blind. They could hunt him down like an animal.

What to do? What to do?

On the road he went with his hands tied behind him, his ankles lashed to the stirrups, and his hest's bridle tied to the pommel of another man's saddle. No chance of escape there. But one must get up after sleep.

He rolled close to Sathi's quiet form as if he were merely turning over in slumber. His lips brushed against the leather bag and he wished it were her face.

"Sathi," he whispered as quietly as he could. "Sathi, don't move, but listen to me."

"Aye," her voice drifted back under the wind and the cold. "Aye, darling."

"I am going to make a break for it when we get up. Help me if you can but don't risk getting hurt. I don't think we can both get away but wait for me in Ganasth!"

She lay silent for a long while. Then, "As you will, Kery. And whatever comes, I love you."

He should have replied but the words stuck in his throat. He rolled back and, quite simply, went to sleep.

A spear butt prodding his side awoke him. He yawned mightily and sat up, loosening his bag around him, tensing every muscle in his body.

"The end of this ride will see us in the city," Mongku said.

Kery rose slowly, gauging distances. A guardsman stood beside him, spear loose in one hand. The rest were scattered around the camp or huddled close to the fire. The hests were a darker shadow bunched on the fringes.

Kery wrenched the spear of the nearest man loose, swinging one booted foot into his belly. He brought the weapon around in a smashing arc, cracking the heavy butt into another's jaw and rammed the head into the throat of a third. Even as he stabbed he was plunging into motion.

A Ganasthian yelled and thrust at him. Sathi threw herself on the shaft, pulling it down. Kery leaped for the hests.

There were two men on guard there. One drew a sword and hewed at the northerner. The keen blade slashed through heavy tunic and undergarments, cutting his shoulder—but not too badly. He came under the fellow's guard and smashed a fist into his jaw. Seizing the weapon he whirled and hacked at the other Dark Lander, beating down the soldier's ax and cutting him across the face.

The rest of the camp was charging at him. Kery bent and cut the hobbles of the hest beside him. A shower of flung spears rained about him as he sprang to the saddleless back. Twisting his left hand into the long mane he kicked the frightened beast in the flanks and plunged free.

Two Ganasthi quartered across his trail. He bent low over the hest's back, spurring the mount with the point of his sword. As he rode down on them he hewed at one and saw him fall with a scream. The other stumbled out of the path of his reckless charge.

"Hai-ah!" shouted Kery.

He clattered away over the stony ice fields toward the shelter of the dark hills looming to the north. Spears and arrows whistled on his trail and he heard, dimly, the shouts of men and the thud of pursuing hoofs.

He was alone in a land of foes, a land of freezing cold where he could scarce see half a mile before him, a land of hunger and swords. They were after him and it would take all the hunter's skill he had learned in Killorn and all the warrior's craftiness taught by the march to evade them. And after that—Ganasth!

VII

The city loomed dark before him reaching with stony fingers for the ever-glittering stars. Of black stone it was, mountainous walls ringing in the narrow streets and the high gaunt houses. A city of night, city of darkness. Kery shivered.

Behind the city rose a mountain, a deeper shadow against the frosty dark of heaven. It was a volcano and from its mouth a red flame flapped in the keening wind. Sparks and smoke streamed over Ganasth. There was a hot smell of sulphur in the bitter air. The fire added a faint blood-like tinge to the cold glitter of moonlight and starlight on the snowfields.

There was a highway leading through the great main gates and the glowing-eyed people of the Dark Lands were trafficking along it. Kery strode directly on his way, through the crowds and ever closer to the city.

He wore the ordinary fur and leather dress of the country that he had stolen from an outlying house. The parka hood was drawn low to shadow his alien features. He went armed, as most men did, sword belted to his waist, and because he went quietly and steadily nobody paid any attention to him.

But if he were discovered and the hue and cry went up that would be the end of his quest.

A dozen sleeps of running and hiding in the wild hills, shivering with cold and hunger, hunting animals which could see where he was blind, and ever the men of Ganasth on his trail—it would all go for naught. He would die and Sathi would be bound to a hateful pledge and Killorn would in time be the home of strangers.

He must finally have shaken off pursuit, he thought. Ranging through the hills he had found no sign of the warriors who had scoured them before. So he had proceeded toward the city on his wild and hopeless mission.

To find a woman and a weapon in the innermost citadel of a foe whose language even was unknown to him—truly the gods must be laughing!

He was close to the gates now. They loomed over him like giants, and the passage through the city wall was a tunnel. Soldiers stood on guard and Kery lowered his head.

Traffic streamed through. No one gave him any heed. But it was black as hell in the tunnel and only a Ganasthian could find his way. Blindly Kery walked ahead, bumping into people, praying that none of the angry glances he got would unmask his pretense.

When he came out into the street the breath was sobbing in his lungs. He pushed on down its shadowy length feeling the wind that howled between the buildings cold on his cheeks.

But where to go now, where to go?

Blindly he struck out toward the heart of town. Most rulers preferred to live at the center.

The Ganasthi were a silent folk. Men stole past in the gloom, noiseless save for the thin snow scrunching under their feet. Crowds eddied dumbly through the great market squares, buying and selling with a gesture or a whispered syllable. City of half-seen ghosts . . . Kery felt more than half a ghost himself, shade of a madman flitting hopelessly to the citadel of the king of hell.

He found the place at last, more by blind blundering through the narrow twisting streets than anything else. Drawing himself into the shadow of a building across the way he stood looking at it, weighing his chances.

There was a high wall around the palace. He could see only its roof but it seemed to be set well back. He spied a gate not too far off, apparently a secondary entrance for it was small and only one sentry guarded it.

Now! By all the gods, now!

For a moment his courage failed him, and he stood sweating and shivering and licking dry lips. It wasn't fear of death. He had lived too long with the dark gods as comrade—he had but little hope of escaping alive from these nighted hills. But he thought of the task before him, and the immensity of it and the ruin that lay in his failure, and his heartbeat nearly broke through his ribs.

What, after all, could he hope to do? What was his plan, anyway? He had come to Ganasth on a wild and hopeless journey, scarcely thinking one sleep ahead of his death-dogged passage. Only now—now he must reach a decision, and he couldn't.

With a snarl, Kery started across the street.

No one else was in sight, there was little traffic in this part of town, but at any moment someone might round either of the corners about which the way twisted and see what he was doing. He had to be fast.

He walked up to the sentry, who gave him a haughty glance. There was little suspicion in it, for what had anyone to fear in the hearth of Ganasth the mighty?

Kery drew his sword and lunged.

The sentry yelled and brought down his pike. Kery batted the shaft aside even as he went by it. His sword flashed, stabbing for the other man's throat. With a dreadful gurgling the guard stumbled and went clattering to earth.

Now quickly!

Kery took the man's helmet and put it on. His own long locks were fair enough to pass for Ganasthian at a casual glance, and the visor would hide his eyes. Shedding his parka he slipped on the bloodstained tunic and the cloak over that. Taking the pike in hand he went through the gate.

Someone cried out and feet clattered in the street and along the garden paths before him. The noise had been heard. Kery looked wildly around at the pale bushes of fungus that grew here under the moon. He crawled between the fleshy fronds of the nearest big one and crouched behind it.

Guardsmen ran down the path. The moonlight blinked like cold silver on their spearheads. Kery wriggled on his stomach through the garden of fungus, away from the trail but toward the black palace.

Lying under a growth at the edge of a frost-silvered expanse of open ground he scouted the place he must next attack. The building was long and rambling, seemingly four stories high, built of polished black marble. There were two guards in sight, standing warily near a door. The rest must have run off to investigate the alarm.

Two—

Kery rose, catching his stride even as he did, and dashed from the garden toward them. The familiar helmet and tunic might assure them for the instant he needed but he had to run lest they notice.

"Vashtung!" shouted one of the men.

His meaning was plain enough. Kery launched his pike at the other, who still looked a bit uncertain. It was an awkward throwing weapon. It brought him down wounded in a clatter of metal. The other roared and stepped forth to meet the assault.

Kery's sword was out and whirring. He chopped at the pikeshaft that jabbed at him, caught his blade in the tough wood and pushed the weapon aside. As he came up face to face he kneed the Ganasthian with savage precision.

The other man reached up and grabbed his ankle and pulled him down. Kery snarled, the rage of battle rising in him. It was as if the pipes of Broina skirled in his head. Fear and indecision were gone. He got his hands on the soldier's neck and wrenched. Even as the spine snapped he was rising again to his feet.

He picked up sword and pike and ran up the stairs and through the door. Now—Sathi! He had one ally in this house of hell.

A long and silent corridor, lit by dim red cressets, stretched before him. He raced down it and his boots woke hollow echoes that paced him through its black length.

Two men in the dress of servants stood in the room into which he burst. They stared wildly at him. He stabbed one but the other fled screaming. He'd give the alarm but there was no time to chase. No time!

A staircase wound up toward the second story and Kery took

it, flying up three steps at a time. Dimly, below him, he heard the frantic tattoo of a giant gong, the alarm signal, but the demon fury was fire and ice in his blood.

Another servant gaped at him. Kery seized him with a rough hand and held the sword at his throat.

"Sathi," he snarled. "Sathi—Ryvan—Sathi!"

The Ganasthian gibbered in a panic that seemed weird with his frozen face. Kery grinned viciously and pinked him with the blade. "Sathi!" he said urgently. "Sathi of Ryvan!"

Shaking, the servant led the way, Kery urging him ungently to greater speed. They went up another flight of stairs and down a hallway richly hung with furs and tapestries. Passing lackeys gaped at them and some ran. Gods, they'd bring all Ganasth down on his neck!

Before a closed door stood a guardsman. Kery slugged the servant when he pointed at that entrance and ran to meet this next barrier. The guard yelled and threw up his pike.

Kery's own long-shafted weapon clashed forth. They stabbed at each other, seeking the vitals. The guardsman had a cuirass and Kery's point grazed off the metal. He took a ripping slash in his left arm. The Ganasthian bored in, wielding his pike with skill, beating aside Kery's guard.

VIII

The Twilight Lander dropped his own weapon, seized the other shaft in both hands, and wrenched. Grimly the Ganasthian hung on. Kery worked his way in closer. Suddenly he released the shaft, almost fell against his enemy, and drew the Dark Lander's sword. The short blade flashed and the sentry fell.

The door was barred. He beat on it frantically, hearing the clatter of feet coming up the stairs, knowing that a thunderstorm of hurled weapons was in its way. "Sathi!" he cried. "Sathi, it is Kery, let me in!"

The first soldiers appeared down at the end of the corridor. Kery threw himself against the door. It opened, and he plunged through and slammed down the bolt.

Sathi stood there and wonder was in her eyes. "Oh, Kery," she breathed, "Kery, you came . . ."

"No time," he rasped. "Where is the pipe of Killorn?"

She fought for calmness. "Mongku has it," she said. "His chambers are on the next floor, above these—"

The door banged and groaned as men threw their weight against it.

Sathi took his hand and led him into the next room. A fire

burned low in the hearth. "I thought it out, against the time you might come," she said. "The only way out is up that chimney. It should take us to the roof and thence we can go down again."

"Oh, well done, lass!" With a sweep of the poker Kery scattered the logs and coals out on the carpet while Sathi barred the door into the next room. Drawing a deep breath the Killorner went into the fireplace, braced feet and back against the sides of the flue and began to clumb up.

Smoke swirled in the chimney. He gasped for breath and his lungs seemed on fire. Night in here, utter dark and choking of fouled air. His heart roared and his strength ebbed from him. Up and up and up, hitch yourself still further up.

"Kery." Her voice came low, broken with coughing. "Kery—I can't. I'm slipping—"

"Hang on!" he gasped. "Here. Reach up. My belt—"

He felt the dragging weight catch at him, there in the smoke-thickened dark, and drew a grim breath and edged himself further, up and up and up.

And out!

He crawled from the chimney and fell to the roof with the world reeling about him and a rushing of darkness in his head. His tormented lungs sucked the bitter air. He sobbed and the tears washed the soot from his eyes. He stood up and helped Sathi to her feet.

She leaned against him, shuddering with strain and with the wind that cried up here under the flickering stars. He looked about, seeking a way down again. Yes, over there, a doorway opening on a small terrace. Quickly now.

They crawled over the slanting, ice-slippery roof, helping each other where they could, fighting a way to the battlement until Kery's grasping fingers closed on its edge and he heaved both of them up onto it.

"Come on!" he snapped. "They'll be behind us any moment now."

"What to do?" she murmured. "What to do?"

"Get the pipes!" he growled, and the demon blood of Broina began to boil in him again. "Get the pipes and destroy them if we can do nothing else."

They went through the door and down a narrow staircase and came to the fourth floor of the palace.

Sathi looked up and down the long empty hallway. "I have been up here before," she said with a coolness that was good to hear. "Let me see—yes, this way, I think—" As they trotted down the hollow length of corridor she said further: "They treated me fairly well here, indeed with honor though I was a prisoner. But oh, Kery, It was like sunlight to see you again!''

He stopped and kissed her, briefly, wondering if he would ever have a chance to do it properly. Most likely not but she would be a good companion on hell-road.

They came into a great antechamber. Kery had his sword out, the only weapon left to him, but no one was in sight. All the royal guards must be out hunting him. He grinned wolfishly and stepped to the farther door.

"Kery—" Sathi huddled close against him. "Kery, do we dare? It may be death—"

A great, richly furnished suite of chambers, dark and still, lay before him. He padded through the first, looking right and left like a questing animal, and into the next.

Two men stood there, talking—Jonan and Mongku.

They saw him and froze, for he was a terrible sight, bloody, black with smoke, fury cold and bitter-blue in his eyes. He grinned, a white flash of teeth in his sooted face, and drew his sword and stalked forward.

"So you have come," said Mongku quietly.

"Aye," said Kery. "Where is the pipe of Killorn?"

Jonan thrust forward, drawing the sword at his belt. "I will hold him, prince," he said. "I will carve him into very bits for you."

Kery met his advance in a clash of steel. They circled, stiff-legged and wary, looking for an opening. There was death here. Sathi knew starkly that only one of those two would leave this room.

Jonan lunged in, stabbing, and Kery skipped back. The officer was better in handling these shortswords than he who was used to the longer blades of the north. He brought his own weapon down sharply, deflecting the thrust. Jonan parried, and then it was bang and crash, thrust and leap and hack with steel clamoring and sparking. The glaives hissed and screamed, the fighters breathed hoarsely and there was murder in their eyes.

Jonan ripped off his cloak with his free hand and flapped it in Kery's face. The northerner hacked out, blinded, and Jonan whipped the cloth around to tangle his blade. Then he rushed in, stabbing. Kery fell to one knee and took the thrust on his helmet, letting it glide off. Reaching up he got Jonan around the waist and pulled the man down on him.

They rolled over, growling and biting and gouging. Jonan clung to his sword and Kery to that wrist. They crashed into a wall and struggled there.

Kery got one leg around Jonan's waist and pulled himself up on the man's chest. He got a two-handed grasp on the enemy's sword arm, slipped the crook of one elbow around, and broke the bone.

Jonan screamed. Kery reached over. He took the sword from his loosening fingers and buried it in Jonan's breast.

He stood up then, trembling with fury, and looked at the pipes of Killorn.

It was almost as if Mongku's expressionless face smiled. The Ganasthian held the weapon cradled in his arms, the mouthpiece near his lips. He nodded. "I got it to working," he said. "In truth it is a terrible thing. Who holds it might well hold the world someday."

Kery stood waiting, the sword hanging limp in one hand.

"Yes," said Mongku. "I am going to play it."

Kery started across the floor—and Mongku blew.

The sound roared forth, wild, cruel, seizing him and shaking him, ripping at nerve and sinew. Bone danced in his skull and night shouted in his brain. He fell to the ground, feeling the horrible jerking of his muscles, seeing the world swim and blur before him.

The pipes screamed. Goodnight, Kery, goodnight, goodnight! It is the dirge of the world he is playing, the coronach of Killorn, it is the end of all things skirling in your body—

Sathi crept forth. She was behind the player, the hell-tune did not strike her so deeply, but even as his senses blurred toward death Kery saw how she fought for every step, how the bronze lamp almost fell from her hand. Mongku had forgotten her. He was playing doom, watching Kery die and noting how the music worked.

Sathi struck him from behind. He fell, dropping the pipes, and turned dazed eyes up to her. She struck him again and again.

Then she fled over to Kery and cradled his head in her arms and sobbed with the horror of it and with the need for haste. "Oh, quickly, quickly, beloved, we have to flee, they will be here now—I hear them in the hallway, come—"

Kery sat up. His head was ringing and thumping, his muscles burned and weakness was like an iron hand on him. But there was that which had to be done and it gave him strength from some forgotten wellspring. He rose on shaky legs and went over and picked up the bagpipe of the gods.

"No," he said.

"Kery . . ."

"We will not flee," he said. "I have a song to play."

She saw the cold remote mask of his face. He was not Kery now of the ready laugh and the reckless bravery and the wistful memories of a lost homestead. He had become something else with the pipe in his hands, something which stood stern and somber and apart from man. There seemed to be ghosts in the vast shadowy room, the blood of his fathers who had been Pipers of Killorn, and he was the guardian now. She shrank against him for protection. There was a small charmed circle which the music did not enter but it was a stranger she stood beside.

Carefully Kery lifted the mouthpiece to his lips and blew. He felt the vibration tremble under his feet. The walls wavered before his eyes as unheard notes shivered the air. He himself heard no more than the barbarian screaming of the war music he had always known but saw death riding out.

A troop of guardsmen burst through the door—halted, stared at the tall piper, and then howled in terror and pain.

Kery played. And as he played Killorn rose before him. He saw the reach of gray windswept moors, light glimmering on high colds tarns, birds winging in a sky of riven clouds. Space and loneliness and freedom, a hard open land of stern and bitter beauty, the rocks which had shaped his bones and the soil which had nourished his flesh. He stood by the great lake of sunset, storms swept in over it, rain and lightning, the waves dashed themselves to angry death on a beach of grinding stones.

He strode forward, playing, and the soldiers of Ganasth died before him. The walls of the palace trembled, hangings fell to the shuddering floor, the building groaned as the demon music sought and found resonance.

He played them a song of the chase, the long wild hunt over the heath, breath gasping in hot lungs and blood shouting in the ears, running drunk with wind after the prey that fled and soared. He played them fire and comradeship and the little huts crouched low under the mighty sky. And the walls cracked around him. Pillars trembled and broke. The roof began to cave in and everywhere they died about him.

He played war, the skirl of pipes and the shout of men, clamor of metal, tramp of feet and hoofs, and the fierce blink of light on weapons. He sang them up an army that rode over the rim of the world with swords aflame and arrows like rain and the whole building tumbled to rubble even as he walked out of it.

Tenderly, dreamily, he played of Morna the fair, Morna who had stood with him on the edge of the lake where it is forever sunset, listening to the chuckle of small wavelets and looking west to the pyre of red and gold and dusky purple, the eyes and the lips and the hair of Morna and what she and he had whispered to each other on that quiet shore. But there was death in that song.

The ground began to shake under Ganasth. There is but little strength in the lungs of one man and yet when that strikes just the right notes, and those small pushes touch off something else far down in the depths of the earth, the world will tremble. The Dark Landers rioted in a more than human fear, in the blind panic which the pipes sang to them.

The gates were closed before him, but Kery played them down. Then he turned and faced the city and played it a song of the wrath of the gods. He played them up rain and cold and scouring wind, glaciers marching from the north in a blind whirl of snow, lightning aflame in the heavens and cities ground to dust. He played them a world gone crazy, sundering continents and tidal waves marching over the shores and mountains flaming into a sky of rain and fire. He played them whirlwinds and dust storms and the relentless sleety blast from the north. He sang them ruin and death and the sun burning out to darkness.

When he ceased, and he and Sathi left the half-shattered city, none stirred to follow. None dared who were still alive. It seemed to the two of them, as they struck out over the snowy plains, that the volcano behind was beginning to grumble and throw its flames a little higher.

IV

He stood alone in the gardens of Ryvan's palace looking out over the city. Perhaps he thought of the hard journey back from the Dark Lands. Perhaps he thought of the triumphant day when they had sneaked back into the fastness and then gone out again, the Piper of Killorn and Red Bram roaring in his wake to smash the siege and scatter the armies of Ganasth and send the broken remnants fleeing homeward. Perhaps he thought of the future—who knew? Sathi approached him quietly, wondering what to say.

He turned and smiled at her, the old merry smile she knew but with something else behind it. He had been the war-god of Killorn and that left its mark on a man.

"So it all turned out well," he said.

"Thanks to you, Kery," she answered softly.

"Oh, not so well at that," he decided. "There were too many good men who fell, too much laid waste. It will take a hundred years before all this misery is forgotten."

"But we reached what we strove for," she said. "Ryvan is

safe, all the Twilight Lands are. You folk of Killorn have the land you needed. Isn't that enough to achieve?''

"I suppose so." Kery stirred restlessly. "I wonder how it stands in Killorn now?"

"And you still want to return?" She tried to hold back the tears. "This is a fair land, and you are great in it, all you people from the north. You would go back to—that?"

"Indeed," he said. "All you say is true. We would be fools to return." He scowled. "It may well be that in the time we yet have to wait most of us will find life better here and decide to stay. But not I, Sathi. I am just that kind of fool."

"This land needs you, Kery. I do."

He tilted her chin, smiling half sorrowfully into her eyes. "Best you forget, dear," he said. "I will not stay here once the chance comes to return."

She shook her head blindly, drew a deep breath, and said with a catch in her voice, "Then stay as long as you can, Kery."

"Do you really mean that?" he asked slowly.

She nodded.

"You are a fool too," he said. "But a very lovely fool."

He took her in his arms.

Presently she laughed a little and said, not without hope, "I'll have a while to change your mind, Kery. And I'll try to do it. I'll try!"

THE WERE-WOLF

By Clemence Housman

The great farm hall was ablaze with the firelight, and noisy with laughter and talk and many-sounding work. None could be idle but the very young and the very old—little Rol, who was hugging a puppy, and old Trella, whose palsied hand fumbled over her knitting. The early evening had closed in, and the farm servants had come in from the outdoor work and assembled in the ample hall, which had space for scores of workers. Several of the men were engaged in carving, and to these were yielded the best place and light; others made or repaired fishing tackle and harness, and a great seine net occupied three pairs of hands. Of the women, most were sorting and mixing eider feather and chopping straw of the same. Looms were there, though not in present use, but three wheels whirred emulously, and the finest and swiftest thread of the three ran between the fingers of the house mistress. Near her were some children, busy, too, plaiting wicks for candles and lamps. Each group of workers had a lamp in its centre, and those farthest from the fire had extra warmth from two braziers filled with glowing wood embers, replenished now and again from the generous hearth. But the flicker of the great fire was manifest to remotest corners, and prevailed beyond the limits of the lesser lights.

Little Rol grew tired of his puppy, dropped it incontinently, and made an onslaught on Tyr, the old wolfhound, who basked, dozing, whimpering and twitching in his hunting dreams. Prone went Rol beside Tyr, his young arms round the shaggy neck, his curls against the black jowl. Tyr gave a perfunctory lick, and stretched with a sleepy sigh. Rol growled and rolled and shoved invitingly, but could gain nothing from the old dog but placid toleration and a half-observant blink. "Take that, then!" said Rol, indignant at this ignoring of his advances, and sent the puppy sprawling against the dignity that disdained him as playmate. The dog took no notice, and the child wandered off to find amusement elsewhere.

The baskets of white eider feathers caught his eye far off in a distant corner. He slipped under the table and crept along on all fours, the ordinary commonplace custom of walking down a room upright not being to his fancy. When close to the women he lay still for a moment watching, with his elbows on the floor and his chin in his palms. One of the women seeing him nodded and smiled, and presently he crept out behind her skirts and passed, hardly noticed, from one to another, till he found opportunity to possess himself of a large handful of feathers. With these he traversed the length of the room, under the table again, and emerged near the spinners. At the feet of the youngest he curled himself round, sheltered by her knees from the observation of the others, and disarmed her of interference by secretly displaying his handful with a confiding smile. A dubious nod satisfied him, and presently he proceeded with the play he had planned. He took a tuft of the white down, and gently shook it free of his fingers close to the whirl of the wheel. The wind of the swift motion took it, spun it round and round in widening circles, till it floated above like a slow white moth. Little Rol's eyes danced, and the row of his small teeth shone in a silent laugh of delight. Another and another of the white tufts was sent whirling round like a winged thing in a spider's web, and floating clear at last. Presently the handful failed.

Rol sprawled forward to survey the room and contemplate another journey under the table. His shoulder thrusting forward checked the wheel for an instant; he shifted hastily. The wheel flew on with a jerk and the thread snapped. "Naughty Rol!" said the girl. The swiftest wheel stopped also, and the house mistress, Rol's aunt, leaned forward and sighting the low curly head, gave a warning against michief, and sent him off to old Trella's corner.

Rol obeyed, and, after a discreet period of obedience, sidled out again down the length of the room farthest from his aunt's eye. As he slipped in among the men, they looked up to see that their tools might be, as far as possible, out of reach of Rol's hands, and close to their own. Nevertheless, before long he managed to secure a fine chisel and take off its point on the leg of the table. The carver's strong objections to this disconcerted Rol, who for five minutes thereafter effaced himself under the table.

During this seclusion he contemplated the many pairs of legs that surrounded him and almost shut out the light of the fire. How very odd some of the legs were; some were curved where they should be straight; some were straight where they should be curved; and as Rol said to himself, "They all seemed screwed on differently." Some were tucked away modestly, under the benches, others were thrust far out under the table, encroaching on Rol's own particular domain. He stretched out his own short legs and regarded them critically, and, after comparison, favorably. Why were not all legs made like his, or like his?

These legs approved by Rol were a little apart from the rest. He crawled opposite and again made comparison. His face grew quite solemn as he thought of the innumerable days to come before his legs could be as long and strong. He hoped they would be just like those, his models, as straight as to bone, as curved as to muscle.

A few moments later Sweyn of the long legs felt a small hand caressing his foot, and looking down met the upturned eyes of his little cousin Rol. Lying on his back, still softly patting and stroking the young man's foot, the child was quiet and happy for a good while. He watched the movements of the strong, deft hands and the shifting of the bright tools. Now and then minute chips of wood puffed off by Sweyn fell down upon his face. At last he raised himself very gently, lest a jog should wake impatience in the carver, and crossing his own legs round Sweyn's ankle, clasping with his arms too, laid his head against the knee. Such an act is evidence of a child's most wonderful hero worship. Quite content was Rol, and more than content when Sweyn paused a minute to joke, and pat his head and pull his curls. Quiet he remained, as long as quiescence is possible to limbs young as his. Sweyn forgot he was near, hardly noticed when his leg was gently released, and never saw the stealthy abstraction of one of his tools.

Ten minutes thereafter was a lamentable wail from low on the floor, rising to the full pitch of Rol's healthy lungs, for his hand was gashed across and the copious bleeding terrified him. Then there was soothing and comforting, washing and binding, and a modicum of scolding, till the loud outcry sank into occasional sobs, and the child, tear-stained and subdued, was returned to the chimney corner, where Trella nodded.

In the reaction after pain and fright, Rol found that the quiet of that fire-lit corner was to his mind. Tyr, too, disdained him no longer, but, roused by his sobs, showed all the concern and sympathy that a dog can by licking and wistful watching. A little shame weighed also upon his spirits. He wished he had not cried quite so much. He remembered how once Sweyn had come home with his arm torn down from the shoulder, and a dead bear; and how he had never winced nor said a word, though his lips turned white with pain. Poor little Rol gave an extra sighing sob over his own faint-hearted shortcomings.

The light and motion of the great fire began to tell strange stories to the child, and the wind in the chimney roared a corroborative note now and then. The great black mouth of the chimney, impending high over the hearth, received the murky coils of smoke and brightness of aspiring sparks as into a mysterious gulf, and beyond, in the high darkness, were muttering and wailing and strange doings, so that sometimes the smoke rushed back in panic, and curled out and up to the roof, and condensed itself to invisibility among the rafters. And then the wind would rage after its lost prey, rattling and shrieking at window and door.

In a lull, after one such loud gust, Rol lifted his head in surprise and listened. A lull had also come on the babble of talk, and thus could be heard with strange distinctness a sound without the door—the sound of a child's voice, a child's hands. "Open, open; let me in!" piped the little voice from low down, lower than the handle, and the latch rattled as though a tip-toe child reached up to it, and soft small knocks were struck. One near the door sprang up and opened it. "No one is here," he said. Tyr lifted his head and gave utterance to a howl, loud, prolonged, most dismal.

Sweyn, not able to believe that his ears had deceived him, got up and went to the door. It was a dark night; the clouds were heavy with snow, that had fallen fitfully when the wind lulled. Untrodden snow lay up to the porch; there was no sight nor sound of any human being. Sweyn strained his eyes far and near, only to see dark sky, pure snow, and a line of black fir trees on a hill brow, bowing down before the wind. "It must have been the wind," he said, and closed the door.

Many faces looked scared. The sound of a child's voice had been so distinct—and the words, "Open, open; let me in!" The wind might creak the wood or rattle the latch, but could not speak with a child's voice; nor knock with the soft plain blows that a plump fist gives. And the strange unusual howl of the wolf-hound was an omen to be feared, be the rest what it might. Strange things were said by one and other, till the rebuke of the house mistress quelled them into far-off whispers. For a time after there was uneasiness, constraint, and silence; then the chill fear thawed by degrees, and the babble of talk flowed on again.

Yet half an hour later a very slight noise outside the door sufficed to arrest every hand, every tongue. Every head was raised, every eye fixed in one direction. "It is Christian; he is late," said Sweyn.

No, no; this is a feeble shuffle, not a young man's tread. With the sound of uncertain feet came the hard tap tap of a stick against the door, and the high-pitched voice of eld, "Open, open; let me in!" Again Tyr flung up his head in a long doleful howl.

Before the echo of the taping stick and the high voice had fairly died way, Sweyn had sprung across to the door and flung it wide. "No one again," he said in a steady voice, though his eyes looked startled as he stared out. He saw the lonely expanse of snow, the clouds swagging low, and between the two the line of dark fir trees bowing in the wind. He closed the door without word of comment, and recrossed the room.

A score of blanched faces were turned to him as though he were the solver of the enigma. He could not be unconscious of this mute eye-questioning, and it disturbed his resolute air of composure. He hesitated, glanced toward his mother, the house mistress, then back at the frightened folk, and gravely, before them all, made the sign of the cross. There was a flutter of hands as the sign was repeated by all, and the dead silence was stirred as by a huge sigh, for the held breath of many was freed as if the sign gave magic relief.

Even the house mistress was perturbed. She left her wheel and crossed the room to her son, and spoke with him for a moment in a low tone that none could overhear. But a moment later her voice was high-pitched and loud, so that all might benefit by her rebuke of the "heathen chatter" of one of the girls. Perhaps she essayed to silence thus her own misgivings and forebodings.

No other voice dared speak now with its natural fullness. Low tones made intermittent murmurs, and now and then silence drifted over the whole room. The handling of tools was as noiseless as might be, and suspended on the instant if the door rattled in a gust of wind. After a time Sweyn left his work, joined the group nearest the door, and loitered there on the pretense of giving advice and help the the unskillful.

A man's tread was heard outside in the porch, "Christian!" said Sweyn and his mother simultaneously, he confidently, she authoritatively, to set the checked wheels going again. But Tyr flung up his head with an appalling howl.

"Open, open; let me in!"

It was a man's voice, and the door shook and rattled as a man's strength beat against it. Sweyn could feel the planks quivering, as on the instant his hand was upon the door, flinging it open, to face the blank porch, and beyond only snow and sky, and firs aslant in the wind.

He stood for a long minute with the open door in his hand. The bitter wind swept in with its icy chill, but a deadlier chill of fear came swifter, and seemed to freeze the beating of hearts. Sweyn snatched up a great bearskin cloak.

"Sweyn, where are you going?"

"No farther than the porch, mother," and he stepped out and closed the door.

He wrapped himself in the heavy fur, and leaning against the most sheltered wall of the porch, steeled his nerves to face the devil and all his works. No sound of voices came from within; but he could hear the crackle and roar of the fire.

It was bitterly cold. His feet grew numb, but he forebore stamping them into warmth lest the sound should strike panic within; nor would he leave the porch, nor print a footmark on the untrodden snow that testified conclusively to no human voices and hands having approached the door since snow fell two hours or more ago. "When the wind drops there will be more snow," thought Sweyn.

For the best part of an hour he kept his watch, and saw no living thing—heard no unwonted sound. "I will freeze here no longer," he muttered, and reentered.

One woman gave a half-suppressed scream as his hand was laid on the latch, and then a gasp of relief as he came in. No one questioned him, only his mother said, in a tone of forced unconcern, "Could you not see Christian coming?" as though she were made anxious only by the absence of her younger son. Hardly had Sweyn stamped near to the fire than clear knocking was heard at the door. Tyr leaped from the hearth—his eyes red as the fire—his fangs showing white in the black jowl—his neck ridged and bristling; and overleaping Rol, ramped at the door, barking furiously.

Outside the door a clear, mellow voice was calling. Tyr's bark made the words undistinguishable.

No one offered to stir toward the door before Sweyn.

He stalked down the room resolutely, lifted the latch, and swung back the door.

A white-robed woman glided in.

No wraith! Living—beautiful—young.

Tyr leapt upon her.

Lithely she balked the sharp fangs with folds of her long fur robe, and snatching from her girdle a small two-edged axe, whirled it up for a blow of defense.

Sweyn caught the dog by the collar and dragged him off, yelling and struggling. The stranger stood in the doorway motionless, one foot set forward, one arm flung up, till the house mistress hurried down the room, and Sweyn, relinquishing to others the furious Tyr, turned again to close the door and offer excuses for so fierce a greeting. Then she lowered her arm, slung the axe in its place at her waist, loosened the furs about her face, and shook over her shoulder the long white robe—all, as it were, with the sway of one movement.

She was a maiden, tall and very fair. The fashion of her dress was strange—half masculine, yet not unwomanly. A fine fur tunic, reaching but little below the knee, was all the skirt she wore; below were the crossbound shoes and leggings that a hunter wears. A white fur cap was set low upon the brows, and from its edge strips of fur fell lappet-wise about her shoulders, two of which at her entrance had been drawn forward and crossed about her throat, but now, loosened and thrust back, left unhidden long plaits of fair hair that lay forward on shoulder and breast, down to the ivory-studded girdle where the axe gleamed.

Sweyn and his mother led the stranger to the hearth without question or sign of curiosity, till she voluntarily told her tale of a long journey to distant kindred, a promised guide unmet, and signals and landmarks mistaken.

"Alone!" exclaimed Sweyn, in astonishment. "Have you journeyed thus far—a hundred leagues—alone?"

She answered, "Yes," with a little smile.

"Over the hills and the wastes! Why, the folk there are savage and wild as beasts."

She dropped her hand upon her axe with a laugh of scorn.

"I fear neither man nor beast; some few fear me," and then she told strange tales of fierce attack and defense, and of the bold, free huntress life she had led.

Her words came a little slowly and deliberately, as though she spoke in a scarce familiar tongue; now and then she hesitated, and stopped in a phrase, as if for lack of some word.

She became the center of a group of listeners. The interest she excited dissipated, in some degree, the dread inspired by the mysterious voices. There was nothing ominous about this bright, fair reality, though her aspect was strange.

Little Rol crept near, staring at the stranger with all his might. Unnoticed, he softly stroked and patted a corner of her soft white robe that reached to the floor in ample folds. He laid his cheek against it caressingly, and then edged close up to her knees.

"What is your name?" he asked.

The stranger's smile and ready answer, as she looked down, saved Rol from the rebuke merited by his question.

"My real name," she said, "would be uncouth to your ears and tongue. The folk of this country have given me another name, and from this"—she laid her hand on the fur robe—"they call me 'White Fell.' "

Little Rol repeated it to himself, stroking and patting as before. "White Fell, White Fell."

The fair face, and soft, beautiful dress pleased Rol. He knelt up, with his eyes on her face and an air of uncertain determination, like a robin's on a doorstep, and plumped his elbows into her lap with a little gasp at his own audacity.

"Rol!" exclaimed his aunt; but, "Oh, let him!" said White Fell, smiling and stroking his head; and Rol stayed.

He advanced farther, and, panting at his own adventurousness, in the face of his aunt's authority, climbed up onto her knees. Her welcoming arms hindered any protest. He nestled happily, fingering the axe head, the ivory studs in her girdle, the ivory clasp at her throat, the plaits of fair hair; rubbing his head against the softness of her fur-clad shoulder, with a child's confidence in the kindness of beauty.

White Fell had not uncovered her head, only knotted the pendant fur loosely behind her neck. Rol reached up his hand toward it, whispering her name to himself, "White Fell, White Fell," then slid his arms round her neck, and kissed her—once—twice. She laughed delightedly and kissed him again.

"The child plagues you?" said Sweyn.

"No, indeed," she answered, with an earnestness so intense as to seem disproportionate to the occasion.

Rol settled himself again on her lap and began to unwind the bandage bound round his hand. He paused a little when he saw where the blood had soaked through, then went on till his hand was bare and the cut displayed, gaping and long, though only skin-deep. He held it up toward White Fell, desirous of her pity and sympathy.

At sight of it and the blood-stained linen she drew in her breath suddenly, clasped Rol to her—hard, hard—til he began to struggle. Her face was hidden behind the boy, so that none could see its expression. It had lighted up with a most awful glee.

Afar, beyond the fir grove, beyond the low hill behind, the absent Christian was hastening his return. From daybreak he had been afoot, carrying summons to a bear hunt to all the best hunters of the farms and hamlets that lay within a radius of twelve miles. Nevertheless, having been detained till a late hour, he now broke into a run, going with a long smooth stride that fast made the miles diminish.

He entered the midnight blackness of the fir grove with scarcely slackened pace, though the path was invisible, and, passing through into the open again, sighted the farm lying a furlong off down the slope. Then he sprang out freely, and almost on the instant gave one great sideways leap and stood still. There in the snow was the track of a great wolf.

His hand went to his knife, his only weapon. He stooped, knelt down, to bring his eyes to the level of a beast, and peered about, his teeth set, his heart beating—a little harder than the pace of his running and had set it. A solitary wolf, nearly always savage and of large size, is a formidable beast that will not hesitate to attack a single man. This wolf track was the largest Christian had ever seen, and, as far as he could judge, recently made. It led from under the fir trees down the slope. Well for him, he thought, was the delay that had so vexed him before; well for him that he had not passed through the dark fir grove when that danger of jaws lurked there. Going warily, he followed the track.

It led down the slope, across a broad ice-bound stream, along the level beyond, leading toward the farm. A less sure knowledge than Christian's might have doubted of it being a wolf track, and guessed it to be made by Tyr or some large dog; but he was sure, and knew better than to mistake between a wolf's and a dog's footmark.

Straight on—straight on toward the farm.

Christian grew surprised and anxious at a prowling wolf daring so near. He drew his knife and pressed on, more hastily, more keenly eyed. Oh, that Tyr were with him!

Straight on, straight on, even to the very door, where the snow failed. His heart seemed to give a great leap and then stop. There the track ended.

Nothing lurked in the porch, and there was no sign of return. The firs stood straight against the sky, the clouds lay low; for the wind had fallen and a few snowflakes came drifting down. In a horror of surprise Christian stood dazed a moment; then he lifted the latch and went in. His glance took in all the old familiar forms and faces, and with them that of the stranger, fur-clad and beautiful. The awful truth flashed upon him. He knew what she was.

Only a few were startled by the rattle of the latch as he

entered. The room was filled with bustle and movement, for it was the supper hour, and all tools were being put aside and trestles and tables shifted. Christian had no knowledge of what he said and did; he moved and spoke mechanically, half thinking that soon he must wake from this horrible dream. Sweyn and his mother supposed him to be cold and dead-tired, and spared all unnecessary questions. And he found himself seated beside the hearth, opposite that dreadful Thing that looked like a beautiful girl, watching her every movement, curdling with horror to see her fondle Rol.

Sweyn stood near them both, intent upon White Fell also, but how differently! She seemed unconscious of the gaze of both— neither aware of the chill dread in the eyes of Christian, nor of Sweyn's warm admiration.

These two brothers, who were twins, contrasted greatly, despite their striking likeness. They were alike in regular profile, fair brown hair, and deep blue eyes; but Sweyn's features were perfect as a young god's, while Christian's showed faulty details. Thus, the line of his mouth was set too straight, the eyes shelved too deeply back, and the contour of the face flowed in less generous curves than Sweyn's. Their height was the same, but Christian was too slender for perfect proportion, while Sweyn's well-knit frame, broad shoulders and muscular arms made him preeminent for manly beauty as well as for strength. As a hunter Sweyn was without rival; as a fisher without rival. All the countryside acknowledged him to be the best wrestler, rider, dancer, singer. Only in speed could he be surpassed, and in that only by his younger brother. All others Sweyn could distance fairly; but Christian could outrun him easily. Ay, he could keep pace with Sweyn's most breathless burst, and laugh and talk the while. Christian took little pride in his fleetness of foot, counting a man's legs to be the least worthy of his limbs. He had no envy of his brother's athletic superiority, though to several feats he had made a moderate second. He loved as only a twin can love—proud of all that Sweyn did, content with all that Sweyn was, humbly content also that his own great love should not be so exceedingly returned, since he knew himself to be so far less loveworthy.

Christian dared not, in the midst of women and children, launch the horror that he knew into words. He waited to consult his brother; but Sweyn did not, or would not, notice the signal he made, and kept his face always turned toward White Fell. Chris-

tian drew away from the hearth, unable to remain passive with
that dread upon him.

"Where is Tyr?" he said, suddenly. Then catching sight of
the dog in a distant corner, "Why is he chained there?"

"He flew at the stranger," one answered.

Christian's eyes glowed. "Yes?" he said interrogatively, and,
rising, went without a word to the corner where Tyr was chained.
The dog rose up to meet him, as piteous and indignant as a dumb
beast can be. He stroked the black head. "Good Tyr! Brave
dog!"

They knew—they only—and the man and the dumb dog had
comfort of each other.

Christian's eyes turned again toward White Fell. Tyr's also,
and he strained against the length of the chain. Christian's hand
lay on the dog's neck, and he felt it ridge and bristle with the
quivering of impotent fury. Then he began to quiver in like
manner, with a fury born of reason, not instinct; as impotent
morally as was Tyr physically. Oh, the woman's form that he
dare not touch! Anything but that, and he with Tyr, would be free
to kill or be killed.

Then he returned to ask fresh questions.

"How long has the stranger been here?"

"She came about half an hour before you."

"Who opened the door to her?"

"Sweyn. No one else dared."

The tone of the answer was mysterious.

"Why?" queried Christian. "Has anything strange happened?
Tell me?"

For answer he was told in a low undertone of the summons at
the door, thrice repeated, without human agency; and of Tyr's
ominous howls, and of Sweyn's fruitless watch outside.

Christian turned toward his brother in a torment of impatience
for a word apart. The board was spread and Sweyn was leading
White Fell to the guest's place. This was more awful! She would
break bread with them under the rooftree.

He started forward and, touching Sweyn's arm, whispered an
urgent entreaty. Sweyn stared, and shook his head in angry
impatience.

Thereupon Christian would take no morsel of food.

His opportunity came at last. White Fell questioned of the
landmarks of the country, and of one Cairn Hill, which was an
appointed meeting place at which she was due that night. The
house mistress and Sweyn both exclaimed.

"It is three long miles away," said Sweyn, "with no place for shelter but a wretched hut. Stay with us this night and I will show you the way to-morrow.''

White Fell seemed to hesitate. "Three miles," she said, "then I should be able to see or hear a signal.''

"I will look out," said Sweyn; "then, if there be no signal, you must not leave us."

He went to the door. Christian silently followed him out.

"Sweyn, do you know what she is?''

Sweyn, surprised at the vehement grasp and low hoarse voice, made answer:

"She? Who? White Fell?''

"Yes.''

"She is a were-wolf.''

Sweyn burst out laughing. "Are you mad?'' he asked.

"No; here, see for yourself.''

Christian drew him out of the porch, pointing to the snow where the footmarks had been—had been, for now they were not. Snow was falling, and every dint was blotted out.

"Well?'' asked Sweyn.

"Had you come when I signed to you, you would have seen for yourself.''

"Seen what?''

"The footprints of a wolf leading up to the door; none leading away.''

It was impossible not to be startled by the tone alone, though it was hardly above a whisper. Sweyn eyed his brother anxiously, but in the darkness could make nothing of his face. Then he laid his hands kindly and reassuringly on Christian's shoulders and felt how he was quivering with excitement and horror.

"One sees strange things," he said, "when the cold has got into the brain behind the eyes; you came in cold and worn out.''

"No," interrupted Christian. "I saw the track first on the brow of the slope, and followed it down right here to the door. This is no delusion.''

Sweyn in his heart felt positive that it was. Christian was given to daydreams and strange fancies, though never had he been possessed with so mad a notion before.

"Don't you believe me?'' said Christian desperately. "You must. I swear it is sane truth. Are you blind? Why, even Tyr knows.''

"You will be clearer-headed to-morrow, after a night's rest. Then come, too, if you will, with White Fell, to the Hill Cairn, and, if you have doubts still, watch and follow, and see what footprints she leaves.''

Galled by Sweyn's evident contempt, Christian turned abruptly to the door. Sweyn caught him back.

"What now, Christian? What are you going to do?"

"You do not believe me; my mother shall."

Sweyn's grasp tightened. "You shall not tell her," he said, authoritatively.

Customarily Christian was so docile to his brother's mastery that it was now a surprising thing when he wrenched himself free vigorously and said as determinedly as Sweyn: "She shall know." But Sweyn was nearer the door, and would not let him pass.

"There has been scare enough for one night already. If this notion of yours will keep, broach it tomorrow." Christian would not yield.

"Women are so easily scared," pursued Sweyn, "and are ready to believe any folly without proof. Be a man, Christian, and fight this notion of a were-wolf by yourself."

"If you would believe me," began Christian.

"I believe you to be a fool," said Sweyn, losing patience. "Another, who was not your brother, might think you a knave, and guess that you had transformed White Fell into a were-wolf because she smiled more readily on me than on you."

The jest was not without foundation, for the grace of White Fell's bright looks had been bestowed on him—on Christian never a whit. Sweyn's coxcombry was always frank and most forgivable, and not without justifiableness.

"If you want an ally," continued Sweyn, "confide in old Trella. Out of her stores of wisdom—if her memory holds good—she can instruct you in the orthodox manner of tackling a were-wolf. If I remember aright, you should watch the suspected person till midnight, when the beast's form must be resumed, and retained ever after if a human eye sees the change; or, better still, sprinkle hands and feet with holy water, which is certain death! Oh, never fear, but old Trella will be equal to the occasion."

Sweyn's contempt was no longer good-humored, for he began to feel excessively annoyed at this monstrous doubt of White Fell. But Christian was too deeply distressed to take offense.

"You speak of them as old wives' tales, but if you had seen the proof I have seen, you would be ready at least to wish them true, if not also to put them to the test."

"Well," said Sweyn, with a laugh that had a little sneer in it, "put them to the test—I will not mind that, if you will only keep your notions to yourself. Now, Christian, give me your word for silence, and we will freeze here no longer."

Christian remained silent.

Sweyn put his hands on his shoulders again and vainly tried to see his face in the darkness.

"We have never quarreled yet, Christian?"

"I have never quarreled," returned the other, aware for the first time that his dictatorial brother had sometimes offered occasion for quarrel, had he been ready to take it.

"Well," said Sweyn, emphatically, "if you speak against White Fell to any other, as tonight you have spoken to me—we shall."

He delivered the words like an ultimatum, turned sharp round and reentered the house. Christian, more fearful and wretched than before, followed.

"Snow is falling fast—not a single light is to be seen."

White Fell's eyes passed over Christian without apparent notice, and turned bright and shining upon Sweyn.

"Nor any signal to be heard?" she queried. "Did you not hear the sound of a sea-horn?"

"I saw nothing and heard nothing; and signal or no signal, the heavy snow would keep you here perforce."

She smiled her thanks beautifully. And Christian's heart sank like lead with a deadly foreboding, as he noted what a light was kindled in Sweyn's eyes by her smile.

That night, when all others slept, Christian, the weariest of all, watched outside the guest chamber till midnight was past. No sound, not the faintest, could be heard. Could the old tale be true of the midnight change? What was on the other side of the door—a woman or a beast—he would have given his right hand to know. Instinctively he laid his hand on the latch, and drew it softly, though believing that bolts fastened the inner side. The door yielded to his hand; he stood on the threshold; a keen gust of air cut at him. The window stood open; the room was empty.

So Christian could sleep with a somewhat lightened heart.

In the morning there was surprise and conjecture when White Fell's absence was discovered. Christian held his peace; not even to his brother did he say how he knew that she had fled before midnight; and Sweyn, though evidently greatly chagrined, seemed to disdain reference to the subject of Christian's fears.

The elder brother alone joined the bear hunt; Christian found pretext to stay behind. Sweyn, being out of humor, manifested his contempt by uttering not one expostulation.

All that day, and for many a day after, Christian would never go out of sight of his home. Sweyn alone noticed how he manoeuvred for this, and was clearly annoyed by it. White Fell's name was never mentioned between them, though not seldom was it heard in general talk. Hardly a day passed without little Rol asking when White Fell would come again; pretty White Fell, who kissed like a snowflake. And if Sweyn answered, Christian would be quite sure that the light in his eyes, kindled by White Fell's smile, had not yet died out.

Little Rol! Naughty, merry, fair-haired little Rol! A day came when his feet raced over the threshold never to return; when his chatter and laugh were heard no more; when tears of anguish were wept by eyes that never would see his bright head again—never again—living or dead.

He was seen at dusk for the last time, escaping from the house with his puppy, in freakish rebellion against old Trella. Later, when his absence had begun to cause anxiety, his puppy crept back to the farm, cowed, whimpering, and yelping—a pitiful, dumb lump of terror—without intelligence or courage to guide the frightened search.

Rol was never found, nor any trace of him. How he had perished was known only by an awful guess—a wild beast had devoured him.

Christian heard the conjecture, "a wolf," and a horrible certainty flashed upon him that he knew what wolf it was. He tried to declare what he knew, but Sweyn saw him start at the words with white face and struggling lips, and, guessing his purpose, pulled him back and kept him silent, hardly, by his imperious grip and wrathful eyes, and one low whisper. Again Christian yielded to his brother's stronger words and will, and against his own judgment consented to silence.

Repentance came before the new moon—the first of the year—was old. White Fell came again, smiling as she entered as though assured of a glad and kindly welcome; and, in truth, there was only one who saw again her fair face and strange white garb without pleasure. Sweyn's face glowed with delight, while Christian's grew pale and rigid as death. He had given his word to keep silence, but he had not thought that she would dare to come again. Silence was impossible—face to face with that Thing—impossible. Irrepressibly he cried out:

"Where is Rol?"

Not a quiver disturbed White Fell's face; she heard, yet remained bright and tranquil—Sweyn's eyes flashed round at his brother dangerously. Among the women some tears fell at the poor child's name, but none caught alarm from its sudden utterance, for the thought of Rol rose naturally. Where was Rol, who had nestled in the stranger's arms, kissing her, and watched for her since, and prattled of her daily?

Christian went out silently. Only one thing there was that he could do, and he must not delay. His horror overmastered any curiosity to hear White Fell's glib excuses and smiling apologies for her strange and uncourteous departure; or her easy tale of the circumstances of her return; or to watch her bearing as she heard the sad tale of little Rol.

The swiftest runner of the countryside had started on his hardest race—little less than three leagues and back, which he reckoned to accomplish in two hours, though the night was moonless and the way rugged. He rushed against the still cold air till it felt like a wind upon his face. The dim homestead sank below the ridges at his back, and fresh ridges of snowlands rose out of the obscure horizon level to drive past him as the stirless air drove, and sink away behind into obscure level again. He took no conscious heed of landmarks, not even when all sign of a path was gone under depths of snow. His will was set to reach his goal with unexampled speed, and thither by instinct his physical forces bore him, without one definite thought to guide.

And the idle brain lay passive, inert, receiving into its vacancy, restless siftings of past sights and sounds; Rol weeping, laughing, playing, coiled in the arms of that dreadful Thing; Tyr—O Tyr!—white fangs in the black jowl; the women who wept on the foolish puppy, precious for the child's last touch; footprints from pinewood to door; the smiling face among furs, of such womanly beauty—smiling—smiling; and Sweyn's face.

"Sweyn, Sweyn, O Sweyn, my brother!"

Sweyn's angry laugh possessed his ear within the sound of the wind of his speed; Sweyn's scorn assailed more quick and keen than the biting cold at his throat. And yet he was unimpressed by any thought of how Sweyn's scorn and anger would rise if this errand were known.

To the younger brother all life was a spiritual mystery, veiled from his clear knowledge by the density of flesh. Since he knew his own body to be linked to the complex and antagonistic forces that constitute one soul, it seemed to him not impossibly strange that one spiritual force should possess divers forms for widely various manifestation. Nor, to him, was it great effort to believe that as pure water washes away all natural foulness, so water holy by consecration must needs cleanse God's world from that supernatural evil Thing. Therefore, faster than ever man's foot had covered those leagues, he sped under the dark, still night, over the waste trackless snow ridges to the faraway church where salvation lay in the holy-water stoop at the door. His faith was as

firm as any that wrought miracles in days past, simple as a
child's wish, strong as a man's will.

He was hardly missed during these hours, every second of
which was by him fulfilled to its utmost extent by extremest
effort that sinews and nerves could attain. Within the homestead
the while the easy moments went bright with words and looks of
unwonted animation, for the kindly hospitable instincts of the
inmates were roused into cordial expression of welcome and
interest by the grace and beauty of the returned stranger.

But Sweyn was eager and earnest, with more than a host's
courteous warmth. The impression that at her first coming had
charmed him, that had lived since through memory, deepened
now in her actual presence. Sweyn, the matchless among men,
acknowledged in this fair White Fell a spirit high and bold as his
own, and a frame so firm and capable that only bulk was lacking
for equal strength. Yet the white skin was molded most smoothly,
without such muscular swelling as made his might evident. Such
love as his frank self-love could concede was called forth by an
ardent admiration for this supreme stranger. More admiration
than love was in his passion, and therefore he was free from a
lover's hesitancy, and delicate reserve and doubts. Frankly and
boldly he courted her favor by looks and tones, and an address
that was his by natural ease.

Nor was she a woman to be wooed otherwise. Tender whispers and sighs would never gain her ear; but her eyes would
brighten and shine if she heard of a brave feat, and her prompt
hand in sympathy fall swiftly on the axe haft and clasp it hard.
That movement ever fired Sweyn's admiration anew; he watched
for it, strove to elicit it and glowed when it came. Wonderful and
beautiful was that wrist, slender and steel-strong; the smooth
shapely hand that curved so fast and firm, ready to deal instant
death.

Desiring to feel the pressure of these hands, this bold lover
schemed with palpable directness, proposing that she should hear
how their hunting songs were sung, with a chorus that signalled
hands to be clasped. So his splendid voice gave the verses, and,
as the chorus was taken up, he claimed her hands, and, even
through the easy grip, felt, as he desired, the strength that was
latent, and the vigor that quickened the very finger tips, as song
fired her, and her voice was caught out of her by the rhythmic
swell and rang clear on the top of the closing surge.

Afterward she sang alone. For contrast, or in the pride of
swaying moods by her voice, she chose a mournful song that
drifted along in a minor chant, sad as a wind that dirges:

"Oh, let me go!
Around spin wreaths of snow;
The dark earth sleeps below.

"Far up the plain
Moans on a voice of pain:
'Where shall my babe be lain?'

"In my white breast
Lay the sweet life to rest!
Lay, where it can be best!

" 'Hush! hush!' it cries;
'Tense night is on the skies;
Two stars are in thine eyes.'

"Come, babe away!
But lie thou till dawn by gray,
Who must be dead by day.

"This cannot last;
But, o'er the sickening blast,
All sorrows shall be past;

"All kings shall be
Low bending at thy knee,
Worshipping life from thee.

"From men long sore
To hope of what's before—
To leave the things of yore.

"Mine, and not thine,
How deep their jewels shine!
Peace laps thy head, not mine!"

Old Trella came tottering from her corner, shaken to additional palsy by an aroused memory. She strained her dim eyes toward the singer, and then bent her head that the one ear yet sensible to sound might avail of every note. At the close, groping forward, she murmured with the high pitched quaver of old age:

"So she sang, my Thora; my last and brightest. What is she like—she, whose voice is like my dead Thora's? Are her eyes blue?"

"Blue as the sky."

"So were my Thora's! Is her hair fair and in plaits to the waist?"

"Even so," answered White Fell herself, and met the advancing hands with her own, and guided them to corroborate her words by touch.

"Like my dead Thora's," repeated the old woman; and then her trembling hands rested on the fur-clad shoulders and she bent forward and kissed the smooth fair face that White Fell upturned, nothing loath to receive and return the caress.

So Christian saw them as he entered.

He stood a moment. After the starless darkness and the icy night air, and the fierce silent two hours' race, his senses reeled on sudden entrance into warmth and light and the cheery hum of voices. A sudden unforeseen anguish assailed him, as now first he entertained the possibility of being overmatched by her wiles and her daring, if at the approach of pure death she should start up at bay transformed to a terrible beast, and achieve a savage glut at the last. He looked with horror and pity on the harmless helpless folk, so unwitting of outrage to their comfort and security. The dreadful Thing in their midst, that was veiled from their knowledge by womanly beauty, was a centre of pleasant interest. There, before him, signally impressive, was poor Old Trelle, weakest and feeblest of all, in fond nearness. And a moment might bring about the revelation of a monstrous horror—a ghastly, deadly danger, set loose and at bay, in a circle of girls and women, and careless, defenseless men.

And he alone of the throng prepared!

For one breathing space he faltered, no longer than that, while over him swept the agony of compunction that yet could not make him surrender his purpose.

He alone? Nay, but Tyr also, and he crossed to the dumb sole sharer of his knowledge.

So timeless is thought that a few seconds only lay between his lifting of the latch and his loosening of Tyr's collar; but in those few seconds succeeding his first glance, as lightning-swift had been the impulses of others, their motion as quick and sure. Sweyn's vigilant eye had darted upon him, and instantly his every fiber was alert with hostile instinct; and half divining, half incredulous, of Christian's object in stooping to Tyr, he came hastily, wary, wrathful, resolute to oppose the malice of his wild-eyed brother.

But beyond Sweyn rose White Fell, blanching white as her furs, and with eyes grown fierce and wild. She leapt down the room to the door, whirling her long robe closely to her. "Hark!" she panted. "The signal horn! Hark, I must go!" as she snatched at the latch to be out and away.

For one precious moment Christian had hesitated on the half-loosened collar; for, except the womanly form were exchanged for the bestial, Tyr's jaws would gnash to rags his honor of manhood. He heard her voice, and turned—too late.

As she tugged at the door, he sprang across grasping his flask, but Sweyn dashed between and caught him back irresistibly, so that a most frantic effort only availed to wrench one arm free. With that, on the impulse of sheer despair, he cast at her with all his force. The door swung behind her, and the flask flew into fragments against it. Then, as Sweyn's grasp slackened, and he met the questioning astonishment of surrounding faces, with a hoarse inarticulate cry: "God help us all!" he said; "she is a were-wolf!"

Sweyn turned upon him, "Liar, coward!" and his hands gripped his brother's throat with deadly force as though the spoken word could be killed so, and, as Christian struggled, lifted him clear off his feet and flung him crashing backward. So furious was he that, as his brother lay motionless, he stirred him roughly with his foot, till their mother came between, crying, "Shame!" and yet then he stood by, his teeth set, his brows knit, his hands clenched, ready to enforce silence again violently, as Christian rose, staggering and bewildered.

But utter silence and submission was more than he expected, and turned his anger into contempt for one so easily cowed and held in subjection by mere force. "He is mad!" he said, turning on his heel as he spoke, so that he lost his mother's look of pained reproach at this sudden free utterance of what was a lurking dread within her.

Christian was too spent for the effort of speech. His hard drawn breath labored in great sobs; his limbs were powerless and unstrung in utter relax after hard service. His failure in this endeavor induced a stupor of misery and despair. In addition was the wretched humiliation of open violence and strife with his brother, and the distress of hearing misjudging contempt expressed without reserve, for he was aware that Sweyn had turned to allay the scared excitement half by imperious mastery, half by explanation and argument that showed painful disregard of brotherly consideration.

Sweyn the while was observant of his brother, despite the continual check of finding, turn and glance where he would, Christian's eyes always upon him, with a strange look of helpless distress, discomposing enough to the angry aggressor. "Like a beaten dog!" he said to himself, rallying contempt to withstand compunction. Observation set him wondering on Christian's exhausted condition. The heavy laboring breath and the slack, inert fall of the limbs told surely of unusual and prolonged exertion. And then why had close upon two hours' absence been followed by manifestly hostile behavior toward White Fell? Suddenly, the fragments of the flask giving a clue, he guessed all, and faced about to stare at his brother in amaze. He forgot that the motive scheme was against White Fell, demanding derision and resentment from him; that was swept out of remembrance by astonishment and admiration for the feat of speed and endurance.

That night Sweyn and his mother talked long and late together, shaping into certainty the suspicion that Christian's mind had lost its balance, and discussing the evident cause. For Sweyn, declaring his own love for White Fell, suggested that his unfortunate brother with a like passion—they being twins in love as in birth—had through jealousy and despair turned from love to hate, until reason failed at the strain, and a craze developed, which the malice and treachery of madness made a serious and dangerous force.

So Sweyn theorized; convincing himself as he spoke; convincing afterward others who advanced doubts against White Fell; fettering his judgment by his advocacy, and by his staunch defenses of her hurried flight, silencing his own inner consciousness of the unaccountability of her action.

But a little time and Sweyn lost his vantage in the shock of a fresh horror at the homestead. Trella was no more, and her end a mystery. The poor old woman crawled out in a bright gleam to visit a bedridden gossip living beyond the fir grove. Under the trees she was last seen halting for her companion, sent back for a forgotten present. Quick alarm sprang, calling every man to the search. Her stick was found among the brushwood near the path, but no track or stain, for a gusty wind was sifting the snow from the branches and hid all sign of how she came by her death.

So panic-stricken were the farm folk that none dared go singly on the search. Known danger could be braced, but not this stealthy Death that walked by day invisible, that cut off alike the child in his play and the aged woman so near to her quiet grave.

"Rol she kissed; Trella she kissed!" So rang Christian's frantic cry again and again, till Sweyn dragged him away and strove to keep him apart from the rest of the household.

But thenceforward all Sweyn's reasoning and mastery could not uphold White Fell above suspicion. He was not called upon to defend her from accusation, when Christian had been brought to silence again; but he well knew the significance of this fact, that her name, formerly uttered freely and often, he never heard now—it was huddled away into whispers that he could not catch.

For a time the twins' variance was marked on Sweyn's part by an air of rigid indifference, on Christian's by heavy downcast silence, and a nervous, apprehensive observation of his brother. Superadded to his remorse and foreboding, Sweyn's displeasure weighed upon him intolerably, and the remembrance of their violent rupture was ceaseless misery. The elder brother, self-sufficient and insensitive, could little know how deeply his unkindness stabbed. A depth and force of affection such as Christian's was unknown to him, and his brother's ceaseless surveillance annoyed him greatly. Therefore, that suspicion might be lulled, he judged it wise to make overtures for peace. Most easily done. A little kindliness, a few evidences of consideration, a slight return of the old brotherly imperiousness, and Christian replied by a gratefulness and relief that might have touched him had he understood all, but instead increased his secret contempt.

So successful was his finesse that when, late on a day, a message summoning Christian to a distance was transmitted by Sweyn no doubt of its genuineness occurred. When, his errand proving useless, he set out to return, mistake or misapprehension was all that he surmised. Not till he sighted the homestead, lying low between the night-gray snow ridges, did vivid recollection of the time when he had tracked that horror to the door rouse an intense dread, and with it a hardly defined suspicion.

His grasp tightened on the bear-spear that he carried as a staff; every sense was alert, every muscle strung; excitement urged him on, caution checked him, and the two governed his long stride, swiftly, noiselessly to the climax he felt was at hand.

As he drew near to the outer gates, a light shadow stirred and went, as though the gray of the snow had taken detached motion. A darker shadow stayed and faced Christian.

Sweyn stood before him, and surely the shadow that went was White Fell.

They had been together—close. Had she not been in his arms, near enough for lips to meet?

There was no moon, but the stars gave light enough to show that Sweyn's face was flushed and elate. The flush remained, though the expression changed quickly at sight of his brother. How, if Christian had seen all, should one of his frenzied outbursts be met and managed—by resolution? by indifference? He halted between the two, and as a result, he swaggered.

"White Fell?" questioned Christian, breathlessly.

"Yes?" Sweyn's answer was a query, with an intonation that implied he was clearing the ground for action.

From Christian came, "Have you kissed her?" like a bolt direct, staggering Sweyn by its sheer, prompt temerity.

He flushed yet darker, and yet half smiled over this earnest of success he had won. Had there been really between himself and Christian the rivalry that he imagined, his face had enough of the insolence of triumph to exasperate jealous rage.

"You dare ask this!"

"Sweyn, O Sweyn, I must know! You have!"

The ring of despair and anguish in his tone angered Sweyn, misconstruing it. Jealousy so presumptuous was intolerable.

"Mad fool!" he said, constraining himself no longer. "Win for yourself a woman to kiss. Leave mine without question. Such a one as I should desire to kiss is such a one as shall never allow a kiss to you."

Then Christian fully understood his supposition.

"I—I—!" he cried. "White Fell—that deadly Thing! Sweyn, are you blind, mad? I would save you from her—a were-wolf!"

Sweyn maddened again at the accusation—a dastardly way of revenge, as he conceived; and instantly, for the second time, the brothers were at strife violently. But Christian was now too desperate to be scrupulous; for a dim glimpse had shot a possibility into his mind, and to be free to follow it the striking of his brother was a necessity. Thank God! he was armed, and so Sweyn's equal.

Facing his assailant with the bear-spear, he struck up his arms, and with the butt end hit so hard that he fell. Then the matchless runner leapt away, to follow a forlorn hope.

Sweyn, on regaining his feet, was as amazed as angry at this unaccountable flight. He knew in his heart that his brother was no coward, and that it was unlike him to shrink from an encounter because defeat was certain, and cruel humiliation from a vindictive victor probable. Of the uselessness of pursuit he was well aware; he must abide his chagrin until his time for advantage should come. Since White Fell had parted to the right, Christian to the left, the event of a sequent encounter did not occur to him.

And now Christian, acting on the dim glimpse he had had, just as Sweyn turned upon him, of something that moved against the sky along the ridge behind the homestead, was staking his only hope on a chance, and his own superlative speed. If what he saw was really White Fell, he guessed she was bending her steps toward the open wastes; and there was just a possibility that, by a straight dash, and a desperate, perilous leap over a sheer bluff, he might yet meet her or head her. And then—he had no further thought.

It was past, the quick, fierce race, and the chance of death at the leap, and he halted in a hollow to fetch his breath and to look—did she come? Had she gone?

She came.

She came with a smooth, gliding, noiseless speed, that was neither walking nor running; her arms were folded in her furs that were drawn tight about her body; the white lappets from her head were wrapped and knotted closely beneath her face; her eyes were set on a far distance. Then the even sway of her going was startled to a pause by Christian.

"Fell!"

She drew a quick, sharp breath at the sound of her name thus mutilated, and faced Sweyn's brother. Her eyes glittered; her upper lip was lifted and showed the teeth. The half of her name, impressed with an ominous sense as uttered by him, warned her of the aspect of a deadly foe. Yet she cast loose her robes till they trailed ample, and spoke as a mild woman.

"What would you?"

Christian answered with his solemn, dreadful accusation:

"You kissed Rol—and Rol is dead! You kissed Trella—she is dead! You have kissed Sweyn, my brother, but he shall not die!"

He added: "You may live till midnight."

The edge of the teeth and the glitter of the eyes stayed a moment, and her right hand also slid down to the axe haft. Then, without a word, she swerved from him, and sprang out and away swiftly over the snow.

And Christian sprang out and away, and followed her swiftly over the snow, keeping behind, but half a stride's length from her side.

So they went running together, silent, toward the vast wastes of snow where no living thing but they two moved under the stars of night.

Never before had Christian so rejoiced in his powers. The gift of speed and the training of use and endurance were priceless to him now. Though midnight was hours away he was confident that go where that Fell Thing would hasten as she would, she could not outstrip him, nor escape from him. Then, when came the time for transformation, when the woman's form made no longer a shield against a man's hand, he could slay or be slain to save Sweyn. He had struck his dear brother in dire extremity, but he could not, though reason urged, strike a woman.

For one mile, for two miles they ran; White Fell ever foremost, Christian ever at an equal distance from her side, so near that, now and again, her outflying furs touched him. She spoke no word; nor he. She never turned her head to look at him, nor swerved to evade him; but, with set face looking forward, sped straight on, over rough, over smooth, aware of his nearness by the regular beat of his feet, and the sound of his breath behind.

In a while she quickened her pace. From the first Christian had judged of her speed as admirable, yet with exulting security in his own excelling and enduring whatever her efforts. But, when the pace increased, he found himself put to the test as never had been done before in any race. Her feet indeed flew faster than his; it was only by his length of stride that he kept his place at her side. But his heart was high and resolute, and he did not fear failure yet.

So the desperate race flew on. Their feet struck up the powdery snow, their breath smoked into the sharp, clear air, and they were gone before the air was cleared of snow and vapor. Now and then Christian glanced up to judge, by the rising of the stars, of the coming of midnight. So long—so long!

White Fell held on without slack. She, it was evident, with confidence in her speed proving matchless, as resolute to outrun her pursuer, as he to endure till midnight and fulfil his purpose. And Christian held on, still self-assured. He could not fail; he would not fail. To avenge Rol and Trella was motive enough for him to do what man could do; but for Sweyn more. She had kissed Sweyn, but he should not die, too—with Sweyn to save he could not fail.

Never before was such a race as this; no, not when in old Greece man and maid raced together with two fates at stake; for the hard running was sustained unabated, while star after star rose and went wheeling up toward midnight—for one hour, for two hours.

Then Christian saw and heard what shot him through with fear. Where a fringe of trees hung round a slope he saw something dark moving, and heard a yelp, followed by a full, horrid cry, and the dark spread out upon the snow—a pack of wolves in pursuit.

Of the beasts alone he had little cause for fear; at the pace he held he could distance them, four-footed though they were. But of White Fell's wiles he had infinite apprehension, for how might she not avail herself of the savage jaws of these wolves, akin as they were to half her nature. She vouchsafed to them nor look nor sign; but Christian, on an impulse, to assure himself that she should not escape him, caught and held the back-flung edge of her furs, running still.

She turned like a flash with a beastly snarl, teeth and eyes gleaming again. Her axe shone on the upstroke, on the down-stroke, as she hacked at his hand. She had lopped it off at the wrist, but that he parried with the bear-spear. Even then she shore through the shaft and shattered the bones of the hand, so that he loosed perforce.

Then again they raced on as before, Christian not losing a pace, though his left hand swung bleeding and broken.

The snarl, indubitably, though modified from a woman's or-gans; the vicious fury revealed in teeth and eyes; the sharp, arrogant pain of her maiming blow, caught away Christian's heed of the beasts behind, by striking into him close, vivid realization of the infinitely greater danger that ran before him in that deadly Thing.

When he bethought him to look behind, lo! the pack had but reached their tracks, and instantly slunk aside, cowed; the yell of pursuit changing to yelps and whines. So abhorrent was that fell creature to beast as to man.

She had drawn her furs more closely to her, disposing them so that, instead of flying loose to her heels, no drapery hung lower than her knees, and this without a check to her wonderful speed, nor embarrassment by the cumbering of the folds. She held her head as before; her lips were firmly set, only the tense nostrils gave her breath; not a sign of distress witnessed to the long sustaining of that terrible speed.

But on Christian by now the strain was telling palpably. His head weighed heavy, and his breath came laboring in great sobs; the bear-spear would have been a burden now. His heart was beating like a hammer, but such a dullness oppressed his brain that it was only by degrees he could realize his helpless state; wounded and weaponless, chasing that Thing, that was a fierce, desperate, axe-armed woman, except she should assume the beast with fangs yet more deadly.

And still the far, slow stars went lingering nearly an hour from midnight.

So far was his brain astray that an impression took him that she was fleeing from the midnight stars, whose gain was by such slow degrees that a time equalling days and days had gone in the race round the northern circle of the world, and days and days as long might last before the end—except she slackened, or except he failed.

But he would not fail yet.

How long had he been praying so? He had started with a self-confidence and reliance that had felt no need for that aid; and now it seemed the only means by which to restrain his heart from swelling beyond the compass of his body; by which to cherish his brain from dwindling and shriveling quite away. Some sharp-toothed creature kept tearing and dragging on his maimed left hand; he never could see it, he could not shake it off, but he prayed it off at times.

The clear stars before him took to shuddering and he knew why; they shuddered at sight of what was behind him. He had never divined before that strange Things hid themselves from men, under pretense of being snow-clad mounds of swaying trees; but now they came slipping out from their harmless covers to follow him, and mock at his impotence to make a kindred Thing resolve to truer form. He knew the air behind him was thronged; he heard the hum of innumerable murmurings together; but his eyes could never catch them—they were too swift and nimble; but he knew they were there, because, on a backward glance, he saw the snow mounds surge as they grovelled flatlings out of sight; he saw the trees reel as they screwed themselves rigid past recognition among the boughs.

And after such glance the stars for a while returned to steadfastness, and an infinite stretch of silence froze upon the chill, gray world, only deranged by the swift, even beat of the flying feet, and his own—slower from the longer stride, and the sound of his breath. And for some clear moments he knew that his only concern was to sustain his speed regardless of pain and distress, to deny with every nerve he had her power to outstrip him or to widen the space between them, till the stars crept up to midnight.

A hideous check came to the race. White Fell swirled about and leapt to the right, and Christian, unprepared for so prompt a lurch, found close at his feet a deep pit yawning, and his own impetus past control. But he snatched at her as he bore past, clasping her right arm with his one whole hand, and the two swung together upon the brink.

And her straining away in self-preservation was vigorous enough to counterbalance his headlong impulse, and brought them reeling together to safety.

Then, before he was verily sure that they were not to perish so, crashing down, he saw her gnashing in wild, pale fury, as she wrenched to be free; and since her right arm was in his grasp, used her axe left-handed, striking back at him.

The blow was effectual enough even so; his right arm dropped powerless, gashed and with the lesser bone broken that jarred with horrid pain when he let it swing, as he leaped out again, and ran to recover the few feet she had gained from his pause at the shock.

The near escape and this new, quick pain made again every faculty alive and intense. He knew that what he followed was most surely Death animate; wounded and helpless, he was utterly at her mercy if so she should realize and take action. Hopeless to avenge, hopeless to save, his very despair for Sweyn swept him on to follow and follow and precede the kiss-doomed to death. Could he yet fail to hunt that Thing past midnight, out of the womanly form, alluring and treacherous, into lasting restraint of the bestial, which was the last shred of hope left from the confident purpose of the outset.

The last hour from midnight had lost half its quarters, and the stars went lifting up the great minutes, and again his greatening heart and his shrinking brain and the sickening agony that swung at either side conspired to appal the will that had only seeming empire over his feet.

Now White Fell's body was so closely enveloped that not a lap nor an edge flew free. She stretched forward strangely aslant, leaning from the upright poise of a runner. She cleared the ground at times by long bounds, gaining an increase of speed that Christian agonized to equal.

He grew bewildered, uncertain of his own identity, doubting of his own true form. He could not be really a man, no more than that running Thing was really a woman; his real form was only hidden under embodiment of a man, but what it was he did not know. And Sweyn's real form he did not know. Sweyn lay fallen at his feet, where he had struck him down—his own brother—he; he stumbled over him and had to overleap him and race harder because she who had kissed Sweyn leapt so fast. "Sweyn—Sweyn—O Sweyn!"

Why did the stars stop to shudder? Midnight else, had surely come!

The leaning, leaping Thing looked back at him a wild, fierce look, and laughed in savage scorn and triumph. He saw in a flash why, for within a time measurable by seconds she would have escaped him utterly. As the land lay a slope of ice sank on the one hand; on the other hand a steep rose, shouldering forward; between the two was space for a foot to be planted, but none for a body to stand; yet a juniper bough, thrusting out, gave a handhold secure enough for one with a resolute grasp to swing past the perilous place, and pass on safe.

Though the first seconds of the last moment were going, she dared to flash back a wicked look, and laugh at the pursuer who was impotent to grasp.

The crisis struck convulsive life into his last supreme effort; his will surged up indomitable, his speed proved matchless yet. He leapt with a rush, passed her before her laugh had time to go out, and turned short, barring the way, and braced to withstand her.

She came hurling desperate, with a feint to the right hand, and then launched herself upon him with a spring like a wild beast when it leaps to kill. And he, with one strong arm and a hand that could not hold, with one strong hand and an arm that could not guide and sustain, he caught and held her even so. And they fell together. And because he felt his whole arm slipping and his whole hand loosing, to slack the dreadful agony of the wrenched bone above, he caught and held with his teeth the tunic at her knee, as she struggled up and wrung off his hands to overleap him victorious.

Like lightning she snatched her axe, and struck him on the neck—deep—once—twice—his life-blood gushed out, staining her feet.

The stars touched midnight.

The death scream he heard was not his, for his set teeth had hardly yet relaxed when it rang out. And the dreadful cry began with a woman's shriek, and changed and ended as the yell of a beast. And before the final blank overtook his dying eyes, he saw the She gave place to It; he saw more, that Life gave place to Death—incomprehensibly.

For he did not dream that no holy water could be more holy, more potent to destroy an evil thing than the life-blood of a pure heart poured out for another in willing devotion.

His own true hidden reality that he had desired to know grew palpable, recognizable. It seemed to him just this: a great, glad, abounding hope that he had saved his brother; too expansive to be contained by the limited form of a sole man, it yearned for a new embodiment infinite as the stars.

What did it matter to that true reality that the man's brain shrank, shrank, till it was nothing; that the man's body could not retain the huge pain of his heart, and heaved it out through the red exit riven at the neck: that hurtling blackness blotted out forever the man's sight, hearing, sense?

* * *

In the early gray of day Sweyn chanced upon the footprints of a man—of a runner, as he saw by the shifted snow; and the direction they had taken aroused curiosity, since a little farther their line must be crossed by the edge of a sheer height. He turned to trace them. And so doing, the length of the stride struck his attention—a stride long as his own if he ran. He knew he was following Christian.

In his anger he had hardened himself to be indifferent to the night-long absence of his brother; but now, seeing where the footsteps went, he was seized with compunction and dread. He had failed to give thought and care to his poor, frantic twin, who might—was it possible?—have rushed to a frantic death.

His heart stood still when he came to the place where the leap had been taken. A piled edge of snow had fallen, too, and nothing lay below when he peered. Along the upper edge he ran for a furlong, till he came to a dip where he could slip and climb down, and then back again on the lower level to the pile of fallen snow. There he saw that the vigorous running had started afresh.

He stood pondering; vexed that any man should have taken that leap where he had not ventured to follow; vexed that he had been beguiled to such painful emotions; guessing vainly at Christian's object in this mad freak. He began sauntering along half-unconsciously following his brother's track, and so in a while he came to the place where the footprints were doubled.

Small prints were these others, small as a woman's, though the pace from one to another was longer than that which the skirts of women allow.

Did not White Fell tread so?

A dreadful guess appalled him—so dreadful that he recoiled from belief. Yet his face grew ashy white, and he gasped to fetch back motion to his checked heart. Unbelievable? Closer attention showed how the smaller footfall had altered for greater speed, striking into the snow with a deeper onset and a lighter pressure on the heels. Unbelievable? Could any woman but White Fell run so? Could any man but Christian run so? The guess became a certainty. He was following where alone in the dark night White Fell had fled from Christian pursuing.

Such villainy set heart and brain on fire with rage and indignation—such villainy in his own brother, till lately loveworthy, praiseworthy, though a fool for meekness. He would kill Christian; had he lives as many as the footprints he had trodden, vengeance should demand them all. In a tempest of murderous hate he followed on in haste, for the track was plain enough;

starting with such a burst of speed as could not be maintained, but brought him back soon to a plod for the spent, sobbing breath to be regulated.

Mile after mile he traveled with a bursting heart; more piteous, more tragic, seemed the case at this evidence of White Fell's splendid supremacy, holding her own so long against Christian's famous speed. So long, so long, that his love and admiration grew more and more boundless, and his grief and indignation therewith also. Whenever the track lay clear he ran, with such reckless prodigality of strength that it was soon spent, and he dragged on heavily, till, sometimes on the ice of a mere, sometimes on a wind-swept place, all signs were lost; but, so undeviating had been their line, that a course straight on, and then short questing to either hand recovered them again.

Hour after hour had gone by through more than half that winter day, before ever he came to the place where the trampled snow showed that a scurry of feet had come and gone! Wolves' feet—and gone most amazingly! Only a little beyond he came to the lopped point of Christian's bear-spear—farther on he would see where the remnant of the useless shaft had been dropped. The snow here was dashed with blood, and the footsteps of the two had fallen closer together. Some hoarse sound of exultation came from him that might have been a laugh had breath sufficed. "O White Fell, my poor brave love! Well struck!" he groaned, torn by his pity and great admiration, as he guessed surely how she had turned and dealt a blow.

The sight of the blood inflamed him as it might a beast that ravens. He grew mad with a desire to once again have Christian by the throat, not to loose this time till he had crushed out his life—or beat out his life—or stabbed out his life—or all of these, and torn him piecemeal likewise—and ah! then, not till then, bleed his heart with weeping, like a child, like a girl, over the piteous fate of his poor lost love.

On—on—on—through the aching time, toiling and straining in the track of those two superb runners, aware of the marvel of their endurance, but unaware of the marvel of their speed that in the three hours before midnight had overpassed all that vast distance that he could only traverse from twilight to twilight. For clear daylight was passing when he came to the edge of an old marlpit, and saw how the two who had gone before had stamped and trampled together in desperate peril on the verge. And here fresh blood stains spoke to him of a valiant defense against his infamous brother; and he followed where the blood had dripped till the cold had staunched its flow, taking a savage gratification from the evidence that Christian had been gashed deeply, maddening afresh with desire to do likewise more excellently and so slake his murderous hate. And he began to know that through all his despair he had entertained a germ of hope, that grew apace, rained upon by his brother's blood.

He strove on as best he might, wrung now by an access of hope—now of despair, in agony to reach the end, however terrible, sick with the aching of the toiled miles that deferred it.

And the light went lingering out of the sky, giving place to uncertain stars.

He came to the finish.

Two bodies lay in a narrow place. Christian's was one, but the other beyond not White Fell's. There where the footsteps ended lay a great white wolf. At the sight Sweyn's strength was blasted; body and soul he was struck down groveling.

The stars had grown sure and intense before he stirred from where he had dropped prone. Very feebly he crawled to his dead brother, and laid his hands upon him, and crouched so, afraid to look or stir further.

Cold—stiff—hours dead. Yet the dead body was his only shelter and stay in that most dreadful hour. His soul, stripped bare of all comfort, cowered, shivering, naked, abject, and the living clung to the dead out of piteous need for grace from the soul that had passed away.

He rose to his knees, lifting the body. Christian had fallen face forward in the snow, with his arms flung up and wide, and so had the frost made him rigid; strange, ghastly, unyielding to Sweyn lifting, so that he laid him down again and crouched above, with his arms fast round him and a low, heart-wrung groan.

When at last he found force to raise his brother's body and gather it in his arms, tight clasped to his breast, he tried to face the Thing that lay beyond. The sight set his limbs in a palsy with horror and dread. His senses had failed and fainted in utter cowardice, but for the strength that came from holding dead Christian in his arms, enabling him to compel his eyes to endure the sight, and take into the brain the complete aspect of the Thing. No wound—only bloodstains on the feet. The great, grim jaws had a savage grin, though dead-stiff. And his kiss—he could bear it no longer, and turned away, nor ever looked again.

And the dead man in his arms, knowing the full horror, had followed and faced it for his sake; had suffered agony and death for his sake; in the neck was the deep death-gash, one arm and both hands were dark with frozen blood, for his sake! Dead he knew him—as in life he had not known him—to give the right meed of love and worship. He longed for annihilation, that so he might lose the agony of knowing himself so unworthy such perfect love. The frozen calm of death on the face appalled him. He dared not touch it with lips that had cursed so lately, with lips fouled by a kiss of the Horror that had been Death.

He struggled to his feet, still clasping Christian. The dead man stood upright within his arms, frozen rigid. The eyes were not quite closed; the head had stiffened, bowed slightly to one side; the arms stayed straight and wide. It was the figure of one crucified, the bloodstained hands also conforming.

So living and dead went back along the track, that one had passed in the deepest passion of love, and one in the deepest passion of hate. All that night Sweyn toiled through the snow, bearing the weight of dead Christian, treading back along the steps he before had trodden when he was wronging with vilest thoughts and cursing with murderous hate the brother who all the while lay dead for his sake.

SWORDS AGAINST THE MARLUK

By Katherine Kurtz

They had not anticipated trouble from the Marluk that summer. In those days, the name of Hogan Gwernach was little more than legend, a vague menace in far-off Tolan who might or might not even materialize as a threat to Brion's throne. Though rumored to be a descendant of the last Deryni sorcerer-king of Gwynedd, Gwernach's line had not set foot in Gweynedd for nearly three generations—not since Duchad Mor's ill-fated invasion in the reign of Jasher Haldane. Most people who knew of his existence at all believed that he had abandoned his claim to Gwynedd's crown.

And so, late spring found King Brion in Eastmarch to put down the rebellion of one of his own earls, with a young, half-Deryni squire named Alaric Morgan riding at his side. Rorik, the Earl of Eastmarch, had defied royal writ and begun to overrun neighboring Marley—a move he had been threatening for years—aided by his brash son-in-law, Rhydon, who was then only *suspected* of being Deryni. Arban Howell, one of the local barons whose lands lay along the line of Rorik's march, sent frantic word to the king of what was happening, then called up his own feudal levies to make a stand until help could arrive.

Only, by the time the royal armies did arrive, Brion's from the capital and an auxiliary force from Claibourne in the north, there was little left to do but assist Arban's knights in the mop-up operation. Miraculously, Arban had managed to defeat and capture Earl Rorik, scattering the remnants of the rebel forces and putting the impetuous Rhydon to flight. Only the formalities remained to be done by the time the king himself rode into Arban's camp.

Trial was held, the accused condemned, the royal sentence carried out. The traitorous Rorik, his lands and titles attainted, was hanged, drawn, and quartered before the officers of the combined armies, his head destined to be returned to his old capital and displayed as a deterrent to those contemplating similar indiscretions in the future. Rhydon, who had assisted his father-in-law's treason, was condemned in absentia and banished. Loyal Arban Howell became the new Earl of Eastmarch for his trouble, swearing fealty to King Brion before the same armies which had witnessed the execution of his predecessor only minutes before.

And so the rebellion ended in Eastmarch. Brion dismissed the Claibourne levies with thanks, wished his new earl godspeed, then turned over command of the royal army to his brother Nigel. Nigel and their uncle, Duke Richard, would see the royal levies back to Rhemuth. Brion, impatient with the blood and killing of the past week, set out for home along a different route, taking only his squire with him.

It was late afternoon when Brion and Alaric found a suitable campsite. Since their predawn rising, there had been little opportunity for rest; and accordingly, riders and horses both were tired and travel-worn when at last they stopped. The horses smelled the water up ahead and tugged at their bits as the riders drew rein.

"God's wounds, but I'm tired, Alaric!" the king sighed, kicking clear of his stirrups and sliding gratefully from the saddle. "I sometimes think the aftermath is almost worse than the battle. I must be getting old."

As Alaric grabbed at the royal reins to secure the horses, Brion pulled off helmet and coif and let them fall as he made his way to the edge of the nearby stream. Letting himself fall face-down, he buried his head in the cooling water. The long black hair floated on the current, streaming down the royal back just past his shoulders as he rolled over and sat up, obviously the better for wear. Alaric, the horses tethered nearby, picked up his master's helm and coif and laid them beside the horses, then walked lightly toward the king.

"Your mail will rust if you insist upon bathing in it, Sire," the boy smiled, kneeling beside the older man and reaching to unbuckle the heavy swordbelt.

Brion leaned back on both elbows to facilitate the disarming, shaking his head in appreciation as the boy began removing vambraces and gauntlets.

"I don't think I shall ever understand how I came to deserve you, Alaric." He raised a foot so the boy could unbuckle greaves and spurs and dusty boots. "You must think me benighted, to ride off alone like this, without even an armed escort other than yourself, just to be away from my army."

"My liege is a man of war and a leader of men," the boy grinned, "but he is also a man unto himself, and must have time away from the pursuits of kings. The need for solitude is a familiar one to me.''

"You understand, don't you?"

Alaric shrugged. "Who better than a Deryni, Sire? Like Your Grace, we are also solitary men on most occasions—though our solitude is not always by choice.''

Brion smiled agreement, trying to imagine what it must be like to be Deryni like Alaric, a member of that persecuted race so feared still by so many. He allowed the boy to pull the lion surcoat off over his head while he thought about it, then stood and shrugged out of his mail hauberk. Discarding padding and singlet as well, he stepped into the water and submerged himself with a sigh, letting the water melt away the grime and soothe the galls of combat and ill-fitting harness and too many hours in the saddle. Alaric joined him after a while, gliding eellike in the dappled shadows. When the light began to fail, the boy was on the bank without a reminder and pulling on clean clothes, packing away the battle-stained armor, laying out fresh garb for his master. Reluctantly, Brion came to ground on the sandy bottom and climbed to his feet, slicked back the long, black hair.

There was a small wood fire waiting when he had dressed, and wild rabbit spitted above the flames, and mulled wine in sturdy leather traveling cups. Wrapped in their cloaks against the growing night chill, king and squire feasted on rabbit and ripe cheese and biscuits only a little gone to mold after a week in the pack. The meal was finished and the camp secured by the time it was fully dark, and Brion fell asleep almost immediately, his head pillowed on his saddle by the banked fire. After a final check of the horses, Alaric slept, too.

It was sometime after moonrise when they were awakened by the sound of hoofbeats approaching from the way they had come. It was a lone horseman—that much Brion could determine, even through the fog of sleep he was shaking off as he sat and reached for his sword. But there was something else, too, and the boy Alaric sensed it. The lad was already on his feet, sword in hand, ready to defend his master if need be. But now he was frozen in the shadow of a tree, sword at rest, his head cocked in an attitude of more than listening.

"Prince Nigel," the boy murmured confidently, returning his sword to its sheath. Brion, used by now to relying on the boy's extraordinary powers, straightened and peered toward the moon-lit road, throwing his cloak around him and groping for his boots in the darkness.

"A Haldane!" a young voice cried.

"Haldane, ho!" Brion shouted in response, stepping into the moonlight to hail the newcomer. The rider reined his lathered horse back on its haunches and half fell from the saddle, tossing the reins in Alaric's general direction as the boy came running to meet him.

"Brion, thank God I've found you!" Nigel cried, stumbling to embrace his older brother. "I feared you might have taken another route!"

The prince was foam-flecked and grimy from his breakneck ride, and his breath came in ragged gasps as he allowed Brion to help him to a seat by the fire. Collapsing against a tree trunk, he gulped the wine that Brion offered and tried to still his trembling hands. After a few minutes, and without attempting to speak, he pulled off one gauntlet with his teeth and reached into a fold of his surcoat. He took a deep breath as he withdrew a folded piece of parchment and gave it over to his brother.

"This was delivered several hours after you and Alaric left us. It's from Hogan Gwernach."

"The Marluk?" Brion murmured. His face went still and strange, the gray Haldane eyes flashing like polished agate, as he held the missive toward the firelight.

There was no seal on the outside of the letter—only a name, written in a fine, educated hand: *Brion Haldane, Pretender of Gwynedd.* Slowly, deliberately, Brion unfolded the parchment, let his eyes scan it as his brother plucked a brand from the fire and held it close for light. The boy Alaric listened silently as the king read.

"*To Brion Haldane, Pretender of Gwynedd, from the Lord Hogan Gwernach of Tolan, Festillic Heir to the Thrones and Crowns of the Eleven Kingdoms. Know that We, Hogan, have determined to exercise that prerogative of birth which is the right of Our Festillic Ancestors, to reclaim the Thrones which are rightfully Ours. We therefore give notice to you, Brion Haldane, that your stewardship and usurpation of Gwynedd is at an end, your lands and Crown forfeit to the House of Festil. We charge you to present yourself and all members of your Haldane Line before Our Royal Presence at Cardosa, no later than the Feast of Saint Asaph, there to surrender yourself and the symbols of your sovereignty into Our Royal Hands.* Sic dicto, Hoganus Rex Regnorum Undecim."

"King of the Eleven Kingdoms?" Alaric snorted, then remembered who and where he was. "Pardon, Sire, but he must be joking!"

Nigel shook his head. "I fear not, Alaric. This was delivered by Rhydon of Eastmarch under a flag of truce."

"The treasonous dog!" Brion whispered.

"Aye." Nigel nodded. "He said to tell you that if you wished to contest this," he tapped the parchment lightly with his fingernail, "the Marluk would meet you in combat tomorrow near the Rustan Cliffs. If you do not appear, he will sack and burn the town of Rustan, putting every man, woman, and child to the sword. If we leave by dawn, we can just make it."

"Our strength?" Brion asked.

"I have my vanguard of eighty. I sent sixty of them ahead to rendezvous with us at Rustan and the rest are probably a few hours behind me. I also sent a messenger ahead to Uncle Richard with the main army. With any luck at all, he'll receive word in time to turn back the Haldane levies to assist. Earl Eawn was too far north to call back, though I sent a rider anyway."

"Thank you. You've done well."

With a distracted nod, Brion laid a hand on his brother's shoulder and got slowly to his feet. As he stood gazing sightlessly into the fire, the light gleamed on a great ruby in his ear, on a wide bracelet of silver clasped to his right wrist. He folded his arms across his chest against the chill, bowing his head in thought. The boy Alaric, with a glance at Prince Nigel, moved to pull the king's cloak more closely around him, to fasten the lion brooch beneath his chin as the king spoke.

"The Marluk does not mean to fight a physical battle. You know that, Nigel," he said in a low voice. "Oh, there may be battle among our various troops in the beginning. But all of that is but prelude. Armed combat is not what Hogan Gwernach desires of me."

"Aye. He is Deryni," Nigel breathed. He watched Brion's slow nod in the firelight.

"But, Brion," Nigel began, after a long pause. "It's been two generations since a Haldane king has had to stand against Deryni magic. Can you do it?"

"I—don't know." Brion, his cloak drawn close about him, sank down beside his brother once again, his manner grave and thoughtful. "I'm sorry if I appear preoccupied, but I keep having this vague recollection that there is something I'm supposed to do now. I seem to remember that Father made some provision, some preparation against this possibility, but—"

He ran a hand through sable hair, the firelight winking again on the silver at his wrist, and the boy Alaric froze, head cocked in a strained listening attitude, eyes slightly glazed. As Nigel nudged his brother lightly in the ribs, the boy sank slowly to his knees. Both pairs of royal eyes stared at him fixedly.

"There is that which must be done," the boy whispered, "which was ordained many years ago, when I was but a babe and you were not yet king, Sire."

"My father?"

"Aye. The key is—the bracelet you wear upon your arm." Brion's eyes darted instinctively to the silver. "May I see it, Sire?"

Without a word, Brion removed the bracelet and laid it in the boy's left hand. Alaric stared at it for a long moment, his pupils dilating until they were pools of inky blackness. Then, taking a deep breath to steel himself for the rush of memories he knew must follow, he bowed his head and laid his right hand over the design incised on the silver. Abruptly he remembered the first time he had seen the bracelet.

He had been just four when it happened, and it was mid-autumn. He had been snuggled down in his bed, dreaming of some childhood fantasy which he would never remember now, when he became aware of someone standing by his couch—and *that* was *not* a dream.

He opened his eyes to see his mother staring down at him intently, golden hair spilling bright around her shoulders, a loose-fitting gown of green disguising the thickening of her body from the child she carried. There was a candle in her hand, and by its light he could see his father standing gravely at her side. He had never seen such a look of stern concentration upon his father's face before, and that almost frightened him.

He made an inquisitive noise in his throat and started to ask what was wrong, but his mother laid a finger against her lips and shook her head. Then his father was reaching down to pull the blankets back, gathering him sleepily into his arms. He watched as his mother followed them out of the room and across the great hall, toward his father's library. The hall was empty even of the hounds his father loved, and outside he could hear the sounds of horses stamping in the yard—perhaps as many as a score of them—and the low-voiced murmur of the soldiers talking their soldier-talk.

At first, he thought the library was empty. But then he noticed an old, gray-haired man sitting in the shadows of his father's favorite armchair by the fireplace, an ornately carved staff cradled in the crook of his arm. The man's garments were rich and costly, but stained with mud at the hem. Jewels winked dimly in the crown of his leather cap, and a great red stone gleamed in his right earlobe. His cloak of red leather was clasped with a massive enameled brooch bearing the figure of a golden lion.

"Good evening, Alaric," the old man said quietly, as the boy's father knelt before the man and turned his son to face the visitor.

His mother made a slight curtsy, awkward in her condition, then moved to stand at the man's right hand, leaning heavily against the side of his chair. Alaric thought it strange, even at that young age, that the man did not invite his mother to sit down—but perhaps the man was sick; he was certainly very old. Curiously, and still blinking the sleep from his eyes, he looked up at his mother. To his surprise, it was his father who spoke.

"Alaric, this is the king," his father said in a low voice. "Do you remember your duty to His Majesty?"

Alaric turned to regard his father gravely, then nodded and disengaged himself from his father's embrace, stood to attention, made a deep, correct bow from the waist. The king, who had watched the preceding without comment, smiled and held out his right hand to the child. A silver bracelet flashed in the firelight as the boy put his small hand into the king's great, scarred one.

"Come and sit beside me, boy," the king said, lifting Alaric to a position half in his lap and half supported by the cavern chair arms. "I want to show you something."

Alaric squirmed a little as he settled down, for the royal lap was thin and bony, and the royal belt bristled with pouches and daggers and other grown-up accouterments fascinating to a small child. He started to touch one careful, stubby finger to the jewel at the end of the king's great dagger, but before he could do it, his mother reached across and touched his forehead lightly with her hand. Instantly, the room took on a new brightness and clarity, became more silent, almost reverberated with expectation. He did not know what was going to happen, but his mother's signal warned him that it was in that realm of special things of which he was never to speak, and to which he must give his undivided attention. In awed expectation, he turned his wide child-eyes upon the king, watched attentively as the old man reached around him and removed the silver bracelet from his wrist.

"This is a very special bracelet, Alaric. Did you know that?"

The boy shook his head, his gray eyes flicking from the king's face to the flash of silver. The bracelet was a curved rectangle of metal as wide as a man's hand, its mirror-sheen broken only by the carved outline of a heraldic rose. But it was the inside which the king turned toward him now—the inner surface, also highly polished but bearing a series of three curiously carved symbols which the boy did not recognize—though at four, he could already read the scriptures and simple texts from which his mother taught him.

The king turned the bracelet so that the first sigil was visible and held his fingernail beneath it. With a piercing glance at the boy's mother, he murmured the word "*One!*" The room spun, and Alaric had remembered nothing more of that night.

But the fourteen-year-old Alaric remembered now. Holding the bracelet in his hands, the old king's successor waiting expectantly beside him, Alaric suddenly knew that this was the key, that *he* was the key who could unlock the instructions left him by a dying man so many years before. He turned the bracelet in his hands and peered at the inside—he knew now that the symbols were runes, though he still could not read them—then raised gray eyes to meet those of his king.

"This is a time which your royal father anticipated, Sire. There are things which I must do, and you, and"—he glanced uneasily at the bracelet before meeting Brion's eyes again—"and somehow he knew that I would be at your side when this time arrived."

"Yes, I can see that now," Brion said softly. " '*There will be a half-Deryni child called Morgan who will come to you in his youth,*' my father said. '*Him you may trust with your life and with all. He is the key who unlocks many doors.*' " He searched Alaric's eyes carefully. "He knew. Even your presence was by his design."

"And was the Marluk also his design?" Nigel whispered, his tone conveying resentment at the implied manipulation, though the matter was now rendered academic.

"*Ancient mine enemy,*" Brion murmured. His face assumed a gentle, faraway air. "No, he did not cause the Marluk to be, Nigel. But he knew there was a possibility, and he planned for *that*. It is said that the sister of the last Festillic king was with child when she was forced to flee Gwynedd. The child's name was—I forget—not that it matters. But his line grew strong in Tolan, and they were never forced to put aside their Deryni powers. The Marluk is said to be that child's descendant."

"And full Deryni, if what they say is true," Nigel replied, his face going sullen. "Brion, we aren't equipped to handle a confrontation with the Marluk. He's going to be waiting for us tomorrow with an army and his *full Deryni powers*. And us? We'll have eighty men of my vanguard, *maybe* we'll have the rest of the Haldane levies, *if* Uncle Richard gets back in time, and you'll have—what?—to stand against a full Deryni Lord who has good reason to want your throne!''

Brion wet his lips, avoiding his brother's eyes, ''Alaric says that Father made provisions. We have no choice but to trust and see. Regardless of the outcome, we must try to save Rustan town tomorrow. Alaric, can you help us?''

''I—will try, Sire.''

Disturbed by the near-clash between the two brothers, and sobered by the responsibility Brion had laid upon him, Alaric laid his right forefinger beneath the first rune, grubby fingernail underscoring the deeply carved sign. He could feel the Haldane eyes upon him as he whispered the word, ''*One!*''

The word paralyzed him, and he was struck deaf and blind to all externals, oblivious to everything except the images flashing through his mind—the face of the old king seen through the eyes of a four-year-old boy—and the instructions, meaningless to the four-year-old, now reengraving themselves in the young man's mind as deeply as the runes inscribed on the silver in his hand.

A dozen heartbeats, a blink, and he was in the world again, turning his gray gaze on the waiting Brion. The king and Nigel stared at him with something approaching awe, their faces washed clean of whatever doubts had remained until that moment. In the moonlight, Alaric seemed to glow a little.

''We must find a level area facing east,'' the boy said. His young brow furrowed in concentration. ''There must be a large rock in the center, living water at our backs, and—and we must gather wildflowers.''

It was nearing first-light before they were ready. A suitable location had been found in a bend of the stream a little way below their camp, with water tumbling briskly along the northern as well as the western perimeter. To the east stretched an unobstructed view of the mountains from behind which the sun would shortly rise. A large, stream-smoothed chunk of granite half the height of a man had been dragged into the center of the clearing with the aid of the horses, and four lesser stones had been set up to mark the four cardinal compass points.

Now Alaric and Nigel were laying bunches of field flowers around each of the cornerstones, in a pattern which Alaric could not explain but which he knew must be maintained. Brion, silent and withdrawn beneath his crimson cloak, sat near the center stone with arms wrapped around his knees, sheathed sword lying beside him. A knot of blazing pine had been thrust into the ground at his right to provide light for what the others did, but

Brion saw nothing, submerged in contemplation of what lay ahead. Alaric, with a glance at the brightening sky, set a small drinking vessel of water to the left of the center stone and dropped to one knee beside the king. An uneasy Nigel snuffed out the torch and drew back a few paces as Alaric took up the bracelet and laid his finger under the second rune.

"*Two!*"

There was a moment of profound silence in which none of the three moved, and then Alaric looked up and placed the bracelet in the king's hand once more.

"The dawn is nearly upon us, Sire," he said quietly. "I require the use of your sword."

"Eh?"

With a puzzled look, Brion glanced at the weapon and picked it up, wrapped the red leather belt more tidily around the scabbard, then scrambled to his feet. It had been his father's sword, and his grandfather's. It was also the sword with which he had been consecrated king nearly ten years before. Since that day, no man had drawn it save himself.

But without further query, Brion drew the blade and formally extended it to Alaric across his left forearm, hilt first. Alaric made a profound bow as he took the weapon, appreciating the trust the act implied, then saluted the king and moved to the other side of the rock. Behind him, the eastern sky was ablaze with pink and coral.

"When the rim of the sun appears above the horizon, I must ward us with fire, my liege," he said. "Please do not be surprised or alarmed at anything which may happen."

Brion nodded, and as he and Nigel drew themselves to respectful attention, Alaric turned on his heel and strode to the eastern limit of the clearing. Raising the sword before him with both hands, he held the cross-hilt level with his eyes and gazed expectantly toward the eastern horizon. And then, as though the sun's movement had not been a gradual and natural thing, dawn was spilling from behind the mountains.

The first rays of sunlight on sword turned the steel to fire. Alaric let his gaze travel slowly up the blade, to the flame now blazing at its tip and shimmering down its length, then extended the sword in salute and brought it slowly to ground before him. Fire leaped up where blade touched sun-parched turf—a fire which burned but did not consume—and a ribbon of flame followed as he turned to the right and walked the confines of the wards.

When he had finished, he was back where he began, all three

of them standing now within a hemisphere of golden light. The boy saluted sunward once again, with hands that shook only a little, then returned to the center of the circle. Grounding the now-normal blade, he extended it to Nigel with a bow, and hilt held crosswise before him. As the prince's fingers closed around the blade, Alaric turned back toward the center stone and bowed his head. Then he held his hands outstretched before him, fingers slightly cupped—gazed fixedly at the space between them.

Nothing appeared to happen for several minutes, though Alaric could feel the power building between his hands. King and prince and squire stared until their eyes watered, then blinked in astonishment as the space between Alaric's hands began to glow. Pulsating with the heartbeat of its creator, the glow coalesced in a sphere of cool, verdant light, swelling to head-size even as they watched. Slowly, almost reverently, Alaric lowered his hands toward the stream-smoothed surface of the center stone; watched as the sphere of light spread bright across the surface.

He did not dare to breathe, so tenuous was the balance he maintained. Drawing back the sleeve of his tunic, he swept his right hand and arm across the top of the stone like an adze, shearing away the granite as though it were softest sand. Another pass to level the surface even more, and then he was pressing out a gentle hollow with his hand, the stone melting beneath his touch like morning frost before the sun.

Then the fire was dead, and Alaric Morgan was no longer the master mage, tapping the energies of the earth's deepest forge, but only a boy of fourteen, staggering to his knees in exhaustion at the feet of his king and staring in wonder at what his hands had wrought. Already, he could not remember how he had done it.

Silence reigned for a long moment, finally broken by Brion's relieved sigh as he tore his gaze from the sheared-off stone. A taut, frightened Nigel was staring at him and Alaric, white-knuckled hands gripping the sword hilt as though it were his last remaining hold on reality. With a little smile of reassurance, Brion laid a hand on his brother's. He felt a little of the tension drain away as he turned back to the young man still kneeling at his feet.

"Alaric, are you all right?"

"Aye, m'lord."

With a weak nod, Alaric brought a hand to his forehead and closed his eyes, murmuring a brief spell to banish fatigue. Another deep breath and it was done. Smiling wanly, he climbed to his feet and took the bracelet from Brion's hands once more,

bent it flat and laid it in the hollow he had made in the rock. The
three runes, one yet unrevealed, shone in the sunlight as he
stretched forth his right hand above the silver.

" *'I form the light and create darkness,'* " the boy whispered.
" *'I make peace and create evil: I the Lord do all these things.'* "

He did not physically move his hand, although muscles and
tendons tensed beneath the tanned skin. Nonetheless, the silver
began to curve away, to conform to the hollow of the stone as
though another, invisible hand were pressing down between his
hand and the metal. The bracelet collapsed on itself and grew
molten then, though there was no heat given off. When Alaric
removed his hand a few seconds later, the silver was bonded to
the hollow like a shallow, silver bowl, all markings obliterated
save the third and final rune. He laid his finger under the sign
and spoke its name.

"Three!"

This time, there was but a fleeting outward hint of the reaction
triggered: a blink, an interrupted breath immediately resumed.
Then he was taking up the vessel of water and turning toward
Brion, gesturing with his eyes for Brion to extend his hands.
Water was poured over them, the edge of Alaric's cloak offered
for a towel. When the king had dried his hands, Alaric handed
him the rest of the water.

"Pour water in the silver to a finger's depth, Sire," he said
softly.

Brion complied, setting the vessel on the ground when he had
finished. Nigel, without being told, moved to the opposite side
of the stone and knelt, holding the sword so that the long,
cross-shadow of the hilt fell across rock and silver.

"Now," Alaric continued, "spread your hands flat above the
water and repeat after me. Your hands are holy, consecrated with
chrism at your coronation just as a priest's hands are consecrated. I am instructed that this is appropriate."

With a swallow, Brion obeyed, his eyes locking with Alaric's
as the boy began speaking.

"I, Brion, the Lord's Anointed, . . ."

"I, Brion, the Lord's Anointed, . . ."

". . . bless and consecrate thee, O creature of water, . . ."

*". . . bless and consecrate thee, O creature of warer, . . . by
the living God, by the true God, by the holy God, . . . by that
God Who in the beginning separated thee by His word from the
dry land, . . . and Whose Spirit moved upon thee."*

"Amen," Alaric whispered.

"Amen," Brion echoed.

"Now, dip your fingers in the water," Alaric began, "and trace on the stone—"

"I *know* this part!" Brion interrupted, his hand already parting the water in the sign of a cross. He, too, was being caught up in that web of recall established so many years before by his royal father, and his every gesture, every nuance of phrasing and pronunciation, was correct and precise as he touched a moistened finger to the stone in front of the silver.

"*Blessed be the Creator, yesterday and today, the Beginning and the End, the Alpha and the Omega.*"

A cross shown wetly on the stone, the Greek letters drawn haltingly but precisely at the east and west aspects.

"*His are the seasons and the ages, to Him glory and dominion through all the ages of eternity. Blessed be the Lord. Blessed be His Holy Name.*"

The signs of the Elementals glistened where Brion had drawn them in the four quadrants cut by the cross—Air, Fire, Water, Earth—and Brion, as he recognized the alchemical signs, drew back his hand as though stung, stared aghast at Alaric.

"How—?" He swallowed. "How did I know that?"

Alaric permitted a wan smile, sharing Brion's discomfiture at being compelled to act upon memories and instructions which he could not consciously remember.

"You, too, have been schooled for this day, Sire," he said. "Now, you have but to carry out the rest of your father's instructions, and take up the power which is rightfully yours."

Brion bowed his head, sleek, raven hair catching the strengthening sunlight. "I—am not certain I know how. From what we have seen and done so far, there must be other triggers, other clues to aid me, but—" He glanced up at the boy. "You must give me guidance, Alaric. You are the master here—not I."

"No, you are the master, Sire," the boy said, touching one finger to the water and bringing a shimmering drop toward Brion's face.

The king's eyes tracked on the fingertip automatically, and as the droplet touched his forehead, the eyes closed. A shudder passed through the royal body and Brion blinked. Then in a daze, he reached to his throat and unfastened the great lion brooch which held his cloak in place. He hefted the piece in his hand as the cloak fell in a heap at his feet and the words came.

> "*Three drops of royal blood on water bright,*
> *To gather flame within a bowl of light.*
> *With consecrated hands, receive the Sight*
> *Of Haldane—'tis thy sacred, royal Right.*"

The king glanced at Alaric unseeing, at Nigel, at the red enameled brooch heavy in his hand. Then he turned the brooch over and freed the golden clasp-pin from its catch, held out a left hand which did not waver.

"*Three drops of royal blood on water bright,*" he repeated. He brought the clasp against his thumb in a swift, sharp jab.

Blood welled from the wound and fell thrice upon the water, rippling scarlet, concentric circles across the silver surface. A touch of tongue to wounded thumb, and then he was putting the brooch aside and spreading his hands above the water, the shadow of the cross bold upon his hands. He closed his eyes.

Stillness. A crystalline anticipation as Brion began to concentrate. And then, as Alaric extended his right hand above Brion's and added his strength to the spell, a deep, musical reverberation, more felt than heard, throbbing through their minds. As the sunlight brightened, so also brightened the space beneath Brion's hands, until finally could be seen the ghostly beginnings of crimson fire flickering on the water. Brion's emotionless expression did not change as Alaric withdrew his hand and knelt.

"*Fear not, for I have redeemed thee,*" Alaric whispered, calling the words from memories not his own. "*I have called thee by name, and thou art mine. When thou walkest through the fire, thou shalt not be burned: neither shall the flame kindle upon thee.*"

Brion did not open his eyes. But as Alaric's words ended, the king took a deep breath and slowly, deliberately, brought his hands to rest flat on the silver of the bowl. There was a gasp from Nigel as his brother's hands entered the flames, but no word or sound escaped Brion's lips to indicate the ordeal he was enduring. Head thrown back and eyes closed, he stood unflinching as the crimson fire climbed his arms and spread over his entire body. When the flames died away, Brion opened his eyes upon a world which would never appear precisely the same again, and in which he could never again be merely mortal.

He leaned heavily on the altar-stone for just a moment, letting the fatigue drain away. But when he lifted his hands from the stone, his brother stifled an oath. Where the royal hands had lain, the silver had been burned away. Only the blackened silhouettes remained, etched indelibly in the hollowed surface of the rock. Brion blanched a little when he saw what he had done, and Nigel crossed himself. But Alaric paid no heed—stood, instead, and turned to face the east once more, extending his arms in a banishing spell. The canopy of fire dissipated in the air.

They were no longer alone, however. While they had worked their magic, some of the men of Nigel's vanguard had found the royal campsite—an even dozen of his crack commanders and tacticians—and they were gathered now by the horses in as uneasy a band as Alaric had ever seen. Brion did not notice them immediately, his mind occupied still with sorting out his recent experience, but Alaric saw them and touched Brion's elbow in warning. As Brion turned toward them in surprise, they went to their knees as one man, several crossing themselves furtively, Brion's brow furrowed in momentary annoyance.

"Did they see?" he murmured, almost under his breath.

Alaric gave a careful nod. "So it would appear, Sire. I suggest you go to them immediately and reassure them. Otherwise, the more timid among them are apt to bolt and run."

"From me, their king?"

"You are more than just a man now, Sire," Alaric returned uncomfortably. "They have seen that with their own eyes. Go to them, and quickly."

With a sigh, Brion tugged his tunic into place and strode across the clearing toward the men, automatically pulling his gauntlets from his belt and beginning to draw them on. The men watched his movements furtively as he came to a halt perhaps a half-dozen steps from the nearest of them. Noting their scrutiny, Brion froze in the act of pulling on the right glove; then, with a smile, he removed it and held his hand toward them, the palm exposed. There was no mark upon the lightly calloused skin.

"You are entitled to an explanation," he said simply, as all eyes fastened on the hand. "As you can see, I am unharmed. I am sorry if my actions caused you some concern. Please rise."

The men got to their feet, only the chinking of their harness breaking the sudden stillness which had befallen the glade. Behind the king, Nigel and Alaric moved to back him, Nigel bearing the royal sword and Alaric the crimson cloak with its lion brooch. The men were silent, a few shifting uneasily, until one of the bolder ones cleared his throat and took a half-step nearer.

"Sire."

"Lord Ralson?"

"Sire," the man shifted from one foot to the other and glanced at his comrades. "Sire, it appears to us that there was magic afoot," he said carefully. "We question the wisdom of allowing a Deryni to influence you so. When we saw—"

"What *did* you see, Gerard?" Brion asked softly.

Gerard Ralson cleared his throat. "Well, I—we—when we

arrived, Sire, you were holding that brooch in your hand," he gestured toward the lion brooch which Alaric held, "and then we saw you prick your thumb with it." He paused. "You looked—not yourself, Sire, as though—something else was commanding you." He glanced at Alaric meaningfully, and several other of the men moved a little closer behind him, hands creeping to rest on the hilts of their weapons.

"I see," Brion said. "And you think that it was Alaric who commanded me, don't you?"

"It appeared so to us, Majesty," another man rumbled, his beard jutting defiantly.

Brion nodded. "And then you watched me hold my hands above the stone, and Alaric hold his above my own. And then you saw me engulfed in flame, and that frightened you most of all."

The speaker nodded tentatively, and his movement was echoed by nearly every head there. Brion sighed and glanced at the ground, looked up at them again.

"My Lords, I will not lie to you. You were witness to very powerful magic. And I will not deny, nor will Alaric, that his assistance was used in what you saw. And Alaric is, most definitely, Deryni."

The men said nothing, though glances were exchanged.

"But there is more that I would have you know," Brion continued, fixing them all with his Haldane stare. "Each of you has heard the legends of my House—how we returned to the throne of Gwynedd when the Deryni Imre was deposed. But if you consider, you will realize that the Haldanes could not have ousted Deryni Lords without some power of their own."

"Are you Deryni, then, Sire?" asked one bold soul from the rear ranks.

Brion smiled and shook his head. "No—or at least, I don't believe I am. But the Haldanes have very special gifts and abilities, nonetheless, handed down from father to son—or sometimes from brother to brother." He glanced at Nigel before continuing. "You know that we can Truth-Read, that we have great physical stamina. But we also have other powers, when they are needed, which enable us to function almost as though we were, ourselves, Deryni. My father, King Blaine, entrusted a few of these abilities to me before his death, but there were others whose very existence he kept secret, for which he left certain instructions with Alaric Morgan *unknown even to him*—and which were triggered by the threat of Hogan Gwernach's challenge which we received last night. Alaric was a child of four when he was instructed by my father—so that even *he* would not remember his instructions until it was necessary—and apparently I was also instructed.

"The result, in part, was what you saw. If there was a commanding force, another influence present within the fiery circle, it was my father's. The rite is now fulfilled, and I am my father's successor *in every way,* with all his powers and abilities."

"Your late *father* provided for all of this?" one of the men whispered.

Brion nodded. "There is no evil in it, Alwyne. You knew my father well. You know he would not draw down evil."

"Aye, he would not," the man replied, glancing at Alaric almost involuntarily. "But what of the Deryni lad?"

"Our fathers made a pact, that Alaric Morgan should come to Court to serve me when he reached the proper age. That bargain has been kept. Alaric Morgan serves me and the realm of Gwynedd."

"But, he is Deryni, Sire! What if he is in league with—"

"He is in league with *me!*" Brion snapped. "He is my liege man, just as all of you, sworn to my service since the age of nine. In that time, he has scarcely left my side. Given the compulsions which my father placed upon him, do you really believe that he could betray me?"

Ralson cleared his throat, stepping forward and making a bow before the king could continue.

"Sire, it is best we do not discuss the boy. None of us here, Your Majesty included, can truly know what is in his heart. You are the issue now. If you were to reassure us, in some way, that you harbor no ill intent, that you have not allied yourself with the Dark Powers—"

"You wish my oath to that effect?" Brion asked. The stillness of his response was, itself, suddenly threatening. "You would be that bold?"

Ralson nodded carefully, not daring to respond by words, and his movement was again echoed by the men standing at his back. After a frozen moment, Brion made a curt gesture for his brother to kneel with the royal sword. As Nigel held up the cross hilt, Brion laid his bare right hand upon it and faced his waiting knights.

"Before all of you and before God, and upon this holy sword, I swear that I am innocent of your suspicions, that I have made no dark pact with any evil power, that the rite which you observed was benevolent and legitimate. I further swear that I have never been, nor am I now, commanded by Alaric Morgan or any other man, human or Deryni; that he is as innocent as I of any evil intent toward the people and Crown of Gwynedd. This is the word of Brion Haldane. If I be forsworn, may this sword break in my hour of need, may all succor desert me, and may the name of Haldane vanish from the earth.''

With that, he crossed himself slowly, deliberately—a motion which was echoed by Alaric, Nigel, and then the rest of the men who had witnessed the oath. Preparations to leave for Rustan were made in total silence.

They met the Marluk while still an hour's ride from Rustan and rendezvous with the rest of Nigel's vanguard. All morning, they had been following the rugged Llegoddin Canyon Trace—a winding trail treacherous with stream-slicked stones which rolled and shifted beneath their horses' hooves. The stream responsible for their footing ran shallow along their right, had crossed their path several times in slimy, fast-flowing fords that made the horses lace back their ears. Even the canyon walls had closed in along the last mile, until the riders were forced to go two abreast. It was a perfect place for an ambush; but Alaric's usually reliable knack for sensing danger gave them almost no warning.

It was cool in the little canyon, the shade deep and refreshing after the heat of the noonday sun, and the echo of steel-shod hooves announced their progress long before they actually reached the end of the narrows. There the track made a sharp turn through the stream again, before widening out to an area of several acres. In the center waited a line of armed horsemen, nearly twice the number of Brion's forces.

They were mailed and helmed with steel, these fighting men of Tolan, and their lances and war axes gleamed in the silent sunlight. Their white-clad leader sat a heavy sorrel destrier before them, lance in hand and banner bright at his back. The blazon left little doubt as to his identity—Hogan Gwernach, called the Marluk. He had quartered his arms with those of Royal Gwynedd.

But there was no time for more than first impressions. Even as Alaric's lips moved in warning, and before more than a handful of Brion's men could clear the stream and canyon narrows, the Marluk lowered his lance and signaled the attack. As the great-horses thundered toward the stunned royal party, picking up momentum as they came, Brion couched his own lance and set spurs to his horse's sides. His men, overcoming their initial dismay with commendable speed, galloped after him in near-order, readying shields and weapons even as they rode.

The earth shook with the force of the charge, echoed with the jingle of harness and mail, the creak of leather, the snorting and labored breathing of the heavy war horses. Just before the two forces met, one of Brion's men shouted, "*A Haldane!*"—a cry which was picked up and echoed instantly by most of his comrades in arms. Then all were swept into the melee, and men were falling and horses screaming riderless and wounded as lances splintered on shield and mail and bone.

Steel clanged on steel as the fighting closed hand-to-hand, cries of the wounded and dying punctuating the butcher sounds of sword and ax on flesh. Alaric, emerging unscathed from the initial encounter, found himself locked shield to shield with a man twice his age and size, the man pressing him hard and trying to crush his helm with a mace. Alaric countered by ducking under his shield and wheeling to the right, hoping to come at his opponent from the other side, but the man was already anticipating his move and swinging in counterattack. At the last possible moment, Alaric deflected the blow with his shield, reeling in the saddle as he tried to recover his balance and strike at the same time. But his aim had been shaken, and instead of coming in from behind on the man's temporarily open right side, he only embedded his sword in the other's high cantle.

He recovered before the blade could be wrenched from his grasp, gripping hard with his knees as his charger lashed out and caught the man in the leg with a driving foreleg. Then, parrying a blow from a second attacker, he managed to cut the other's girth and wound his mount, off-handedly kicking out at yet a third man who was approaching from his shield side. The first knight hit the ground with a yelp as his horse went down, narrowly missing death by trampling as one of his own men thundered past in pursuit of one of Brion's wounded.

Another strike, low and deadly, and Alaric's would-be slayer was, himself, the slain. Drawing ragged breath, Alaric wheeled to scan the battle for Brion, and to defend himself from renewed attack by the two men on foot.

The king himself was in little better circumstances. Though still mounted and holding his own, Brion had been swept away from his mortal enemy in the initial clash, and had not yet been able to win free to engage with him. Nigel was fighting at his brother's side, the royal banner in his shield hand, but the banner only served to hamper Nigel and to tell the enemy where Gwynedd's monarch was. Just now, both royal brothers were sore beset, half a dozen of the Marluk's knights belaboring them from every side but skyward. The Marluk, meantime, was busily slaying a hundred yards away—content, thus far, to spend his time slaughtering some of Brion's lesser warriors, and shunning Brion's reputed superior skill. As Brion and Nigel beat back their attackers, the king glanced across the battlefield and saw his enemy, dispatched one of his harriers with a brutal thrust, raised his sword and shouted the enemy's name:

"Gwernach!"

The enemy turned in his direction and jerked his horse to a rear, circled his sword above his head. His helmet was gone, and pale hair blew wild from beneath his mail coif.

"The Haldane is mine!" the Marluk shouted, spurring toward Brion and cutting down another man in passing. "Stand and fight, usuper! Gwynedd is mine by right!"

The Marluk's men fell back from Brion as their master pounded across the field, and with a savage gesture, Brion waved his own men away and urged his horse toward the enemy. Now was the time both had been waiting for—the direct, personal combat of the two rival kings. Steel shivered against steel as the two men met and clashed in the center of the field, and the warriors of both sides drew back to watch, their own hostilities temporarily suspended.

For a time, the two seemed evenly matched. The Marluk took a chunk out of the top of Brion's shield, but Brion divested the Marluk of a stirrup, and nearly a foot. So they continued, neither man able to score a decisive blow, until finally Brion's sword found the throat of the Marluk's mount. The dying animal collapsed with a liquid scream, dumping its rider in a heap. Brion, pursuing his advantage, tried to ride down his enemy then and there.

But the Marluk rolled beneath his shield on the first pass and nearly tripped up Brion's horse, scrambling to his feet and bracing as Brion wheeled viciously to come at him again. The second pass cost Brion his mount, its belly ripped out by the Marluk's sword. As the horse went down, Brion leaped clear and whirled to face his opponent.

For a quarter hour the two battled with broadsword and shield, the Marluk with the advantage of weight and height, but Brion with youth and greater agility in his favor. Finally, when both men could barely lift their weapons for fatigue, they drew apart and leaned on heavy swords, breath coming in short, ragged gasps. After a moment, golden eyes met steely gray ones. The Marluk flashed a brief, sardonic grin at his opponent.

"You fight well, for a Haldane," the Marluk conceded, still breathing heavily. He gestured with his sword toward the waiting men. "We are well matched, at least in steel, and even were we to cast our men into the fray again, it would still come down to the same—you against me."

"Or my power against yours," Brion amended softly. "That is your eventual intention, is it not?"

The Marluk started to shrug, but Brion interrupted.

"No, you would have slain me by steel if you could," he said. "To win by magic exacts greater payment, and might not give you the sort of victory you seek if you would rule my human kingdom and not fear for your throne. The folk of Gwynedd would not take kindly to a Deryni king after your bloody ancestors."

The Marluk smiled. "By force, physical or arcane—it matters little in the long reckoning. It is the victory itself which will command the people after today. But you, Haldane, your position is far more precarious than mine, dynastically speaking. Do you see yon riders, and the slight one dressed in blue?"

He gestured with his sword toward the other opening of the clearing from which he and his men had come, where half a score of riders surrounded a pale, slight figure on a mouse-gray palfrey.

"Yonder is my daughter and heir, Haldane," the Marluk said smugly. "Regardless of the outcome here today, she rides free— you cannot stop her—to keep my name and memory until another time. But you—your brother and heir stands near, his life a certain forfeit if I win." He gestured toward Nigel, then rested the tip of his sword before him once more. "And the next and final Haldane is your Uncle Richard, a childless bachelor of fifty. After him, there are no others."

Brion's grip tightened on the hilt of his sword, and he glared across at his enemy with something approaching grudging respect. All that the Marluk had said was true. There *were* no other male Haldanes beyond his brother and his uncle, at least for now. Nor was there any way that he or his men could prevent the escape of the Marluk's heir. Even if he won today, the Marluk's daughter would remain a future menace. The centuries-long struggle for supremacy in Gwynedd would not end here—unless, of course, Brion lost.

The thought sobered him, cooled the hot blood racing through his veins and slowed his pounding heart. He must answer this usurper's challenge, and now, and with the only card he had left.

They had fought with force of steel before, and all for naught. Now they must face one another with other weapons.

Displaying far more confidence than he felt, for he would never play for higher stakes than life and crown, Brion let fall his shield and helm and strode slowly across half the distance separating him from his mortal enemy. Carefully, decisively, he traced an equal-armed cross in the dust with the tip of his sword, the first arm pointing toward the Marluk.

"I, Brion, Anointed of the Lord, King of Gwynedd and Lord of the Purple March, call thee forth to combat mortal, Hogan Gwernach, for that thou hast raised hostile hand against me and, through me, against my people of Gwynedd. This I will defend upon my body and my soul, to the death, so help me, God."

The Marluk's face had not changed expression during Brion's challenge, and now he, too, strode to the figure scratched in the dust and laid his sword tip along the same lines, retracing the cross.

"And I, Hogan Gwernach, descendant of the lawful kings of Gwynedd in antiquity, do return thy challenge, Brion Haldane, and charge that thou art base pretender to the throne and crown thou holdest. And this I will defend upon my body and my soul, to the death, so help me, God."

With the last words, he began drawing another symbol in the earth beside the cross—a detailed, winding interlace which caught and held Brion's concentration with increasing power. Only just in time, Brion recognized the spell for what it was and, with an oath, dashed aside the Marluk's sword with his own, erasing the symbol with his boot. He glared at the enemy standing but a sword's length away, keeping his anger in check only with the greatest exertion of will.

If I let him get me angry, he thought, *I'm dead.*

Biting back his rage, he forced his sword arm to relax.

The Marluk drew back a pace and shrugged almost apologetically at that—he had not really expected his diversion to work so well—then saluted with his sword and backed off another dozen paces. Brion returned the salute with a sharp, curt gesture and likewise withdrew the required distance. Then, without further preliminaries, he extended his arms to either side and murmured the words of a warding spell. As answering fire sprang up crimson at his back, the Marluk raised a similar defense, blue fire joining crimson to complete the protective circle. Beneath the canopy of light thus formed, arcs of energy began to crackle sword to sword, ebbing and flowing, as arcane battle was joined.

The circle brightened as they fought, containing energies so immense that all around it would have perished had the wards not held it in. The very air within grew hazy, so that those without could no longer see the principals who battled there. So it remained for nearly half an hour, the warriors of both sides drawing mistrustfully together to watch and wait. When, at last, the fire began to flicker erratically and die down, naught could be seen within the circle but two ghostly, fire-edged figures in silhouette, one of them staggering drunkenly.

They could not tell which was which. One of them had fallen to his knees and remained there, sword upraised in a last, desperate, warding-off gesture. The other stood poised to strike, but something seemed to hold him back. The tableau remained frozen that way for several heartbeats, the tension growing between the two; but then the kneeling one reeled sidewards and let fall his sword with a cry of anguish, collapsing forward on his hands to bow his head in defeat. The victor's sword descended as though in slow motion, severing head from body in one blow and showering dust and victor and vanquished with blood. The fire dimmed almost to nonexistence, and they could see that it was Brion who lived.

Then went up a mighty cheer from the men of Gwynedd. A few of the Marluk's men wheeled and galloped away across the field toward the rest of their party before anyone could stop them, but the rest cast down their weapons and surrendered immediately. At the mouth of the canyon beyond, a slender figure on a gray horse turned and rode away with her escort. There was no pursuit.

Brion could not have seen them through the haze, but he knew. Moving dazedly back to the center of the circle, he traced the dust-drawn cross a final time and mouthed the syllables of a banishing spell. Then, as the fiery circle died away, he gazed long at the now-empty canyon mouth before turning to stride slowly toward his men. They parted before him as he came, Gwynedd and Tolan men alike.

Perhaps a dozen men remained of Brion's force, a score or less of the Marluk's, and there was a taut, tense silence as he moved among them. He stopped and looked around him, at the men, at the wounded lying propped against their shields, at Nigel and Alaric still sitting upon their blood-bespattered war horses, at the bloody banner still in Nigel's hand. He stared at the banner for a long time, no one daring to break the strained silence. Then he let his gaze fall on each man in turn, catching and holding each man's attention in rapt, unshrinking thrall.

"We shall not speak of the details of this battle beyond this

place,'' he said simply. The words crackled with authority,
compulsion, and Alaric Morgan, of all who heard, knew the
force behind that simple statement. Though most of them would
never realize that fact, every man there had just been touched by
the special Haldane magic.

Brion held them thus for several heartbeats, no sound or
movement disturbing their rapt attention. Then Brion blinked and
smiled and the otherworldliness was no more. Instantly, Nigel
was springing from his horse to run and clasp his brother's arm.
Alaric, in a more restrained movement, swung his leg over the
saddle and slid to the ground, walked stiffly to greet his king.

"Well fought, Sire," he murmured, the words coming with
great difficulty.

"My thanks for making that possible, Alaric," the king replied, "though the shedding of blood has never been my wish."

He handed his sword to Nigel and brushed a strand of hair
from his eyes with a blood-streaked hand. Alaric swallowed and
made a nervous bow.

"No thanks are necessary, Sire. I but gave my service as I
must." He swallowed again and shifted uneasily, then abruptly
dropped to his knees and bowed his head.

"Sire, may I crave a boon of you?"

"A boon? You know you have but to ask, Alaric. I pray you,
stand not upon ceremony."

Alaric shook his head, brought his gaze to meet Brion's. "No,
this I will and must do, Sire." He raised joined hands before
him. "Sire, I would reaffirm my oath of fealty to you."

"Your oath?" Brion began. "But you have already sworn to
serve me, Alaric, and have given me your hand in friendship,
which I value far more from you than any oath."

"And I, Sire," Alaric nodded slightly. "But the fealty I gave
you before was such as any liegeman might give his Lord and
King. What I offer now is fealty for the powers which we share.
I would give you my fealty as Deryni."

There was a murmuring around them, and Nigel glanced at his
brother in alarm, but neither king nor kneeling squire heard. A
slight pause, a wry smile, and then Brion was taking the boy's
hands between his own blood-stained ones, gray eyes meeting
gray as he heard the oath of the first man to swear Deryni fealty
to a human king in nearly two centuries.

"I, Alaric Anthony, Lord Morgan, do become your liegeman
of life and limb and earthy worship. And faith and truth I will
bear unto you, *with all the powers at my command*, so long as
there is breath within me. This I swear upon my life, my honor,

and my faith and soul. If I be forsworn, may my powers desert me in my hour of need.''

Brion swallowed, his eyes never leaving Alaric's. ''And I for my part, pledge fealty to you, Alaric Anthony, Lord Morgan, to protect and defend you, and any who may depend upon you, *with all the powers at my command,* so long as there is breath within me. This I swear upon my life, my throne, and my honor as a man. And if I be forsworn, may dark destruction overcome me. This is the promise of Brion Donal Cinhil Urien Haldane, King of Gwynedd, Lord of the Purple March, and friend of Alaric Morgan.''

With these final words, Brion smiled and pressed Alaric's hands a bit more closely between his own, then released them and turned quickly to take back his sword from Nigel. He glanced at the stained blade as he held it before him.

''I trust you will not mind the blood,'' he said with a little smile, ''since it is through the shedding of this blood that I am able to do what I do now.''

Slowly he brought the flat of the blade to touch the boy's right shoulder.

''Alaric Anthony Morgan,'' the sword rose and crossed to touch the other shoulder, ''I create thee Duke of Corwyn, by right of thy mother,'' the blade touched the top of his head lightly and remained there. ''And I confirm thee in this title, for thy life and for the surviving issue of thy body, for so long as there shall be Morgan seed upon the earth.'' The sword was raised and touched to the royal lips, then reversed and brought to ground. ''So say I, Brion of Gwynedd. Arise, Duke Alaric.''

NOT LONG BEFORE
THE END

By Larry Niven

A swordsman battled a sorcerer, once upon a time.

In that age such battles were frequent. A natural antipathy exists between swordsmen and sorcerers, as between cats and small birds, or between rats and men. Usually the swordsman lost, and humanity's average intelligence rose some trifling fraction. Sometimes the swordsman won, and again the species was improved; for a sorcerer who cannot kill one miserable swordsman is a poor excuse for a sorcerer.

But this battle differed from the others. On one side, the sword itself was enchanted. On the other, the sorcerer knew a great and terrible truth.

We will call him the Warlock, as his name is both forgotten and impossible to pronounce. His parents had known what they were about. He who knows your name has power over you, but he must speak your name to use it.

The Warlock had found his terrible truth in middle age.

By that time he had traveled widely. It was not from choice. It was simply that he was a powerful magician, and he used his power, and he needed friends.

He knew spells to make people love a magician. The Warlock had tried these, but he did not like the side effects. So he commonly used his great power to help those around him, that they might love him without coercion.

He found that when he had been ten to fifteen years in a place, using his magic as whim dictated, his powers would weaken. If he moved away, they returned. Twice he had had to move, and twice he had settled in a new land, learned new customs, made new friends. It happened a third time, and he prepared to move again. But something set him to wondering.

Why should a man's powers be so unfairly drained out of him?

It happened to nations too. Throughout history, those lands which had been richest in magic had been overrun by barbarians

242

carrying swords and clubs. It was a sad truth, and one that did not bear thinking about, but the Warlock's curiosity was strong.

So he wondered, and he stayed to perform certain experiments.

His last experiment involved a simple kinetic sorcery set to spin a metal disc in midair. And when that magic was done, he knew a truth he could never forget.

So he departed. In succeeding decades he moved again and again. Time changed his personality, if not his body, and his magic became more dependable, if less showy. He had discovered a great and terrible truth, and if he kept it secret, it was through compassion. His truth spelled the end of civilization, yet it was of no earthly use to anyone.

So he thought. But some five decades later (the date was on the order of 12,000 B.C.) it occurred to him that all truths find a use somewhere, sometime. And so he built another disc and recited spells over it, so that (like a telephone number already dialed but for one digit) the disc would be ready if ever he needed it.

The name of the sword was Glirendree. It was several hundred years old, and quite famous.

As for the swordsman, his name is no secret. It was Belhap Sattlestone Wirldess ag Miracloat roo Cononson. His friends, who tended to be temporary, called him Hap. He was a barbarian, of course. A civilized man would have had more sense than to touch Glirendree, and better morals than to stab a sleeping woman. Which was how Hap had acquired his sword. Or vice versa.

The Warlock recognized it long before he saw it. He was at work in the cavern he had carved beneath a hill, when an alarm went off. The hair rose up, tingling, along the back of his neck. "Visitors," he said.

"I don't hear anything," said Sharla, but there was an uneasiness to her tone. Sharla was a girl of the village who had come to live with the Warlock. That day she had persuaded the Warlock to teach her some of his simpler spells.

"Don't you feel the hair rising on the back of your neck? I set the alarm to do that. Let me just check . . ." He used a sensor like a silver hula hoop set on edge. "There's trouble coming. Sharla, we've got to get you out of here."

"But . . ." Sharla waved protestingly at the table where they had been working.

"Oh, that. We can quit in the middle. That spell isn't dangerous.'' It was a charm against love-spells, rather messy to work, but safe and tame and effective. The Warlock pointed at the spear of light glaring through the hoop-sensor. ''That's dangerous. An enormously powerful focus of mana power is moving up the west side of the hill. You go down the east side.''

''Can I help? You've taught me *some* magic.''

The magician laughed a little nervously. ''Against that? That's Glirendree. Look at the size of the image, the color, the shape. No. You get out of here, and right now. The hill's clear on the eastern slope.''

''Come with me.''

''I can't. Not with Glirendree loose. Not when it's already got hold of some idiot. There are obligations.''

They came out of the cavern together, into the mansion they shared. Sharla, still protesting, donned a robe and started down the hill. The Warlock hastily selected an armload of paraphernalia and went outside.

The intruder was halfway up the hill: a large but apparently human being carrying something long and glittering. He was still a quarter of an hour downslope. The Warlock set up the silver hula hoop and looked through it.

The sword was a flame of mana discharge, an eye-hurting needle of white light. Glirendree, right enough. He knew of other, equally powerful mana foci, but none were portable, and none would show as a sword to the unaided eye.

He should have told Sharla to inform the Brotherhood. She had that much magic. Too late now.

There was no colored borderline to the spear of light.

No green fringe effect meant no protective spells. The swordsman had not tried to guard himself against what he carried. Certainly the intruder was no magician, and he had not the intelligence to get the help of a magician. Did he know *nothing* about Glirendree?

Not that that would help the Warlock. He who carries Glirendree was invulnerable to any power save Glirendree itself. Or so it was said.

''Let's test that,'' said the Warlock to himself. He dipped into his armload of equipment and came up with something wooden, shaped like an ocarina. He blew the dust off it, raised it in his fist and pointed it down the mountain. But he hesitated.

The loyalty spell was simple and safe, but it did have side effects. It lowered its victim's intelligence.

''Self-defense,'' the Warlock reminded himself, and blew into the ocarina.

The swordsman did not break stride. Glirendree didn't even glow; it had absorbed the spell that easily.

In minutes the swordsman would be here. The Warlock hurriedly set up a simple prognostics spell. At least he could learn who would win the coming battle.

No picture formed before him. The scenery did not even waver.

"Well, now," said the Warlock. "*Well,* now!" And he reached into his clutter of sorcerous tools and found a metal disc. Another instant's rummaging produced a double-edged knife, profusely inscribed in no known language, and very sharp.

At the top of the Warlock's hill was a spring, and the stream from that spring ran past the Warlock's house. The swordsman stood leaning on his sword, facing the Warlock across that stream. He breathed deeply, for it had been a hard climb.

He was powerfully muscled and profusely scarred. To the Warlock it seemed strange that so young a man should have found time to acquire so many scars. But none of his wounds had impaired motor functions. The Warlock had watched him coming up the hill. The swordsman was in top physical shape.

His eyes were deep blue and brilliant, and half an inch too close together for the Warlock's taste.

"I am Hap," he called across the stream. "Where is she?"

"You mean Sharla, of course. But why is that your concern?"

"I have come to free her from her shameful bondage, old man. Too long have you—"

"Hey, hey, hey. Sharla's my *wife.*"

"Too long have you used her for your vile and lecherous purposes. Too—"

"She stays of her own free will, you nit!"

"You expect me to believe that? As lovely a woman as Sharla, could she love an old and feeble warlock?"

"Do I look feeble?"

The Warlock did not look like an old man. He seemed Hap's age, some twenty years old, and his frame and his musculature were the equal of Hap's. He had not bothered to dress as he left the cavern. In place of Hap's scars, his back bore a tattoo in red and green and gold, an elaborately curlicued pentagramic design, almost hypnotic in its extradimensional involutions.

"Everyone in the village knows your age," said Hap. "You're two hundred years old, if not more."

"Hap," said the Warlock. "Belhap something-or-other roo Cononson. Now I remember. Sharla told me you tried to bother

her last time she went to the village. I should have done something about it then.''

''Old man, you lie. Sharla is under a spell. Everybody knows the power of a warlock's loyalty spell.''

''I don't use them. I don't like the side effects. Who wants to be surrounded by friendly morons?'' The Warlock pointed to Glirendree. ''Do you know what you carry?''

Hap nodded ominously.

''Then you ought to know better. Maybe it's not too late. See if you can transfer it to your left hand.''

''I tried that. I can't let go of it.'' Hap cut at the air, restlessly, with his sixty pounds of sword. ''I have to sleep with the damned thing clutched in my hand.''

''Well, it's too late then.''

''It's worth it,'' Hap said grimly. ''For now I can kill you. Too long has an innocent woman been subjected to your lecherous—''

''I know, I know.'' The Warlock changed languages suddenly, speaking high and fast. He spoke thus for almost a minute, then switched back to Rynaldese. ''Do you feel any pain?''

''Not a twinge,'' said Hap. He had not moved. He stood with his remarkable sword at the ready, glowering at the magician across the stream.

''No sudden urge to travel? Attacks of remorse? Change of body temperature?'' But Hap was grinning now, not at all nicely. ''I thought not. Well, it had to be tried.''

There was an instant of blinding light.

When it reached the vicinity of the hill, the meteorite had dwindled to the size of a baseball. It should have finished its journey at the back of Hap's head. Instead, it exploded a millisecond too soon. When the light had died, Hap stood within a ring of craterlets.

The swordsman's unsymmetrical jaw dropped, and then he closed his mouth and started forward. The sword hummed faintly.

The Warlock turned his back.

Hap curled his lip at the Warlock's cowardice. Then he jumped three feet backward from a standing start. A shadow had pulled itself from the Warlock's back.

In a lunar cave with the sun glaring into its mouth, a man's shadow on the wall might have looked that sharp and black. The shadow dropped to the ground and stood up, a humanoid outline that was less a shape than a window view of the ultimate blackness beyond the death of the universe. Then it leapt.

Glirendree seemed to move of its own accord. It hacked the demon once lengthwise and once across, while the demon seemed to batter against an invisible shield, trying to reach Hap even as it died.

"Clever," Hap panted. "A pentagram on your back, a demon trapped inside."

"That's clever," said the Warlock, "but it didn't work. Carrying Glirendree works, but it's not clever. I ask you again, do you know what you carry?"

"The most powerful sword ever forged." Hap raised the weapon high. His right arm was more heavily muscled than his left, and inches longer, as if Glirendree had been at work on it. "A sword to make me the equal of any warlock or sorceress, and without the help of demons, either. I had to kill a woman who loved me to get it, but I paid that price gladly. When I have sent you to your just reward, Sharla will come to me—"

"She'll spit in your eye. Now will you listen to me? Glirendree *is* a demon. If you had an ounce of sense, you'd cut your arm off at the elbow."

Hap looked startled. "You mean there's a demon imprisoned in the metal?"

"Get it through your head. *There is no metal.* It's a demon, a bound demon, and it's a parasite. It'll age you to death in a year unless you cut it loose. A warlock of the northlands imprisoned it in its present form, then gave it to one of his bastards, Jeery of Something-or-other. Jeery conquered half this continent before he died on the battlefield, of senile decay. It was given into the charge of the Rainbow Witch a year before I was born, because there never was a woman who had less use for people, especially men."

"That happens to have been untrue."

"Probably Glirendree's doing. Started her glands up again, did it? She should have guarded against that."

"A year," said Hap. "One year."

But the sword stirred restlessly in his hand. "It will be a glorious year," said Hap, and he came forward.

The Warlock picked up a copper disc. "Four," he said, and the disc spun in midair.

By the time Hap had sloshed through the stream, the disc was a blur of motion. The Warlock moved to keep it between himself and Hap, and Hap dared not touch it, for it would have sheared through anything at all. He crossed around it, but again the Warlock had darted to the other side. In the pause he snatched up something else: a silvery knife, profusely inscribed.

"Whatever that is," said Hap, "it can't hurt me. No magic can affect me while I carry Glirendree."

"True enough," said the Warlock. "The disc will lose its force in a minute anyway. In the meantime, I know a secret that I would like to tell, one I could never tell to a friend."

Hap raised Glirendree above his head and, two-handed, swung it down on the disc. The sword stopped jarringly at the disc's rim.

"It's protecting you," said the Warlock. "If Glirendree hit the rim now, the recoil would knock you clear down to the village. Can't you hear the hum?"

Hap heard the whine as the disc cut the air. The tone was going up and up the scale.

"You're stalling," he said.

"That's true. So? Can it hurt you?"

"No. You were saying you knew a secret." Hap braced himself, sword raised, on one side of the disc, which now glowed red at the edge.

"I've wanted to tell someone for such a long time. A hundred and fifty years. Even Sharla doesn't know." The Warlock still stood ready to run if the swordsman should come after him. "I'd learned a little magic in those days, not much compared to what I know now, but big, showy stuff. Castles floating in the air. Dragons with golden scales. Armies turned to stone, or wiped out by lightning, instead of simple death spells. Stuff like that takes a lot of power, you know?"

"I've heard of such things."

"I did it all the time, for myself, for friends, for whoever happened to be king, or whomever I happened to be in love with. And I found that after I'd been settled for a while, the power would leave me. I'd have to move elsewhere to get it back."

The copper disc glowed bright orange with the heat of its spin. It should have fragmented, or melted, long ago.

"Then there are the dead places, the places where a warlock dares not go. Places where magic doesn't work. They tend to be rural areas, farmlands and sheep ranges, but you can find the old cities, the castles built to float which now lie tilted on their sides, the unnaturally aged bones of dragons, like huge lizards from another age.

"So I started wondering."

Hap stepped back a bit from the heat of the disc. It glowed pure white now, and it was like a sun brought to earth. Through the glare Hap had lost sight of the Warlock.

"So I built a disc like this one and set it spinning. Just a simple kinetic sorcery, but with a constant acceleration and no limit point. You know what mana is?"

"What's happening to your voice?"

"Mana is the name we give to the power behind magic." The Warlock's voice had gone weak and high.

A horrible suspicion came to Hap. The Warlock had slipped down the hill, leaving his voice behind! Hap trotted around the disc, shading his eyes from its heat.

An old man sat on the other side of the disc. His arthritic fingers, half-crippled with swollen joints, played with a rune-inscribed knife. "What I found out—oh, there you are. Well, it's too late now."

Hap raised his sword, and his sword changed.

It was a massive red demon, horned and hooved, and its teeth were in Hap's right hand. It paused, deliberately, for the few seconds it took Hap to realize what had happened and to try to jerk away. Then it bit down, and the swordsman's hand was off at the wrist.

The demon reached out, slowly enough, but Hap in his surprise was unable to move. He felt the taloned fingers close his windpipe.

He felt the strength leak out of the taloned hand, and he saw surprise and dismay spread across the demon's face.

The disc exploded. All at once and nothing first, it disintegrated into a flat cloud of metallic particles and was gone, flashing away as so much meteorite dust. The light was as lightning striking at one's feet. The sound was its thunder. The smell was vaporized copper.

The demon faded, as a chameleon fades against its background. Fading, the demon slumped to the ground in slow motion, and faded further, and was gone. When Hap reached out with his foot, he touched only dirt.

Behind Hap was a trench of burnt earth.

The spring had stopped. The rocky bottom of the stream was drying in the sun.

The Warlock's cavern had collapsed. The furnishings of the Warlock's mansion had gone crashing down into that vast pit, but the mansion itself was gone without trace.

Hap clutched his messily severed wrist, and he said, "But what happened?"

"Mana," the Warlock mumbled. He spat out a complete set of blackened teeth. "Mana. What I discovered was that the

power behind magic is a natural resource, like the fertility of the
soil. When you use it up, it's gone.''

"But—"

"Can you see why I kept it a secret? One day all the wide
world's mana will be used up. No more mana, no more magic.
Do you know that Atlantis is tectonically unstable? Succeeding
sorcerer-kings renew the spells each generation to keep the whole
continent from sliding into the sea. What happens when the
spells don't work anymore? They couldn't possibly evacuate the
whole continent in time. Kinder not to let them know.''

"But . . . that disc."

The Warlock grinned with his empty mouth and ran his hands
through snowy hair. All the hair came off in his fingers, leaving
his scalp bare and mottled. "Senility is like being drunk. The
disc? I told you. A kinetic sorcery with no upper limit. The disc
keeps accelerating until all the mana in the locality has been used
up.''

Hap moved a step forward. Shock had drained half his strength.
His foot came down jarringly, as if all the spring were out of his
muscles.

"You tried to kill me."

The Warlock nodded. "I figured if the disc didn't explode and
kill you while you were trying to go around it, Glirendree would
strangle you when the constraint wore off. What are you complaining about? It cost you a hand, but you're free of Glirendree.''

Hap took another step, and another. His hand was beginning
to hurt, and the pain gave him strength. "Old man," he said
thickly. "Two hundred years old. I can break your neck with the
hand you left me. And I will.''

The Warlock raised the inscribed knife.

"That won't work. No more magic.'' Hap slapped the Warlock's hand away and took the Warlock by his bony throat.

The Warlock's hand brushed easily aside, and came back, and
up. Hap wrapped his arms around his belly and backed away
with his eyes and mouth wide open. He sat down hard.

"A knife always works,'' said the Warlock.

"Oh,'' said Hap.

"I worked the metal myself, with ordinary blacksmith's tools,
so the knife wouldn't crumble when the magic was gone. The
runes aren't magic. They only say—''

"Oh,'' said Hap. "Oh." He toppled sideways.

The Warlock lowered himself onto his back. He held the knife
up and read the markings, in a language only the Brotherhood
remembered.

AND THIS, TOO, SHALL PASS AWAY. It was a very old platitude, even then.

He dropped his arm back and lay looking at the sky.

Presently the blue was blotted by a shadow.

"I told you to get out of here," he whispered.

"You should have known better. What's *happened* to you?"

"No more youth spells. I knew I'd have to do it when the prognostics spell showed blank." He drew a ragged breath. "It was worth it. I killed Glirendree."

"Playing hero, at your age! What can I do? How can I help?"

"Get me down the hill before my heart stops. I never told you my true age—"

"I knew. The whole village knows." She pulled him to sitting position, pulled one of his arms around her neck. It felt dead. She shuddered, but she wrapped her own arm around his waist and gathered herself for the effort. "You're so thin! Come on, love. We're going to stand up." She took most of his weight onto her, and they stood up.

"Go slow. I can hear my heart trying to take off."

"How far do we have to go?"

"Just to the foot of the hill, I think. Then the spells will work again, and we can rest." He stumbled. "I'm going blind," he said.

"It's a smooth path, and all downhill."

"That's why I picked this place. I knew I'd have to use the disc someday. You can't throw away knowledge. Always the time comes when you use it, because you have to, because it's there."

"You've changed so. So—so ugly. And you smell."

The pulse fluttered in his neck, like a hummingbird's wings. "Maybe you won't want me, after seeing me like this."

"You can change back, can't you?"

"Sure. I can change to anything you like. What color eyes do you want?"

"I'll be like this myself someday," she said. Her voice held cool horror. And it was fading; he was going deaf.

"I'll teach you the proper spells, when you're ready. They're dangerous. Blackly dangerous."

She was silent for a time. Then: "What color were *his* eyes? You know, Belhap Sattlestone whatever."

"Forget it," said the Warlock, with a touch of pique.

And suddenly his sight was back.

But not forever, thought the Warlock as they stumbled through the sudden daylight. When the mana runs out, I'll go like a blown candle flame, and civilization will follow. No more magic, no more magic-based industries. Then the whole world will be barbarian until men learn a new way to coerce nature, and the swordsmen, the damned stupid swordsmen will win after all.

MAUREEN BIRNBAUM, BARBARIAN SWORDSPERSON

(as told to Bitsy Spiegelman)
By George Alec Effinger

The last time I saw Muffy Birnbaum was, let me see, last December—no, make that last January, because it was right after exams and before Mums and I spent a couple of dreadful weeks at the B and T in Palm Beach. So that makes it ten months almost, and she told me to wait a year before I revealed this to the world, to use her exact words. But I don't think Muffy will mind that I'm two months early. She's long ago and far away, if you believe her story. Do I believe her story? Look. She was missing for a full week, and then I get this telegram—a telegram, can you believe it? Not a phone call. Meet me under the Clock, 15 January, noonish. Come alone. Trust me. Kisses, Muffy. What was I supposed to think? I show up and she's not there, but there's a note waiting for me: Come to Room 1623. *Just too mysterious, but up I go. The door's open and I walk in, and there's goddamn Maureen Danielle Birnbaum practically* naked, *wearing nothing but these leather straps across her shoulders and a little gold G-string, and she's got this goddamn* sword *in one hand like she was expecting the Sheriff of Nottingham or something to come through the door instead of her best friend and roommate. I couldn't think of anything to say at first, so she called down for some ice, pointed to a chair, and began to tell me this story. I'll give it to you just the way it is on my tape; then you tell me if you believe it.*

So listen, I'm telling you this story. Believe me, I'd *had* it, absolutely *had* it. School was a *complete* bore and I was absolutely falling to pieces. Absolutely. I needed a vacation and I told Daddy that a little intense skiing action would shape me up very nicely, and so, just like that, I found myself at Mad River Glen, looking very neat, I thought, until I saw some of the competition, the collegiate talent. They were deadly cute and they knew it, and all you had to do was ask them and they'd tell you all about it. You could just about tell where they went to

school, like they were wearing uniforms. The Vassar girls were
the ones sort of flouncing downhill wearing their circle pins on
the front of their hundred-dollar goose-down ski parkas. The
Bennington girls were the ones looking rugged and trying to ski
back *uphill*. Definitely Not Our Kind, sweetie.

Are those your cigarettes, Bitsy? Mind if I—no, just toss me
the whole pack. I have matches here in the ashtray. My *God*. I
haven't had a cigarette in *so long*—

Where was I? Vermont, right. So I was staring down this
goddamn hill, if you can believe it, and I'm all set to push off
and go barreling down the mountain at some outrageous speed,
when I stop. I look up at the sky—it's starting to get dark, you
know, and absolutely clear and kind of sweet, but *cold*—when I
feel this weird feeling inside. First I thought I was going to die,
just absolutely *die*. Then I thought, "My God, I know what it is.
And they always say nothing can happen if—" You know. But I
was wrong both times. The next thing I knew I was standing
stark naked in the snow beside my body, which was still dressed
up in this cute outfit from L.L. Bean, and I thought, "Muffy,
you've *had* it." I thought I was dead or something, but I didn't
understand why I was so goddamn *cold*. Then I looked up into
the sky and this bright red dot caught my eye and I sort of
shivered. I knew right then, I said to myself, "That is where I'm
going." Heaven or Hell, here I come. And just like that I felt
this whushing, and dizziness and everything, and I opened my
eyes, and I wasn't in Vermont anymore but I was still cold.

I'm drinking Bloody Marys. It isn't too early for you, is it?
Then you try calling down for ice, I've given up on them. Are
you hungry? We'll have lunch later. I'm putting myself on a
diet, but I'll go with you and you can have something.

Anyway, they didn't prepare me at the Greenberg School for
what was waiting for me when I opened my eyes. Here I was on
some weirdo planet out in space, for God's sake. Say, Bitsy, you
have any gum or what? Chiclets? Yuck. Let me have—no, just
one, thanks. A weirdo planet, if you can believe that. I was
standing there at the top of the run one second, having this
unbelievable fight with the zipper on the ski jacket Pammy—
that's Daddy's new wife—bought me for Christmas—and the
next minute I'm up to my ankles in orange grunge. And I was so
cold I thought I would freeze to death. I was cold because—
we're just going to have to live without the ice, I think, Bitsy,
because this hotel probably has a goddamn *policy* against it or
something, so just pour it in the glass—I was standing there in
the proverbial buff! Me! Three years living with me at the

Greenberg School, and even *you* never saw my pink little derrière. And here I am starko for the whole world to see. What world it was I didn't know, so I didn't know *who* could see, but believe me, Bitsy, I didn't particularly care. Right then I had two or three pressing problems on my mind, and getting dressed was high on the list. I really missed that ski outfit. It was cold as hell.

All around me there was nothing but this gross orange stuff on the ground. I don't know what it was. It wasn't grass, I know that. It felt more like the kind of sponge the cleaning woman keeps under your sink for a couple of years. Gross. And there was nothing else to see except some low hills off in one direction. I decided to head that way. There sure wasn't anything any other way, and—who knew?—there may have been a Bloomingdale's on the other side of the hills. At that point I would have settled for Lamston's, *believe* me.

You're going to die laughing when I tell you this, absolutely die. When I took a step I went sailing up into the air. Just like a balloon, and I thought, "Muffy, honey, *what* did they put in your *beer?*" When I settled back down I tried it again, and I flew away again. It took me absolutely an hour to figure out how to walk and run and all that. I still don't know why it was. One of those lame boys from Brush-Bennett would know, right off the bat, but it wasn't all that important to me. I just needed to learn to handle it. So in a while, still freezing my completely cute buns off, I got to the top of the first hill and I looked down on my new world.

You want to know what I saw? Was that the door? *You* better get it, Bitsy, because even though Daddy stays here *all* the time the staff has been just *too* dreary for words. You should have heard what they said about my sword. They talked about my sword a lot, because they were too embarrassed to mention my costume. I think it's—who? The ice? Would you be a dear and leave the boy something? I don't have a goddamn *penny*. I mean, you don't see any pockets, do you?

There was more orange crud all the way to the whatyoucall— the horizon. But there was a little crowd of people down there about a quarter of a mile away. It looked to me like a little tailgate party, like we used to have with your parents in New Haven before the Harvard game. I thought, "That's nice, they'll be able to drive me to a decent motel or something until I can get settled." But then I wondered how I was going to walk up to them all naked and glowing with health and frostbite and all. I thought about covering up the more strategic areas with the orange stuff from the ground, but I didn't even know if I could rip it loose. I was standing there thinking when I heard this girl scream. She sounded like Corkie the time we threw that dead fish into the shower with her. There was something *awful* going on down there, a mugging or a purse-snatching or something terrible, so what does yours truly do? I started running downhill toward them. Don't look so *surprised*. It's just something you do when you find yourself on a creepy planet, undressed and stone cold, with nothing else around except the two moons in the sky. Did I mention that there were two moons? Well, there were. I ran toward the people because I needed a lift into town, wherever it was, and if I helped the poor girl out maybe her daddy would let me stay at their place for a while.

When I got closer I saw that I had made just a little bitty mistake. The station wagon and the Yalies turned into a drastic and severe kind of fight, a brawl, really, except everybody was using one of these swords and they were using them for *real*. I mean, Bitsy, my *God*, blood was pouring all over *everywhere* and people were actually *dying* and it was all kind of heroic and all that and *very* horrible and dramatic. It was people against big, giant things with four arms. No, really. *Really*. Bitsy, stop *laughing*. There were these huge old creatures with four arms, and they were chopping away at the normal-sized people, everybody fighting away with these *intense* grins on their faces. I never did find out about that, why they were all *smiling* while they were whacking away at each other. Anyway, while I stood there the two groups just about wiped each other out, all the giant creatures except one and all the people except this one positively *devastating* guy. All the other guys and girls were lying very dead on the orange stuff, and it wasn't really *surprising*. I mean, just imagine something that's twelve feet tall and has arms slashing swords around up where you can barely *see*, for God's sake. And then this *darling* boy goes and tangles his adorable legs and falls over backwards.

Bitsy, are you listening to this, or what? I mean, I don't know why I even bothered—no, look. I didn't *have* to send you the telegram. I could have called Mother. Except she would have had *kittens* if she had seen me like this. Do you understand? This was a very moving moment for me, Bitsy, I mean, watching these kids fighting like that and all, and even though I didn't know them, I got very emotional and everything. So I'd appreciate it, I really would, if you'd show a little respect. *You've* never had to fight for *anything* except with the burger-brained Amherst freshman you went out with senior year. *Of course* I remember him. He reminds me a lot of these four-armed things.

Well, if anything *terminal* happened to my blond hero, that monster was coming after *me* next. So, perky little thing that I am, I run up and grab a sword—this sword, I call her "Old Betsy" because that's what Davy Crockett called his rifle or something—I grab Old Betsy and I stand there trying not to look that . . . thing in the eye. This was very easy, believe me, because his eyes are *at least* six feet over my head. And I'm all nice and balanced—*you* remember, you were there, you remember how *tremendous* I was in that six weeks of fencing we had sophomore year, with what's-her-name, Miss Duplante. You remember how she was absolutely terrified of me? Anyway, picture me standing there *en garde* waiting for this four-armed darling to settle into position. But he *doesn't*, that's what's so scary, he just goes *whacko!* and takes a wide swipe at my goddamn head.

Only I'm not there anymore, I'm about fifty feet away. I remembered that I could jump, but *really*. So I hop around for a minute or two to get my bearings and to stay away from the thing's sword. I hop, and I jump, bounce, bounce, bounce, all around the landscape. And the creature is watching me, *mad as hell*. My blond dream is still on the ground, and *he's* watching too. "Get a *sword*, dummy," I yell at him, and he nods. That's something else I forgot to tell you, Bitsy. All the people on this planet speak English. It's really neat and very convenient. So between the two of us we finished the monster off. No, it's just *too awful* to think about, stabbing and bleeding and hacking and all like that. Fencing was a lot tidier—you know, just a kind of polite poking around with a sharp stick. And *I* had to do all the *heavyweight* hacking because my boyfriend couldn't reach anything terribly vital on the four-armed thing. He was taking mighty swings at the giant's knees, and meanwhile good old Muffy is cutting its pathetic little head off. Just altogether *unreal*.

Well, that's the dynamic, exciting carnage part. After I took care of the immediate danger, the boy starts to talk to me. "Hello," he goes. "You were excellent."

"Thanks," I go. At this point I feel like I'm riding on a horse with only one rocker, but I don't let it show. The old Greenberg School *pride*, Bitsy.

He goes, "My name is Prince Van."

"Uh-huh," I go, "I'm Maureen Birnbaum. My daddy is a contract lawyer and I live with my mother. We raise golden retrievers."

"How nice," the prince goes. Let me tell you what this guy *looked* like! You wouldn't *believe* it! Do you remember that boy who came down to visit that drecky redhead from Staten Island? No, not the boy from Rutgers, the one from—where was it? That place I never *heard* of—Colby College, in Maine? Sounds like a goddamn *cheese* factory or something? Anyway, standing beside me on the orange stuff is something just like him, only the prince is awesome. He is tall and strong and blond with perfect teeth and eyes like Paul Newman and he's wearing, well, you see what *I'm* wearing. Just *imagine*, honey, if that isn't just too devastating for you. He is *beautiful*. And his name is Prince Van. I always told you that someday my prince would—

Okay, okay. I didn't really know what to say to him or anything. I mean, we'd just had this sort of pitched battle and all, and there were all these unpleasant *bodies* lying around—we were stepping over people here and there, and I was trying not to notice. We stopped and he bent down and took this harness for me from someone he said had been his sister. He didn't seem sad or anything. He was very brave, *intensely* brave, no tears for Sis, the gang back at the palace wouldn't approve. And all the dead boys looked just like him, all blond and large and uncomfortably cute, and all the girls looked just like Tri-Delts, with feathered blond hair and perfect teeth. They had been his retinue, Prince Van explained, and he said I shouldn't grieve. He could get another one.

"Where to?" I go. The palace couldn't be too far away, I thought.

"Well," he says—and his voice was like a handful of Valium; I just wanted to curl up and listen to it—he says, like, "my city is two thousand miles *that* way," he pointed, "but there is a closer city one thousand miles *that* way." He pointed behind us.

I go, "*Thousand?* You've *got* to be kidding."

He says, like, "I have never seen anyone like you." And he smiled. Bitsy, that was just the kind of thing my mother had *warned* me about, and I had begun to think it didn't really exist. I think I was in love.

"I'm from another world," I go. I tried to sound like I partied around in space quite a bit.

"That explains it," he goes. "It explains your strength and agility and your exotic beauty. I am captivated by your raven tresses. No one on our world has hair your color. It is very beautiful." *Raven tresses*, for God's sake! I think I blushed, and I think he wanted me to. We were holding hands by now. I was thinking about one or two thousand miles alone with Prince Van of Who-Knows-Where. I wondered what boys and girls did on this planet when they were alone. I decided that it was the same everywhere.

We walked for a long time and I asked a lot of questions. He must have thought I was just *really* lame, but he never laughed at me. I learned that the cities were so far because we were walking across the bottom of what had once been a great ocean, years and years before. There weren't oceans and lakes and things on this planet now. They have all their water delivered or something. I thought, "There's *oil* down there." I wanted to remember that for when we got to the palace. I don't think anyone had realized it yet.

"Then where do you go sailing?" I go.

"Sailing?" he asked innocently.

"What about swimming?"

"Swimming?"

He was cute, absolutely *tremendous* in fact, but life without sailing and swimming would be just too terribly *triste*, you know? And I think he was just being polite before when I mentioned golden retrievers.

I say, like, "Is there somwhere where I can pick up some clothes?" I figured that although his city was two thousand miles away, there were probably isolated little ocean-bottom suburbs along the way or shopping malls where all the blond people came to buy new straps and swords and stuff.

"Clothes?" he goes. I knew he was going to say that, I just *knew* it, but as gross as it was I had to hear it from his own lips.

I walked along for a while, dying, absolutely *dying* for a cigarette, not saying anything. Then I couldn't stand it any longer. "Van," I go, "listen. It isn't like it hasn't been wonderful with you, cutting up that big old monster and all. But, like, there are some things about this relationship that are totally the worst, but *really*."

"Relationship?" he goes. He kept smiling. I think I could eventually see enough of it.

I explained it all to him. There were no horses. There was no sailing, no swimming, no skiing, no raquetball. There were no penny loafers, no mixers at the boys' schools, no yearbooks. There was no Junior Year Abroad, no Franny and Zooey Glass, no Nantucket Island, *no Coors*. There was no Sunday *Times*, no Godiva chocolates, no Dustin Hoffman. There was no Joni Mitchell and no food processors and no golden retrievers and no little green Triumphs.

There were no clothes. Bitsy, *there was no shopping!*

So kind of sadly I kissed him on the cheek and told myself
that his couldn't-be-cuter expression was a little sad, too. I say,
like, "*Adieu, mon cher*," and I give him a little wave. Then I
stretched myself out toward the sky again—oh, yes, just a little
late I told myself that I wasn't absolutely sure about what I was
doing, that I might end up God only knew where—and waited to
whush back to the snowy mountaintop in Vermont. I missed. But
fortunately it wasn't as bad as it could have been. I mean, I
didn't land on *Saturn* or anything. I turned up at the corner of
Eighth Avenue and 45th Street. No one noticed me very much; I
fit right into that neighborhood.

So if I can just ask you a little favor, Bitsy, then I'll be on my
way. Yes, on my way, goddamn it, I'm going back. I'm not
going to leave that but *totally* attractive Prince Van to those
perky blond hometown honeys—he is *mine*. I kept my harness
and Old Betsy on the way here, so I think I know how to get
back there again with anything I want to take with me. So I want
to pick up a few things first. My daddy always told me to Be
Prepared. He said that all the time, he's a Mason or something.
He sure was prepared when he met Pammy, and he's close to
fifty years old.

Never mind. Anyway, let's go rummage in a bin somewhere
and suit me up with a plaid skirt or two and some cute jeans and
some sweaters and some alligator shirts and Top-Siders and a
brand-new insulated ski jacket and sunglasses and some *Je Reviens*
and stuff. It'll be fun!

Oh. And a circle pin. My old one wore out.

*We went shopping at Saks and Bloomingdale's—I went to
Korvettes and got her some cheaper clothes first, though. I
didn't want to walk around midtown Manhattan with Muffy while
she was wearing nothing but suspenders and no pants. We
charged four hundred dollars to Mum's cards, and let me tell
you I heard about that a few weeks later. But I was sworn to
secrecy. Now Muffy's gone again, back to her secret paradise in
the sky, back to Prince Van of the terribly straight teeth. I hope
she's happy. I hope she comes back someday to tell me her
adventures. I hope she pays me back the four hundred dollars.
Perhaps only time will tell. . . .*

THURIGON AGONISTES

By Ardath Mayhar

The bath-slaves held the great towels high to wrap his dripping nakedness. Thurigon smiled beneath his white beard, for he knew that they also turned their eyes aside from his hard-muscled body. Such vigor at his advanced age was proof to them, more even than his position as Chief of the Council, that he was, indeed, a terribly potent sorcerer.

He stepped onto the velvet rug and stretched himself on the padded couch. He could hear the patter of bare feet as the slaves left the bath to him and Ankush, his masseur. At the ripple of the hanging beside him, he looked up and grinned at the huge man who loomed over the couch.

"So, Ankush. Another day and we still live. A miracle, perhaps?"

The big black face was grim. "To this point, Sorcerer. But tongues wag in the marketplace. Pernicious rumors fly through the streets with the bats at nightfall. Your seeing was not false. One comes. An enemy to fear, for even the weakliest of the wizardlings have felt his approach."

"You are my ear, Ankush. If I could trust those on the Council as I can rely upon you, things would not seem so grim. How, I wonder, in a land that breeds magicians in abundance, can one lone wanderer pose a threat? Yet my heart chills when I think of him. My inner eye cannot see his face, only a lean shape in leather and steel. And the studded ball upon a chain that dangles from his belt, swinging with every step. Why does that frighten me, who heads the Council of Sorcerers?"

"Best ask your fellows, Sorcerer. I am a simple man of the people. My talents are not those of your kind." The scarred face wrinkled in a fierce grin, and Thurigon shuddered. He had seen Ankush tear the head from the shoulders of a living man almost as large as he, at the past winter's Games.

At times the thought of those tremendous hands moving upon his aged skin made the wizard shiver. Hands that had slain many. Hands that could tear him apart, for all his vigor, as easily

as they could a kitten. Yet there was something subtly exciting,
too, about being massaged by a proven killer of men. And at his
age excitement was too infrequent to relinquish.

Now he sighed. "I hate portents," he said. "I have seen them
come many times before, and they never prove easy or benefi-
cial. Not to the city; not to the Council; not, most emphatically,
to me. Yet this is the strongest portent that I have known in all
my years on the Council. Listen closely, Ankush, as you go
about the markets and the wineshops. And in three days—not
more, mind you—come back to my house. It is in my mind that
I will need your strength and your skills more than any of those I
or my comrades possess."

Ankush grunted and put his strength to the task of loosening
the old man's muscles, relaxing his nerves. When the oil had
been used up, and Thurigon was gleaming pinkly, he held out
his hand to the sorcerer.

When Thurigon was sitting, the big man hunkered down
beside the couch and put his head close to that of the wizard. "I
will be here in three days, Sorcerer. But look to your spells.
Even I, untalented as any in the land, feel something terrible
about this one who comes. Ghosts dance among my bones when
I think of him. Look well into your glazen bowls of water. Cast
your ivory pieces carefully. This that comes frightens me. Even
me! But you need not tell that about." He stood and took his
silver tray of unguents. Without another word or glance, he
parted the draperies. The swish as they fell together again was
the only sound he made.

Thurigon found himself compelled to follow the Black's advice. Once his robers had done with him, he went directly to the
tower that he had fallen heir to as head of the Council. One spell
was required to open the door. Another took him through the
invisible shield that hung just inside it. And there he felt, for the
time, secure.

Truly, Ankush knew little of sorcery. The bowls and the
ivories were the tools of the journeymen at his trade. He was a
Master and needed no toys. Yet even he must have some aid in
wresting the secrets of the past and present and future from the
fabric of the world. His most secret thing was a mirror.

Touching a spring that hid beneath a carven stag on a pedestal,
he turned to watch as a painting slipped aside into the wall,
revealing a glass that stood a man's height and more than a
man's width. Such a clear, true substance had never before been
seen in Gereon, and his possession of such a treasure was a
secret that only he held. For more than one reason.

He faced the clear depths. Yet only a faint haze of color reflected from the room about him. His own shape was even less distinct. Instead, the mirror was focused upon a rough track that cut through hills that were covered with stunted growth. "The Hills of Hurthal," the sorcerer murmured to himself. He had followed that selfsame track on his journey back to Gereon with the mirror.

For a moment he thought that no moving shape was there in the glass. Then he realized that it was just now moving near enough to see. A mere speck in the distance, it grew rapidly to the shape of a tall figure, striding steadily toward him. Thurigon flinched, the merest hint of a motion. Then he sighed.

"There is still time. Three days, even at that pace. In three days, all the forces of our power will be marshaled to hold back whatever ill that marcher brings." His voice was not so sure as his words.

He watched for a long time. In that interval, the leather-clad warrior came very near, seemingly marching into the reverse of the glass. Then the perspective shifted, and once more it was a speck in the distance, one hill-slope nearer the City of Gereon-Prime. There was a shrine beside the track, midway between the oncomer and his watcher. Its three-tiered roof peaked above the two-walled enclosure that held a stone carving of the Sorcerers' God, Jephal. For the first time in hand-spans of years, Thurigon sent a prayer toward his patron.

"Lend us your strength, Jephal-Mage. We who are your distant children will have need of it." His voice died away, and his piercing eyes turned again toward the approaching shape. The steadiness of the stride was frightening. One could surmise that a person who marched so, without rest or hesitation, over such rough terrain must be more like a mechanism than a man. He seemed armed with more-than-human determination.

The light was dying from the room, as the sun sank. Thurigon touched the spring that returned the mirror to its concealment. With a grimace, he turned from the room and made for his own chamber, where a light meal waited for him.

The handmaid cringed behind the draperies of the window, waiting for his commands and dreading them, he knew, with the terror common to the talentless kind. The thought gave him pleasure, which had grown even less frequent than excitement in these days of his age. He would have liked to give her real reason to shudder, but it had been long since a woman had roused him to passion. For this reason, and others even more pressing, he hated the sex with maliciousness.

Now he thought of a thing that would tear the heart from that useless quiver of robes and tresses. He turned his head toward the curtains and gestured with his chin, one curt bob.

Telessa came at once, dropping to her knees before him.

"Tonight," Thurigon said in his most honey-sweet voice; "I would take pleasure. Bring me your son Deran."

Her golden tan face paled to the shade of muddy water. A shudder ran from head to heel. Her hands clasped together, but she knew—who better?—that to appeal his word would lead to worse than death for her and her son. She bowed her head. He could almost see the hidden tears, the freezing of her blood.

Thurigon laughed, as the draperies swished together behind her. He felt invigorated at the thought of the evening to come. A double-edged pleasure was seldom met with, now, and the suffering of the son, added to that of the mother, would be a feast for his dulled senses.

When the dying child was carried from his chamber, he lay for a long time, savoring the exquisite pleasure of mishandling the boy. Deran's terror had added much to the pleasure of the moment, and Telessa's agony had reached him even from the slaves' hall to which he had sent her. Surfeited, he waited for sleep.

Instead there came a vision. The dim flambeaux glimmered to dullness. A midnight cloud seemed to fill the room. The old Sorcerer tried to sit, but a stifling weight lay upon his chest, and he could not move.

He could feel the darkness against his skin, as a fog in his nostrils, a pressure in his ears. Terror brought sweat, a mad pumping of his heart. But a spark of light grew before his eyes. Bright. Forming a face in the midst of the bubble of light.

"Jephal!" he gasped, as the familiar face came clear. The stony eyes turned in their sockets, seeing him even as he lay in darkness. The furrowed brow bent into deep crevices. The narrow lips tightened. Then they opened.

"This world was dedicated to wizardry, to be ruled by those with the Gift. The Other Gods, busy with their many works, believed that those who court wisdom and practice the Great Arts would serve the ungifted people well. Much power was entrusted to them. To you, Thurigon Tor En-Ne. You knew, in the beginning, that that power was not without restriction. You also knew, once, that you were not unobserved, even in the busy-ness of the gods. I am their observer. I have watched as you went from wisdom to folly, from virtue to villainy. Yet I believed that, given time, you would see your own error and return to the paths that lead to wisdom and kindness. To learn the truths of the universe is to become loving of the poor morsels of flesh who must exist within that cold continuum.

"There was within you a potential for the greatest goodness. But you chose that other potential—that for the greatest possible ill. We have been patient. Too patient, while your people suffer beneath your unwisdom and through your jaded appetites. You have weakened your powers, Sorcerer. Wicked self-indulgence, when it is not allowed to touch the flesh, corrodes the soul. You will find that you no longer control those potent gifts that were yours. In two days' time, you will need all that you possess . . . and they may well be insufficient for your needs. Beware, Thurigon. We who set you in your place no longer sustain you!"

The face was gone. The blackness retreated, and the room glimmered with the soft light he demanded. Struggling to sit among his cushions, he saw the empty wine-jar on the carpet beside him. Ahh. Much is induced by wine, he thought, and he lay back, turned on his side, and slept deeply.

In the next days he avoided thinking of that nightmare. Jephal was lifeless stone. He had proven that to his own satisfaction. The thrice-yearly rituals were intended to keep the ungifted ones awe-stricken and devoted. But deep in his innermost self, he felt the unease of that marching figure. He could not eradicate it—indeed, it grew. So it was with relief that he woke on the third morning to find Ankush beside him.

"The day," said the big Black, folding his arms over his muscle-bound belly and frowning fiercely. "Have you considered well?"

"I have watched as the challenger has approached, hill by hill, valley and meadow and wood. I have practiced my arts, strengthened the spells at my command. Yet I have not determined the identity of the one who comes, for it is cloaked by sorcery. I do know that he will enter the main gate at midmorning. The guard is armed and ready." Here Ankush sneered slightly. The caliber of the Guard was well known. Indeed, it was the subject of much ribald amusement in the city. "And I want you to wait at the door of my House. I will be inside, for it is not fitting for me to take notice of any chance wanderer who might come to my door."

Long before midmorning, Thurigon was sitting in his tall Chair in the great House raised for the reigning sorcerer of Gereon-Prime. Dry wind blew across the plain from the hills, and its hot breath found him, even in the cool deeps of his hearing-chamber. Sweat beaded his face. Apprehension, more than heat, sent it trickling down his spine.

The voices in the street told him when the walker entered the gates. They, too, waited, for the merest hedge-wizard among them had seen his coming for weeks. Now the people waited in the shade of the overhanging balconies, watching and talking.

Thurigon closed his eyes. Then he opened them, rose, and strode to the doorway, his robe fluttering behind him. On the step he paused to watch the dusty warrior striding easily up the street toward him. The face was invisible beneath a scarf that was drawn about the chin and mouth to keep out the dusty wind. A leather cap with metal studding covered the head. The shape was tall and lean, and the ease of the steps told of tough muscles and fine training. Yet he was almost a child, when compared with Ankush, and that relieved Thurigon. He almost smiled, but he stood quietly, waiting.

As the warrior approached, the spike-studded ball swung from its chain with the motion of his stride. Its pendulumlike arc set up some strange rhythm in the mind. Thurigon shook his head slightly, to clear it, as the warrior stopped at the foot of the steps and looked up the marble tiers at the wizard.

"You are Thurigon Tor En-Ne, Chief Sorcerer of Gereon-Prime? Thief and rapist and murderer?" The set of the man's head was arrogant, for all his slightness.

Thurigon felt his face go hot. Anger such as he had not felt in thirty years filled his aged veins, swelled in his throat.

"Who comes uninvited to my city, to my very steps, to speak such ill-chosen words? I am Thurigon, Chief Sorcerer. Who calls me thief? Who dares to call me rapist?"

"Very few," came the dry-voiced reply. "Yet I know you to be such. The mirror that stands in the wall of your tower came from my father's house. He, too, was Chief Sorcerer—of Gereon-Duo. Until you skewered him with a poisoned dagger, raped my mother, and fled with the mirror that was the greatest treasure of our family and our city. Since that day I have worked and studied and trained myself for this day. I watched you at your bloody work in my home. Though I was but a child, I remembered and I hated. My mother was a sorceress, and she taught me all that she knew, that my father had known. She strangled your ill-gotten brat with her own hands, when it came to birth, and we swore an oath in its blood. Thirty years ago . . . this very day . . . you visited my home. Today I visit yours."

The blood that had rushed to his head now rushed down again. He felt dry and empty, drained of will and potency. The sweat chilled on his skin as he stared down at the figure that stood on the lowest of the six steps.

"There was no male child. I would have killed him!"

"Indeed. And with good reason. You have done enough such deeds to know about vengeance, I have no doubt." A leather-gloved hand swept off the cap, pulled down the scarf. Bronze braids tumbled out to hang waist-length. A thin face glared up at the sorcerer. "My mother had one child, when you visited us. I am she."

Relief flooded through Thurigon. Only a woman! And to send such forebodings before her! There was Talent there, no doubt. But only a woman. He nodded to Ankush.

The burly Black came forward from his position by the doors. "You are not allowed to speak so to the Chief Sorcerer of Gereon-Prime. Go back, Woman. Else you must face me, and few men, even, will consent to do that."

She laughed. The wild peal echoed eerily among the peak-roofed houses and along the balconied streets. "Think you that I have not heard of Ankush? Come into the street, man-killer. See if you are able to kill me!"

The big face furrowed angrily. Ankush descended the steps, rushing her. She sidestepped lightly, and when he turned to face her the chain of the morning-star was in her hand. The spiked ball was swinging in a deadly arc toward his head. Only instinct sent him ducking in time.

"Skeara Gan Na-Li greets you," she shouted, dancing aside from his attack. "I lengthened my arm, just for you, Man-Killer. I knew years ago that you would outreach me." The ball whizzed again. Ankush was forced to leap high, for it cut at his thighs.

It was a weird battle, there in the dusty street. Thurigon watched as if from a daze. Then he recalled himself and formed a spell in his mind, though a fateful feeling in his gut told him that Ankush had met his match, at last. A spell to aid the Black!

But none would come into his mind. Not even the simplest formulae that he had learned as a child. Nothing. Where the well of strange energies had lived inside him, there was now a void that echoed with mocking memories. Could the woman be so talented that her powers damped his own? Dimly he recalled something—bright, forbidding. The face of Jephal. The words of Jephal! Then all thought drained away as if his mind were a sieve.

Ankush was no fool. Stumbling backward, he found that one of the Guard was thrusting a sword-hilt into his hand. He grasped it gratefully. Then he darted forward, feinting at her head, shifting the stroke to slice into one leather-covered calf. She spun away, her morning-star ripping around so that it arced toward his own skull. He dropped to his knees beneath the stroke. That was the last mistake of his life, for she followed through on the spin of the ball, whirling in a circle and catching him in the face with all the added force of the circular motion.

There was shocked silence in the street. Skeara coiled the chain neatly and attached the weapon to her belt. It dripped slowly, leaving a scarlet trail on her leather and splotches in the dust at her feet. Her other calf oozed blood. She didn't seem to notice it.

Thurigon stared at the Black, prone in the dust. His last defender. The Guard had been gutted by his own will, for those who wield swords can bring down sorcerers. No hand would be lifted in his defense. He raised his eyes to meet those of the woman. He remembered, now. A child that crouched, silent and big-eyed, in a corner while he took his pleasure of the woman there. He had dismissed her as merely female.

His most terrible error!

She mounted the steps slowly, moving with deliberation. He threw up one hand and made a potent Sign. She deflected the spark with one derisive twitch of her fingers. That would have been difficult for him at any time. And that last spark of the old power drained him entirely.

She was facing him now. She looked him up and down scornfully. "I came to kill you," she said. "Yet now I know that that is not the cruelest punishment. You have cheated the years, Thurigon. Now I give them leave to take their toll." Her hand moved, her lips moved. She whispered something that was lost in the sudden clamor of the crowd.

The wizard flinched backward. A terrible sensation held him now, and he felt his skin begin crawling—into wrinkles! Thousands of them, covering him with tracks of the years he had held at bay. His leg muscles quivered, weakening. He felt the skin beneath his chin sag against his neck. He saw the alteration of his appearance in the recoil of those who stood nearest. His back bent, and he caught at the doorpost for support.

"Kill me!" he tried to shout at the woman, who now stood a half-head taller than he. The voice came out as a quaver.

She smiled, and even he stepped back at the cruelty of that grimace.

Then she turned to face those in the street. "I leave you your sorcerer. Much good may he do you!" Her face turned toward the tower in which the mirror was hidden. Her brows drew together in concentration. There was a terrible **crack** from the place, and light flashed momentarily from the windows, dimming even the sunlight.

"A mirror that he has sullied cannot again be used for good purposes," she said. "I leave to him the shards."

She came down the steps, and the Guard backed away from her dusty shape and her swinging, bloody weapon. The people in the street melted into doorways and alleys as she passed. The very gateway seemed to shrink away from her as she went through.

Thurigon watched her go, the tears of age seeping from his wrinkled eyesockets. Curses babbled from his lips, and his hands gestured feebly, but there was no power left. Not even enough to know that Telessa was approaching from the rear. With a knife.

VAULT OF SILENCE

By Lin Carter

I
Green Eyes

From the gates of Grand Khev the road stretches east across the open grassy plains of Sarkovy to the mountains. From thence, it twists and crawls like a dusty gray serpent through the foothills, rising ever higher and higher to the Arul Pass. It was there, at the height of the pass, that Carthalla came to the end of her strength and fell to her knees in the sharp stones.

All day she had run behind the shaggy, horned ponies of her captors. It was soon after dawn that the Thungoda war party had attacked the company of a dozen knights her father had sent to escort her on her way. The ugly little men in greasy furs had lain hidden in the tall grasses. They rose to their feet, loosing a shower of barbed arrows on the astonished knights, and sprang howling upon them, pulling them down one by one.

Carthalla alone they spared. The reason was obvious: she was a woman—young, fresh, and beautiful.

They lashed her wrists together with a leather thong and galloped off toward the mountains. She was forced to run on foot in the dust of their hooves. If she fell, and she fell several times, she must scramble to her feet again however she might, and go on, or lie and be dragged to death.

The life of a Prince's daughter is luxurious and silken. Carthalla had never known fatigue, save as a languid weariness after an all-night ball. Nor had she ever known pain, save as a small discomfort or a childish illness soon dispelled by her father's court physician. But now she knew such pain and weariness as she never dreamed flesh could endure.

Her lungs ached as if on fire. Every breath she drew with dry, sobbing lips was agony. The furious torment of the tight thongs about her wrists soon died to a numbness. But it was her feet and legs—*there* was pain, pain beyond thought. Her fashionable riding boots of Ordovic leather had seized the fancy of the squat, leering little Thungoda leader: so he had stripped them from her legs, leaving her feet bare. The long road was harsh and cindery with the height of summer. And her slim little feet were soft and tender. Soon, very soon, they were bruised and sore. Ere long they left a wet, red trail in the road dust.

But now, as they came almost to the crest of the pass, she could go no farther. She fell to her knees, crying out sharply as the thongs bit cruelly into her swollen wrists. But the Thungoda did not stop. They dragged her through the dust, and the one to whose horned horse she was tethered turned and grinned back. Her gown was torn and disarranged from the pawing of dirty Thungoda hands, when they had searched her for gems. Now, through the rents in the long skirt, her bare limbs gleamed white. Sharp rocks gashed her thighs and knees. Harsh road dust rasped her tender flanks, leaving them raw.

In her exhaustion and torment and despair, she called aloud on her god. His name was Changlamar. A little god of the sea was he, and seldom worshiped in these dark days. But it was his sign had reigned at her nativity, and the Prince her father had vowed her to his phratry.

She called, then, out of the depths of her hopelessness. Nor did she expect an answer.

But then the horned horse stopped.

She lay wearily in the dust, bedrabbled with blood, gasping with dust-smirched lips for breath. It was no use: she could not rise; let them kill her here. Or rape her, or do to her whatever things the brutal Thungoda did to the Sarkovian women they seized. But none came to boot her to her feet. Instead, she heard the warriors muttering to each other ahead. She lifted her head from the dust of the road and peered forward.

It was nearly sundown and the immense curve of the sky was dim crimson fire. Against the dark flame of the sky, ahead of them at the crest of the pass, stood a tall man.

She could not see him clearly, for the light was dim and her eyes were watering from the dust. But he was no Thungoda: six feet and more he was, tall, and lean, and straight as a spear. His sinewy limbs were naked under the tunic of supple black leather cinched in at the waist with a girdle of iron plates. Heavy bands of iron clasped his right wrist and his upper arm. He wore boots, but no spurs. And a huge black cloak with bat-winged collar flapped in the rising wind about him.

He stood silent, grim, looking them over: the nine mounted Thungoda warriors, who eyed him belligerently, yet uneasily, as they fingered their sword hilts; and the helpless girl with flame-red hair who sprawled in the dust of the road, and who raised wondering eyes in a pleading gaze to his. He neither moved nor spoke for a time: he stood, leaning on a tall iron-shod staff of heavy black wood, regarding them with strange burning eyes set in a dark, clean-shaven and impassive face.

His eyes. They were the first odd thing Carthalla noticed about him. In her father's realm of Sarkovy, people had blue or gray eyes. But his were *green*—cold, burning eyes of weird green flame. They blazed in his dark-skinned, gaunt face. It was hard, that face, too harsh and somber to be handsome. A long thin white scar crooked down from his hairline to his black, scowling brows. She shivered involuntarily as the gaze of those burning green eyes paused to rest momentarily on her, before lifting to bend their lambent scrutiny upon her uneasy captors.

And then she saw his hand. His right hand. It wore a glove of black leather; but the left hand, that clasped the black staff, went bare.

Then she noticed yet a third odd thing about him. He had the hard, dangerous look of a warrior, but he was none, for he wore no sword—not even an empty scabbard. Nor—now that she thought of it—was his thick black hair woven into a warrior's single braid. Instead, it swung loose about his lean face in a tangle of witchlocks, stirring to the touch of the wind, which had suddenly turned chill.

He loomed like an apparition against the dark flame of the sky. One lone man, unarmed; yet there was something about him that held the Thungoda back. They chittered uneasily among themselves, casting half-frightened, half-challenging glances at him from their squinting, slitted eyes. Any other man who stood in their path, they would have ridden down, whooping and slashing with curved steel. This man . . . they did not like to face. It was all very curious.

It was even a little frightening.

II

The Black Wolf

Kugal, chief of the Thungoda war party, felt his prestige ebb as he hesitated before the grim, dark man who blocked their path. He reined his horned horse forward, drawing his curved sword.

"Who are you, man?" he demanded harshly, letting him see naked steel.

"I am Kellory," the stranger said in a low voice. And: "Release the girl."

"*Hai!*" Kugal crowed, grinning. "One man—no steel—and you give orders to Thungoda!" He laughed, thin lips peeling back to reveal discolored tusks. Then, in the way of his Horde, his temper changed. He snarled, spitting viciously, and suddenly his narrow slitted eyes were cold with venom.

"I cut your guts out with this," he spat, showing Kellory the sword again, "and make you eat them!"

Kellory did not move. His green eyes were wintry and his voice was as low as a whisper as he said:

"Set the girl free and go your way, Thungoda. Or you shall kneel at the feet of Pnom in the Kingdom of Shadows before the world's an hour older."

It was not a boast; not even a threat. There was the quiet ring of certitude to his words. It was a promise.

Kugal grimaced, and spat again, and made his shaggy-maned steed rear a little. He should have squalled a war cry and ridden the tall man down. But, somehow, he didn't. He didn't even try.

"You Sarkoy-man?" he demanded.

Kellory shook his head, witchlocks tangling. "I am a man of the north," he said impassively.

"Barbarian?"

Kellory's eyes blazed up at an old memory.

"My people were the Black Wolf nation," he said softly. "The Thungoda Horde butchered them to the last babe ten years since. I have never forgotten the face of the leader, Mnar."

Kugal grinned again.

"Prince Mnar? He rules all Thungoda now. He cut down Black Wolves of Thedric Ironmane: soon all Sarkovy fall to steel of Thungoda, like this girl. City Khev run red with blood of Sarkovymen. We kill all—all!"

His greasy, swart face flushed dark at the thought of the blood to come. Kugal was no longer intimidated by the somber mien and burning witch-eyes of the tall man. Suddenly, without a moment's warning, he jerked his horned horse forward and swung at Kellory's face, steel flashing in the sunset light.

Lightning flared!

Blinding, dazzling, a blaze of intolerable blue-white light flashed from the black wood staff in Kellory's hand. The spark of lightning caught the curved sword as it swung for his face. In a splatter of flying droplets of molten steel, the saber flew from Kugal's hand. He was dead from the bolt before he had time to scream, sprawling under the heels of his own horse, which bucked and jumped from the nearness of the dark man, fled back down the pass, blundering into the eight other Thungoda warriors, knocking them this way and that. Struggling with the reins, snatching at sword-hilts, squalling and spitting with fury and surprise, they lurched against the sides of the pass. And flash after flash from the black staff lit the gloomy way as Kellory struck them down.

It was over almost as soon as it had begun. Nine twisted corpses lay huddled against the rough stone. The fresh air of early evening was heavy with the stench of burnt man-flesh, and the weird metallic odor of ozone hung on the wind.

Kellory strode to where Carthalla lay frozen and cut her bonds. She stared up at him, her pale, dust-smeared face white with shock, her enormous eyes filled with disbelief.

"Are you wizard . . . or warrior?" she whispered faintly.

"I am both," he said, helping her to her feet. He used only his left hand in so doing, leaning the black staff against the rocky wall of the pass. His right hand, which wore the glove of black leather, was inert and stiff.

"Can you walk, or shall I carry you?" he grunted.

"To where?"

He nodded in the direction.

"There is a cave up under the ledges of the cliff. I will make a fire. Night will be upon us soon, and these are the Ghoul-Haunted Hills. Come—let me help you."

And then great winds awoke and rose, and shouldered aside the thick-piled clouds, and showed forth great bright furnaces of sunset gold.

III

"My Name is Vengeance!"

When Carthalla woke next morning, she was alone in the cave. The fire had burned to cold ash sometime in the night, but she had slept warmly in the furs he had given her. With a little shiver, the girl recalled the weird manner with which Kellory had made the fire. He had simply laid his left hand on the pile of wood—the left hand, which wore a small iron ring on the middle finger, a ring engraved with a glyph in no language she had ever seen—and he had spoken a Word. And fire blazed up! It was uncanny. She wondered idly, stretching and yawning under the warm furs, why he had not used his terrible black staff—his "blasting wand," as he called it. If it could melt the Thungoda chieftain's sword like a lightning bolt, surely it could set the twigs afire. But, then, perhaps too much fire was worse than none at all; perhaps the lightnings of the staff could not be so finely controlled; and had he been so foolish as to use the staff, the cave might have been shattered to rubble. She shivered again. What a strange, grim man he was!

At length she stirred and got up. It was the custom of Sarkovy for men and women to sleep naked, but she had slept in the torn remnants of her gown, since she did not wish to bare her body before Kellory. She had expected to be raped and murdered by the Thungoda warriors who had seized her on the road; escaping their lusts, she did not wish to risk her maidenhead by tempting the manhood of the strange silent man who had saved her. He was not of Sarkovy; he was not even a warrior, or at least he did not wear his hair in a warrior's braid. Sarkovy women are taught to despise the touch of foreign men—even those who, like herself, a Prince's daughter, are expected to wed foreign Princes. And, anyway, she did not like Kellory. She was used to the gallant, laughing young knights and nobles of Grand Khev, with their fresh, fair coloring and bright blue eyes and golden hair. This Black Wolf—he was aptly born!—was too harsh and grim, too dark and cold and hard for her tastes. She felt a small delicious shiver run over her at the thought of those strong hard hands on her body—and that right hand, gloved in black, and useless.

Thinking of Kellory made Carthalla wonder where he was. For he was not in the small cave, and the black cloak, whereon he had lain all night at her side, was gone. Surely he had not departed! Why, today he was going to take her back to the court of her father—or so, at least, she expected.

She found him sitting outside the cave mouth, staring down at the dim plains through the blur of morning mist. His staff lay beside him, ready to his hand. His arms were wrapped around his knees, and his brooding face rested upon them, as he stared thoughtfully down at the land of Sarkovy spread out to the dawn.

"I feared you might have gone, and left me," she said, when it became obvious he had not noticed her standing behind her. He grunted something. But he did not turn to greet her, and neither did he rise.

After a few moments of silence, she awkwardly sat down near him.

"Where is Khev?" she asked, more to make conversation than to gain the fact. He gestured with the gloved hand.

"There," he grunted.

"My father will be astonished when I return home," she said. "He would have thought me halfway to Aijan by now."

"Why were you going to Aijan, anyway?" he asked. "We talked but little last night, you were so tired."

She busied her hands, trying to get her bright hair neat.

"I am trothed to the Prince of Aijan," she said coolly, "and yesterday was my seventeenth birthday. Since I am now of age, my father, the Prince Valemyr, dispatched me to the court of my future husband, the Prince Shio. Oh, my father will be enraged when he hears how the Thungoda attacked our party scarce an hour's ride from the city gates! Never have I known the Thungoda to dare strike so close to Khev. They grow bolder. It is time the knights of Valemyr taught them a lesson!"

His emerald gaze brooded on the mist-drenched land below.

He nodded toward the plains of Sarkovy, witchlocks stirring.

"Not Valemyr, but Fear, is king over this land," he said.

She raised her head to look at him with surprise. He went on, after a moment:

"It is time that Valemyr and all the Seven Princes of Sarkovy realized the truth," he said. "For a hundred years, now, the Thungoda have been drifting down from the north. First they came in small war parties, and scarce ventured south of Ulgoth River. Then in larger and ever larger parties. Then they stayed, some of them, building their wood-walled *mengli*. They settled far from the Seven Cities, and no one cared: the plains of Sarkovy are vast, and there is room for all—or so the Princes thought, the fools!"

Anger flashed briefly in Carthalla's wide blue eyes. She tossed her head a little, flame-bright hair catching the sun.

"Why 'fools'?" she demanded.

"Because they confuse that which they *wish* to be true with that which *is* true," he replied harshly. "The Thungoda are here to stay. And they are only the vanguard. Millions more will follow, and one by one the great stone cities will go down before them, unless one of the Princes moves against them now."

Anger made red patches burn in her cheeks.

"Of course *you* are wiser than the Lords of Sarkovy!" she observed tartly. He turned his cold green gaze on her. But there was no anger in his voice when he spoke.

"Listen, girl. I was born beyond those mountains you see marching like a purple wall to the north—in the land you citydwellers speak of, contemptuously, as 'Barbaria.' Well, a hundred years before the first Thungoda parties began seeping through the mountains into Sarkovy, they began drifting into my homeland, too, and in the same manner; first scattered parties, then whole tribes. They came down from the ultimate north, out of the Desolate Land. And they came to stay. First they built their palisaded camps, their *mengli*. Then they decided to take hold of a city—''

"*Are* there cities in Barbaria?" she asked, almost tauntingly. Again this detestable, cold hard man refused to rise to the bait.

"There were cities in the north when all *this* land was empty fields," he said grimly. "Surely you have heard of Illyrion, the City of the High Kings?"

She bridled a little.

"Yes . . . of course! I had forgotten that Lost Illyrion was a northern city . . . but that was long before Barbaria was—Barbaria!"

He ignored this.

"The city they took was called Amyris, the White City. It was famous for its poets and philosophers. Old statues of mellow ivory dreamed in the purple shadows of the long arcades of Amyris, and the great Theater, where once the plays of Kesirion and Scoupher were first performed, could hold ten thousand citizens. The Thungoda turned the White City red with the blood of the slaughtered. They hacked the ivory statues of the Kings to pieces; they fired the Golden House to rubble; the great bowl of the Theater they used for an arena and pitted the legions that had surrendered to their lies against mandragons and theladars captured on the black shores of the Kynellarian Sea. There was not one man, woman, or child alive in Amyris when they were done with their red work. Thus it will be with Sarkovy, too, in time.''

She did not say anything. He noticed that the color had drained from her face.

He went on.

"We fought them. For sixty years, we fought them. But it was too late by then. The time to fight was when they were but few, and scattered. We, in our vanity and foolishness, had let ninety thousand warriors of the Thungoda Horde enter into our land. And they crushed us. City by city, castle by castle, tribe by tribe. My people were a tribe of half-naked savages when I was born; but my father's father had been High King of Illyrion. You may have heard of him, if you paid any attention to your tutors: Niodronicus, seventh of that name.''

"Niodronicus of the Glory?" she whispered faintly. He nodded, and his eyes were cold and somber.

"Even as savage tribesmen they would not let us live in the land which had once been ours, and which had now become theirs," he continued. "Tribe by tribe they crushed us into the mire. They breed like rats in the sewers: there were a hundred forty thousand of them by that time. My people, the Black nation, were the last to go under. My father had led us into the hills at the edge of the mountains. We were hard to find, and harder yet to fight. But they found us, and they fought us. They have no reverence for life. They will spend the lives of a hundred warriors to drag down a single man of your people or of mine. In the end, they had us all. My brothers they spitted on pikes, and those that were too young to walk yet were tossed alive into the torture fires. My father they flayed before my eyes, before they burned him alive. *My mother*—"

His lips clamped together against the terrible words. They were white from the pressure. She did not dare to meet his eyes: the withering blaze in them was not human. And she cursed her wanton tongue that had taunted and baited him earlier.

He went on, in a very low tone.

"Only I lived. They let me live. It was a whim of their warlord, Mnar: him that is now their Prince. I remember how he sat on his black stallion, the light of burning men flickering on the polished steel of his spiked helm, grinning down at the last of the line of ancient Kings—a naked, frightened boy of ten, bound and helpless in the dust. 'Let one live,' he laughed—I will hear that laugh until the hour I perish from the world—'let one live, to remember our clemency.' *Clemency!*" He spat, as if the word was slime in his mouth.

"What—happened then?" she asked in a faint whisper.

"They let me loose," he growled. "But first they held my hand—my right hand—my *sword* hand—in the fire till it was black and dead. It was so that I could never bear a sword against them, they said. It was the fire my father was dying in. He yet lived—a little. He looked down at me from the stake, and he breathed out one word: *live!* He spoke in the Old Tongue, so the swine could not understand. The pain in my hand was very great. I had never known such pain. But I remember the rage and the fury in his eyes, and the sorrow in them, and the pride. And I whispered one word so that he could hear it as he died. I said *kel-lor-ri*. It is the Old Tongue, and its meaning is: *I will avenge*."

"Your name . . ."

He shook his head, witchlocks blowing about his lean jaw. "I had another name then. An old and proud name: Kings had borne it once. But now my name is Vengeance."

He turned his cold, brooding gaze upon the girl who sat pale and silent at his side, there on the rocky ledge overlooking the plains of Sarkovy.

"And now you know why I cannot spare the time to take you

back to Khev. I have been watching since dawn. There are three hundred warriors of the Horde down on those plains between here and the city. My power is not strong enough to permit the two of us to fight through them—*yet.* But soon I will be strong enough, aye, powerful enough to reach into the City of Terror and pull down black Mnar from his high place and send his foul spirit down to squeal and flop on the red-hot floors of hell, where it belongs! Soon—very soon, now, if my god is with me, I shall become the greatest sorcerer that this world has seen since the high days of old . . .''

"What do you mean?"

"With this useless hand, I could not become a warrior. So I became a wizard—a *warlock,* warrior and wizard combined in one man. Old Phazdaliom the Green Enchanter was my teacher: I came to him a naked, crippled savage. He taught me the Nine Arts and thus I entered into the Brotherhood of Darkness.''

Carthalla had heard of the Brotherhood of Darkness, the ancient and worldwide fellowship of sorcerers. Great was their power and their mastery over the Invisible World that lies beyond this world of the living, but she also had heard that initiates of the Brotherhood of Darkness are sworn on terrible oaths never to employ their dreadful power to meddle in the flow of world history. She said as much, and Kellory nodded.

"True. But my need is great. I shall go up in war against the Thungoda filth, and I shall tread them down under my heel. If I cannot do it with the sword, I shall do it with the staff! And the gods may do with my miserable spirit what they will, in the end.''

His voice was hoarse, as hard and dry as crumbling desert rocks under the baking skies of the desert.

And not for the first time that day, Carthalla found herself shivering in the old grim presence of this dark and terrible man.

IV

The Ride to Black River

The sun was high in the noonward sky before Kellory would turn aside to break their fast and rest a little. They had ridden all morning on the shaggy little horn-horses Kellory had tethered in the pass. These were the horses of the Thungoda war party from whom he had rescued Carthalla yesterday at sunset: but the Thungoda would ride them no more.

When they set out, he had explained the mission whereon he

was bound. Once (he said), ages ago, there had been a mighty magician by the name of Yaohim. "Lord of Shadows," his name meant, in the Old Tongue, for he alone possessed mastery of a secret art. This art he had used once against the Sea Devils when they had come thundering down Turisan River to loot and ravage and burn.

Carthalla had heard vaguely of the Sea Devils. They were wild and savage and bloody corsairs who had infested the Hundred Isles that lay many leagues off the shores of Sarkovy in the midst of the great green sea. Their lean black galleys had glided by night through the deep but narrow river, and dawn found them at the walls of Gorovod, foremost and eldest of the Seven Cities. In their thousands, the wild corsairs took the city by storm. But Amric, Prince of Gorovod, fled by the secret way and rode with a small band of followers seven nights and seven days across the plains of Sarkovy, giving warning to his brother Princes that the Sea Devils had landed in great force and were sworn to pull down the Seven Cities, one by one.

South of Grand Khev, Black River crawls like a sluggish stream of pitch from the southernmost of the mountains. And somewhere, beyond Black River, dwelt Yaohim the Lord of Shadows. The master magician was no friend of the Princes of Sarkovy, but he well knew that if the cities fell, all they who dwelt in this land would go in peril of their lives—even a magician.

So he rode back to whelmed and broken Gorovod with Amric at his side. Within the stone-walled city, the devil pirates of the Hundred Isles feasted and swilled red wine and tortured and raped, not knowing the hour of their doom was upon them. And that night, in the dark of the three moons, Yaohim worked a mighty feat of shadow magic. No man knows what he did nor what followed upon his calling, but with dawn a sight of horror met the eyes of Prince Amric and his men.

Six thousand corsairs had swilled and sung within the walls of Gorovod with sunset. With dawn, six thousand madmen mewled and tittered in the ravaged halls.

And, without thanks nor payment, the Lord of Shadows had ridden back to his tower beyond Black River and vanished from the memory of men.

But Kellory remembered.

He reasoned that a magic strong enough to whelm the wild pirates of the Isles in all their bloody thousands could strike down the numberless warriors of the Thungoda Horde as well.

Thus was he bound for the tower of the magician, or whatever remained thereof. For among the ruins of the tower (his tutor and master had whispered) lay to this hour the Grimoire of Yaohim, the Book of Shadows, wherein the secret of this mighty magic lay.

And Kellory would find it or die.

There was something of the gallant and the heroic in this lonely quest of one man for a secret that could destroy the foul and numberless vermin that imperiled the world. Carthalla felt the thrill of it: this was the stuff of songs. Whether Kellory the Warlock won or lost, someday the bards would sing of his long quest, that now was nearly done.

. . . Save that, if he lost, the Thungoda would leave alive no bards to sing nor Sarkovymen to listen to that song.

Nor did she mind any longer that he would not turn aside from his quest to return her to the city of her father. At first, hearing that she must ride with him or be left behind to fare as she might, she had railed and ranted. To her tears and threats alike, Kellory had remained unmoved. To him it was very simple: they could not fight their way through the war parties that now infested the road between the pass and Grand Khev. To detour far to the south was the only safe way. And south lay the region whereunto he was bound, on a mightier and more important mission than merely bringing a lost girl home to her father's hearth, be she Princess or no.

And, since they must go south in any case, why not finish the quest and bring forth the Book of Shadows ere riding to the gates to Khev? It was perfectly simple.

And, to tell the truth, something within the girl's heart responded to the plan. How glorious it would be to ride into Khev, bearing the salvation of the world! How pleased her father would be, and how proud of her! She knew him well: a good man, but not overly strong. His land lay in peril from the numberless Thungoda that swarmed in every-increasing hordes across the plains. And he knew it well, and worried over it. But the cities of Sarkovy were few, as yet. Men were new-come into these plains; only five centuries before, Roldomar the Mighty had led the peoples into Sarkovy from the lost realm of the south, long since overrun by the Ghost Legions loosed during the Wizard's War of the last age, when the Gold City fell before the Witchmen. As yet, the warriors of Sarkovy were too few to face in battle the Thungoda—even were the Seven Princes to become convinced of the ever-growing peril.

Thus, as they lunched on Kellory's packet of dried meats and black Cryphax wine, the girl became enwrapped deeper and

deeper in the vision of the glory to come when she rode with
Kellory and the Book under the frowning battlements of Grand
Khev, to lead the knights of Sarkovy to a magnificent victory
over the brutish little beastmen of the Horde.

They mounted and rode on.

By starfall they had passed Black River at the ancient ford,
and that night they slept on the edge of the valley of the Wizard.

V

The Crawling Slime

When dawn rose over the edges of the world and flooded the
land with pale gold light, Carthalla went down to the edge of
Black River without waking Kellory. She was filthy with the dust
and grime of travel, and her body stank of sweat. She *must*
bathe, and be the water black or not, at least it was wet. In the
shelter of overhanging ferns she stripped off her filthy gown,
which was, by now, little more than rags. She handled it despair-
ingly. She would scrub it as clean as possible—but later. First
the bath. However, she could not resist ripping the remnants of
the hem away: from thigh down the gown was in long ribbons
which entangled her legs when she walked. So she tore the
soiled cloth and made an abbreviated, but more travel-worthy,
garment from what was left. Then, with a heartfelt sigh of
pleasure, she waded through the rushes and slid into the cold wet
caress of the ebon waters.

For a time she drifted, swimming idly, blissfully enjoying the
intimate touch of the cold water. Strange beyond telling was this
river: black as ink its waters, and no man knew why, though
some said it flowed up out of the Kingdom of Shadows at the
bottom of the world, the place where the shadows of dead men
went who were not welcome in the Higher World of the gods . . .

Then a cold hand closed around her ankle and she screamed!

Another hand locked around her left wrist, and a long slick
limb or member—it felt like a serpent—slid around her waist.
Carthalla went wild with terror and shrieked again and again,
kicking frantically and beating the water in a desperate effort to
free herself from the embrace of the unknown thing beneath the
black waters. But it clung with incredible strength, and when
with wild effort, she dragged her left hand above the surface she
saw with an indescribable thrill of horror that a rope of moving
slime was locked about it!

Like some vile grayish jelly it was, and transparent, for the light struck through it if but dimly. The very touch of the slime thing against her flesh was loathsome, and she fought it with every strength in her young body.

Luckily, she had not ventured very far out into Black River. Her feet still touched bottom, and with this for leverage she somehow managed to struggle nearer in to shore, so that she stood partway out of the water. Looking down, she saw with a gasp of terror and revulsion the thing that held her in its unbreakable grip.

A gigantic mass of quaking, blubbery slime met her eyes. It had no limbs, no head, no eyes. Somehow it could shape extensions of itself, and three of these long tentaclelike extrusions of hard jelly were looped about her. Even as she watched, bulges appeared in the glistening, smooth surface of the slime thing. They grew out like nipples—then extended farther, like wriggling feelers. She knew they would grow larger and become yet more arms to ensnare her and drag her down to a hideous death on the murky floors of Black River.

Suddenly, Kellory was there.

Her cries had awakened him and he had sprung to his feet in answer to her call so swiftly that he had not thought to seize up his blasting wand. Now as he saw the jelly thing that had already half enveloped the naked, struggling girl, a wild black rage awoke within him.

He lifted up his arms to the morning skies and cried in a great voice:

"Go back down, *shoiggua!* Go back down, I am a warlock of the Secret Flame. My circle is the Ninth; my sphere the Sphere of Darkness; my god is Azzamungandyr the Lord of the Mysteries. *You—may—not—take—the—girl!*"

It seemed to Carthalla almost as if the quivering mass of slime had ears and could hear his words. It—hesitated. It—waited. And it seemed to her that Kellory was grown greater than before: his Power enveloped him like a mighty mantle he could draw on at will.

But the slime monster did not obey. It did not withdraw. Seeing this, Kellory drew in his breath and called upon the inmost resources of his being—hidden wells of strength few mortal men ever disturb. There within him, deeply hidden, as it lies hidden with every man, is a Power which links him to the unseen maze of forces and alignments that constitutes the Plenum— the Totality, the All, the Complete Universe of Space and Time. He called now upon that Power: few men dare call upon it; but he dared.

It seemed to Carthalla that his face and figure darkened to utter blackness. In this blackness his weird green eyes burned like emerald suns—blazing with intolerable brilliance. The sky above him drew dark, though it was day. He seemed to grow taller—taller—beyond the height of man. Like a tower of ultimate darkness he loomed up into the sky, and his eyes were like great windows that looked in upon the seething flames of hell.

"Go back down, *shioggua!* This girl is mine! You may not take her for your foul pleasure. Need I call upon the Timeless Ones—the Guardians of the Balance? I speak the Name ASSA-THYA-IOQQUNQUANDAR! ZAOTH! PHUOL LUMNIVUUR! Go back down, Foulness, lest I smite thee with the Secret Flame!"

Thunder cracked in the pitch-black night above them, and sulfurous flames of no lightning ever seen by man licked at the edges of the roiling black clouds.

But suddenly the thing was gone. The slime slid back into the depths of Black River and Carthalla stood free.

Suddenly she was very conscious of her body, with the eyes of Kellory upon her. She crooked one forearm across her full young breasts and covered her lap with the palm of her other hand, in the immemorial posture of woman surprised.

But Kellory—now no longer sky-tall and terrible—was no longer looking at her. His dark lean face was pale and drawn and it glistened wetly. He looked, suddenly, exhausted to the point of collapse. Indded, he staggered and almost fell to his knees.

Her modesty forgotten, Carthalla came up out of the water and seized his arm.

"What is wrong? Are you hurt?" she cried. He tried to speak but could not; then, all at once, his full weight was against her and she saw that he had swooned. Could it be the feat of magic that had so greatly unmanned him? Staggering under his dead weight, the girl half carried and half dragged him back to their camp. She wished that she knew more about magic, and the ways of magicians.

A little wine revived him, although he still looked pale and drawn. His green eyes were strangely colorless, empty and without their usual fire, as he looked up, thanking her with a long glance. She smiled back, anxiously: she had not bothered to retrieve her gown, but had wrapped her wet body in his long black warlock cloak.

"I will be all right," he said hoarsely.

"What was that—that *thing?*" Carthalla asked with a little grimace of revulsion.

"A *shioggua*—a Guardian Demon, summoned from the Water Element. Old Yaohim left his land . . . protected."

She shivered uncontrollably, perhaps from the morning wind on her wet nakedness under the cloak, or perhaps from the memory of that dread embrace. "It was . . . horrible!"

He nodded weakly. Then the faint shadow of a smile crossed his hard mouth.

"Now you know better than to bathe in Black River," he said.

VI

The Valley of Silence

Toward midmorn they reached the wizard's tower. A little rest and some wine and food had restored Kellory's strength—or most of it. Only he knew how terribly his reserves of Power had been drained in fighting off the *shioggua*. He dreaded the next adversary, for surely the Lord of Shadows had left more than one guardian to stand watch over his demesne.

But—and this was very odd—they met with no more supernatural encounters on their path. Kellory found this disquieting in the extreme. Surely, an Air Elemental should have been set to watch over the treasures of Yaohim. Or, most terrible of all, a Demon of the Earth, with the iron mineral strength of the earth itself slumbering in its vast, misshapen limbs. But no other Being asccosted them, and they went forward into the morning.

The valley was silent and dim, for all the blaze of noon above. Tall trees shadowed the path, but no birds sang in their branches and the leaves rustled not in the breeze. It was as if a spell of silence had been set over the wizard's vale. Kellory did not like it at all.

Perhaps (he thought) the force he had aroused when he put forth his full Power and called upon That which is not summoned lightly had driven the other guardians into hiding. The inhabitants of the Invisible World had senses other than the nine known to him. The release of such Power as he had summoned forth disturbs the equilibrium of the Other World, and dark things far from the site of such a calling-forth are made aware of it: as a stone thrown into a pond sends ripples traveling to the farthest shores of a lake. Perhaps this was the answer.

Perhaps . . .

And then the tower of Yaohim stood before them, dark and tall and forbidding in the blaze of noon sun.

Most curiously, although more than three hundred years must have passed since the death of the master magician, his tower yet stood unshaken by the tides of time. He paused, and stopped, and stood there for a time, frowning thoughtfully on the tower of Yaohim. For seven years he had striven to stand in this place. For although his master, Phazdaliom, had known much of the history of the Lord of Shadows, he had not known where in the wide-wayed world his wizard's fortress stood. Long and hard had Kellory searched in the years since he had left the castle of Phazdaliom. At length, only two months ago in the last days of spring, he had come upon a crumbling parchment map of the southlands below Sarkovy. He had found it in the ruins of an abandoned monastery in the mountain country, north of the Arul Pass, many leagues from the place where he had rescued the Princess Carthalla from her abductors. Once, the moldering ruins had housed a hundred monks of the Brotherhood of Light, the priestly equivalent of his own sorcerous fraternity. But long since roving bands of Thungoda had come upon the monastery: the harmless and holy men they had doubtless tortured to death with the ghoulish glee their vile kind feel when bringing agony and black death to Servants of the Higher World. And the monastery itself they had ravished, besoiling the holy books and precious documents with the dirt of their bowels, before giving the ancient structure over to the red embrace of the fire. But this map had not burned: a hand of Power had inscribed it on a sheet of pliable metal, such as men no longer knew how to fashion. The kiss of the flames had not tarnished the imperishable flexive steel, nor dimmed the ancient traceries of a long-dead hand. Thus had Kellory at last learned of the location of Yaohim's demesne.

He stood and looked at the tower.

Strange it was, builded by magic; no hand of man had taken part in its raising. It was all of one piece, like something molded out of thick heavy dark glass, or like something that had lived and grown to this shape. The organic curves of the soaring pylon were uncanny: no structure on earth that Kellory had ever seen was so shapen. It swelled and curved and tapered to a narrow spire wherein one long, pointed window looked forth on the wilderness through which they had come. Dim was that window, shadowed, like the dusty socket of an empty skull.

But even as Kellory looked, he thought he discerned something that moved within that tall, peaked window. He looked again and there was nothing there. Perhaps it had been only his imagination, or a trick of light and shadow. He comforted himself with the thought, but he was not deceived: his eye *had* caught the flicker of movement, that he knew. For a moment, a something had stood within that tall narrow window and had gazed down at them, and had passed from their view. It was a disquieting thought; perhaps he should leave the girl behind, and press forward alone to enter the shadow-haunted tower of the long-dead mage. But no: if any guardians lurked in this cursed vale of shadow and silence, it was only from fear of his Power that they kept from the girl.

Kellory's jaw tightened. Well did he know the strange lusts of the shadowy denizens of the Invisible World; and all too well could he guess to what repulsive and degrading uses they would twist Carthalla's slim young body—and mind—and soul. No: they must go forward together, and go back. And he would not go back, not even if he knew for very certain that a dark and grisly death awaited him in that strange tall house in the vale.

So they went forward into the tower of Yaohim.

VII

Dark Citadel

There were no gates, no door. The portal stood open and empty. They went through into a dimness and a silence greater even than that which reigned over the strange valley beyond. Kellory walked softly, the staff of his Power in his hand, and his eyes roamed from side to side, searching every nook and corner. His ears strained for the whisper of a voice or the echo of a football, but there came no sound to his ears other than that which they made. And with other senses he searched as well, senses denied to the girl at his side: the tendrils of his mind reached out through the Web of the Worlds and hearkened after tremors that should disturb—ever so slightly—the intricate and interlocking balance of forces that is the Universe. He sensed, however, nothing but the smell of ancient magics, the shadow of long-gone presences, and the resonance of once-spoken Words and Names, many of which he himself would not wish to speak aloud, far less to call upon.

The first floor was completely empty. A mere featureless oval chamber unbroken by window or doorway. An unrailed stairway glided up the curve of the wall to the second story, and Kellory and the Princess ascended by it. The girl, not daring to speak aloud lest she break Kellory's concentration, marveled much at the strange, sleek, glassy substance of the walls. It was most like

a ceramic, she thought: she had seen enameled vases from the
kilns of far Charabys with this kind of finish . . . but her
imagination shuddered back from contemplating how vast must
have been the furnace in which this tower was fired! The flaming
hell of her religion itself would not be vast enough . . .

On the second floor they found naught but the rubble of
decayed furniture, a few shards of pottery, scattered rags of
rotten cloth, and scraps of old parchment that fell to dust at a
touch. These, and cobwebs thick with the dust of centuries, and
nothing more.

They searched the spaces above. One story must have been the
librarium of the sorcerer, for broken and collapsing shelves of
some nameless scarlet wood lined the curving walls, and a few
heaps of moldering trash littered the corners, among which they
found verdigris-eaten clasps and bits of oddly shaped metal such
as those with which sealed and locked books are bound. But the
Book of Shadows they found not. Nor on the next story, which
had once been a laboratorium of some nature, for procelain
benches and iron tables and broken crockery still lay about,
surviving the corrosion and decay of centuries. Particles of glass
crunched under the step of Kellory's boot. But there were no
books.

When they had searched the tower from top to bottom, they
returned at length to the first floor, dispirited and weary and
much besmirched with dust.

"The Book must have crumbled to dust," Carthalla said,
"like those we found in the librarium above."

"Not so, girl," he grunted. He felt an inward restlessness; his
eyes roved about and he prowled the room from wall to wall,
pacing like a caged brute.

Exasperated with his curtness, the Princess demanded: "Why
'not so'?"

"Hush: do not disturb my thoughts," he growled. "There is
something that I have forgotten, or something that has been
hidden from my remembrance, one or the other. Something that
I should recall . . . it has been years since I was last in the
citadel of an enchanter . . . but I remember well the castle of
Phazdaliom, my master . . . what it is that I have overlooked?"

At length he shrugged and gave up. "There is something that
should be here. I *know* it should be here. But, by the Nine Faces
and the Hidden Face Itself, I cannot bring it to mind. Curse that
vile *shioggua!* In driving it down I dangerously depleted my
Inward Self . . . I have not that acuity of mind that I must have
to find the secret!"

He tried a bit more, and finally growled and spat, and turned on his heel.

"Come on! We had best be out of here before nightfall. I cannot think of the thing that eludes me, curse the foul luck!"

"Well, then perhaps you can tell me now why the Book of Shadows would not have fallen to mold and filth, while every other book in this place has done so," she demanded tartly. Her temper was not improved by his unspoken criticism of her behavior at dawn: curse the *shioggua* indeed—and curse her for daring to bathe without asking his permission first!

"Is that what's bothering you?" he barked a curt laugh. "A grimoire—a wizard's own book—is embued with his own vitality, which is more than human. Every fiber of the pages thereof, every drop of ink, is filled with supermortal energy. It takes a thousand years for wind and rain to deface a carven stone; but the grimoire of a master magician can outlive the eon itself."

"Thank you for the information," she said coldly. "I will forever treasure the morsels of wisdom you let fall in my presence. And when I come to stand before the throne of my father, I will tell him of your courtesy and—and—"

She broke off, staring at him. For suddenly a grin of incredulous joy spread over his features. It was the first genuine smile she had ever seen on his face, and the dark somberness of him was lightened, made warm, and even human, thereby. Even his grim cold eyes of lambent emerald fire suddenly seemed those of a man and not the shining orbs of some implacable demon of revenge.

"Bless you for your temper, Carthalla," he said. And the girl flushed crimson although she did not really know why: it was the first time he had ever called her by her name, and there was warmth in his voice.

"What—?"

"You said your father's *throne;* of course, your father has a throne, a Seat of Power, for he is a mighty Prince. But a magician is princely, too. How said my old master once? 'A wizard is a king of nature,' those were his words. And well do I remember my master seated on his chair of green crystal atop the dais of nine steps: enthroned in his Seat of Power, the magician rules the forces of the Invisible. *But where, in all this tower, is Yaohim's Seat?*"

VIII

The Whispering Shadow

It took Kellory the better part of an hour to find the secret door. No ordinary man could have found the invisible crack that sundered the smooth fabric of the tower's base: but Kellory could search the molecular structure of the substance with the inner eye of a warlock and find that which was hidden to men. And once found, it was no great matter to gain entry. The utterance of a Word sufficed, albeit a Word that human throat and mouth were never shaped to speak.

But he had a clue that greatly eased his search: since all the tower was empty above, the throneroom of the master magician must lie below ground. And thus it was.

As the sound of the Word died in eerie echoes, a vast square of the floor lifted, revealing a dark yawning abyss. Up from the mouth of darkness beat a slow pulse of dim uncolored light. By this throbbing illumination, the warlock and the Princess could dimly perceive a flight of glassy steps that descended into the maw of pallidly lit blackness.

Down the stairs they went, Kellory in the lead. He held the great black staff of his Power before him to ward off whatever ghostly guardians the long-dead archimage might have set to watch over his magical treasures. But they descended to the dim floor of the subterranean hall without trouble.

The room was huge and long and filled with darkness. Dim shapes loomed about them in the gloom, and Kellory feared lest a careless step precipitate them into a mantrap of some kind. So he spake a Word and a dull sphere of luminance gathered out of nothingness and floated above his left shoulder, steadily growing brighter. Waves of light pulsed from it, driving back the darkness. It was a small task to sustain the witchlight on this plane of being, and Kellory did not begrudge the slight effort—although every such work of magic took its toll of his remaining strength.

By the cold phosphorescent fire of the witchlight they could now observe a mighty throne that stood at the far end of the room. It rested atop a huge cube of black glistening glass or crystal. When they stepped closer to observe it more carefully, Kellory saw that the upmost surface, of the cube bore markings. Into the substance of the dark, glittering stuff had been inset talismans of great potency—the Seals of Two Palorities, the Sigils of the Three Worlds, the Signs of the Four Elements, and the Signets of the Five Divinities of Darkness. Woven about these talismans, encompassing them all, was a strip of shining metal in the shape of the Quadridecagram—the Fourteen-Pointed Star.

In the center of this star stood the wizard's Throne of Power: a huge, ancient chair of black wood, carven with leering masks and devilish faces and queer glyphs. Enthroned therein, his staff in his hand, within reach of the great talismans, Yaohim had once sat in the midst of his Power. But that was centuries ago.

About the foot of the dark, glistening cube rose small squat pedestals of stone. These bore the consecrated Instruments of the Magical Art—the Burin, the Arthame, the Bolline and the Arctrave, the stone called Ematille, the Cruse and Aspergillus, the Speculum, the Annulus, and others. Despite the tension of the moment, Kellory stared at them with admiration. They were superbly made, and beautifully crafted by a master hand. Each instrument represented many years of patient labor. To make the Arthame alone, as the Wizard's Knife was called, took seven years. Never had he seen such perfect craftsmanship!

The waxing and waning light came from the mighty staff of Yaohim, which leaned against his Place of Power. A dim halo surrounded it. The pulsations of light throbbed like a living heart.

He did not see the Book. But he noticed that one pedestal was empty.

The Throne was not.

He stiffened, sucking in his breath. Beside him, the girl clutched his bare arm, as she saw it too.

A vague shadow sat within the chair of ancient black wood. It had no shape, no form: merely a blur of darkness, but in that darkness burned twin sparks of crimson fire like the eyes of jungle beasts.

As they watched, frozen, the shadow darkened . . . thickened . . . gathering substance unto itself. The flaming eyes burned more fiercely now, like crimson stars.

Now, with his subtle senses, Kellory grew conscious of a Presence of Power. Power steamed from that shadow-shape, and power was centered therein. Vast, terrific power, with illimitable depths and strengths.

And the shadow . . . *whispered!*

At first he could not make out words. Naught but a faint susurration like an uneasy wind prowling through dead dry leaves. But even as the shadow took on shape and substance, so too did its whispering voice grow stronger. Now he could hear it plain.

"Unwise wast thou, warlock, to intrude upon mine slumbers."

The shadow spake in the Old Tongue, that is used only by wizards, priests, and Kings. Summoning his courage, Kellory replied in the same tongue:

"Thou art the shade of Yaohim?"

The shadow laughed faintly. *"I am he! Aye and verily, I that once was Lord of the Shadows am become but a shadow myself. Thus, with such ironies, doth fate play with the spirits of the dead!"*

The shadow had taken full form by now. It wore the likeness of an aged man, tall and gaunt, and wrapped in tattered robes like the cerements of the grave. A tangled mane of snowy witchlocks flowed about the skull-like head of the apparition, floating on an unfelt wind. Within deep, enshadowed sockets, eyes burned red and blazing.

And the staff was held now in the hand of the shadow.

"Wrongly didst thou seek to plunder mine sepulcher of its treasures, warlock. For I shall smite thee with mine wrath and bear thee down into the Kingdom of Darkness . . ."

Before Kellory could move or speak, the shadow pointed its staff at him and uttered a potent syllable. A cold force closed about his body: a constriction that gripped and held him helpless as in a vise. By his side, the girl voiced an involuntary cry of fear as the cold uncanny force enclosed her as well.

Kellory knew this spell; it was called the Curse of Chains. His spirits sank within him and he tasted the bitterness of despair. If he could have moved, his head would have sunk on his chest; he faltered and his courage sagged. *Alas!* he thought, *that it should come to a trial of strength: and I am already weary . . .*

But there was but one thing to do, and Kellory did it. He released his spirit self from its housing of flesh and sank into the World of Darkness.

IX

Battle in the Halfworld

Only once before, during his training under the Green Enchanter, had Kellory ventured into the shadowy realm. And then was he fresh and well prepared. Now, still inwardly exhausted from his great struggle with the *shioggua*, and feeling the strain of the several times he had been forced to use his Power since entering the Valley of Silence, he was in no fit condition to duel between the planes of being.

His body left behind on the physical plain, the First World, he ventured into the Dubious Land as a shape of light. This peculiar, region, which lay between the world of living men and the Other World where the spirits of the dead dwell, together with certain Beings that were never alive, was not real and true. Here illusion reigned, and here all things were but symbols and representations of True Realities.

So he passed through a dim gray forest where no birds sang and naught moved or lived. The ground underfoot was a level plain, colorless as ashes, and the trees were unnaturally symmetrical. When he looked closely at them he could see they were not trees at all: but when looked at obliquely, or in passing, they seemed like enough to trees.

There were circular holes in the ashen floor: perfect circles, pits of blackness. He knew all too well what creatures sometimes dwelt in the Under Pits, and he avoided them with great care.

There was no sky overhead; no vast unending vault above the trees. The air was thick as if with mist, and the mist thickened above the treetops until the sight could probe no farther. It was just as well. His sanity might have been endangered had he looked beyond that curtain of mist to the sky wherein black stars burned like titanic eyes.

He knew the shadow of Yaohim would sense his flight and follow him into the Halfworld. And, ere long—as time is measured in a region that exists out of time—a shadow-shape stepped from the gray trees to confront him.

The shape of light that was the astral body of Kellory, and which went armed with a shaft of lightning brilliance that was the symboling of his warlock's staff in this realm of mystery, stood facing the astral self of Yaohim.

In the Halfworld, Yaohim was still a shadow. But now he stood as a towering mass of utter blackness, and his staff was a rod of ultimate darkness.

They did not speak, for here no speech was possible. But here they could fight—and fight they did!

The rod of darkness swung to strike him, and Kellory parried it, lifting the shaft of brilliance just in time. The shock of the blow, which was not a physical impact, shook him to the core of his being. But he fought on, knowing he would never be stronger than he was now, and that with every timeless moment that passed his strength would ebb away. *Best to battle at the beginning,* he thought. But he had few hopes of surviving that battle.

The shaft of light and the rod of utter darkness flickered in an eerie dueling. Then the shadow struck the glowing shaft aside and closed with the shape of light.

Wings of darkness enfolded the dazzling shape that was the astral self of Kellory. He struck out, a cloud of blazing splendor, coiling about the dark thing that opposed him. His shimmering tendrils sank into the darkness, and the darkness drank them in, and stifled their radiance.

Now the webs of shadow encircled Kellory and his glory dimmed, as if the darkness sought to bury and extinguish the light. Rather than struggle futilely against the slithering shadowy coils, Kellory permitted himself to be drawn into the smothering embrace of the ebon cloud. For a plan had come to him—a desperate scheme.

He felt his fires dim. Black, stifling veils of coldness closed about him. He was lost in the depths of an utter darkness and a terrific cold such as reigns unchallenged in the black spaces between the stars.

Even as his Power failed, half fainting, he struck to the core of the shadow—and seized it.

Like a black flame it burned, the Dark Star that was the inmost being of Yaohim. Every man has three bodies, Kellory knew. The first body is the physical; within that as within a shell of flesh, lies the astral; and within that, like a star of eternal fire, the etheric. Each body has its place and being on each of the Three Worlds. And now Kellory, with all his waning strength, seized upon the etheric star of Yaohim and caught it within his shape of light.

The Dark Star writhed within his grasp, but he held it nonetheless. And now bright tendrils probed into the central fires, seizing upon the *chakras*, the etheric organs that are the centers of power. One by one he mastered them.

The shadow shape dissolved in drifting patches of umbra. The Dark Flame burned and slithered in Kellory's grasp, but he held it fast and probed within. He was greatly weakened—more than two-thirds of his strength was gone. Where he had been a shape of splendor, now he was a fog-wraith of dimming light. Soon—soon—he must return to the First World, or drift here in the Halfworld forever, a ghost of light.

Exhausted, he released the Dark Star and it fled.

With the very dregs of his Power, he made the return passage between the worlds.

And fell limp and cold as a dead thing at the feet of Carthalla.

X

The Quest Goes On

There were times when he perceived a girl's face bending above him and heard, faint and far off, a voice calling his name. But then the light would die in a wash of shadows and the voice would fade from his hearing.

And then, a long while later, he became conscious of sunshine. He was lying, pillowed on leaves, in the brilliance of open day. Birds were twittering and the scent of grass and flowers came to him. He felt very weary, but he felt—whole.

She came to him, there in the wizard's garden behind the tower of Yaohim, and gave him fresh water to drink, and fruit. He was content to rest and to take food from her hands, without words. He could see well enough what had happened.

The tower rose beyond him. Already its shining surface was pitted and veined with black jagged cracks. And the luster of the shimmering stuff whereof it was composed had dimmed.

Birds sang again in the woods of the valley of silence. And, after a while, he slept.

Day followed day and night followed night. They were comfortable enough in the shelter of the crumbling tower. Silence and shadows ruled therein no longer; neither did the undying shadow of Yaohim dwell forever on its Throne of Power. For in conquering the master magician in that nightmare world between life and death, he had banished it forever from the world of men.

"It began almost at once—just after you collapsed and the shadow was gone from the chair," Carthalla said. "I thought you were dead. The invisible bonds no longer held me and I fled up the stairs and out into the valley. And it was no longer a dead place! The boughs tossed in the wind, birds sang and fluttered, and there were small things scuttling through the grass. So I took courage and went back and found you breathing."

"How long have you tended me like this?" he asked.

"I am not sure. It was a week before you opened your eyes, and weeks more before you spoke to me. The better part of a month, I guess. You are better now?"

"Day by day my strength grows. Soon I will be able to stand. And then—" His face was dark and there was bitterness in the grim set of his jaw. "Then I must go on again."

"Whither?"

"South; into the desert country," he muttered. "For at the last, as I probed into the centers of his being, I read that Yaohim had given over the Book of Shadows into the hands of his disciple, Pnomphet, a sorcerer who dwells in Ashangabar, the Dead City. There must I quest still, in search of the Book of Shadows.''

There was dark defeat and great weariness in his eyes and he stared broodingly toward the mountains of the south.

The girl, who sat near him, the grimy rags of her gown scarce covering her beauty, looked down at him and said softly:

"I will go with you . . ."

Her face was very close to his. But he made no answer, merely looking up at her from the sterile depths of his bitterness. He had never known the love of woman, and never thought to do so. For his name was Vengeance, and Vengeance was his god.

But he stared, and hoped he could always remember the exact, exquisite color of her soft limpid eyes . . . no matter how the Quest ended thereafter.

THE OTHER ONE

By Karl Edward Wagner

There is a story, so it is told, of certain bandits who took shelter beneath a tree, and as the darkness and the storm closed over them, they gathered about their fire and said to their leader: "Tell us a tale, to pass the night hours in this lonely place"; and their leader spoke to them: "Once certain bandits took shelter beneath a tree, and as the darkness and the storm closed over them, they gathered about their fire and said to their leader: 'Tell us a tale, to pass the night hours in this lonely place'; and their leader spoke to them: 'Once certain bandits took shelter beneath a tree . . .' "

Blacker against the darkening sky, the thousand-armed branches of the huge banyan swayed and soughed before the winds of the storm. Tentative spats of rain struck the barren stones beyond their shelter—streaking like the ranging shots of massed archers from the lowering thunderheads that marched toward them from across the desolate plain beyond.

Someone got a fire going. Yellow flames crackled and spat as the damp twigs caught; gray smoke crawled through the roof of banyan limbs, to be whipped away by the winds. There were more than ten of them about the fire—outlaws and renegades whose dirty mail and mismatched weapons showed the proof of hard and bloody service.

Another hundred of them might have gathered beneath the banyan, pressed between its pillared maze of limbs and roots. The tree had spread its limbs and stabbed downward its roots, growing upward and outward for imperturbable centures. Behind— along the trail the outlaws had followed—lay unbroken miles of tropical forest. Beyond—toward which their path led—stretched a miles-wide plain of utter desolation. Beneath the gray curtain of the approaching storm could be glimpsed the walls of forest that enclosed the farther perimeters of the plain.

Across the jungle-girded plain, new forest crept through where a century before had been carefully tilled fields, crawled over

297

flattened stones and heaps of broken rubble where once had reared a great city. Of the city, no walls or towers remained; so utter was its destruction that scarcely one stone yet stood upon its base. It was an expanse of total annihilation—a wasteland of toppled stone and fire-scarred rubble. After more than a century, only scrub and vine and secondary forest had invaded the ruin. More than another century would pass before the last mound of shattered wall would vanish beneath the conquering forest.

They gathered about their fire, laying aside their well-worn gear, pulling out such as they had to make their evening meal. Three days march, or maybe four—and their leader promised them more plunder than they might carry. This night the prospects did not bring the usual chatter of anticipation. Uneasily, the men watched the closing storm, gloomily considered the plain of ruins beside which they were camped. For these were the ruins of Andalar the Accurst, and no man cared to linger in this place.

"The greatest city of the land," one of them murmured pensively. "Nothing now but broken stone and rotted bone. Not even pickings to tempt a vulture there now."

"Once there was pickings as rich as you'd dare dream," another commented. "Andalar was the proudest city in the world."

"And the gods destroyed Andalar for its pride," a third intoned, with less scorn than had he spoken in another place than this. "Or so I've heard."

"I've heard a number of tales," the first bandit argued. "No one seems to remember anymore."

"I remember," their leader murmured.

"Do you indeed know the tale of the doom that came to this city? Pray, tell us the tale."

Their leader laughed, as at a bitter jest, and began.

The news of the death of Andalar's king came as no great surprise to Kane. Luisteren VII was late into his eighth decade. Nor was the news—at first—any tragic blow to Kane; for he had taken certain measures to ensure that Andalar's ruler would never enter his ninth decade. Kane, as Lord Minister of Andalar, was well known to be a great favorite of the senile king's half-witted heir, and, although it was less well known, the king's youngest wife, Haeen, was a great favorite of Kane.

As the first shrill rumors of Luisteren's impending death sped through the palace, and the funeral trumpets of the priests of Inglarn howled a tocsin throughout the twilit streets of the city, Kane smiled, filled his golden chalice and drank a silent toast to the memory of the departed. The king's death had fallen several months earlier than his plans called for. Perhaps he should have administered the powders more conservatively, or possibly the aged despot's heart had simply choked in its dusty blood. Whatever, Luisteren VII was dead. Kane's position was secure. When the king's favorite son mounted the throne as Middosron III, the new king would be only too content for Kane to manage the affairs of Andalar as he pleased.

Kane finished the brandy, leaned his massive body back in his chair, and reflected upon the past year. It had been a heady rise to power, even by Kane's standards—but then, Andalar had been a prize ripe for the picking, and it mattered little to Kane that his course had been so formularized as to be tedious to him.

As captain of a band of mercenaries, Kane had entered Andalar's service not quite a year before. Success in battle had brought him to the king's attention, and his rise to general of the city-state's armies had quickly followed. Andalar's border wars victoriously concluded, Kane used the king's favor to advance to high office in the royal court. A judicious prescription of certain esoteric elixirs known to Kane restored the aged king's vigor and virility, assuring Kane's influence over Luisteren. After that, it was only a matter of cunning statecraft: after Kane's chief rivals were exposed (by Kane) to be conspiring against the king, Kane's rise to Lord Minister of the city-state was as inevitable as the king's imminent decease.

While it was hardly a novel situation for Kane, he did feel a certain pride of accomplishment in that never before had an outlander risen so fast or so far in Andalar's power structure. Andalar was the oldest and grandest of the scattered city-states that held suzerainty over this jungle-locked region, and if a pronounced obsession with traditions and a decided xenophobia accompanied that proud heritage, so had an incalculable fortune accumulated in the royal coffers over the centuries. Kane was amusing himself with idle schemes as to the use he would make of Andalar's bounty, when Haeen dashed into his chambers.

Luisteren's youngest wife had not a quarter of her royal husband's years. Haeen was slender, close to Kane's six feet of height—but neither boyish nor coltish. Her figure was as precisely formed as that of a marble goddess, and she moved with a dancer's poise—for she had once been a dancer in the temple of Inglarn. She had the rare combination of bright green eyes and hair of luminous black. At the moment her long hair was disordered, her elfin features bleak with despair. Kane wondered at her tears, for Haeen had shown no such evidence of wifely devotion during their own clandestine trysts.

"You know?" she said, coming to his arms in a swirl of silks.

Kane wondered at the lifelessness of her tone. There was no need for such convention in his private chambers. "I was told he had lapsed deeper into stupor about dawn. When the priests started their damned caterwaul a moment ago, I drank to your widowhood."

Haeen made a choking sound beneath Kane's red beard, wrapped her arms about his barrel chest. "If only he could have withstood this last fever. We might have had so many more nights from which to steal an hour of ecstasy."

Kane laughed urbanely. "Well, of course propriety will dictate a judicious interval of mourning, but after . . ."

She stopped his laugh with her kiss. "One last embrace, beloved! They will be coming for us in another moment."

"What are you talking about?" Kane began, suddenly aware that her despair was all too real.

But already they had come for them.

Gaudy in their flame-hued cloaks, the priests of Inglarn filed into Kane's private chambers. Their faces were pallid beneath sooty ritual designs of mourning; their expressions were unreadable as they regarded the pair.

"Come, O Beloved of the King," intoned their leader. "Your master summons you to dwell with him now in the Palace of Inglarn in the Paradise of the Chosen."

"I left orders that I was not to be disturbed," Kane snarled, groping for understanding. His personal bodyguard—all hand-picked men—should have thrown these fools from his threshold, given alarm had Kane's secret designs miscarried. But a glance beyond the doorway showed Kane's soldiers calmly withdrawing from their stations.

The contempt in his tone cut through the sonorous phrases of the high priest. "You are an outlander, Lord Kane. You hold high office such as no stranger before has been entrusted. Yet, outlander that you are, there remains the final and highest duty that you must perform to your master."

Kane had newly come to this land, had only a sketchy impression of its innumerable laws and traditions. If they suspected poison, why had come priests instead of armed guards?

"What is this, Haeen?"

"Don't you know?" Haeen told him dully. "It is the Law of Inglarn. When the king of Andalar is summoned into Paradise, his household and his chief counselors must accompany him. Thus they will continue to serve their master in the Palace of Inglarn, and the new king will begin his holy reign untainted by the ties that the departed king had established."

"Of course," Kane agreed blandly, while behind his impassive face his thoughts were chaotic. His knowledge of this tradition-bound land was incomplete. Inglarn was purely a local deity, and Kane had not troubled to learn the secrets of his cult. Luisteren VII had ascended the throne as a child, more than seventy years before. In his concern with court intrigue, Kane had not delved overmuch into events beyond the memory of almost everyone in the city.

"Come with us now to the temple of Inglarn," the high priest invited. His two fellows produced the ritual fetters of gold. "This night you will pay a final earthly court to your master upon his pyre. On the morrow you will pass through the flame to join him in the Blessed Palace of Inglarn."

"Of course," Kane smiled. Save for the priests, the hallway beyond his quarters was for the moment deserted. One does not intrude upon a sacred ritual.

The high priest's neck snapped with a sound no louder than his gasp of surprise. Kane flung his corpse aside as carelessly as a child discards a doll, and his open fist made lethal impact with the neck of the second priest, even as the man stood goggle-eyed in disbelief. The third priest spun for the open doorway, sucking breath to shout; Kane caught him with an easy bound, and steel-like fingers stifled outcry and life.

Haeen raised her voice in a shrill scream of horror.

It was not a time for reason. Kane's blow rocked her head back with almost killing force. Pausing only to strap his sword across his back, Kane bundled the unconscious girl in his cloak and fled like a shadow from the palace.

Darkness, and the initial chaos as news of the king's death stunned the city, made possible Kane's escape. That, and the fact that Kane's sacrilege was so unthinkable that the tradition-bound folk of Andalar at first could not react to so monstrous a crime.

Kane made the city gates before Haeen had fully recovered consciousness, and before knowledge of his outrage had alerted the confused guard at the wall. He would have ridden beyond Andalar's bourne before pursuit could be organized, but forest trails are treacherous in the night, and while Kane might see in the darkness, his horse could not.

Kane swore and sent his crippled horse stumbling off into the darkness. The false trail might throw off pursuit for long enough to let him make good his escape. Haeen still seemed to be in shock—either from his fist or from his sacrilege—but she followed him silently as Kane struck out on foot.

They walked for a timeless interval through clutching darkness—Kane holding his pace to Haeen's—until at last a taint of grayness began to erode the starless roof of trees.

There was a muffled thunder of water somewhere ahead of them, and a breath of cold mist. In the grayness of false dawn, they crept toward the rim of a gorge. Kane slowed his pace, uncertain how to reach the river below. He had campaigned along the borders of the city-state's holdings, and had a fair idea as to his bearings, although he did not recognize this vicinity of the forest.

Haeen huddled miserably on a boulder, watching as Kane prowled about along the mist-lapped escarpment.

"We'll find a way down once it's daylight," he told her. "There are rapids along here, but if we follow the river farther down, it flows smoothly enough to float a raft. We'll lash some drift together and float beyond Andalar's borders before the fools can guess where to search for us."

"Kane, Kane," Haeen moaned hopelessly. "You can't escape. You don't even know what sin you propose. Kane, this is *wrong!*"

He gave her an impatient scowl that—in the half-light—she could only sense from his tone. "Haeen, I have not lived this long to end my life in some priestly ritual. Let the fools burn the living with the dead, as tradition demands. You and I will laugh together in lands where Andalar is a realm unknown."

"Kane." She shook her midnight mane. "You don't understand. You're an outsider. You *can't* understand."

"I understand that your customs and sacred laws are sham and empty mummery. And I understand that I love you. And you love me."

"Oh, Kane." Haeen's face was tortured. "You scorn our laws. You scorn our gods. But this you *must* understand."

"Haeen, if you really want to die for the greater glory of a husband whose senile touch you loathed . . ."

"*Kane!*" Her cry tore across his sneer. "This is *evil!*"

"So is adultery in some social structures," Kane laughed, trying to break her mood.

"Will you *listen* to me! What you mock is a part of me."

"Of course."

"Andalar is the oldest city in the world."

"One of the wealthiest, I'll grant you—but far from the oldest."

"Kane! How can I make you understand, when you only mock me!"

"I'm sorry. Please go on." Kane thought he could see a path that might lead downward, but the mist was too thick to be sure.

"Andalar was built by Inglarn in the dawn of the world." She seemed to recite a catechism.

"And Andalar worships Inglarn to this day," Kane prompted her. It was not uncommon to find local deities worshiped as the supreme god in isolated regions such as this.

"When Inglarn departed in a Fountain of Flame to the Paradise Beyond the Sun," Haeen recited, "he left a portion of his sacred fire in the flesh of the kings of Andalar."

Kane had heard portions of the legend. But he had long since lost interest in the innumerable variations of the solar myth.

"Therefore," Haeen continued, "the personal household of each king of Andalar is sacred unto the Fire of Inglarn. And when the Fire Made Flesh of the king transcends the Flesh and must return to the Fire of Inglarn, then so must all of those who are a part of the king's Radiance enter with their king into the Fire, to be reborn in the Paradise of the Chosen."

"There must be a way down to the river not far from here," Kane mused aloud. "It might be best if I seek it out by myself, then come back for you."

"Kane, will you listen! This is the sin *you* have committed! You have defied the Sacred Law of Inglarn. You have sought to escape the fate that Inglarn has ordained for you. And the Law decrees that should any of the king's household so blaspheme Inglarn as to flee from their holy duty to their king and their god, then shall Inglarn come back from the Fire—return to utterly destroy Andalar and all its people!"

Kane sensed her agony, listened to her anguished phrases, tried to make himself understand. But Kane was a man who defied all gods, who knew no reverence to any god or law. And he knew that they must make good their escape within the next few hours, or be encircled by their frantic pursuers.

"I have heard such legends in a hundred lands," he told her carefully. But he now understood that the people of Andalar would spare no effort to capture them for the pyre.

"But this is *my* land."

"No longer. I'll take you to a thousand more."

"Only hold me for this moment."

And Kane took Haeen then, on the moss-robed boulders of the gorge—while the river rumbled beneath them, and the skies tattered with gray above them. And Haeen cried out her joy to the dying stars, and Kane for an instant forgot the loneliness of immortality.

And after, Kane unbound their spent bodies, and kissed her.
"Wait here until I return. You're safe—they'll need full light to
find our trail. Before then I'll have found a path down to the
river. We'll see the last of Andalar's borders and its mad customs before another dawn."

And she kissed him, and murmured.

It was late morning before Kane finally discovered a path into
the gorge that he was confident Haeen could traverse. They
could follow the river for a space—throwing off pursuit—until
he could fashion a raft to carry them beyond Andalar's territories. While this avenue of escape was by no means as certain as
Kane had given Haeen to believe, Kane knew their chances were
better than even. Cautiously Kane retraced his steps to the
boulders where he had hidden her.

At first Kane tried to tell himself that he had missed his
landmarks, but then he found the message Haeen had scratched
onto the boulder.

"I cannot let my city be destroyed through my sin. Go your
own way, Kane. You are an outsider, and Inglarn will forgive."

Kane uttered a wordless snarl of pain, and turned his baleful
gaze toward Andalar.

Kane followed her trail, recklessly, hoping that some fool
might challenge his course, praying for a mount. He found
where Haeen had met their pursuers, and where their horses
turned to gallop back to Andalar.

But by the time he limped to within sight of the walls of
Andalar, the funeral pyre of King Luisteren VII and all his
household had blackened the skies. . . .

The skies were black with night and the lowering storm, as
their leader concluded his tale. Rain sought them through the
massed banyan limbs, hissed into the fire. They looked upon the
ruins of Andalar the Accurst, and shivered from more than the
rain.

"But the legend then was true?" one bandit asked their leader.
"Did Inglarn destroy the city because of the sacrilege the outlander had committed?"

"No. Their *god* spared their city," Kane told him bitterly.
"But *I* returned with an army of a hundred thousand. And I
spared not a soul, nor left one stone standing, in all of Andalar."

THE AGE OF THE WARRIOR

By Hank Reinhardt

The chatter and gaiety of the feast had been stilled, and although the candles still burned brightly, fear and apprehension darkened the Great Hall of Castle Glaun. Rank was forgotten as lord and lady, townsman and guardsman mingled in small, quiet clusters. The low murmur of their voices would still as the door to the ducal chambers opened, but picked up as soon as only a servingman or maid appeared.

The evening had started out well enough. Lyulf II, King of Lyvane, accompanied by his retinue and the Duke of Jagai, had arrived earlier in the day. The Duke of Glaun had been well prepared for his royal guests, and the feast he had served was splendid. The recent treaty between King Lyulf II and Togai, King of the Shang, was an event to be well remembered, and the Duke had spared no expenses to celebrate it.

It was right after an impromptu wrestling match, won by Asgalt, Duke of Jagai, against a young guardsman, that the blow fell. A messenger arrived bearing the ill news that the Shang had invested Castle Kels, and it looked as if the castle would fall within a few days.

Pandemonium broke loose, and the King with his closest Advisors retired to the private chambers of the Duke of Glaun.

In the chambers the King sat hunched over a table, poring over a map as if seeking to change the very lay of the land with his thoughts. Around the table stood several of his ministers, while in the corner the two Dukes engaged in a heated argument.

The King glanced with annoyance at the two men, and with a tone of less than regal forebearance snarled, "Will you two stop that damned bickering and get over here! The whole kingdom is threatened and you two argue over propriety!"

Asgalt, about to make a point, stopped in midsentence and looked at the King. "Sire, I do not argue, I merely defend myself."

The Duke of Glaun, Colwen by name, bowed from the waist

305

and answered. "Your Pardon, Sire, but I feel that it is unseemly for a Duke of the Realm to wrestle a common guardsman, even if the man is a champion."

Asgalt grunted in disgust. "Bah, you only object because I win." Lyulf glared at the two, then in his most Kingly voice, "We do not care about wrestling, or the proprieties. We do care about advice!"

Colwen, Duke of Glaun, walked over with dignity and stationed himself behind the King. He was a tall man, with hair as white as snow, and a face lined with years of care and worry.

However, the Duke of Jagai merely ambled over to the front of the King, and stood looking down at him. He saw a man full grown, calm and stern, well suited to rule, but in his mind's eyes he also saw a young boy, gawping up at him in awe and wonder.

Asgalt pointed to the map. "Look, you can see what has to be done, or at least tried."

The King shook his head. "I said no."

Asgalt slapped his thighs with anger. He was a large man, with cold blue eyes shaded by iron-gray hair. Thick-necked, running into massive shoulders and chest, with arms to match. Only the iron gray of his hair and the thickening midsection betrayed his age. He turned away, then turned back again.

"You young puppy, were you not a man grown I'd shake some sense into you, King or no. By Kimwalt's Eyes, all you have to do is look!"

The ministers glanced at each other in embarrassed silence, but the Duke of Glaun spoke up in shocked reprimand.

"Your Grace! You can't speak to the King like that! It isn't proper!"

Asgalt swelled and roared. "Proper! Proper! With Shang soon to be riding through every hamlet, butchering and pillaging till their black hearts' content, and you say 'Proper'!" He shook his head in wonder, then continued in the same roaring voice. "Colwen, you were one of the best fighting men I have ever seen, but—" His voice trailed, and he spoke to the King in a lower voice. "Do you remember when Colwen and I held the breach during the siege of this castle? Fifteen years ago it was, and he wanted me to stand to the left rear, as he was born to the Ducal Chair!"

The King, despite his woes, grinned. He had heard this story at least once a month for the past fifteen years. But then reality returned, and his face tightened.

"Enough of this. Togai has broken the treaty, the Shang are marching, and the Kingdom has to be warned and the levy raised. I don't have time to sit and listen to your constant bickering.''

Asgalt nodded, dropped his pretended fury and spoke seriously. ''No, you don't. Nor do you have time to send a messenger the long way around the Blue Mountains. The Shang are already at Kels, and before you can move the long way around, they will be here, and the main army will be moving. Before the levy is raised, Lyvane will be open.''

He continued. ''The only way to better the time is over the Pass of Jagai. Once through, and the Shang can be avoided by a good man, the levy can be raised by the time the Shang reach here. We could easily catch them here. And there is only one man who knows the pass, me.''

Lyulf sat and never spoke. All there knew his concern. Asgalt had been a close friend and advisor to his father, indeed, he was responsible for his father gaining back the throne after the rebellion. But Asgalt had aged, and the journey he spoke of so easily was hard on even a much younger man, and the Shang were out in force.

In the end it was Colwen who forced the issue. ''Sire, the Duke is right. 'Tis the only chance that we have! The course of action is plain. You leave at once taking the long road, and Asgalt leaves, for the Pass.''

Lyulf nodded in final agreement. He looked at Asgalt and his face softened. ''Have a care, Old Warrior. Remember that a young king still needs old friends.''

The Duke grinned back at him, and for a moment his hard, craggy face looked boyish.

''Old? Ask that young guardsman. He thought I was old . . . but his back and shoulder will tell him different this night.''

''Then take him with you. He looked tough as boot leather.''

Asgalt ruefully answered, ''He is.''

The morning sun had not yet risen as the King and Duke Glaun watched Asgalt and Flan ride from the castle.

The King shook his head in fear, and spoke to his companion. '' 'Tis a fear, good Duke, that we may not see Asgalt again. Strange, that yet again the fate of this land rests on the shoulders of an outlander.''

Colwen nodded his agreement. ''There are no stronger ones for it to rest on.'' He paused, then continued. ''He seemed more than merely eager to go. Is it that he fears his age, or is it his hatred for the Shang?''

The morning fog had lifted and now the sun shone warm. They rode at a steady pace, rarely speaking, each in his own

thoughts. At noon they dismounted for a quick meal, and to walk
the horses. Flan, the guardsman, was a tall youth, wide and
rangy in appearance, with jet black hair and matching eyes. He
eyed the Duke, then spoke.

"Tell me, Your Grace. How is it that a chief of the Haga Hai
becomes a Duke of Lyvane?"

"That, lad, would take some telling. I'm not a Haga Hai, but
a Birkit. I joined one of their raiding parties to settle a personal
score against the Shang. Well, one thing led to another, and I
ended up as Chief. It was a good life, all the Haga Hai want to
do is drink and fight. I'd probably be there still, but a Shang
raiding party hit us one night. They killed everyone but me. They
planned on strangling me, then stuffing the carcass." He chuckled. "That was a mistake. I broke loose, killed a few more.

"I wandered a few years, then ended up in Lyvane serving in
the Army. It was at Iron Mountain that I met Old Lyulf. The line
broke, and it was clear that the rebels were winning, so when the
whole army broke and ran, I tried to stay alive. Couple of days
later I came on a man trying to fight four of the rebels and
protect a boy. I killed the rebels, and the man followed me." He
laughed outright. "It was a damn month before I found out it
was the King. Old Lyulf was a cagey devil."

His mind drifted back over the years, and he spoke in a low
reverie, forgetting he had an audience, talking more to himself
than to Flan.

"Five years we wandered and fought. Hiding out in hills and
caves and with a few loyal to the Crown. Finally we had an
army, and we caught Morgaun at Whitewater Flats. What a
battle that was! I killed Morgaun, damn well cut him near in
half! But enough of me. How is it that a man of Lyvale ends up
in Lyvane?"

Flan smiled. "Not much to tell, Your Grace. The wanderlust
that hits many a young son of a poor farmer. I roamed awhile,
tried the sea, but my stomach didn't care for it. I fought with
Lord Conlenach, was with him at Colnar Ridge. Got away,
wandered a bit more, then ended up in Glaun. The Duke hired
me," he then added with a smile. "He was impressed with my
wrestling!"

Asgalt laughed, a full-throated bellow. "I knew that old devil
was trying to set me up! And he damn near did. You almost had
me, but I tricked you. You wrestle well; all you lack is age and
experience."

"Next time, Your Grace, I'll try not to be tricked."

They continued on, and soon the land began to change. The

rolling hills gave way to open woodland, and this in turn to lowlands, with rich and fertile valleys. This was beautiful land, but now the beauty was marred by signs of war; burnt farms, scattered livestock, and whole villages put to the sword. The occasional stink of death they encountered as they passed a burnt-out steading soon gave way to a horrible stench, that filled the air and seemed to get into their very pores. Death was all about them.

Asgalt reined in his mount. ''Now 'tis time to arm. Shang are all about, and we'd best keep a sharp eye.''

Quickly they stripped the pack pony and each donned his mail shirt, steel helmet, and slipped their shields onto their backs. Their spears they set horizontally, so that they wouldn't project upward and give warning of their presence.

The Duke cut the pack pony loose and sent it running with a slap on the rump.

''From here it's two days' ride. Then a climb up the mountain, across the bridge, and it's over with. All we need to do now is avoid the Shang.''

The stench grew worse as they neared the outskirts of a small village. They passed death in its most grotesque forms, bodies lying with complete abandonment, bloated bellies thrusting at the sun. Neither spoke. Flan, with grim indifference, passed the scene, but Asgalt's face grew flint-hard, and no expression crossed it.

As they neared the crest of a small hill, they could hear the sounds of battle on the other side, screams and curses and yells of agony. Quickly they reined in and slipped from their horses, crawling stealthily to the top of the hill. The last act was played as they watched. One man still stood, jabbing feebly at the circling Shang warriors. At his feet lay a young girl, wide-eyed with terror. A warrior casually parried the spear, then slashed downward and the man fell, blood spurting high in the air from a severed neck artery.

The Shang circled the girl, making false attempts to grab her, and laughing at her frantic movements.

Flan started to rise, but Asgalt pulled him down. He turned angrily.

''Why? There are only five and we can hit them before they know what's happening.''

Asgalt pointed to his left. In the distance a large party of mounted men could be seen.

''I feel like you do, but I've a kingdom to worry about. If we're caught, it could happen to the whole land.''

The girl's screams caused them to look up. The Shang were now close about her, poking with their spears.

Suddenly Asgalt stood up, and now his fury was real. He reached down and dragged the startled Flan to his feet with one hand. "Kimwalt's balls. The day I can't kill five and outride a hundred the kingdom can fall! Ride, damn you, ride. Grab the girl and ride."

The Shang were still laughing and jabbing at the girl when the two hit them. The first died never knowing what the strange pointed thing was that suddenly grew from his chest. The second turned, saw a flash, then nothingness engulfed him. The third screamed, parried a slashing sword, then had his neck broken by the edge of a shield. The fourth saw only a gray-haired demon suddenly appear and kill three of his companions, when a sword lashed out, and cut deep into his side. He looked up in bewilderment, saw a pair of jet black eyes, then life left him. The fifth almost made it, turning and galloping for the body of men in the distance. He fled for his life, but Asgalt wanted it also, and his sword took the man cleanly at the juncture of neck and shoulder.

Asgalt reined in the Shang horse and led it back to Flan and the girl.

"Mount up and ride. They've seen us." He nodded over his shoulder. "Into the hills; we can cut over and hit the main trail by tomorrow."

The night was cold and Asgalt cursed the Shang, the damp and the very small fire. He was tired. The ride had been long and hard, but so far they had outdistanced the Shang. He looked at the two across the fire from him, the girl and Flan huddled close under a cloak and Flan obviously enjoying it.

The girl, Eithne, a baker's daughter, had been visiting an uncle when the Shang attacked. She had fled with several others only to be caught out in the open. The girl shivered under the blanket as Flan asked, "Do you think we've gotten away?"

Flan shrugged, "Ask the Duke. I've never even seen Shang until today."

"The Duke," and her eyes grew wide. "Your Grace," and she made a motion as if to rise.

"Stay seated, girl. It's too cold and late for such nonsense." Asgalt warmed his hands on the small blaze. "No, one thing you can say for the Shang, they never quit. I'm surprised that that one tried to run away. Never saw one break and run before. They're out there. My fear is that they know where we're headed."

Flan snuggled the girl closer and asked. "Why? And what is this pass of Jagai that we're headed to?"

"It's a pass up the mountain. No one knew of it until old Lyulf and I stumbled on it. The Shang can't use it, as they're cavalry, and no way you can get horses up it. We got to the top, then found there was a damn deep gorge. All the way to the bottom of the mountain it falls. I managed to get across it. That is how we got back into Lyvane after the Rebellion. Later we built a bridge.

"Once across, we're in Jagai. I keep a way station about three miles down the mountain, so it'll be an easy walk and an easy ride to Jagai Castle. If they realize that's where we're headed, they'll have the whole army trying to stop us. Once we get across, the army can be raised and the whole attack is ruined."

Asgalt looked longingly at the fire wishing it were larger, then doused it. "Now get some sleep. Tomorrow is going to be a bad day."

Dawn broke cold and clear, and when Asgalt awoke, Flan and the girl had already made another small fire. He was stiff and his back hurt. "Damn ill-trained horse," he muttered as he tried to stretch himself into some semblance of a man rather than an aching mass of bones. He was peeved that they had awakened before he did. Usually he awoke first and fully alert. But now he felt that he needed more hours of sleep. He was groggy and only half awake as he munched his meager breakfast. They mounted, and began a slow, tiring ride up the hill.

The terrain was rocky, with little clefts and culverts, down a short, steep incline, then up a longer steeper one. But slowly they climbed higher and higher. They rounded a bad bend and the mountain loomed forbiddingly over them.

They paused to rest the horses, and Asgalt was quite pleased when Flan suggested it. While the horses drank from a small mountain stream the Duke looked back down the trail.

"Flan, come take a look. I can't make out anything, but do you see something? Seems to be some movement?"

Flan shaded his eyes. "Shang. A large party. Anywhere from fifty to a hundred."

"They know. Best get moving."

They camped that night under an overhanging rock. Not having planned on the girl, they found their supplies were quickly giving out. The Shang horse had had no food bag. It seemed to Asgalt that he had just fallen asleep when Eithne was shaking him. "Your Grace, time to be moving. The Shang followed into the night."

Asgalt rose quickly, and his body protested. Pain shot through his back, and his elbows and shoulders felt as if they were locked in irons. "What? How do you know?"

Flan spoke quietly. "I awoke early, slipped down the trail. Saw them. They gained quite a bit on us."

The Duke nodded. "Let the horse go. From here on up we have to climb. One more day, then we can be over the bridge by midmorning of the next."

Flan discarded his armor and shield, keeping only his sword and spear. He suggested that Asgalt do the same, but the Duke shook his head.

"No. I've had both for twenty years, and when they build my cairn I want them inside. And I need the axe."

The climb was slow and painful. Asgalt watched with envy as Flan made his way up, his breathing never quickening nor his stride faltering. Asgalt felt as if he weighed a ton, but stubbornly refused to discard his armor. He cursed the soft living, and resolved to spend more time in the field, refusing to admit that age had anything to do with it.

The land leveled and the going became easier. Asgalt pointed. "There's a stream over there. Good place to rest a moment. Afterwards, it's a bad climb, but we'll have a good place to sleep. It eases off in the morning."

Eithne greeted the small stream and pond with a cry of pleasure. Quickly she ran and jumped in it. Flan and Asgalt both smiled, and Flan quickly followed the girl. Asgalt slipped off his armor, and the release from the weight felt good. Then he, too, slipped into the pool.

But knowledge of what was ahead of them and what was behind them made the stay brief. Asgalt brought the spears back, leaned them against the rock and spread their clothes to dry. They finished the last of the food, drank some water, then slowly dressed.

Just as they had finished dressing, Flan looked back up the stream, and his voice was cold and flat.

"Well, we're in it now!"

Asgalt followed his gaze. There, beside his armor and the only way out, stood three Shang warriors.

The Duke grunted and spat disgustedly. "Three, fully armed, and us with only spears."

He glanced around, and the bare rock walls loomed mockingly over him. He turned, plucked a knife from his belt, and casually tossed it to Eithne. "Here, girl, in case we fail."

Asgalt and Flan watched stoically as the three Shang closed their ranks and began a slow march toward them.

Fully armed, the two would have been more than a match for the three. Fully armed, one alone might have won, but armed with nothing but a spear apiece, and with no armor, their future looked dim indeed. Both were too experienced in combat to feel they had much chance.

Suddenly the Shang stopped, and one pointed with his sword: "Old Man!" he yelled, "Do you know me? Look well and long, for I mean to give your dead eyes a better view on the end of my lance!"

Asgalt snarled and roared, "You spawn of a snake. I missed you once, but I won't now!"

He then spoke quietly to Flan.

"I know that dog. We fought once before, and my horse bolted before I could kill him. Then a Spaewoman said he would never die by my hand. Since then he's hoped to meet me." His voice grew low and urgent. "Listen, we may stand a chance. He's convinced that I want to kill him myself. What I want you to do is charge with me, then before we hit, fall back, and stab whatever comes open. I'll hit alone. But whatever you do, keep glancing at Artor, the one with the red shield."

The two gripped their spears and started forward. Their right hands gripped the butts, holding them tight and close to the hip, while their left hands were extended along the shaft.

Their pace quickened, and both pairs of eyes glanced left. Artor the Shang muttered low to his men, and their gait increased.

Suddenly Asgalt broke into a run, and Flan quickly caught up with him, but just as contact was to be made, Flan dropped back. Asgalt, spear pointed directly at the man in the center, but eyes constantly glancing left, leaped forward, spun, and drove his spear directly into the face of the man on his right. The spearhead skimmed the top of the shield, smashed upward through the roof of the mouth, and stuck in the bone of the skull. Wrenching his spear loose, he barely slid aside in time to avoid the shearing stroke of a sword. Off balance from missing his blow, the man stumbled. Asgalt grabbed his shield with one hand, spun him around, and drove his spear into his back. The Duke looked up in time to see Artor's sword about to descend, when Flan, in a clean hard lunge, drove his spear through the body of the Shang. The spear caught Artor under the arm, and actually pierced the shield on the other side of his body.

Artor staggered, shock and pain clouded his face. He looked at Flan, then back to Asgalt. "*You* didn't kill me," he muttered. Then his eyes glazed, he fell heavily, twitched and lay still.

*   *   *

The rest of the climb was brutal. It seemed to Asgalt that he must have completely forgotten just how much physical exertion it required. He was thankful that the girl was sturdy, so that only a few times were they required to actually lift her. When they reached the ledge where they would make their camp, only pride kept him from collapsing at once. The Shang had all carried food bags, so at least there was now plenty to eat. The fare was plain, but all thought they had never tasted better.

"Asgalt, what do we face tomorrow?"

"A short climb, then it's merely a hard walk. Once we reach the top, it'll be over."

Flan looked quizzical. "How did you build a bridge?"

"We didn't build a bridge the first time we crossed. There used to be a tree, and we got a rope caught in it, and I swung across. We built it from the other side. It was while we were trying to raise an army. It was a good place to escape to if there was need. He was determined to keep the Royal blood alive, and we could hole up, then dash across. We built the bridge from the other side, and Old Lyulf, cagey he was, designed it so that it would be easy to chop through from this side. Other side has rock foundations."

Conversation died, and the stars shone down, diamond-bright in the crisp, clear night air. Asgalt leaned back against the rock and tried to sleep, but for a change sleep eluded him. He watched Eithne and Flan, heard the low muted laughter, saw the looks into each other's eyes. He smiled to himself, and he remembered another girl, one with hair black as night, and lips that were red, and eyes that laughed. Another night, long ago, when he had sat with her, and their eyes had met. He could still hear her laugh, see her smile, and feel the touch of her hand. How the people had gasped when he had married her and made her a Duchess! The life they had was good. The pain of losing her was still with him. It had been hard, but she had given him two strong sons and two beautiful daughters, and he must see that they were taken care of.

He sat up and shook off the inexplicable nostalgia.

"Flan. Let me interrupt you children." He took off his Ducal ring. "Take this. It's foolish for me to pretend I'm not bone-tired, and the two of you can make better time down the mountain to the way station than I can. Take this, show it to the guard there, and grab two fast horses and go on to Castle Jagai. Give the ring to Olwen, and have him send riders out to raise the levy. He'll know what to do."

Flan took the ring. "Aye, and I'll have him prepare a Hero's Welcome for his Lord."

Asgalt laughed. "A hero, a hero. . . . Hell, have him prepare for a tired old man! And Lyulf will have parades and pageants after this is over. Now let me get some sleep."

But the sleep was brief, and this time Asgalt awakened with both Eithne and Flan. Food was gulped hurriedly and the last leg of the journey was begun.

The last of the climb was hard, but quick. As they reached the top, as if planned, all three turned in unison and looked back down the trail; sun glinted off Shang armor.

Shaking his head in disgust, the Duke muttered, "We're a lot alike, the Shang and I, we never let up, and we never forget."

The last portion was made at a dogtrot over flat firm earth. A quick turn, a small hill, and the bridge was before them. It spanned a chasm that was only the width of five tall men, but it extended out of sight on either side, and the eye was lost in the distance to the bottom.

The bridge was a simple, crude affair, no railings, but two ropes on either side gave some security.

"Flan. Go cut the ropes on that end while I undo these." He knelt and began working on the thick rope. By the time he had finished, Flan had cut both and was standing beside him.

Asgalt stripped off his armor and began to fashion a sling to go around his body and between his legs. Once this was done he turned to Flan and Eithne.

"You two go on ahead. I can cut the bridge loose from this side and cross on the two remaining ropes. This was in case we ever got caught on this side. I told you old Lyulf was cagey."

Flan shook his head. "Let me climb down. I can cut them quicker than you."

"No, I helped build it. I'll cut it down. Now get on across."

Asgalt secured the rope and lowered himself until he was even with the supporting posts of the bridge. He swung out and back until he had grasped a beam, then wedged himself between it and the cliff, wrapping his legs tight around the wood.

He leaned back. He was tired and wanted to rest for a few minutes, but there wasn't time. He removed the axe from his belt and began to chop.

The space was narrow, and the cut had to be made close to his body, so that there was little room for a full swing. He swung the axe in short, hard blows, wrenching it to clear the blade on each stroke. His hand cramped and his forearm began to quiver with strain, but he never ceased his relentless rhythm. It seemed to him that with each stroke the wood grew harder and the axe duller.

But slowly, ever so slowly, the cut widened and deepened. He stopped, thrust the axe back through his belt and massaged his aching hand and forearm.

A few more should do it, he thought. *Damn, will I be glad to rest in a bed again, beside a nice warm fire.*

He hooked his knees about the beam, and trusting to the thick rope, leaned out, swinging the axe upward in vicious strokes, as if the wood were a personal enemy.

The wood cracked and broke loose, and Asgalt kicked out and swung free in case the whole bridge broke loose, but it sagged, creaked and held.

The Duke ignored the yawning chasm below him, and cursed with a fervor and feeling that was awesome in its intensity. Still cursing, he pulled himself back up the rope, attached it on the other side, and began the whole process over.

Sweat stung his eyes, and his back began to ache from the strained unnatural position. He worked more slowly, and would stop after several strokes to gauge the depth of the cut, and to clear his vision. The bridge creaked and sagged even further as the amount of wood holding it grew less. After what seemed hours, the top began to splinter and snap. He quickly slipped off the beam and as he kicked back and away, swung the axe once more. The axe bit, the wood cracked, and the bridge slipped downward, grabbing the axe, flipping it loose from his grip. Then bridge and axe fell end over end into the depths below.

Asgalt watched the dwindling shapes. "Hmmuph, man could starve before he hit bottom," he thought.

Again he pulled himself up the rope, this time more slowly. A shout greeted him, and he saw Flan and Eithne wave from the other side.

"Well done, Lord Duke, Well done!"

Asgalt waved tiredly. Even his bones ached. His forearms quivered uncontrollably, and his knees were flaccid, almost unable to bear his weight. He sat down heavily, his body worn and his eyes dulled with fatigue. His hand aimlessly gripped the hilt of his sword; he gazed blindly at the mail shirt, helmet and shield that lay at his feet.

Wearily he rose and walked back along the path. Far down he could see the first of the Shang as they made the turn, walking cautiously, expecting an ambush behind every rock.

"Still time," he muttered under his breath.

He walked back and picked up his mail, slipped it on, and

buckled the sword about his waist. The familiar weight felt comforting, an old friend.

Once again he sat down on the rock, ignoring the urgent shouts from Flan and Eithne.

He chuckled to himself. *They're right, I'm growing old. Old Lyulf was right, it comes before you know, and soon you don't even care.*

He looked across the gorge to Flan and Eithne, and their youthful figures brought back a flood of memories, and his past life fled across his mind's eye. He remembered the aimless wanderings, the battles; he stood again on the walls of Castle Gluan, with Colwen beside him, holding the breach against attack after attack, until the enemy fell back, dismayed and broken and not being able to break two men. He wandered again, guarding the life of the King and the young Prince, and he remembered the final charge in the battle for the Crown. The foes falling before him until he had reached the Standard, cutting down the bearer, and then with one stroke cutting through the helmet, head and chest of Mergaun.

He realized suddenly that life had been good to him, that he had achieved a great deal, and that now the battles were over. All he had to do was walk across that rope bridge. There would be parades, and feasts, and even tournaments, all in his honor. And once that was over, there would be a quiet life for the remainder of his years. He would grow old, and slightly fat, and honors would still be heaped on him. His sons were near grown, and his daughters already promised. The Kingdom was secure, no new threats, no new battles.

He thought of how nice it would be, to sleep in a soft bed, to take an attractive serving girl to the same bed. . . . Yes, life would be pleasant until that final sleep in that same soft bed.

The Duke of Jagai stood and wearily reached for his helmet and shield, an old man, gray hair glinting in the sun, and tired beyond belief.

The sword flashed in a short, bright arc, and the rope parted and twisted its way downward.

The years and fatigue seemed to melt from his body as he buckled his helmet and dressed his shield on his arm. He stood straight and tall and strong, and his eyes were hell-bright!

With a strong and steady stride, Asgalt, Duke of Jagai, marched down to meet the Shang.

BEYOND THE BLACK RIVER

By Robert E. Howard

1.
Conan Loses His Ax

The stillness of the forest trail was so primeval that the tread of a soft-booted foot was a startling disturbance. At least it seemed so to the ears of the wayfarer, though he was moving along the path with the caution that must be practiced by any man who ventures beyond Thunder River. He was a young man of medium height, with an open countenance and a mop of tousled tawny hair unconfined by cap or helmet. His garb was common enough for that country—a coarse tunic, belted at the waist, short leather breeches beneath, and soft buckskin boots that came short of the knee. A knife-hilt jutted from one boot-top. The broad leather belt supported a short, heavy sword and a buckskin pouch. There was no perturbation in the wide eyes that scanned the green walls which fringed the trail. Though not tall, he was well built, and the arms that the short wide sleeves of the tunic left bare were thick with corded muscle.

He tramped imperturbably along, although the last settler's cabin lay miles behind him, and each step was carrying him nearer the grim peril that hung like a brooding shadow over the ancient forest.

He was not making as much noise as it seemed to him, though he well knew that the faint tread of his booted feet would be like a tocsin of alarm to the fierce ears that might be lurking in the treacherous green fastness. His careless attitude was not genuine; his eyes and ears were keenly alert, especially his ears, for no gaze could penetrate the leafy tangle for more than a few feet in either direction.

But it was instinct more than any warning by the external senses which brought him up suddenly, his hand on his hilt. He stood stock-still in the middle of the trail, unconsciously holding his breath, wondering what he had heard, and wondering if indeed he had heard anything. The silence seemed absolute. Not a squirrel chattered or bird chirped. Then his gaze fixed itself on a mass of bushes beside the trail a few yards ahead of him. There was no breeze, yet he had seen a branch quiver. The short hairs on his scalp prickled, and he stood for an instant undecided, certain that a move in either direction would bring death streaking at him from the bushes.

A heavy chopping crunch sounded behind the leaves. The bushes were shaken violently, and simultaneously with the sound, an arrow arched erratically from among them and vanished among the trees along the trail. The wayfarer glimpsed its flight as he sprang frantically to cover.

Crouching behind a thick stem, his sword quivering in his fingers, he saw the bushes part, and a tall figure stepped leisurely into the trail. The traveler stared in surprise. The stranger was clad like himself in regard to boots and breeks, though the latter were of silk instead of leather. But he wore a sleeveless hauberk of dark mesh-mail in place of a tunic, and a helmet perched on his black mane. That helmet held the other's gaze; it was without a crest, but adorned by short bull's horns. No civilized hand ever forged that headpiece. Nor was the face below it that of a civilized man: dark, scarred, with smoldering blue eyes, it was a face as untamed as the primordial forest which formed its background. The man held a broadsword in his right hand, and the edge was smeared with crimson.

"Come on out," he called, in an accent unfamiliar to the wayfarer. "All's safe now. There was only one of the dogs. Come on out."

The other emerged dubiously and stared at the stranger. He felt curiously helpless and futile as he gazed on the proportions of the forest man—the massive iron-clad breast, and the arm that bore the reddened sword, burned dark by the sun and ridged and corded with muscles. He moved with the dangerous ease of a panther; he was too fiercely supple to be a product of civilization, even of that fringe of civilization which composed the outer frontiers.

Turning, he stepped back to the bushes and pulled them apart. Still not certain just what had happened, the wayfarer from the east advanced and stared down into the bushes. A man lay there, a short, dark, thickly muscled man, naked except for a loincloth, a necklace of human teeth and a brass armlet. A short sword was thrust into the girdle of the loincloth, and one hand still gripped a heavy black bow. The man had long black hair; that was about all the wayfarer could tell about his head, for his features were a mask of blood and brains. His skull had been split to the teeth.

"A Pict, by the gods!" exclaimed the wayfarer.

The burning blue eyes turned upon him.

"Are you surprised?"

"Why, they told me at Velitrium, and again at the settlers' cabins along the road, that these devils sometimes sneaked across the border, but I didn't expect to meet one this far in the interior."

"You're only four miles east of Black River," the stranger informed him. "They've been shot within a mile of Velitrium. No settler between Thunder River and Fort Tuscelan is really safe. I picked up this dog's trail three miles south of the fort this morning, and I've been following him ever since. I came up behind him just as he was drawing an arrow on you. Another instant and there'd have been a stranger in Hell. But I spoiled his aim for him."

The wayfarer was staring wide-eyed at the larger man, dumbfounded by the realization that the man had actually tracked down one of the forest devils and slain him unsuspected. That implied woodsmanship of a quality undreamed, even for Conajohara.

"You are one of the fort's garrison?" he asked.

"I'm no soldier. I draw the pay and rations of an officer of the line, but I do my work in the woods. Valannus knows I'm of more use ranging along the river than cooped up in the fort."

Casually the slayer shoved the body deeper into the thickets with his foot, pulled the bushes together and turned away down the trail. The other followed him.

"My name is Balthus," he offered. "I was at Velitrium last night. I haven't decided whether I'll take up a hide of land, or enter fort service."

"The best land near Thunder River is already taken," grunted the slayer. "Plenty of good land between Scalp Creek—you crossed it a few miles back—and the fort, but that's getting too devilish close to the river. The Picts steal over to burn and murder—as that one did. They don't always come singly. Some day they'll try to sweep the settlers out of Conajohara. And they may succeed—probably will succeed. This colonization business is mad, anyway. There's plenty of good land east of the Bossonian marches. If the Aquilonians would cut up some of the big estates of their barons, and plant wheat where now only deer are hunted, they wouldn't have to cross the border and take the land of the Picts away from them."

"That's queer talk from a man in the service of the governor of Conajohara," objected Balthus.

"It's nothing to me," the other retorted. "I'm a mercenary. I sell my sword to the highest bidder. I never planted wheat and never will, so long as there are other harvests to be reaped with the sword. But you Hyborians have expanded as far as you'll be allowed to expand. You've crossed the marches, burned a few villages, exterminated a few clans and pushed back the frontier to Black River; but I doubt if you'll even be able to hold what you've conquered, and you'll never push the frontier any further westward. Your idiotic king doesn't understand conditions here. He won't send you enough reinforcements, and there are not enough settlers to withstand the shock of a concerted attack from across the river."

"But the Picts are divided into small clans," persisted Balthus. "They'll never unite. We can whip any single clan."

"Or any three or four clans," admitted the slayer. "But some day a man will rise and unite thirty or forty clans, just as was done among the Cimmerians, when the Gundermen tried to push the border northward, years ago. They tried to colonize the southern marches of Cimmeria: destroyed a few small clans, built a fort-town, Venarium—you've heard the tale."

"So I have indeed," replied Balthus, wincing. The memory of that red disaster was a black blot in the chronicles of a proud and warlike people. "My uncle was at Venarium when the Cimmerians swarmed over the walls. He was one of the few who escaped that slaughter. I've heard him tell the tale, many a time. The barbarians swept out of the hills in a ravening horde, without warning, and stormed Venarium with such fury none could stand before them. Men, women, and children were butchered. Venarium was reduced to a mass of charred ruins, as it is to this day. The Aquilonians were driven back across the marches, and have never since tried to colonize the Cimmerian country. But you speak of Venarium familiarly. Perhaps you were there?"

"I was," grunted the other. "I was one of the horde that swarmed over the walls. I hadn't yet seen fifteen snows, but already my name was repeated about the council fires."

Balthus involuntarily recoiled, staring. It seemed incredible that the man walking tranquilly at his side should have been one of those screeching, blood-mad devils that had poured over the walls of Venarium on that long-gone day to make her streets run crimson.

"Then you, too, are a barbarian!" he exclaimed involuntarily.

The other nodded, without taking offense.

"I am Conan, a Cimmerian."

"I've heard of you." Fresh interest quickened Balthus' gaze.
No wonder the Pict had fallen victim to his own sort of subtlety!
The Cimmerians were barbarians as ferocious as the Picts, and
much more intelligent. Evidently Conan had spent much time
among civilized men, though that contact had obviously not
softened him, nor weakened any of his primitive instincts. Balthus'
apprehension turned to admiration as he marked the easy catlike
stride, the effortless silence with which the Cimmerian moved
along the trail. The oiled links of his armor did not clink, and
Balthus knew Conan could glide through the deepest thicket or
most tangled copse as noiselessly as any naked Pict that ever
lived.

"You're not a Gunderman?" It was more assertion than
question.

Balthus shook his head. "I'm from the Tauran."

"I've seen good woodsmen from the Tauran. But the Bossonians
have sheltered you Aquilonians from the outer wilderness for too
many centuries. You need hardening."

That was true; the Bossonian marches, with their fortified
villages filled with determined bowmen, had long served Aquilonia
as a buffer against the outlying barbarians. Now among the
settlers beyond Thunder River there was growing up a breed of
forest men capable of meeting the barbarians at their own game,
but their numbers were still scanty. Most of the frontiersmen
were like Balthus—more of the settler than the woodsman type.

The sun had not set, but it was no longer in sight, hidden as it
was behind the dense forest wall. The shadows were lengthening, deepening back in the woods as the companions strode on
down the trail.

"It will be dark before we reach the fort," commented Conan
casually; then: "Listen!"

He stopped short, half crouching, sword ready, transformed
into a savage figure of suspicion and menace, poised to spring
and rend. Balthus had heard it too—a wild scream that broke at
its highest note. It was the cry of a man in dire fear or agony.

Conan was off in an instant, racing down the trail, each stride
widening the distance between him and his straining companion.
Balthus puffed a curse. Among the settlements of the Tauran he
was accounted a good runner, but Conan was leaving him behind
with maddening ease. Then Balthus forgot his exasperation as
his ears were outraged by the most frightful cry he had ever
heard. It was not human, this one; it was a demoniacal caterwauling

of hideous triumph that seemed to exult over fallen humanity and find echo in black gulfs beyond human ken.

Balthus faltered in his stride, and clammy sweat beaded his flesh. But Conan did not hesitate; he darted around a bend in the trail and disappeared, and Balthus, panicky at finding himself alone with that awful scream still shuddering through the forest in grisly echoes, put on an extra burst of speed and plunged after him.

The Aquilonian slid to a stumbling halt, almost colliding with the Cimmerian, who stood in the trail over a crumpled body. But Conan was not looking at the corpse which lay there in the Crimson-soaked dust. He was glaring into the deep woods on either side of the trail.

Balthus muttered a horrified oath. It was the body of a man which lay there in the trail, a short, fat man, clad in the gilt-worked boots and (despite the heat) the ermine-trimmed tunic of a wealthy merchant. His fat, pale face was set in a stare of frozen horror; his thick throat had been slashed from ear to ear as if by a razor-sharp blade. The short sword still in its scabbard seemed to indicate that he had been struck down without a chance to fight for his life.

"A Pict?" Balthus whispered, as he turned to peer into the deepening shadows of the forest.

Conan shook his head and straightened to scowl down at the dead man.

"A forest devil. This is the fifth, by Crom!"

"What do you mean?"

"Did you ever hear of a Pictish wizard called Zogar Sag?"

Balthus shook his head uneasily.

"He dwells in Gwawela, the nearest village across the river. Three months ago he hid beside this road and stole a string of pack-mules from a pack-train bound for the fort—drugged their drivers, somehow. The mules belonged to this man"—Conan casually indicated the corpse with his foot—"Tiberias, a merchant of Velitrium. They were loaded with ale-kegs, and old Zogar stopped to guzzle before he got across the river. A woodsman named Soractus trailed him, and led Valannus and three soldiers to where he lay dead drunk in a thicket. At the importunities of Tiberias, Valannus threw Zogar Sag into a cell, which is the worst insult you can give a Pict. He managed to kill his guard and escape, and sent back word that he meant to kill Tiberias and the five men who captured him in a way that would make Aquilonians shudder for centuries to come.

"Well, Soractus and the soldiers are dead. Soractus was killed on the river, the soldiers in the very shadow of the fort. And now Tiberias is dead. No Pict killed any of them. Each victim—except Tiberias, as you see—lacked his head—which no doubt is now ornamenting the altar of Zogar Sag's particular god."

"How do you know they weren't killed by the Picts?" demanded Balthus.

Conan pointed to the corpse of the merchant.

"You think that was done with a knife or a sword? Look closer and you'll see that only a talon could have made a gash like that. The flesh is ripped, not cut."

"Perhaps a panther—" began Balthus, without conviction.

Conan shook his head impatiently.

"A man from the Tauran couldn't mistake the mark of a panther's claws. No. It's a forest devil summoned by Zogar Sag to carry out his revenge. Tiberias was a fool to start for Velitrium alone, and so close to dusk. But each one of the victims seemed to be smitten with madness just before doom overtook him. Look here; the signs are plain enough. Tiberias came riding along the trail on his mule, maybe with a bundle of choice otter pelts behind his saddle to sell in Velitrium, and the *thing* sprang on him from behind that bush. See where the branches are crushed down.

"Tiberias gave one scream, and then his throat was torn open and he was selling his otter skins in Hell. The mule ran away into the woods. Listen! Even now you can hear him thrashing about under the trees. The demon didn't have time to take Tiberias' head; it took fright as we came up."

"As *you* came up," amended Balthus. "It must not be a very terrible creature if it flees from one armed man. But how do you know it was not a Pict with some kind of a hook that rips instead of slicing? Did you see it?"

"Tiberias was an armed man," grunted Conan. "If Zogar Sag can bring demons to aid him, he can tell them which men to kill and which to let alone. No, I didn't see it. I only saw the bushes shake as it left the trail. But if you want further proof, look here!"

The slayer had stepped into the pool of blood in which the dead man sprawled. Under the bushes at the edge of the path there was a footprint, made in blood on the hard loam.

"Did a man make that?" demanded Conan.

Balthus felt his scalp prickle. Neither man nor any beast that he had ever seen could have left that strange, monstrous, three-toed print, that was curiously combined of the bird and the reptile, yet a true type of neither. He spread his fingers above the print, careful not to touch it, and grunted explosively. He could not span the mark.

"What is it?" he whispered. "I never saw a beast that left a spoor like that."

"Nor any other sane man," answered Conan grimly. "It's a swamp demon—they're thick as bats in the swamps beyond Black River. You can hear them howling like damned souls when the wind blows strong from the south on hot nights."

"What shall we do?" asked the Aquilonian, peering uneasily into the deep blue shadows. The frozen fear on the dead countenance haunted him. He wondered what hideous head the wretch had seen thrust grinning from among the leaves to chill his blood with terror.

"No use to try to follow a demon," grunted Conan, drawing a short woodsman's ax from his girdle. "I tried tracking him after he killed Soractus. I lost his trail within a dozen steps. He might have grown himself wings and flown away, or sunk down through the earth to Hell. I don't know. I'm not going after the mule, either. It'll either wander back to the fort, or to some settler's cabin."

As he spoke Conan was busy at the edge of the trail with his ax. With a few strokes he cut a pair of saplings nine or ten feet long, and denuded them of their branches. Then he cut a length from a serpentlike vine that crawled among the bushes near by, and making one end fast to one of the poles, a couple of feet from the end, whipped the vine over the other sapling and interlaced it back and forth. In a few moments he had a crude but strong litter.

"The demon isn't going to get Tiberias' head if I can help it," he growled. "We'll carry the body into the fort. It isn't more than three miles. I never liked the fat fool, but we can't have Pictish devils making so cursed free with white men's heads."

The Picts were a white race, through swarthy, but the border men never spoke of them as such.

Balthus took the rear end of the litter, onto which Conan unceremoniously dumped the unfortunate merchant, and they moved on down the trail as swiftly as possible. Conan made no more noise laden with their grim burden than he had made when unencumbered. He had made a loop with the merchant's belt at the end of the poles, and was carrying his share of the load with one hand, while the other gripped his naked broadsword, and his restless gaze roved the sinister walls about them. The shadows were thickening. A darkening blue mist blurred the outlines of the foliage. The forest deepened in the twilight, became a blue haunt of mystery sheltering unguessed things.

They had covered more than a mile, and the muscles in Balthus' sturdy arms were beginning to ache a little, when a cry rang shuddering from the woods whose blue shadows were deepening into purple.

Conan started convulsively, and Balthus almost let go the poles.

"A woman!" cried the younger man. "Great Mitra, a woman cried out then!"

"A settler's wife straying in the woods," snarled Conan, setting down his end of the litter. "Looking for a cow, probably, and—stay here!"

He dived like a hunting wolf into the leafy wall. Balthus' hair bristled.

"Stay here alone with this corpse and a devil hiding in the woods?" he yelped. "I'm coing with you!"

And suiting action to words, he plunged after the Cimmerian. Conan glanced back at him, but made no objection, though he did not moderate his pace to accommodate the shorter legs of his companion. Balthus wasted his wind in swearing as the Cimmerian drew away from him again, like a phantom between the trees, and then Conan burst into a dim glade and halted crouching, lips snarling, sword lifted.

"What are we stopping for?" panted Balthus, dashing the sweat out of his eyes and gripping his short sword.

"That scream came from this glade, or nearby," answered Conan. "I don't mistake the location of sounds, even in the woods. But where—"

Abruptly the sound rang out again—*behind them*; in the direction of the trail they had just quitted. It rose piercingly and pitifully, the cry of a woman in frantic terror—and then, shockingly, it changed to a yell of mocking laughter that might have burst from the lips of a fiend of lower Hell.

"What in Mitra's name—" Balthus' face was a pale blur in the gloom.

With a scorching oath Conan wheeled and dashed back the way he had come, and the Aquilonian stumbled bewilderedly after him. He blundered into the Cimmerian as the latter stopped dead, and rebounded from his brawny shoulders as though from an iron statue. Gasping from the impact, he heard Conan's breath hiss through his teeth. The Cimmerian seemed frozen in his tracks.

Looking over his shoulder, Balthus felt his hair stand up

stiffly. Something was moving through the deep bushes that fringed the trail—something that neither walked nor flew, but seemed to glide like a serpent. But it was not a serpent. Its outlines were indistinct, but it was taller than a man, and not very bulky. It gave off a glimmer of weird light, like a faint blue flame. Indeed, the eerie fire was the only tangible thing about it. It might have been an embodied flame moving with reason and purpose through the blackening woods.

Conan snarled a savage curse and hurled his ax with ferocious will. But the thing glided on without altering its course. Indeed it was only a few instants' fleeting glimpse they had of it—a tall, shadowy thing of misty flame floating through the thickets. Then it was gone, and the forest crouched in breathless stillness.

With a snarl Conan plunged through the intervening foliage and into the trail. His profanity, as Balthus floundered after him, was lurid and impassioned. The Cimmerian was standing over the litter on which lay the body of Tiberias. And that body no longer possessed a head.

"Tricked us with its damnable caterwauling!" raved Conan, swinging his great sword about his head in his wrath. "I might have known! I might have guessed a trick! Now there'll be five heads to decorate Zogar's altar."

"But what thing is it that can cry like a woman and laugh like a devil, and shines like witch-fire as it glides through the trees?" gasped Balthus, mopping the sweat from his pale face.

"A swamp devil," responded Conan morosely. "Grab those poles. We'll take in the body, anyway. At least our load's a bit lighter."

With much grim philosophy he gripped the leathery loop and stalked down the trail.

2

The Wizard of Gwawela

Fort Tuscelan stood on the eastern bank of Black River, the tides of which washed the foot of the stockade. The latter was of logs, as were all the buildings within, including the donjon (to dignify it by that appellation), in which were the governor's quarters, overlooking the stockade and the sullen river. Beyond that river lay a huge forest, which approached jungle-like density along the spongy shores. Men paced the runways along the log parapet day and night, watching that dense green wall. Seldom a menacing figure appeared, but the sentries knew that they too were watched, fiercely, hungrily, with the mercilessness of ancient hate. The forest beyond the river might seem desolate and vacant of life to the ignorant eye, but life teemed there, not alone of bird and beast and reptile, but also of men, the fiercest of all the hunting beasts.

There, at the fort, civilization ended. Fort Tuscelan was the last outpost of a civilized world; it represented the westernmost thrust of the dominant Hyborian races. Beyond the river the primitive still reigned in shadowy forests, brush-thatched huts where hung the grinning skulls of men, and mud-walled enclosures where fires flickered and drums rumbled, and spears were whetted in the hands of dark, silent men with tangled black hair and the eyes of serpents. Those eyes often glared through the bushes at the fort across the river. Once dark-skinned men had built their huts where that fort stood, yes, and their huts had risen where now stood the fields and log cabins of fair-haired settlers, back beyond Velitrium, that raw, turbulent frontier town on the banks of Thunder River, to the shores of that other river that bounds the Bossonian marches. Traders had come, and priests of Mitra who walked with bare feet and empty hands, and died horribly, most of them; but soldiers had followed, and men with axes in their hands and women and children in ox-drawn wains. Back to Thunder River, and still back, beyond Black River, the aborigines had been pushed, with slaughter and massacre. But the dark-skinned people did not forget that once Conajohara had been theirs.

The guard inside the eastern gate bawled a challenge. Through a barred aperture torchlight flickered, glinting on a steel headpiece and suspicious eyes beneath it.

"Open the gate," snorted Conan. "You see it's I, don't you?"

Military discipline put his teeth on edge.

The gate swung inward and Conan and his companion passed through. Balthus noted that the gate was flanked by a tower on each side, the summits of which rose above the stockade. He saw loopholes for arrows.

The guardsmen grunted as they saw the burden borne between the men. Their pikes jangled against each other as they thrust shut the gate, chin on shoulder, and Conan asked testily: "Have you never seen a headless body before?"

The faces of the soldiers were pallid in the torchlight.

"That's Tiberias," blurted one. "I recognize that fur-trimmed tunic. Valerius here owes me five lunas. I told him Tiberias had heard the loon call when he rode through the gate on his mule, with his glassy stare. I wagered he'd come back without his head.''

Conan grunted enigmatically, motioned Balthus to ease the litter to the ground, and then strode off toward the governor's quarters, with the Aquilonian at his heels. The tousle-headed youth stared about him eagerly and curiously, noting the rows of barracks along the walls, the stables, the tiny merchants' stalls, the towering blockhouse, and the other buildings, with the open square in the middle where the soldiers drilled, and where, now, fires danced and men off duty lounged. These were now hurrying to join the morbid crowd gathered about the litter at the gate. The rangy figures of Aquilonian pikemen and forest runners mingled with the shorter, stockier forms of Bossonian archers.

He was not greatly surprised that the governor received them himself. Autocratic society with its rigid caste laws lay east of the marches. Valannus was still a young man, well knit, with a finely chiseled countenance already carved into sober cast by toil and responsibility.

"You left the fort before daybreak, I was told," he said to Conan. "I had begun to fear that the Picts had caught you at last.''

"When they smoke my head the whole river will know it," grunted Conan. "They'll hear Pictish women wailing their dead as far as Velitrium—I was on a lone scout. I couldn't sleep. I kept hearing drums talking across the river.''

"They talk each night," reminded the governor, his fine eyes shadowed, as he stared closely at Conan. He had learned the unwisdom of discounting wild men's instincts.

"There was a difference last night," growled Conan. "There has been ever since Zogar Sag got back across the river.''

"We should either have given him presents and sent him home, or else hanged him," sighed the governor. "You advised that, but—''

"But it's hard for you Hyborians to learn the ways of the outlands," said Conan. "Well, it can't be helped now, but there'll be no peace on the border so long as Zogar lives and remembers the cell he sweated in. I was following a warrior who slipped over to put a few white notches on his bow. After I split his head I fell in with this lad whose name is Balthus and who's come from the Tauran to help hold the frontier.''

Valannus approvingly eyed the young man's frank countenance and strongly knit frame.

"I am glad to welcome you, young sir. I wish more of your people would come. We need men used to forest life. Many of

our soldiers and some of our settlers are from the eastern provinces and know nothing of woodcraft, or even of agricultural
life.''

"Not many of that breed this side of Velitrium," grunted
Conan. "That town's full of them, though. But listen, Valannus,
we found Tiberias dead on the trail." And in a few words he
related the grisly affair.

Valannus paled. "I did not know he had left the fort. He must
have been mad!''

"He was," answered Conan. "Like the other four; each one,
when his time came, went mad and rushed into the woods to
meet his death like a hare running down the throat of a python.
Something called to them from the deeps of the forest, something
the men call a loon, for lack of a better name, but only the
doomed ones could hear it. Zogar Sag has made a magic that
Aquilonian civilization can't overcome.''

To this thrust Vlannus made no reply; he wiped his brow with
a shaky hand.

"Do the soldiers know of this?''

"We left the body by the eastern gate.''

"You should have concealed the fact, hidden the corpse somewhere in the woods. The soldiers are nervous enough already.''

"They'd have found it out some way. If I'd hidden the body,
it would have been returned to the fort as the corpse of Soractus
was—tied up outside the gate for the men to find in the morning.''

Valannus shuddered. Turning, he walked to a casement and
stared silently out over the river, black and shiny under the glint
of the stars. Beyond the river the jungle rose like an ebony wall.
The distant screech of a panther broke the stillness. The night
pressed in, blurring the sounds of the soldiers outside the blockhouse, dimming the fires. A wind whispered through the black
branches, rippling the dusky water. On its wings came a low,
rhythmic pulsing, sinister as the pad of a leopard's foot.

"After all," said Valannus, as if speaking his thoughts aloud,
"what do we know—what does anyone know—of the things that
jungle may hide? We have dim rumors of great swamps and
rivers, and a forest that stretches on and on over everlasting
plains and hills to end at last on the shores of the western ocean.
But what things lie between this river and that ocean we dare not
even guess. No white man has ever plunged deep into that
fastness and returned alive to tell us what he found. We are wise
in our civilized knowledge, but our knowledge extends just so
far—to the western bank of that ancient river! Who knows what

shapes earthly and unearthly may lurk beyond the dim circle of light our knowledge has cast?

"Who knows what gods are worshipped under the shadows of that heathen forest, or what devils crawl out of the black ooze of the swamps? Who can be sure that all the inhabitants of that black country are natural? Zogar Sag—a sage of the eastern cities would sneer at his primitive magic-making as the mummery of a fakir; yet he has driven mad and killed five men in a manner no man can explain. I wonder if he himself is wholly human."

"If I can get within ax-throwing distance of him I'll settle that question," growled Conan, helping himself to the governor's wine and pushing a glass toward Balthus, who took it hesitatingly, and with an uncertain glance toward Valannus.

The governor turned toward Conan and stared at him thoughtfully.

"The soldiers, who do not believe in ghosts or devils," he said, "are almost in a panic of fear. You, who believe in ghosts, ghouls, goblins, and all manner of uncanny things, do not seem to fear any of the things in which you believe."

"There's nothing in the universe cold steel won't cut," answered Conan. "I threw my ax at the demon, and he took no hurt, but I might have missed in the dusk, or a branch deflected its flight. I'm not going out of my way looking for devils; but I wouldn't step out of my path to let one go by."

Valannus lifted his head and met Conan's gaze squarely.

"Conan, more depends on you than you realize. You know the weakness of this province—a slender wedge thrust into the untamed wilderness. You know that the lives of all the people west of the marches depend on this fort. Were it to fall, red axes would be splintering the gates of Velitrium before a horseman could cross the marches. His Majesty, or his Majesty's advisers, have ignored my plea that more troops be sent to hold the frontier. They know nothing of border conditions, and are averse to expending any more money in this direction. The fate of the frontier depends upon the men who now hold it.

"You know that most of the army which conquered Conajohara has been withdrawn. You know the force left me is inadequate, especially since that devil Zogar Sag managed to poison our water supply, and forty men died in one day. Many of the others are sick, or have been bitten by serpents or mauled by wild beasts which seem to swarm in increasing numbers in the vicinity of the fort. The soldiers believe Zogar's boast that he could summon the forest beasts to slay his enemies.

"I have three hundred pikemen, four hundred Bossonian archers, and perhaps fifty men who, like yourself, are skilled in woodcraft. They are worth ten times their number of soldiers, but there are so few of them. Frankly, Conan, my situation is becoming precarious. The soldiers whisper of desertion; they are low-spirited, believing Zogar Sag has loosed devils on us. They fear the black plague with which he threatened us—the terrible black death of the swamplands. When I see a sick soldier I sweat with fear of seeing him turn black and shrivel and die before my eyes.

"Conan, if the plague is loosed upon us, the soldiers will desert in a body! The border will be left unguarded and nothing will check the sweep of the dark-skinned hordes to the very gates of Velitrium—maybe beyond! If we cannot hold the fort, how can they hold the town?

"Conan, Zogar Sag must die, if we are to hold Conajohara. You have penetrated the unknown deeper than any other man in the fort; you know where Gwawela stands, and something of the forest trails across the river. Will you take a band of men tonight and endeavor to kill or capture him? Oh, I know it's mad. There isn't more than one chance in a thousand that any of you will come back alive. But if we don't get him, it's death for us all. You can take as many men as you wish."

"A dozen men are better for a job like that than a regiment," answered Conan. "Five hundred men couldn't fight their way to Gwawela and back, but a dozen might slip in and out again. Let me pick my men. I don't want any soldiers."

"Let me go!" eagerly exclaimed Balthus. "I've hunted deer all my life on the Tauran."

"All right. Valannus, we'll eat at the stall where the foresters gather, and I'll pick my men. We'll start within an hour, drop down the river in a boat to a point below the village and then steal upon it through the woods. If we live, we should be back by daybreak."

3

The Crawlers in the Dark

The river was a vague trace between walls of ebony. The paddles that propelled the long boat creeping along in the dense shadow of the eastern bank dipped softly into the water, making no more noise than the beak of a heron. The broad shoulders of the man in front of Balthus were a blue in the dense gloom. He knew that not even the keen eyes of the man who knelt in the prow would discern anything more than a few feet ahead of them. Conan was feeling his way by instinct and an intensive familiarity with the river.

No one spoke. Balthus had had a good look at his companions in the fort before they slipped out of the stockade and down the bank into the waiting canoe. They were of a new breed growing up in the world on the raw edge of the frontier—men whom grim necessity had taught woodcraft. Aquilonians of the western provinces to a man, they had many points in common. They dressed alike—in buckskin boots, leathern breeks and deerskin shirts, with broad girdles that held axes and short swords; and they were all gaunt and scarred and hard-eyed; sinewy and taciturn.

They were wild men, of a sort, yet there was still a wide gulf between them and the Cimmerian. They were sons of civilization, reverted to a semibarbarism. He was a barbarian of a thousand generations of barbarians. They had acquired stealth and craft, but he had been born to these things. He excelled them even in lithe economy of motion. They were wolves, but he was a tiger.

Balthus admired them and their leader and felt a pulse of pride that he was admitted into their company. He was proud that his paddle made no more noise than did theirs. In that respect at least he was their equal, though woodcraft learned in hunts on the Tauran could never equal that ground into the souls of men on the savage border.

Below the fort the river made a wide bend. The lights of the outpost were quickly lost, but the canoe held on its way for nearly a mile, avoiding snags and floating logs with almost uncanny precision.

Then a low grunt from their leader, and they swung its head about and glided toward the opposite shore. Emerging from the black shadows of the brush that fringed the bank and coming into the open of the midstream created a peculiar illusion of rash exposure. But the stars gave little light, and Balthus knew that unless one were watching for it, it would be all but impossible for the keenest eye to make out the shadowy shape of the canoe crossing the river.

They swung in under the overhanging bushes of the western shore and Balthus groped for and found a projecting root which he grasped. No word was spoken. All instructions had been given before the scouting-party left the fort. As silently as a great panther, Conan slid over the side and vanished in the bushes. Equally noiseless, nine men followed him. To Balthus, grasping

the root with his paddle across his knee, it seemed incredible that
ten men should thus fade into the tangled forest without a sound.

He settled himself to wait. No word passed between him and
the other man who had been left with him. Somewhere, a mile or
so to the northwest, Zogar Sag's village stood girdled with thick
woods. Balthus understood his orders; he and his companion
were to wait for the return of the raiding-party. If Conan and his
men had not returned by the first tinge of dawn, they were to
race back up the river to the fort and report that the forest had
again taken its immemorial toll of the invading race. The silence
was oppressive. No sound came from the black woods, invisible
beyond the ebony masses that were the overhanging bushes.
Balthus no longer heard the drums. They had been silent for
hours. He kept blinking, unconsciously trying to see through the
deep gloom. The dank night-smells of the river and the damp
forest oppressed him. Somewhere, near by, there was a sound as
if a big fish had flopped and splashed the water. Balthus thought
it must have leaped so close to the canoe that it had struck the
side, for a slight quiver vibrated the craft. The boat's stern began
to swing, slightly away from the shore. The man behind him
must have let go of the projection he was gripping. Balthus
twisted his head to hiss a warning, and could just make out the
figure of his companion, a slightly blacker bulk in the blackness.

The man did not reply. Wondering if he had fallen asleep,
Balthus reached out and grasped his shoulder. To his amaze-
ment, the man crumpled under his touch and slumped down in
the canoe. Twisting his body half about, Balthus groped for him,
his heart shooting into his throat. His fumbling fingers slid over
the man's throat—only the youth's convulsive clenching of his
jaws choked back the cry that rose to his lips. His finger encountered a gaping, oozing wound—his companion's throat had been
cut from ear to ear.

In that instant of horror and panic Balthus started up—and
then a muscular arm out of the darkness locked fiercely about his
throat, strangling his yell. The canoe rocked wildly. Balthus'
knife was in his hand, though he did not remember jerking it out
of his boot, and he stabbed fiercely and blindly. He felt the blade
sink deep, and a fiendish yell rang in his ear, a yell that was
horribly answered. The darkness seemed to come to life about
him. A bestial clamor rose on all sides, and other arms grappled
him. Borne under a mass of hurtling bodies the canoe rolled
sidewise, but before he went under with it, something cracked
against Balthus' head and the night was briefly illuminated by a

blinding burst of fire before it gave way to a blackness where not even stars shone.

4

The Beasts of Zogar Sag

Fires dazzled Balthus again as he slowly recovered his senses. He blinked, shook his head. Their glare hurt his eyes. A confused medley of sound rose about him, growing more distinct as his senses cleared. He lifted his head and stared stupidly about him. Black figures hemmed him in, etched against crimson tongues of flame.

Memory and understanding came in a rush. He was bound upright to a post in an open space, ringed by fierce and terrible figures. Beyond that ring fires burned, tended by naked, dark-skinned women. Beyond the fires he saw huts of mud and wattle, thatched with brush. Beyond the huts there was a stockade with a broad gate. But he saw these things only incidentally. Even the cryptic dark women with their curious coiffures were noted by him only absently. His full attention was fixed in awful fascination on the men who stood glaring at him.

Short men, broad-shouldered, deep-chested, lean-hipped, they were naked except for scanty loin-clouts. The firelight brought out the play of their swelling muscles in bold relief. Their dark faces were immobile, but their narrow eyes glittered with the fire that burns in the eyes of a stalking tiger. Their tangled manes were bound back with bands of copper. Swords and axes were in their hands. Crude bandages banded the limbs of some, and smears of blood were dried on their dark skins. There had been fighting, recent and deadly.

His eyes wavered away from the steady glare of his captors, and he repressed a cry of horror. A few feet away there rose a low, hideous pyramid: it was built of gory human heads. Dead eyes glared glassily up the black sky. Numbly he recognized the countenances which were turned toward him. They were the heads of the men who had followed Conan into the forest. He could not tell if the Cimmerian's head were among them. Only a few faces were visible to him. It looked to him as if there must be ten or eleven heads at least. A deadly sickness assailed him. He fought a desire to retch. Beyond the heads lay the bodies of half a dozen Picts, and he was aware of a fierce exultation at the sight. The forest runners had taken toll, at least.

Twisting his head away from the ghastly spectacle, he became aware that another post stood near him—a stake painted black as was the one to which he was bound. A man sagged in his bonds there, naked except for his leathern breeks, whom Balthus recognized as one of Conan's woodsmen. Blood trickled from his mouth, oozed sluggishly from a gash in his side. Lifting his head as he licked his livid lips, he muttered, making himself heard with difficulty above the fiendish clamor of the Picts: "So they got you, too!"

"Sneaked up in the water and cut the other fellow's throat," groaned Balthus. "We never heard them till they were on us. Mitra, how can anything move so silently?"

"They're devils," mumbled the frontiersman. "They must have been watching us from the time we left midstream. We walked into a trap. Arrows from all sides were ripping into us before we knew it. Most of us dropped at the first fire. Three or four broke through the bushes and came to hand-grips. But there were too many. Conan might have gotten away. I haven't seen his head. Been better for you and me if they'd killed us outright. I can't blame Conan. Ordinarily we'd have gotten to the village without being discovered. They don't keep spies on the river-bank as far down as we landed. We must have stumbled into a big party coming up the river from the south. Some devilment is up. Too many Picts here. These aren't all Gwaweli; men from the western tribes here and from up and down the river."

Balthus stared at the ferocious shapes. Little as he knew of Pictish ways, he was aware that the number of men clustered about them was out of proportion to the size of the village. There were not enough huts to have accommodated them all. Then he noticed that there was a difference in the barbaric tribal designs painted on their faces and breasts.

"Some kind of devilment," muttered the forest runner. "They might have gathered here to watch Zogar's magic-making. He'll make some rare magic with our carcasses. Well, a border-man doesn't expect to die in bed. But I wish we'd gone out along with the rest."

The wolfish howling of the Picts rose in volume and exultation, and from a movement in their ranks, an eager surging and crowding, Balthus deduced that someone of importance was coming. Twisting his head about, he saw that the stakes were set before a long building, larger than the other huts, decorated by human skulls dangling from the eaves. Through the door of that structure now danced a fantastic figure.

"Zogar!" muttered the woodsman, his bloody countenance set in wolfish lines as he unconsciously strained at his cords. Balthus saw a lean figure of middle height, almost hidden in ostrich plumes set on a harness of leather and copper. From amidst the plumes peered a hideous and malevolent face. The plumes puzzled Balthus. He knew their source lay half the width of a world to the south. They fluttered and rustled evilly as the shaman leaped and cavorted.

With fantastic bounds and prancings he entered the ring and whirled before his bound and silent captives. With another man it would have seemed ridiculous—a foolish savage prancing meaninglessly in a whirl of feathers. But that ferocious face glaring out from the billowing mass gave the scene a grim significance. No man with a face like that could seem ridiculous or like anything except the devil he was.

Suddenly he froze to statuesque stillness; the plumes rippled once and sank about him. The howling warriors fell silent. Zogar Sag stood erect and motionless, and he seemed to increase in height—to grow and expand. Balthus experienced the illusion that the Pict was towering above him, staring contemptuously down from a great height, though he knew the shaman was as tall as himself. He shook off the illlusion with difficulty.

The shaman was talking now, a harsh, guttural intonation that yet carried the hiss of a cobra. He thrust his head on his long neck toward the wounded man on the stake; his eyes shone red as blood in the firelight. The frontiersman spat full in his face.

With a fiendish howl Zogar bounded convulsively into the air, and the warriors gave tongue to a yell that shuddered up to the stars. They rushed toward the man on the stake, but the shaman beat them back. A snarled command sent men running to the gate. They hurled it open, turned and raced back to the circle. The ring of men split, divided with desperate haste to right and left. Balthus saw the women and naked children scurrying to the huts. They peeked out of doors and windows. A broad lane was left to the open gate, beyond which loomed the black forest, crowding sullenly in upon the clearing, unlighted by the fires.

A tense silence reigned as Zogar Sag turned toward the forest, raised on his tiptoes and sent a weird inhuman call shuddering out into the night. Somewhere, far out in the black forest, a deeper cry answered him. Balthus shuddered. From the timbre of that cry he knew it never came from a human throat. He remembered what Valannus had said—that Zogar boasted that he could summon wild beasts to do his bidding. The woodsman was livid beneath his mask of blood. He licked his lips spasmodically.

The village held its breath. Zogar Sag stood still as a statue, his plumes trembling faintly about him. But suddenly the gate was no longer empty.

A shuddering gasp swept over the village and men crowded hastily back, jamming one another between the huts. Balthus felt the short hair stir on his scalp. The creature that stood in the gate was like the embodiment of nightmare legend. Its color was of a curious pale quality which made it seem ghostly and unreal in the dim light. But there was nothing unreal about the low-hung savage head, and the great curved fangs that glistened in the firelight. On noiseless padded feet it approached like a phantom out of the past. It was a survival of an older, grimmer age, the ogre of many an ancient legend—a saber-tooth tiger. No Hyborian hunter had looked upon one of those primordial brutes for centuries. Immemorial myths lent the creatures a supernatural quality, induced by their ghostly color and their fiendish ferocity.

The beast that glided toward the men on the stakes was longer and heavier than a common, striped tiger, almost as bulky as a bear. Its shoulders and forelegs were so massive and mightily muscled as to give it a curiously top-heavy look, though its hindquarters were more powerful than that of a lion. Its jaws were massive, but its head was brutishly shaped. Its brain capacity was small. It had room for no instincts except those of destruction. It was a freak of carnivorous development, evolution run amuck in a horror of fangs and talons.

This was the monstrosity Zogar Sag had summoned out of the forest. Balthus no longer doubted the actuality of the shaman's magic. Only the black arts could establish a domination over that tiny-brained, mighty-thewed monster. Like a whisper at the back of his consciousness rose the vague memory of the name of an ancient god of darkness and primordial fear, to whom once both men and beasts bowed and whose children—men whispered— still lurked in dark corners of the world. New horror tinged the glare he fixed on Zogar Sag.

The monster moved past the heap of bodies and the pile of gory heads without appearing to notice them. He was no scavenger. He hunted only the living, in a life dedicated solely to slaughter. An awful hunger burned greenly in the wide, unwinking eyes; the hunger not alone of belly-emptiness, but the lust of death-dealing. His gaping jaws slavered. The shaman stepped back; his hand waved toward the woodsman.

The great cat sank into a crouch, and Balthus numbly remembered tales of its appalling ferocity: of how it would spring upon an elephant and drive its swordlike fangs so deeply into the titan's skull that they could never be withdrawn, but would keep it nailed to its victim, to die by starvation. The shaman cried out shrilly, and with an ear-shattering roar the monster sprang.

Balthus had never dreamed of such a spring, such a hurtling of incarnated destruction embodied in that giant bulk of iron thews and ripping talons. Full on the woodsman's breast it struck, and the stake splintered and snapped at the base, crashing to the earth under the impact. Then the saber-tooth was gliding toward the gate, half dragging, half carrying a hideous crimson hulk that only faintly resembled a man. Balthus glared almost paralyzed, his brain refusing to credit what his eyes had seen.

In that leap the great beast had not only broken off the stake, it had ripped the mangled body of its victim from the post to which it was bound. The huge talons in that instant of contact had disemboweled and partially dismembered the man, and the giant fangs had torn away the whole top of his head, shearing through the skull as easily as through flesh. Stout rawhide thongs had given way like paper; where the thongs had held, flesh and bones had not. Balthus retched suddenly. He had hunted bears and panthers, but he had never dreamed the beast lived which could make such a red ruin of a human frame in the flicker of an instant.

The saber-tooth vanished through the gate, and a few moments later a deep roar sounded through the forest, receding in the distance. But the Picts still shrank back against the huts, and the shaman still stood facing the gate that was like a black opening to let in the night.

Cold sweat burst suddenly out on Balthus' skin. What new horror would come through that gate to make carrion-meat of *his* body? Sick panic assailed him and he strained futilely at his thongs. The night pressed in very black and horrible outside the firelight. The fires themselves glowed lurid as the fires of Hell. He felt the eyes of the Picts upon him—hundreds of hungry, cruel eyes that reflected the lust of souls utterly without humanity as he knew it. They no longer seemed men; they were devils of this black jungle, as inhuman as the creatures to which the fiend in the nodding plumes screamed through the darkness.

Zogar sent another call shuddering through the night, and it was utterly unlike the first cry. There was a hideous sibilance in it—Balthus turned cold at the implication. If a serpent could hiss that loud, it would make just such a sound.

This time there was no answer—only a period of breathless silence in which the pound of Balthus' heart strangled him; and then there sounded a swishing outside the gate, a dry rustling that sent chills down Balthus' spine. Again the firelit gate held a hideous occupant.

Again Balthus recognized the monster from ancient legends. He saw and knew the ancient and evil serpent which swayed there, its wedge-shaped head, huge as that of a horse, as high as a tall man's head, and its palely gleaming barrel rippling out behind it. A forked tongue darted in and out, and the firelight glittered on bared fangs.

Balthus became incapable of emotion. The horror of his fate paralyzed him. That was the reptile that the ancients called Ghost Snake, the pale, abominable terror that of old glided into huts by night to devour whole families. Like the python it crushed its victim, but unlike other constrictors its fangs bore venom that carried madness and death. It too had long been considered extinct. But Valannus had spoken truly. No white man knew what shapes haunted the great forests beyond Black River.

It came on silently, rippling over the ground, its hideous head on the same level, its neck curving back slightly for the stroke. Balthus gazed with glazed, hypnotized stare into that loathsome gullet down which he would soon be engulfed, and he was aware of no sensation except a vague nausea.

And then something that glinted in the firelight streaked from the shadows of the huts, and the great reptile whipped about and went into instant convulsions. As in a dream Balthus saw a short throwing-spear transfixing the mighty neck, just below the gaping jaws; the shaft protruded from one side, the steel head from the other.

Knotting and looping hideously, the maddened reptile rolled into the circle of men who stove back from him. The spear had not severed its spine, but merely transfixed its great neck muscles. Its furiously lashing tail mowed down a dozen men and its jaws snapped convulsively, splashing others with venom that burned like liquid fire. Howling, cursing, screaming, frantic, they scattered before it, knocking each other down in their flight, trampling the fallen, bursting through the huts. The giant snake rolled into a fire, scattering sparks and brands, and the pain lashed it to more frenzied efforts. A hut wall buckled under the ramlike impact of its flailing tail, disgorging howling people.

Men stampeded through the fires, knocking the logs right and left. The flames sprang up, then sank. A reddish dim glow was all that lighted that nightmare scene where the giant reptile whipped and rolled, and men clawed and shrieked in frantic flight.

Balthus felt something jerk at his wrists, and then, miraculously, he was free, and a strong hand dragged him behind the post. Dazedly he saw Conan, felt the forest man's iron grip on his arm.

There was blood on the Cimmerian's mail, dried blood on the sword in his right hand; he loomed dim and gigantic in the shadowy light.

"Come on! Before they get over their panic!"

Balthus felt the haft of an ax shoved into his hand. Zogar Sag had disappeared. Conan dragged Balthus after him until the youth's numb brain awoke, and his legs began to move of their own accord. Then Conan released him and ran into the building where the skulls hung. Balthus followed him. He got a glimpse of a grim stone altar, faintly lighted by the glow outside; five human heads grinned on that altar, and there was a grisly familiarity about the features of the freshest; it was the head of the merchant Tiberias. Behind the altar was an idol, dim, indistinct, bestial, yet vaguely manlike in outline. Then fresh horror choked Balthus as the shape heaved up suddenly with a rattle of chains, lifting long misshapen arms in the gloom.

Conan's sword flailed down, crunching through flesh and bone, and then the Cimmerian was dragging Balthus around the altar, past a huddled shaggy bulk on the floor, to a door at the back of the long hut. Through this they burst, out into the enclosure again. But a few yards beyond them loomed the stockade.

It was dark behind the altar-hut. The mad stampede of the Picts had not carried them in that direction. At the wall Conan halted, gripped Balthus, and heaved him at arm's length into the air as he might have lifted a child. Balthus grasped the points of the upright logs set in the sun-dried mud and scrambled up on them, ignoring the havoc done his skin. He lowered a hand to the Cimmerian, when around a corner of the altar-hut sprang a fleeing Pict. He halted short, glimpsing the man on the wall in the faint glow of the fires. Conan hurled his ax with deadly aim, but the warrior's mouth was already open for a yell of warning, and it rang loud above the din, cut short as he dropped with a shattered skull.

Blinding terror had not submerged all ingrained instincts. As that wild yell rose above the clamor, there was an instant's lull, and then a hundred throats bayed ferocious answer and warriors came leaping to repel the attack presaged by the warning.

Conan leaped high, caught not Balthus' hand but his arm near the shoulder, and swung himself up. Balthus set his teeth against the strain, and then the Cimmerian was on the wall beside him, and the fugitives dropped down on the other side.

5

The Children of Jhebbal Sag

"Which way is the river?" Balthus was confused.

"We don't dare try for the river now," grunted Conan. "The woods between the village and the river are swarming with warriors. Come on! We'll head in the last direction they'll expect us to go—west!"

Looking back as they entered the thick growth, Balthus beheld the wall dotted with black heads as the savages peered over. The Picts were bewildered. They had not gained the wall in time to see the fugitives take cover. They had rushed to the wall expecting to repel an attack in force. They had seen the body of the dead warrior. But no enemy was in sight.

Balthus realized that they did not yet know their prisoner had escaped. From other sounds he believed that the warriors, directed by the shrill voice of Zogar Sag, were destroying the wounded serpent with arrows. The monster was out of the shaman's control. A moment later the quality of the yells was altered. Screeches of rage rose in the night.

Conan laughed grimly. He was leading Balthus along a narrow trail that ran west under the black branches, stepping as swiftly and surely as if he trod a well-lighted thoroughfare. Balthus stumbled after him, guiding himself by feeling the dense wall on either hand.

"They'll be after us now. Zogar's discovered you're gone, and he knows my head wasn't in the pile before the altar-hut. The dog! If I'd had another spear I'd have thrown it through him before I struck the snake. Keep to the trail. They can't track us by torchlight, and there are a score of paths leading from the village. They'll follow those leading to the river first—throw a cordon of warriors for miles along the bank, expecting us to try to break through. We won't take to the woods until we have to. We can make better time on his trail. Now buckle down to it and run as you never ran before."

"They got over their panic cursed quick!" panted Balthus, complying with a fresh burst of speed.

"They're not afraid of anything, very long," grunted Conan.

For a space nothing was said between them. The fugitives devoted all their attention to covering distance. They were plunging deeper and deeper into the wilderness and getting farther away from civilization at every step, but Balthus did not question Conan's wisdom. The Cimmerian presently took time to grunt: "When we're far enough away from the village we'll swing back to the river in a big circle. No other village within miles of Gwawela. All the Picts are gathered in that vicinity. We'll circle wide around them. They can't track us until daylight. They'll pick up our path then, but before dawn we'll leave the trail and take to the woods."

They plunged on. The yells died out behind them. Balthus' breath was whistling through his teeth. He felt a pain in his side, and running became torture. He blundered against the bushes on each side of the trail. Conan pulled up suddenly, turned and stared back down the dim path.

Somewhere the moon was rising, a dim white glow amidst a tangle of branches.

"Shall we take to the woods?" panted Balthus.

"Give me your ax," murmured Conan softly. "Something is close behind us."

"Then we'd better leave the trail!" exclaimed Balthus.

Conan shook his head and drew his companion into a dense thicket. The moon rose higher, making a dim light in the path.

"We can't fight the whole tribe!" whispered Balthus.

"No human being could have found our trail so quickly, or followed us so swiftly," muttered Conan. "Keep silent."

There followed a tense silence in which Balthus felt that his heart could be heard pounding for miles away. Then abruptly, without a sound to announce its coming, a savage head appeared in the dim path. Balthus' heart jumped into his throat; at first glance he feared to look upon the awful head of the saber-tooth. But this head was smaller, more narrow; it was a leopard which stood there, snarling silently and glaring down the trail. What wind there was was blowing toward the hiding men, concealing their scent. The beast lowered his head and snuffed the trail, then moved forward uncertainly. A chill played down Balthus' spine. The brute was undoubtedly trailing them.

And it was suspicious. It lifted its head, its eyes glowing like balls of fire, and growled low in its throat. And at that instant Conan hurled the ax.

All the weight of arm and shoulder was behind the throw, and the ax was a streak of silver in the dim moon. Almost before he realized what had happened, Balthus saw the leopard rolling on the ground in its death-throes, the handle of the ax standing up from its head. The head of the weapon had split its narrow skull.

Conan bounded from the bushes, wrenched his ax free and dragged the limp body in among the trees, concealing it from the casual glance.

"Now let's go, and go fast!" he grunted, leading the way southward, away from the trail. "There'll be warriors coming after that cat. As soon as he got his wits back Zogar sent him after us. The Picts would follow him, but he'd leave them far behind. He'd circle the village until he hit our trail and then come after us like a streak. They couldn't keep up with him, but they'll have an idea as to our general direction. They'd follow, listening for his cry. Well, they won't hear that, but they'll find the blood on the trail, and look around and find the body in the brush. They'll pick up our spoor there, if they can. Walk with care."

He avoided clinging briars and low-hanging branches effortlessly, gliding between trees without touching the stems and always planting his feet in the places calculated to show least evidence of his passing; but with Balthus it was slower, more laborious work.

No sound came from behind them. They had covered more than a mile when Balthus said: "Does Zogar Sag catch leopard-cubs and train them for bloodhounds?"

Conan shook his head. "That was a leopard he called out of the woods."

"But," Balthus persisted, "if he can order the beasts to do his bidding, why doesn't he rouse them all and have them after us? The forest is full of leopards; why send only one after us?"

Conan did not reply for a space, and when he did it was with a curious reticence.

"He can't command all the animals. Only such as remember Jhebbal Sag."

"Jhebbal Sag?" Balthus repeated the ancient name hesitantly. He had never heard it spoken more than three or four times in his whole life.

"Once all living things worshipped him. That was long ago, when beasts and men spoke one language. Men have forgotten him; even the beasts forget. Only a few remember. The men who remember Jhebbal Sag and the beasts who remember are brothers and speak the same tongue."

Balthus did not reply; he had strained at a Pictish stake and seen the nighted jungle give up its fanged horrors at a shaman's call.

"Civilized men laugh," said Conan. "But no one can tell me how Zogar Sag can call pythons and tigers and leopards out of the wilderness and make them do his bidding. They would say it is a lie, if they dared. That's the way with civilized men. When they can't explain something by their half-baked science, they refuse to believe it."

The people on the Tauran were closer to the primitive than most Aquilonians; superstitions persisted, whose sources were lost in antiquity. And Balthus had seen that which still prickled his flesh. He could not refute the monstrous thing which Conan's words implied.

"I've heard that there's an ancient grove sacred to Jhebbal Sag somewhere in this forest," said Conan. "I don't know. I've never seen it. But more beasts *remember* in this country than any I've ever seen."

"Then others will be on our trail?"

"They are now," was Conan's disquieting answer. "Zogar would never leave our tracking to one beast alone."

"What are we to do, then?" asked Balthus uneasily, grasping his ax as he stared at the gloomy arches above him. His flesh crawled with the momentary expectation of ripping talons and fangs leaping from the shadows.

"Wait!"

Conan turned, squatted and with his knife began scratching a curious symbol in the mold. Stooping to look at it over his shoulder, Balthus felt a crawling of the flesh along his spine, he knew not why. He felt no wind against his face, but there was a rustling of leaves above them and a weird moaning swept ghostily through the branches. Conan glanced up inscrutably, then rose and stood staring somberly down at the symbol he had drawn.

"What is it?" whispered Balthus. It looked archaic and meaningless to him. He supposed that it was his ignorance of artistry which prevented his identifying it as one of the conventional designs of some prevailing culture. But had he been the most erudite artist in the world, he would have been no nearer the solution.

"I saw it carved in the rock of a cave no human had visited for a million years," muttered Conan, "in the uninhabited mountains beyond the Sea of Vilayet, half a world away from this spot. Later I saw a black witch-finder of Kush scratch it in the sand of a nameless river. He told me part of its meaning—it's sacred to Jhebbal Sag and the creatures which worship him. Watch!"

They drew back among the dense foliage some yards away and waited in tense silence. To the east drums muttered and somewhere to north and west other drums answered. Balthus shivered, though he knew long miles of black forest separated him from the grim beaters of those drums whose dull pulsing was a sinister overture that set the dark stage for bloody drama.

Balthus found himself holding his breath. Then with a slight shaking of the leaves, the bushes parted and a magnificent panther came into view. The moonlight dappling through the leaves shone on its glossy coat rippling with the play of the great muscles beneath it.

With its head low it glided toward them. It was smelling out their trail. Then it halted as if frozen, its muzzle almost touching the symbol cut in the mold. For a long space it crouched motionless; it flattened its long body and laid its head on the ground before the mark. And Balthus felt the short hairs stir on his scalp. For the attitude of the great carnivore was one of awe and adoration.

Then the panther rose and backed away carefully, belly almost to the ground. With his hindquarters among the bushes he wheeled as if in sudden panic and was gone like a flash of dappled light.

Balthus mopped his brow with a trembling hand and glanced at Conan.

The barbarian's eyes were smoldering with fires that never lit the eyes of men bred to the ideas of civilization. In that instant he was all wild, and had forgotten the man at his side. In his burning gaze Balthus glimpsed and vaguely recognized pristine images and half-embodied memories, shadows from Life's dawn, forgotten and repudiated by sophisticated races—ancient, primeval fantasms unnamed and nameless.

Then the deeper fires were masked and Conan was silently leading the way deeper into the forest.

"We've no more to fear from the beasts," he said after a while, "but we've left a sign for men to read. They won't follow our trail very easily, and until they find that symbol they won't know for sure we've turned south. Even then it won't be easy to smell us out without the beasts to aid them. But the woods south of the trail will be full of warriors looking for us. If we keep moving after daylight, we'll be sure to run into some of them. As soon as we find a good place we'll hide and wait until another night to swing back and make the river. We've got to warn Valannus, but it won't help him any if we get ourselves killed."

"Warn Valannus?"

"Hell, the woods along the river are swarming with Picts! That's why they got us. Zogar's brewing war-magic; no mere raid this time. He's done something no Pict has done in my memory—united as many as fifteen or sixteen clans. His magic did it; they'll follow a wizard farther than they will a war-chief. You saw the mob in the village; and there were hundreds hiding along the riverbank that you didn't see. More coming, from the farther villages. He'll have at least three thousand fighting-men. I lay in the bushes and heard their talk as they went past. They mean to attack the fort; when, I don't know, but Zogar doesn't dare delay long. He's gathered them and whipped them into a frenzy. If he doesn't lead them into battle quickly, they'll fall to quarreling with one another. They're like blood-mad tigers.

"I don't know whether they can take the fort or not. Anyway, we've got to get back across the river and give the warning. The settlers on the Velitrium road must either get into the fort or back to Velitrium. While the Picts are besieging the fort, war parties will range the road far to the east—might even cross Thunder River and raid the thickly settled country behind Velitrium."

As he talked he was leading the way deeper and deeper into the ancient wilderness. Presently he grunted with satisfaction. They had reached a spot where the underbrush was more scattered, and an outcropping of stone was visible, wandering off southward. Balthus felt more secure as they followed it. Not even a Pict could trail them over naked rock.

"How did you get away?" he asked presently.

Conan tapped his mail-shirt and helmet.

"If more borderers would wear harness there'd be fewer skulls hanging on the altar-huts. But most men make noise if they wear armor. They were waiting on each side of the path, without moving. And when a Pict stands motionless, the very beasts of the forest pass him without seeing him. They'd seen us crossing the river and got in their places. If they'd gone into ambush after we left the bank, I'd have had some hint of it. But they were waiting, and not even a leaf trembled. The devil himself couldn't have suspected anything. The first suspicion I had was when I heard a shaft rasp against a bow as it was pulled back. I dropped and yelled for the men behind me to drop, but they were too slow, taken by surprise like that.

"Most of them fell at the first volley that raked us from both sides. Some of the arrows crossed the trail and struck Picts on the other side. I heard them howl." He grinned with vicious satisfaction. "Such of us as were left plunged into the woods and closed with them. When I saw the others were all down or taken, I broke through and outfooted the painted devils through the darkness. They were all around me. I ran and crawled and sneaked, and sometimes I lay on my belly under the bushes while they passed me on all sides.

"I tried for the shore and found it lined with them, waiting for just such a move. But I'd have cut my way through and taken a chance on swimming, only I heard the drums pounding in the village and knew they'd taken somebody alive.

"They were all so engrossed in Zogar's magic that I was able to climb the wall behind the altar-hut. There was a warrior supposed to be watching at that point, but he was squatting behind the hut and peering around the corner at the ceremony. I came up behind him and broke his neck with my hands before he knew what was happening. It was his spear I threw into the snake, and that's his ax you're carrying.''

"But what was that—that thing you killed in the altar-hut?" asked Balthus, with a shiver at the memory of the dim-seen horror.

"One of Zogar's gods. One of Jhebbal's children that didn't remember and had to be kept chained to the altar. A bull ape. The Picts think they're sacred to the Hairy One who lives on the moon—the gorilla-god of Gullah.

"It's getting light. Here's a good place to hide until we see how close they're on our trail. Probably have to wait until night to break back to the river.''

A low hill pitched upward, girdled and covered with thick trees and bushes. Near the crest Conan slid into a tangle of jutting rocks, crowned by dense bushes. Lying among them they could see the jungle below without being seen. It was a good place to hide or defend. Balthus did not believe that even a Pict could have trailed them over the rocky ground for the past four or five miles, but he was afraid of the beasts that obeyed Zogar Sag. His faith in the curious symbol wavered a little now. But Conan had dismissed the possibility of beasts tracking them.

A ghostly whiteness spread through the dense branches; the patches of sky visible altered in hue, grew from pink to blue. Balthus felt the gnawing of hunger, though he had slaked his thirst at a stream they had skirted. There was complete silence, except for an occasional chirp of a bird. The drums were no longer to be heard. Balthus' thoughts reverted to the grim scene before the altar-hut.

"Those were ostrich plumes Zogar Sag wore," he said. "I've seen them on the helmets of knights who rode from the East to visit the barons on the marches. There are no ostriches in this forest, are there?"

"They came from Kush," answered Conan. "West of here,

many marches, lies the seashore. Ships from Zingara occasionally come and trade weapons and ornaments and wine to the coastal tribes for skins and copper ore and gold dust. Sometimes they trade ostrich plumes they got from the Stygians, who in turn got them from the black tribes of Kush, which lies south of Stygia. The Pictish shamans place great store by them. But there's much risk in such trade. The Picts are too likely to try to seize the ship. And the coast is dangerous to ships. I've sailed along it when I was with the pirates of the Barachan Isles, which lie southwest of Zingara.''

Balthus looked at his companion with admiration.

''I knew you hadn't spent your life on this frontier. You've mentioned several far places. You've traveled widely?''

''I've roamed far; farther than any other man of my race ever wandered. I've seen all the great cities of the Hyborians, the Shemites, the Stygians, and the Hyrkanians. I've roamed in the unknown countries south of the black kingdoms of Kush, and east of the Sea of Vilayet. I've been a mercenary captain, a corsair, a *kozak*, a penniless vagabond, a general—hell, I've been everything except a king of a civilized country, and I may be that, before I die.'' The fancy pleased him, and he grinned hardly. Then he shrugged his shoulders and stretched his mighty figure on the rocks. ''This is as good a life as any. I don't know how long I'll stay on the frontier; a week, a month, a year. I have a roving foot. But it's as well on the border as anywhere.''

Balthus set himself to watch the forest below them. Momentarily he expected to see fierce painted faces thrust through the leaves. But as the hours passed no stealthy footfall disturbed the brooding quiet. Balthus believed the Picts had missed their trail and given up the chase. Conan grew restless.

''We should have sighted parties scouring the woods for us. If they've quit the chase, it's becasue they're after bigger game. They may be gathering to cross the river and storm the fort.''

''Would they come this far south if they lost the trail?''

''They've lost the trail, all right; otherwise they'd have been on our necks before now. Under ordinary circumstances they'd scour the woods for miles in every direction. Some of them should have passed without sight of this hill. They must be preparing to cross the river. We've got to take a chance and make for the river.''

Creeping down the rocks Balthus felt his flesh crawl between his shoulders as he momentarily expected a withering blast of arrows from the green masses above them. He feared that the Picts had discovered them and were lying about in ambush. But

Conan was convinced no enemies were near, and the Cimmerian was right.

"We're miles to the south of the village," grunted Conan. "We'll hit straight through for the river. I don't know how far down the river they've spread. We'll hope to hit it below them."

With haste that seemed reckless to Balthus they hurried eastward. The woods seemed empty to life. Conan believed that all the Picts were gathered in the vicinity of Gwawela, if, indeed, they had not already crossed the river. He did not believe they would cross in the daytime, however.

"Some woodsman would be sure to see them and give the alarm. They'll cross above and below the fort, out of sight of the sentries. Then others will get in canoes and make straight across for the river wall. As soon as they attack, those hidden in the woods on the east shore will assail the fort from the other sides. They've tried that before, and got the guts shot and hacked out of them. But this time they've got enough men to make a real onslaught of it."

They pushed on without pausing, though Balthus gazed longingly at the squirrels flitting among the branches, which he could have brought down with a cast of his ax. With a sigh he drew up his broad belt. The everlasting silence and gloom of the primitive forest was beginning to depress him. He found himself thinking of the open groves and sun-dappled meadows of the Tauran, of the bluff cheer of his father's steep-thatched, diamond-paned house, of the fat cows browsing through the deep, lush grass, and the hearty fellowship of the brawny, bare-armd plowmen and herdsmen.

He felt lonely, in spite of his companion. Conan was as much a part of this wilderness as Balthus was alien to it. The Cimmerian might have spent years among the great cities of the world; he might have walked with the rulers of civilization; he might even achieve his wild whim someday and rule as king of a civilized nation; stranger things had happened. But he was no less a barbarian. He was concerned only with the naked fundamentals of life. The warm intimacies of small, kindly things, the sentiments and delicious trivialities that make up so much of civilized men's lives were meaningless to him. A wolf was no less a wolf because a whim of chance caused him to run with the watchdogs. Bloodshed and violence and savagery were the natural elements of the life Conan knew; he could not, and would never, understand the little things that are so dear to civilized men and women.

The shadows were lengthening when they reached the river

and peered through the masking bushes. They could see up and down the river for about a mile each way. The sullen stream lay bare and empty. Conan scowled across at the other shore.

"We've got to take another chance here. We've got to swim the river. We don't know whether they've crossed or not. The woods over there may be alive with them. We've got to risk it. We're about six miles south of Gwawela."

He wheeled and ducked as a bowstring twanged. Something like a white flash of light streaked through the bushes. Balthus knew it was an arrow. Then with a tigerish bound Conan was through the bushes. Balthus caught the gleam of steel as he whirled his sword, and heard a death scream. The next instant he had broken through the bushes after the Cimmerian.

A Pict with a shattered skull lay face-down on the ground, his fingers spasmodically clawing at the grass. Half a dozen others were swarming about Conan, swords and axes lifted. They had cast away their bows, useless at such deadly close quarters. Their lower jaws were painted white, contrasting vividly with their dark faces, and the designs on their muscular breasts differed from any Balthus had ever seen.

One of them hurled his ax at Balthus and rushed after it with lifted knife. Balthus ducked and then caught the wrist that drove the knife licking at his throat. They went to the ground together, rolling over and over. The Pict was like a wild beast, his muscles hard as steel strings.

Balthus was striving to maintain his hold on the wild man's wrist and bring his own ax into play, but so fast and furious was the struggle that each attempt to strike was blocked. The Pict was wrenching furiously to free his knife hand, was clutching at Balthus' ax, and driving his knees at the youth's groin. Suddenly he attempted to shift his knife to his free hand, and in that instant Balthus, struggling up on one knee, split the painted head with a desperate blow of his ax.

He sprang up and glared wildly about for his companion, expecting to see him overwhelmed by numbers. Then he realized the full strength and ferocity of the Cimmerian. Conan bestrode two of his attackers, shorn half asunder by that terrible broadsword. As Balthus looked he saw the Cimmerian beat down a thrusting shortsword, avoid the stroke of an ax with a catlike sidewise spring which brought him within arm's length of a squat savage stooping for a bow. Before the Pict could straighten, the red sword flailed down and clove him from shoulder to midbreastbone, where the blade stuck. The remaining warriors rushed in, one from either side. Balthus hurled his ax with an accuracy that reduced the attackers to one, and Conan, abandoning his efforts to free his sword, wheeled and met the remaining Pict with his bare hands. The stocky warrior, a head shorter than his tall enemy, leaped in, striking with his ax, at the same time stabbing murderously with his knife. The knife broke on the Cimmerian's mail, and the ax checked in midair as Conan's fingers locked like iron on the descending arm. A bone snapped loudly, and Balthus saw the Pict wince and falter. The next instant he was swept off his feet, lifted high above the Cimmerian's head—he writhed in midair for an instant, kicking and thrashing, and then was dashed headlong to the earth with such force that he rebounded, and then lay still, his limp posture telling of splintered limbs and a broken spine.

"Come on!" Conan wrenched his sword free and snatched up an ax. "Grab a bow and a handful of arrows, and hurry! We've got to trust to our heels again. That yell was heard. They'll be here in no time. If we tried to swim now, they'd feather us with arrows before we reached midstream!"

6

Red Aces of the Border

Conan did not plunge deeply into the forest. A few hundred yards from the river, he altered his slanting course and ran parallel with it. Balthus recognized a grim determination not to be hunted away from the river which they must· cross if they were to warn the men in the fort. Behind them rose more loudly the yells of the forest men. Balthus believed the Picts had reached the glade where the bodies of the slain men lay. Then further yells seemed to indicate that the savages were streaming into the woods in pursuit. They had left a trail any Pict could follow.

Conan increased his speed, and Balthus grimly set his teeth and kept on his heels, though he felt he might collapse anytime. It seemed centuries since he had eaten last. He kept going more by an effort of will than anything else. His blood was pounding so furiously in his ear-drums that he was not aware when the yells died out behind them.

Conan halted suddenly. Balthus leaned against a tree and panted.

"They've quit!" grunted the Cimmerian, scowling.

"Sneaking—up—on—us!" gasped Balthus.

Conan shook his head.

"A short chase like this they'd yell every step of the way. No. They've gone back. I thought I heard somebody yelling behind them a few seconds before the noise began to get dimmer. They've been recalled. And that's good for us, but damned bad for the men in the fort. It means the warriors are being summoned out of the woods for the attack. Those men we ran into were warriors from a tribe down the river. They were undoubtedly headed for Gwawela to join in the assault on the fort. Damn it, we're father away than ever, now. We've got to get across the river."

Turning east he hurried through the thickets with no attempt at concealment. Balthus followed him, for the first time feeling the sting of lacerations on his breast and shoulder where the Pict's savage teeth had scored him. He was pushing through the thick bushes that fringed the bank when Conan pulled him back. Then he heard a rhythmic splashing, and peering through the leaves, saw a dugout canoe coming up the river, its single occupant paddling hard against the current. He was a strongly built Pict with a white heron feather thrust in a copper band that confined his square-cut mane.

"That's a Gwawela man," muttered Conan. "Emissary from Zogar. White plume shows that. He's carried a peace talk to the tribes down the river and now he's trying to get back and take a hand in the slaughter."

The lone ambassador was now almost even with their hiding place, and suddenly Balthus almost jumped out of his skin. At his very ear had sounded the harsh gutturals of a Pict. Then he realized that Conan had called to the paddler in his own tongue. The man started, scanned the bushes and called back something, then cast a startled glance across the river, bent low and sent the canoe shooting in toward the western bank. Not understanding, Balthus saw Conan take from his hand the bow he had picked up in the glade, and notch an arrow.

The Pict had run his canoe in close to the shore, and staring up into the bushes, called out something. His answer came in the twang of the bowstring, the streaking flight of the arrow that sank to the feathers in his broad breast. With a choking gasp he slumped sidewise and rolled into the shallow water. In an instant Conan was down the bank and wading into the water to grasp the drifting canoe. Balthus stumbled after him and somewhat dazedly crawled into the canoe. Conan scrambled in, seized the paddle and sent the craft shooting toward the eastern shore. Balthus noted with envious admiration the play of the great muscles beneath the sunburnt skin. The Cimmerian seemed an iron man, who never knew fatigue.

"What did you say to the Pict?" asked Balthus.

"Told him to pull into shore; said there was a white forest runner on the bank who was trying to get a shot at him."

"That doesn't seem fair," Balthus objected. "He thought a friend was speaking to him. You mimicked a Pict perfectly—"

"We needed his boat," grunted Conan, not pausing in his exertions. "Only way to lure him to the bank. Which is worse—to betray a Pict who'd enjoy skinning us both alive, or betray the men across the river whose lives depend on our getting over?"

Balthus mulled over this delicate ethical question for a moment, then shrugged his shoulders and asked: "How far are we from the fort?"

Conan pointed to a creek which flowed into Black River from the east, a few hundred yards below them.

"That's South Creek; it's ten miles from its mouth to the fort. It's the southern boundary of Conajohara. Marshes miles wide south of it. No danger of a raid from across them. Nine miles above the fort North Creek forms the other boundary. Marshes beyond that, too. That's why an attack must come from the west, across Black River. Conajohara's just like a spear, with a point nineteen miles wide, thrust into the Pictish wilderness."

"Why don't we keep to the canoe and make the trip by water?"

"Because, considering the current we've got to brace, and the bends in the river, we can go faster afoot. Besides, remember Gwawela is south of the fort; if the Picts are crossing the river we'd run right into them."

Dusk was gathering as they stepped upon the eastern bank. Without pause Conan pushed on northward, at a pace that made Balthus' sturdy legs ache.

"Valannus wanted a fort built at the mouths of North and South Creeks," grunted the Cimmerian. "Then the river could be patrolled constantly. But the Government wouldn't do it.

"Soft-bellied fools sitting on velvet cushions with naked girls offering them iced wine on their knees—I know the breed. They can't see any farther than their palace wall. Diplomacy—hell! They'd fight Picts with theories of territorial expansion. Valannus and men like him have to obey the orders of a set of damned fools. They'll never grab any more Pictish land, any more than they'll ever rebuild Venarium. The time may come when they'll see the barbarians swarming over the walls of the eastern cities!"

A week before, Balthus would have laughed at any such

preposterous suggestion. Now he made no reply. He had seen the unconquerable ferocity of the men who dwelt beyond the frontiers.

He shivered, casting glances at the sullen river, just vsible through the bushes, at the arches of the trees which crowded close to its banks. He kept remembering that the Picts might have crossd the river, and be lying in ambush between them and the fort. It was fast growing dark.

A slight sound ahead of them jumped his heart into his throat, and Conan's sword gleamed in the air. He lowered it when a dog, a great, gaunt, scarred beast, slunk out of the bushes and stood staring at them.

"That dog belonged to a settler who tried to build his cabin on the bank of the river a few miles south of the fort," grunted Conan. "The Picts slipped over and killed him, of course, and burned his cabin. We found him dead among the embers, and the dog lying senseless among three Picts he'd killed. He was almost cut to pieces. We took him to the fort and dressed his wounds, but after he recovered he took to the woods and turned wild. —What now, Slasher, are you hunting the men who killed your master?"

The massive head swung from side to side and the eyes glowed greenly. He did not growl or bark. Silently as a phantom he slid in behind them.

"Let him come," muttered Conan. "He can smell the devils before we can see them."

Balthus smiled and laid his hand caressingly on the dog's head. The lips involuntarily writhed back to display the gleaming fangs; then the great beast bent his head sheepishly, and his tail moved with jerky uncertainty, as if the owner had almost forgotten the emotions of friendliness. Balthus mentally compared the great gaunt hard body with the fat sleek hounds tumbling vociferously over one another in his father's kennel yard. He sighed. The frontier was no less hard for beasts than for men. This dog had almost forgotten the meaning of kindness and friendliness.

Slasher glided ahead, and Conan let him take the lead. The last tinge of dusk faded into stark darkness. The miles fell away under their steady feet. Slasher seemed voiceless. Suddenly he halted, tense, ears lifted. An instant later the men heard it—a demoniac yelling up the river ahead of them, faint as a whisper.

Conan swore like a madman.

"They've attacked the fort! We're too late! Come on!"

He increased his pace, trusting to the dog to smell out ambushes ahead. In a flood of tense excitement Balthus forgot his hunger and weariness. The yells grew louder as they advanced, and above the devilish screaming they could hear the deep shouts of the soldiers. Just as Balthus began to fear they would run into the savages who seemed to be howling just ahead of them, Conan swung away from the river in a wide semicircle that carried them to a low rise from which they could look over the forest. They saw the fort, lighted with torches thrust over the parapets on long poles. These cast a flickering, uncertain light over the clearing, and in that light they saw throngs of naked, painted figures along the fringe of the clearing. The river swarmed with canoes. The Picts had the fort completely surrounded.

An incessant hail of arrows rained against the stockade from the woods and the river. The deep twanging of the bowstrings rose above the howling. Yelling like wolves, several hundred naked warriors with axes in their hands ran from under the trees and raced toward the eastern gate. They were within a hundred and fifty yards of their objective when a withering blast of arrows from the wall littered the ground with corpses and sent the survivors fleeing back to the trees. The men in the canoes rushed their boats toward the river-wall, and were met by another shower of clothyard shafts and a volley from the small ballistae mounted on towers on that side of the stockade. Stones and logs whirled through the air and splintered and sank half a dozen canoes, killing their occupants, and the other boats drew back out of range. A deep roar of triumph rose from the walls of the fort, answered by bestial howling from all quarters.

"Shall we try to break through?" asked Balthus, trembling with eagerness.

Conan shook his head. He stood with his arms folded, his head slightly bent, a somber and brooding figure.

"The fort's doomed. The Picts are blood-mad, and won't stop until they're all killed. And there are too many of them for the men in the fort to kill. We couldn't break through, and if we did, we could do nothing but die with Valannus."

"There's nothing we can do but save our own hides, then?"

"Yes. We've got to warn the settlers. Do you know why the Picts are not trying to burn the fort with fire-arrows? Because they don't want a flame that might warn the people to the east. They plan to stamp out the fort, and then sweep east before anyone knows of its fall. They may cross Thunder River and take Velitrium before the people know what's happened. At least they'll destroy every living thing between the fort and Thunder River.

"We've failed to warn the fort, and I see now it would have

done no good if we had succeeded. The fort's too poorly manned. A few more charges and the Picts will be over the walls and breaking down the gates. But we can start the settlers toward Velitrium. Come on! We're outside the circle the Picts have thrown around the fort. We'll keep clear of it.''

They swung out in a wide arc, hearing the rising and falling of the volume of the yells, marking each charge and repulse. The men in the fort were holding their own; but the shrieks of the Picts did not diminish in savagery. They vibrated with a timbre that held assurance of ultimate victory.

Before Balthus realized they were close to it, they broke into the road leading east.

"Now run!" grunted Conan. Balthus set his teeth. It was nineteen miles to Velitrium, a good five to Scalp Creek, beyond which began the settlements. It seemed to the Aquilonian that they had been fighting and running for centuries. But the nervous excitement that rioted through his blood stimulated him to herculean efforts.

Slasher ran ahead of them, his head to the ground, snarling low, the first sound they had heard from him.

"Picts ahead of us!" snarled Conan, dropping to one knee and scanning the ground in the starlight. He shook his head, baffled. "I can't tell how many. Probably only a small party. Some that couldn't wait to take the fort. They've gone ahead to butcher the settlers in their beds! Come on!"

Ahead of them presently they saw a small blaze through the trees, and heard a wild and ferocious chanting. The trail bent there, and leaving it, they cut across the bend, through the thickets. A few moments later they were looking on a hideous sight. An ox-wain stood in the road piled with meager household furnishings; it was burning; the oxen lay near with their throats cut. A man and a woman lay in the road, stripped and mutilated. Five Picts were dancing about them with fantastic leaps and bounds, waving bloody axes; one of them brandished the woman's red-smeared gown.

At the sight a red haze swam before Balthus. Lifting his bow he lined the prancing figure, black against the fire, and loosed. The slayer leaped convulsively and fell dead with the arrow through his heart. Then the two white men and the dog were upon the startled survivors. Conan was animated merely by his fighting spirit and an old, old racial hate, but Balthus was afire with wrath.

He met the first Pict to oppose him with a ferocious swipe that split the painted skull, and sprang over his falling body to grapple with the others. But Conan had already killed one of the two he had chosen, and the leap of the Aquilonian was a second late. The warrior was down with the long sword through him even as Balthus' ax was lifted. Turning toward the remaining Pict, Balthus saw Slasher rise from his victim, his great jaws dripping blood.

Balthus said nothing as he looked down at the pitiful forms in the road beside the burning wain. Both were young, the woman little more than a girl. By some whim of chance the Picts had left her face unmarred, and even in the agonies of an awful death it was beautiful. But her soft young body had been hideously slashed with many knives—a mist clouded Balthus' eyes and he swallowed chokingly. The tragedy momentarily overcame him. He felt like falling upon the ground and weeping and biting the earth.

"Some young couple just hitting out on their own," Conan was saying as he wiped his sword unemotionally. "On their way to the fort when the Picts met them. Maybe the boy was going to enter the service; maybe take up land on the river. Well, that's what will happen to every man, woman, and child this side of Thunder River if we don't get them into Velitrium in a hurry."

Balthus' knees trembled as he followed Conan. But there was no hint of weakness in the long easy stride of the Cimmerian. There was a kinship between him and the great gaunt brute that glided beside him. Slasher no longer growled with his head to the trail. The way was clear before them. The yelling on the river came faintly to them, but Balthus believed the fort was still holding. Conan halted suddenly, with an oath.

He showed Balthus a trail that led north from the road. It was an old trail, partly grown with new young growth, and this growth had recently been broken down. Balthus realized this fact more by feel than sight, though Conan seemed to see like a cat in the dark. The Cimmerian showed him where broad wagon tracks turned off the main trail, deeply indented in the forest mold.

"Settlers going to the licks after salt," he grunted. "They're at the edges of the marsh, about nine miles from here. Blast it! They'll be cut off and butchered to a man! Listen! One man can warn the people on the road. Go ahead and wake them up and herd them into Velitrium. I'll go and get the men gathering the salt. They'll be camped by the licks. We won't come back to the road. We'll head straight through the woods."

With no further comment Conan turned off the trail and hurried down the dim path, and Balthus, after staring after him for a few moments, set out along the road. The dog had re-

mained with him, and glided softly at his heels. When Balthus
had gone a few rods he heard the animal growl. Whirling, he
glared back the way he had come, and was startled to see a
vague ghostly glow vanishing into the forest in the direction
Conan had taken. Slasher rumbled deep in his throat, his hackles
stiff and his eyes balls of green fire. Balthus remembered the
grim apparition that had taken the head of the merchant Tiberias
not far from that spot, and he hesitated. The thing must be
following Conan. But the giant Cimmerian had repeatedly dem-
onstrated his ability to take care of himself, and Balthus felt his
duty lay toward the helpless settlers who slumbered in the path
of the red hurricane. The horror of the fiery phantom was
overshadowed by the horror of those limp, violated bodies beside
the burning ox-wain.

He hurried down the road, crossed Scalp Creek and came in
sight of first settler's cabin—a long, low structure of ax-hewn
logs. In an instant he was pounding on the door. A sleepy voice
inquired his pleasure.

"Get up! The Picts are over the river!"

That brought instant response. A low cry echoed his words
and then the door was thrown open by a woman in a scanty shift.
Her hair hung over her bare shoulders in disorder; she held a
candle in one hand an an ax in the other. Her face was colorless,
her eyes wide with terror.

"Come in!" she begged. "We'll hold the cabin."

"No. We must make for Velitrium. The fort can't hold them
back. It may have fallen already. Don't stop to dress. Get your
children and come on."

"But my man's gone with the others after salt!" she wailed,
wringing her hands. Behind her peered three tousled youngsters,
blinking and bewildered.

"Conan's gone after them. He'll fetch them through safe. We
must hurry up the road to warn the other cabins."

Relief flooded her countenance.

"Mitra be thanked!" she cried. "If the Cimmerian's gone
after them, they're safe if mortal man can save them!"

In a whirlwind of activity she snatched up the smallest child
and herded the others through the door ahead of her. Balthus
took the candle and ground it out under his heel. He listened an
instant. No sound came up the dark road.

"Have you got a horse?"

"In the stable," she groaned. "Oh, hurry!"

He pushed her aside as she fumbled with shaking hands at the
bars. He led the horse out and lifted the children on its back,

telling them to hold to its mane and to one another. They stared at him seriously, making no outcry. The woman took the horse's halter and set out up the road. She still gripped her ax and Balthus knew that if cornered she would fight with the desperate courage of a she-panther.

He held behind, listening. He was oppressed by the belief that the fort had been stormed and taken; that the dark-skinned hordes were already streaming up the road toward Velitrium, drunken on slaughter and mad for blood. They would come with the speed of starving wolves.

Presently they saw another cabin looming ahead. The woman started to shriek a warning, but Balthus stopped her. He hurried to the door and knocked. A woman's voice answered him. He repeated his warning, and soon the cabin disgorged its occupants—an old woman, two young women, and four children. Like the other woman's husband, their men had gone to the salt licks the day before, unsuspecting of any danger. One of the young women seemed dazed, the other prone to hysteria. But the old woman, a stern old veteran of the frontier, quieted them harshly; she helped Balthus get out the two horses that were stabled in a pen behind the cabin and put the children on them. Balthus urged that she herself mount with them, but she shook her head and made one of the younger women ride.

"She's with child," grunted the old woman. "I can walk— and fight, too, if it comes to that."

As they set out, one of the young women said: "A young couple passed along the road about dusk; we advised them to spend the night at our cabin, but they were anxious to make the fort tonight. Did—did—"

"They met the Picts," answered Balthus briefly, and the woman sobbed in horror.

They were scarcely out of sight of the cabin when some distance behind them quavered a long high-pitched yell.

"A wolf!" exclaimed one of the women.

"A painted wolf with an ax in his hand," muttered Balthus. "Go! Rouse the other settlers along the road and take them with you. I'll scout along behind."

Without a word the old woman herded her charges ahead of her. As they faded into the darkness, Balthus could see the pale ovals that were the faces of the children twisted back over their shoulders to stare toward him. He remembered his own people on the Tauran and a moment's giddy sickness swam over him. With momentary weakness he groaned and sank down in the road; his muscular arm fell over Slasher's massive neck and he felt the dog's warm moist tongue touch his face.

He lifted his head and grinned with a painful effort.

"Come on, boy," he mumbled, rising. "We've got work to do."

A red glow suddenly became evident through the trees. The Picts had fired the last hut. He grinned. How Zogar Sag would froth if he knew his warriors had let their destructive natures get the better of them. The fire would warn the people farther up the road. They would be awake and alert when the fugitives reached them. But his face grew grim. The women were traveling slowly, on foot and on the overloaded horses. The swift-footed Picts would run them down within a mile, unless—he took his position behind a tangle of fallen logs beside the trail. The road west of him was lighted by the burning cabin, and when the Picts came he saw them first—black furtive figures etched against the distant glare.

Drawing a shaft to the head, he loosed and one of the figures crumpled. The rest melted into the woods on either side of the road. Slasher whimpered with the killing lust beside him. Suddenly a figure appeared on the fringe of the trail, under the trees, and began gliding toward the fallen timbers. Balthus' bowstring twanged and the Pict yelped, staggered and fell into the shadows with the arrow through his thigh. Slasher cleared the timber with a bound and leaped into the bushes. They were violently shaken and then the dog slunk back to Balthus' side, his jaws crimson.

No more appeared in the trail; Balthus began to fear they were stealing past his position through the woods, and when he heard a faint sound to his left he loosed blindly. He cursed as he heard the shaft splinter against a tree, but Slasher glided away as silently as a phantom, and presently Balthus heard a thrashing and a gurgling; then Slasher came like a ghost through the bushes, snuggling his great, crimson-stained head against Blathus' arm. Blood oozed from a gash in his shoulder, but the sounds in the wood had ceased for ever.

The men lurking on the edges of the road evidently sensed the fate of their companion, and decided that an open charge was preferable to being dragged down in the dark by a devil-beast they could neither see nor hear. Perhaps they realized that only one man lay behind the logs. They came with a sudden rush, breaking cover from both sides of the trail. Three dropped with arrows through them—and the remaining pair hesitated. One turned and ran back down the road, but the other lunged over the breastwork, his eyes and teeth gleaming in the dim light, his ax lifted. Balthus' foot slipped as he sprang up, but the slip saved his life. The descending ax shaved a lock of hair from his head, and the Pict rolled down the logs from the force of his wasted blow. Before he could regain his feet Slahser tore his throat out.

Then followed a tense period of waiting, in which time Balthus wondered if the man who had fled had been the only survivor of the party. Obviously it had been a small band that had either left the fighting at the fort, or was scouting ahead of the main body. Each moment that passed increased the chances for safety of the women and children hurrying toward Velitrium.

Then without warning a shower of arrows whistled over his retreat. A wild howling rose from the woods along the trail. Either the survivor had gone after aid, or another party had joined the first. The burning cabin still smoldered, lending a little light. Then they were after him, gliding through the trees beside the trail. He shot three arrows and threw the bow away. As if sensing his plight, they came on, not yelling now, but in deadly silence except for a swift pad of many feet.

He fiercely hugged the head of the great dog growling at his side, muttered: "All right, boy, give 'em hell!" and sprang to his feet, drawing his ax. Then the dark figures flooded over the breastworks and closed in a storm of flailing axes, stabbing knives and ripping fangs.

7

The Devil in the Fire

When Conan turned from the Velitrium road, he expected a run of some nine miles and set himself to the task. But he had not gone four when he heard the sounds of a party of men ahead of him. From the noise they were making in their progress he knew they were not Picts. He hailed them.

"Who's there?" challenged a harsh voice. "Stand where you are until we know you, or you'll get an arrow through you."

"You couldn't hit an elephant in this darkness," answered Conan impatiently. "Come on, fool; it's I—Conan. The Picts are over the river."

"We suspected as much," answered the leader of the men, as they strode forward—tall, rangy men, stern-faced, with bows in their hands. "One of our party wounded an antelope and tracked it nearly to Black River. He heard them yelling down the river and ran back to our camp. We left the salt and the wagons, turned the oxen loose, and came as swiftly as we could. If the Picts are besieging the fort, war-parties will be ranging up the road toward our cabins.''

"Your families are safe," grunted Conan. "My companion went ahead to take them to Velitrium. If we go back to the main road we may run into the whole horde. We'll strike southeast, through the timber. Go ahead. I'll scout behind.''

A few moments later the whole band was hurrying southeast-ward. Conan followed more slowly, keeping just within earshot. He cursed the noise they were making; that many Picts or Cimmerians would have moved through the woods with no more noise than the wind makes as it blows through the black branches.

He had just crossed a small glade when he wheeled, answering the conviction of his primitive instincts that he was being fol-lowed. Standing motionless among the bushes he heard the sound of the retreating settlers fade away. Then a voice called faintly back along the way he had come: "Conan! Conan! Wait for me, Conan!''

"Balthus!" he swore bewideredly. Cautiously he called: "Here I am!''

"Wait for me, Conan!" the voice came more distinctly.

Conan moved out of the shadows, scowling. "What the devil are you doing here?—*Crom!*''

He half crouched, the flesh prickling along his spine. It was not Balthus who was emerging from the other side of the glade. A weird glow burned through the trees. It moved toward him, shimmering weirdly—a green witchfire that moved with purpose and intent.

It halted some feet away and Conan glared at it, trying to distinguish its fire-misted outlines. The quivering flame had a solid core; the flame was but a green garment that masked some animate and evil entity; but the Cimmerian was unable to make out its shape or likeness. Then, shockingly, a voice spoke to him from amidst the fiery column.

"Why do you stand like a sheep waiting for the butcher, Conan?''

The voice was human but carried strange vibrations that were not human.

"Sheep?" Conan's wrath got the best of his momentary awe. "Do you think I'm afraid of a damned Pictish swamp devil? A friend called me.''

"I called in his voice," answered the other. "The men you follow belong to my brother; I would not rob his knife of their blood. But you are mine. O fool, you have come from the far gray hills of Cimmeria to meet your doom in the forests of Conajohara.''

"You've had your chance at me before now," snorted Conan. "Why didn't you kill me then, if you could?"

"My brother had not painted a skull black for you and hurled it into the fire that burns forever on Gullah's black altar. He had not whispered your name to the black ghosts that haunt the uplands of the Dark Land. But a bat has flown over the Mountains of the Dead and drawn your image in blood on the white tiger's hide that hangs before the long hut where sleep the Four Brothers of the Night. The great serpents coil about their feet and the stars burn like fireflies in their hair.''

"Why have the gods of darkness doomed me to death?" growled Conan.

Something—a hand, foot or talon, he could not tell which, thrust out from the fire and marked swiftly on the mold. A symbol blazed there, marked with fire, and faded, but not before he recognized it.

"You dared make the sign which only a priest of Jhebal Sag dare make. Thunder rumbled through the black Mountain of the Dead and the altar-hut of Gullah was thrown down by a wind from the Gulf of Ghosts. The loon which is messenger to the Four Brothers of the Night flew swiftly and whispered your name in my ear. Your race is run. You are a dead man already. Your head will hang in the altar-hut of my brother. Your body will be eaten by the black-winged, sharp-beaked Children of Jhil.''

"Who the devil is your brother?" demanded Conan. His sword was naked in his hand, and he was subtly loosening the ax in his belt.

"Zogar Sag; a child of Jhebbal Sag who still visits his sacred groves at times. A woman of Gwawela slept in a grove holy to Jhebbal Sag. Her babe was Zogar Sag. I too am a son of Jhebbal Sag, out of a fire-being from a far realm. Zogar Sag summoned me out of the Misty Lands. With incantations and sorcery and his own blood he materialized me in the flesh of his own planet. We are one, tied together by invisible threads. His thoughts are my thoughts; if he is struck, I am bruised. If I am cut, he bleeds. But I have talked enough. Soon your ghost will talk with the ghosts of the Dark Land, and they will tell you of the old gods which are not dead, but sleep in the outer abysses, and from time to time awake.''

"I'd like to see what you look like," muttered Conan, working his ax free, "you who leave a track like a bird, who burn like a flame and yet speak with a human voice."

"You shall see," answered the voice from the flame, "see, and carry the knowledge with you into the Dark Land."

The flames leaped and sank, dwindling and dimming. A face began to take shadowy form. At first Conan thought it was Zogar Sag himself who stood wrapped in green fire. But the face was higher than his own, and there was a demoniac aspect about it—Conan had noted various abnormalities about Zogar Sag's features—an obliqueness of the eyes, a sharpness of the ears, a wolfish thinness of the lips: these peculiarites were exaggerated in the apparition which swayed before him. The eyes were red as coals of living fire.

More details came into view: a slender torso, covered with snaky scales, which was yet manlike in shape, with manlike arms, from the waist upward; below, long cranelike legs ended in splay, three-toed feet like those of some huge bird. Along the monstrous limbs the blue fire fluttered and ran. He saw it as through a glistening mist.

Then suddenly it was towering over him, though he had not seen it move toward him. A long arm, which for the first time he noticed was armed with curving, sicklelike talons, swung high and swept down at his neck. With a fierce cry he broke the spell and bounded aside, hurling his ax. The demon avoided the cast with an unbelievably quick movement of its narrow head and was on him again with a hissing rush of leaping flames.

But fear had fought for it when it slew its other victims, and Conan was not afraid. He knew that any being clothed in material flesh can be slain by material weapons, however grisly its form may be.

One flailing talon-armed limb knocked his helmet from his head. A little lower and it would have decapitated him. But fierce joy surged through him as his savagely driven sword sank deep in the monster's groin. He bounded backward from a flailing stroke, tearing his sword free as he leaped. The talons raked his breast, ripping through mail-links as if they had been cloth. But his return spring was like that of a starving wolf. He was inside the lashing arms and driving his sword deep in the monster's belly—felt the arms lock about him and the talons ripping the mail from his back as they sought his vitals—he was lapped and dazzled by blue flame that was chill as ice—then he had torn fiercely away from the weakneing arms and his sword cut the air in a tremendous swipe.

The demon staggered and fell sprawling sidewise, its head

hanging only by a shred of flesh. The fires that veiled it leaped fiercely upward, now red as gushing blood, hiding the figure from view. A scent of burning flesh filled Conan's nostrils. Shaking the blood and sweat from his eyes, he wheeled and ran staggering through the woods. Blood trickled down his limbs. Somewhere, miles to the south, he saw the faint glow of flames that might mark a burning cabin. Behind him, toward the road, rose a distant howling that spurred him to greater efforts.

8

Conajohara No More

There had been fighting on Thunder River; fierce fighting before the walls of Velitrium; ax and torch had been plied up and down the bank, and many a settler's cabin lay in ashes before the painted horde was rolled back.

A strange quiet followed the storm, in which people gathered and talked in hushed voices, and men with red-stained bandages drank their ale silently in the taverns along the river bank.

There, to Conan the Cimmerian, moodily quaffing from a great wineglass, came a gaunt forester with a bandage about his head and his arm in a sling. He was the one survivor of Fort Tuscelan.

"You went with the soldiers to the ruins of the fort?"

Conan nodded.

"I wasn't able," murmured the other. "There was no fighting?"

"The Picts had fallen back across Black River. Something must have broken their nerve, though only the devil who made them knows what."

The woodsman glanced at his bandaged arm and sighed.

"They saw there were no bodies worth disposing of."

Conan shook his head. "Ashes. The Picts had piled them in the fort and set fire to the fort before they crossed the river. Their own dead and the men of Valannus."

"Valannus was killed among the last—in the hand-to-hand fighting when they broke the barriers. They tried to take him alive, but he made them kill him. They took ten of the rest of us prisoners when we were so weak from fighting we could fight no more. They butchered nine of us then and there. It was when Zogar Sag died that I got my chance to break free and run for it."

"Zogar Sag's dead?" ejaculated Conan.

"Aye. I saw him die. That's why the Picts didn't press the fight against Velitrium as fiercely as they did against the fort. It was strange. He took no wounds in battle. He was dancing among the slain, waving an ax with which he'd just brained the last of my comrades. He came at me, howling like a wolf—and then he staggered and dropped the ax, and began to reel in a circle screaming as I never heard a man or beast scream before. He fell between me and the fire they'd built to roast me, gagging and frothing at the mouth, and all at once he went rigid and the Picts shouted that he was dead. It was during the confusion that I slipped my cords and ran for the woods.

"I saw him lying in the firelight. No weapon had touched him. Yet there were red marks like the wounds of a sword in the groin, belly, and neck—the last as if his head had been almost severed from his body. What do you make of that?"

Conan made no reply, and the forester, aware of the reticence of barbarians on certain maters, continued: "He lived by magic, and somehow, he died by magic. It was the mystery of his death that took the heart out of the Picts. Not a man who saw it was in the fighting before Velitrium. They hurried back across Black River. Those that struck Thunder River were warriors who had come on before Zogar Sag died. They were not enough to take the city by themselves.

"I came along the road, behind their main force, and I know none followed me from the fort. I sneaked through their lines and got into the town. You brought the settlers through all right, but their women and children got into Velitrium just ahead of those painted devils. If the youth Balthus and old Slasher hadn't held them up awhile, they'd have butchered every woman and child in Conajohara. I passed the place where Balthus and the dog made their last stand. They were lying amid a heap of dead Picts—I counted seven, brained by his ax, or disemboweled by the dog's fangs, and there were others in the road with arrows sticking in them. Gods, what a fight that must have been!"

"He was a man," said Conan. "I drink to his shade, and to the shade of the dog, who knew no fear." He quaffed part of the wine, then emptied the rest upon the floor, with a cruious heathen gesture, and smashed the goblet. "The heads of ten Picts shall pay for his, and seven heads for the dog, who was a better warrior than many a man."

And the forester, staring into the moody, smoldering blue eyes, knew the barbaric oath would be kept.

"They'll not rebuild the fort?"

"No; Conajohara is lost to Aquilonia. The frontier has been pushed back. Thunder River will be the new border."

The woodsman sighed and stared at his calloused hand, worn from contact with ax-haft and sword-hilt. Conan reached his long arm for the wine jug. The forester stared at him, comparing him with the men about them, the men who had died along the lost river, comparing him with those other wild men over that river. Conan did not seem aware of his gaze.

"Barbarism is the natural state of mankind," the borderer said, still staring somberly at the Cimmerian. "Civilization is unnatural. It is a whim of circumstance. And barbarism must always ultimately triumph."

ABOUT THE EDITORS

Robert Adams lives in Seminole County, Florida. He is the author of the best-selling *Horseclans* series and the *Castaways in Time* series (both available in Signet editions), and is the co-editor, with Andre Norton, of an anthology series, *Magic in Ithkar*. Like the characters in his books, he is partial to fencing and fancy swordplay, hunting and riding, good food and drink. At one time Robert could be found slaving over a hot forge, making a new sword or busily reconstructing a historically accurate military costume, but, unfortunately, he no longer has time for this as he's far too busy writing.

Martin H. Greenberg has been called (in *The Science Fiction and Fantasy Book Review*) "The King of the Anthologists"; to which he replied—"It's good to be the King!" He has produced more than one hundred of them, usually in collaboration with a multitude of co-conspirators. A Professor of Regional Analysis and Political Science at the University of Wisconsin–Green Bay, he is still trying to publish his weight.

Charles G. Waugh is a Professor of Psychology and Communications at the University of Maine at Augusta who is still trying to figure out how he got himself into all this. He has also worked with many collaborators, since he is basically a very friendly fellow. He has done some sixty-five anthologies and single-author collections, and especially enjoys locating unjustly ignored stories. He also claims that he met his wife via computer dating—her choice was an entire fraternity or him, and she has only minor regrets.